Attempts
to Join
Society

Attempts to Join Society

A NOVEL

Richard Thornley

BEAUFORT BOOKS
Publishers
New York

Library of Congress Cataloging-in-Publication Data

Thornley, Richard, 1950–
Attempts to join society

I. Title.
PR6070.H692A9 1986 823'.914 85-26778
ISBN 0-8253-0351-6

The author and publishers would like to thank the following for use of
copyright material: on p. 27 the cover copy of *Point Blank* by Richard Stark ap-
pears by permission of Fawcett Books, an imprint of Ballantine Books, New
York; on p. 213 the news report is reprinted by permission of Associated Press
Ltd, London. Quotations from the plays of Eugene O'Neill are attributable
thus: *The Iceman Cometh*, p. 190, lines 4-5, 19-21, p. 195, lines 23-30, p. 287, lines
30-1; *Long Day's Journey into Night*, p.190, line 38 to p. 191, line 4, p. 243, lines
30-3; *A Moon for the Misbegotten*, p. 197, line 17.
  The original version of Chapter 27 appeared in *Firebird 3*, published by
Penguin Books Ltd in 1984.

Published in the United States by Beaufort Books Publishers, New York.

Printed in the U.S.A.   First American Edition, 1986

10   9   8   7   6   5   4   3   2   1

PART
1

Pale Grey:
Martin

1

There was plenty of sun, the sea was passably clean. If you didn't like the sea, the hotel had a swimming-pool. If you didn't want to stay near the hotel, you could rent a car and drive off round the island. If you didn't want to listen to the nightly flamenco music, you could sit on your balcony and watch the electric storms flashing across the water.

I was due to go to university, my sister was carelessly preparing for her last year at school; she swam and slacked and groaned. Aunt Jane and uncle Philip, our adoptive parents for the fourteen years since our real parents died, sat beside us. My uncle looked at the headlines in the *Financial Times* that he had walked down to Palma Nova to fetch. My aunt applied herself to Solzhenitsyn's *The First Circle*. She wasn't sure whether or not she liked it. I carried *A History of Western Philosophy* from the bedroom to the swimming-pool, carefully moving the bookmark forward some thirty pages each morning.

We lay on our backs in the sun. I considered a paragraph of ideas randomly extracted from whatever page the bookmark chose. I would do this with much furrowing of brow, narrowing of eyes, pursing of lips; and my aunt Jane would say, 'Don't you think you've done enough for one day?' and I would reluctantly agree, shutting the book, pushing it under the reclining chair, and my uncle Philip would fold his *Financial Times* and we would lie on our backs with our eyes closed, facing the sun, and my kid sister would say, 'God, it's hot.'

She had class, my sister Annie. She was very beautiful and only half liked being aware of it. She seemed to give a lot of people the feeling that they weren't quite up to standard. We liked each other because I knew that she had no idea what she wanted, and she knew that I knew. She thought that I was 'mental', whatever that meant. 'Mad' was too obvious for her; so I was 'mental'.

I was looking at another girl. I knew that she was called Laura. Laura had long dark hair which shone and a white bikini which slashed twice across her chocolate suntan. I was daymaring urgently; or duskmaring. My uncle and aunt had retired to dress for dinner.

'Who do you fancy?' my kid sister demanded.

'*She's* nice,' I said, wishing that Annie would be replaced by Laura.

'Oh you're mental!'

'I'm not.'

'She's more boring than I am.'

'That's impossible.'

'*I'm* not boring.'

'You *are*.'

'How do *you* know? You're mental.'

'What does that mean?' I asked angrily.

'Well, look at you. And look at the way you move that stupid bookmark forward every day. I suppose you think we're all as mental as you are. We know, you know. Why don't you bend the corner of the page over? And you ought to draw lines down the margin. That's what I do, and they never get suspicious. Anyway, you wouldn't want to marry someone like her, would you?'

'I don't know. Maybe.'

'I can remember when you said that you'd like to marry someone like me.'

'That was probably when I was mental.'

Annie scowled and we laughed. She said that she had prickly heat and she was going up to her room, and if I had to look at the girl in the white bikini at least try not to stare or look dumb, otherwise people might think that our whole family had just come out of the loony bin.

Annie played ten to my thirteen. That's how we were when my uncle decided that I should be sent away to school, and that's how we stopped.

I couldn't go on and on looking at this Laura; and I certainly couldn't say anything to her. Of course she might just notice my book and then, with a book with that title, I wouldn't have to say anything. We would immediately enjoy each other's company, a waiter would appear with her kind of drink, and we would gradually become aware that we were fulfilling each other.

But she got out of her chair; she put on her robe and collected her creams and walked down the other side of the pool and into the hotel.

Girls are so self-contained. You often wonder if they have

any wayward feelings at all; they just seem to have alliances, then they have fiancés, then they have husbands who pay for the central heating.

It was pretty pointless sitting out there by the pool. Most of the other people were lighting cigarettes and I didn't smoke cigarettes. And it was a lot more professional to draw lines down the margin.

Annie and I now showed up just before dinner. We didn't show up for the hour's drinking which preceded dinner. We did so at first, but it was dreadful. Having lain around all day, everybody suddenly stood rigid and mastered the art of talking about nothing. If we were there, our uncle and aunt would usually get round to talking about us: 'Annie's such and such ... ', 'he's going to do such and such ... ' And they'd always tag on 'aren't you?' at the end – like a bad ventriloquist making sure that the audience's attention switches to the dummy. So we always had these one-syllable introductory speeches to other people. The conversation ran: 'So and so, such and such, so and so, such and such ... aren't you?' And we said: 'Yes.' You know that this isn't really anyone's fault; or it's your fault for being stupid enough to be there in the first place.

But. If, on the other hand, my uncle and aunt could be guided surreptitiously towards parents who had daughters in white bikinis; then I could say, 'Yes', while my eyes said, 'You're so beautiful!'

I practised this in my room until Annie knocked on the door and came in. 'It's the boring hour,' she said. Nevertheless she had got herself done up and she even sat quite stiffly on the bed.

I had a strange feeling that it wouldn't work. There was one chance in a hundred that it would work, if I hit it just right.

'Say something, Annie; and then say "aren't you?" at the end of it.'

'Why?' Annie was intrigued.

'It's just a thing.'

'Is it a joke?'

'No.'

'It's not some stupid thing where you throw water over me, is it?'

11

'No, it's serious.'

'Promise?'

'Yes.' I hurried her. She could see that I was preparing to perform.

'So what is it again?' she asked. 'What do you want me to say?'

'Something, something, something, *aren't you?*'

'What kind of thing?'

'Anything, anything you want,' I urged.

'All right. The sea is green, aren't you?' she inquired.

My God. Sisters.

'What's wrong? Is that it? I don't understand it.' Annie gave out the mental look.

'I wasn't ready. Do it again.'

'One … two … three … The sea is green, *aren't you?*'

One … two … three. 'Yes!' Pause. Flood of knowing tenderness. We mean so much to each other, you and I, how absurd this world is, we could slip away for a Martini and your eyes, so beautiful.

'What do you think?' I demanded from Annie, the verdict.

'Well,' she considered, 'it's *quite* scary. You can do worse ones than that. When you curl your top lip up over your gum.'

'Do you want to play cards, Annie?'

'Oh all right, let's sit on the balcony.'

2

My aunt discovered Billy. Or he discovered us.

Annie and I had been in the pool and were laid out like a couple of sausages on a grill-pan. The sun was at its highest and brightest; the end of my nose felt as though it had been scraped with a blunt razor-blade. I lay with my eyes shut and thought about retreating to the bedroom, where there would be nothing else to do but to read that book. Over on the other side of Annie, my aunt got involved in some kind of a chair-moving disturbance.

Nothing ever happened at the pool. A chair-moving disturbance was an incident. (A man once dropped a plate of risotto, but that was different, that was like the assassination of President Kennedy.)

I heard the scraping of metal chair legs along the tiles. I could imagine my aunt smiling and not wanting to be a nuisance and everyone English apologising like mad and laughing nervously and shuffling and arranging. I could imagine the escalation of politeness, and the more people who got involved the more of an incident it would be, especially if any of the other people were Germans. My aunt could never quite understand how it was that, when we had won the war, there were still Germans taking the same holidays as us; she didn't like to be reminded of Germans. When we had moved into her house and Annie was growing up, I used to check under Annie's bed to make sure that Hitler wasn't hiding there.

Anyway, the hour before dinner was sufficient for chatting to holiday acquaintances of any nationality. No one came too close to the family. The chair incident died. I felt my uncle sit up and pay attention. He noted that things were arranged satisfactorily, he asked and was assured and lay back down again. I supposed that we would have another half-hour's cooking before we went inside for lunch. The Swedes and the English usually decamped to the dining-room. Poolside eating had been taken over by other nationalities, we found their jocundity a bit oppressive.

I wondered if I could stand the heat for another half-hour. I could spend the half-hour not wondering, if I was left alone with this blank white sun-induced screen at the back of my mind and there was no projection and Annie didn't groan too much.

All in all I was liquefied. The arms of the chair kept me from oozing over the edge. Until I, or my attention, was tilted slowly.

It wasn't just that my aunt was involved in a conversation. Or that the conversation – very little of which I could hear clearly – seemed at times to escape the usual well-beaten track, no matter how sternly she pegged its boundaries. This was strange enough. But more strange was the irrepressible animation which reached over her and spread along the family line.

And then, in a swirl, Annie became involved; and Annie was actually sitting up, which was unheard of for Annie.

13

The voice was louder now and American; it laughed a bit much and a bit brash. It was one of those growly, cigaretted voices. I reckoned that it would probably stop at Annie – a lot of voices chose to do so.

But the animation reached and reached; my aunt laughed and Annie said something; she was interested, and the animation was obviously seeping through to my uncle because he was stirring as though someone had passed a pheasant casserole under his nose.

I sat up to see what was going on. I looked straight at a man. He was something of a short cross between Cock Robin and a sleazy film producer. He was all hairy chest and tan and gold chain around his neck. A loose-lipped mouth and white teeth; a totem-pole nose. Bloodshot eyes. And a slimy manner which surely wouldn't have fooled anyone.

'And this is your son? I'm very pleased to meet you. And you, sir,' he took in my blinking uncle on the same round of handshake. We didn't have time to go through all the usual explanations.

It was all so phoney and suave. I couldn't believe it; and I couldn't believe that he got us all into having a poolside drink before lunch, introducing us to his friend and manager Donald, and then he said that he'd see us back at the pool after lunch if that was fine by us. We all mumbled that we didn't know what we were doing that afternoon, but probably, and aren't you, Annie, and yes.

'I'm sure that he doesn't mean to be slimy; I think he's interesting,' Annie decided in the corridor.

'And what's his name?'

'Bill. But he wants to be called Billy.'

'Why does he want to be called Billy?'

'Search me; he just does. How old do you think he is?'

'Thirty-five.'

'That's what I thought. He's a bit too old for me. It's a pity really.'

We went into our respective rooms to hang our damp costumes over our respective balconies.

Annie sat a little straighter at lunch and stopped shovelling her food. My uncle announced his intention of ducking out of the afternoon session, my aunt thought that it would be a good idea if we went into town to buy some postcards. Annie saw

14

the plot before it was half-way out. My uncle warned about sunburn; my aunt needed company.

We acquiesced, and trailed down into Palma Nova. After postcards there seemed to be a need for suntan oil, and maybe souvenirs and maybe a bikini for Annie. Annie was half-irritable, but then she was never averse to having things bought for her. Everything that could get bought got bought, and we were down to looking round a church, but Annie was turned away because of her short dress and that was apparently the reason for heading back to the hotel.

My uncle was sitting with this Billy by the pool; other chairs were reserved for us.

Annie appeared in her new bikini, as though there should have been trumpets. Sickening. It was four-thirty and everyone agreed to catch the last of the sun.

No one talked.

My uncle announced that he was going inside, and did so.

Annie had no desire to swim. Twice. Apparently the launching of a new bikini is a very private affair. In case the rivets come loose and the whole tub sinks modestly. Oh well.

Annie disappeared and my aunt disappeared, I stayed. The sun was disappearing. We were on the western side of a promontory, the hotel was on top of some rocks with a dozen steps down from the pool area to the sea; and the main block of land to the west cut off the sun at an early hour. We were pale grey when in the distance the sea was still blue and sunny. The air kept warm and your eyes could focus now that the glare had gone. It was like an English summer evening. Annie thought that this time was morbid, but it was my favourite time. I liked the warm grey, the shadow of the land mass and the brilliant dancing sea with the odd fishing boat.

I didn't know how this Billy felt about it. I didn't really want him there but he stayed. His manager clucked and disappeared, everyone else had gone to get dressed up. I felt peculiarly weak and indecisive. He waited. I couldn't see that he would appreciate soft beauty. He shocked. The pale grey wasn't at ease this evening; it was intruded on, the touch of a calloused hand. He had cigarettes and a drink that clinked with ice.

'It's beautiful,' he drawled.

'It *is*!' I claimed, protectively; thinking him easy or cynical

15

or flippant. Feeling gauche, immediately, or pretentious. Boring sea and sky, package tour, gangly body like a child's toy. If he doesn't touch me I shall twitch, and if he does I shall be repulsed.

'Hey,' he said, laying his hand on my arm and I thought, who the hell are you to do that. 'Take it easy.'

What do you want? With my breath shallow and the blood rushing to my lips. Don't touch me. 'It *is* beautiful,' I said, holding my arms out nervously.

He laughed, a brash honest bray, like a bulldozer careering through a scrapyard. 'Of course it is, sure it is, we just shared it, it's beautiful!' He regained my arm and saw that I wasn't sure about this. 'Oh hell, I'm sorry.' I didn't know whether it was okay or not. There was something about surrendering and I couldn't do it gracefully.

'What do you do?' he asked. His eyes looked as though they were picking me out of a crowd. But there was no one else there. I didn't understand it. There was no way of acting with him, he was very physical and very close.

'I'm going to university.'

'That's good.'

'Yes.' I had never thought about it until now, it just seemed like what I was going to do, it had never seemed either good or bad.

'You're damn lucky.'

'What do you do?' I asked him.

'I'm an actor. I started the best nightclub in New York. I like your family.'

'Yes?' I'd never thought about liking my family. 'Annie?'

'She's cute. And Jane. She's a warm woman. You're very lucky. I have a sister, you'd like her. We love each other a lot.'

'What does she do?' Why doesn't he go away?

'Oh she's a dancer, she enjoys herself. Have you ever been to New York?'

'No. I've never been to America.'

'You will; and if you want to see America, you want to see New York.'

'What about Vietnam?' I said.

'There's a hell of a lot of good in our country,' he started, 'and a lot of young people are standing up to fight for it. There's a lot of older people who don't know what the hell they're

16

doing. It isn't all bad though. And you don't have to pretend that little England is full of angels, you don't believe that self-righteous crap.' He watched me. 'If you don't know what America's like you should have enough politeness to come and see before you judge. We have problems we're going to get through, we don't ignore them.'

I sat numb.

'Are you coming inside, Billy? It's kind of cold out here when the sun's finished.' Donald had come out of the hotel. He stood, unsure, at Bill's shoulder, his hands in his pockets. Bill and I sat face to face, looking at our mutual dislike.

There was a tightly clenched fist behind his eyes. And yet he was watching the effect he had. He was still watching me.

'Oh Donald.' Bill turned his head away, and then came back to me. 'He's always fussing.'

'Well, we'd better think about eating, Billy; or do you want to carry on out here? *I* don't know.'

'He wants to get out on the town with his Danes, don't you, Don. Come on now. That's the only reason he goes on these holidays!' Bill exulted. Donald hid away.

'Well you know *that's* not true – '

'I think I'd better be going in,' I said.

'Hell, we'll all go in. We'll eat and talk; we'll get there.'

'I didn't want to disturb anything.'

'Don, you certainly have a good way of not disturbing anything.' Bill put an arm round Donald's shoulder, laughing. Donald had a loafing schoolboy saunter beside Bill's leopard tread. 'Don't forget your book,' Bill told me. We parted in the foyer; I waited for the lift, the two of them went on into the bar.

In my room I tried to categorise Bill. Suave, obnoxious, something to prove. His gestures were performed. The smile went on too long. I didn't believe in it. Broad shoulders. Violent laugh. He screwed his eyes up. He didn't frown. He was too tanned, his teeth were too white, he was too hairy. He reached too much. He punctured. He was too ugly and too naked. His face was too heavy, his mouth was too fleshy. He laughed too coarsely. Gold around his neck and a gold tooth. Chipped toenails. Couldn't keep himself to himself. From my balcony I watched women in clinging swimwear.

'I like him,' Annie said, 'there's something about him.'

'He's a character,' my uncle allowed.

'Oh I should think he's a terror, that Billy,' my aunt shook her head, smiling. 'It's lucky for him that Donald keeps an eye on him.'

'Donald's obviously the businessman. He was making transatlantic telephone calls all afternoon. It must cost him a fortune. I think his company has something to do with electronics. I couldn't find out exactly what he does.'

'We couldn't really. That Bill … '

'Billy!'

'He talks so much, we really had no chance to talk to Donald.'

'*He's* strange,' Annie announced, 'definitely.'

We sat in the clink and scrape of a not very softly lit dinner. The dining-room was rectangular and the dining hours were very confined, as was the menu.

'They don't seem to be here,' Annie looked around, 'can you see them?'

They weren't in the dining-room. I didn't search, but the room hadn't had the feel of Bill when we'd stood by the door waiting to be assigned to a table. We didn't have our own table; that was another black mark, nobody had their own table.

'They said they were going out on the town,' I told everybody, while we were eating.

'What a nuisance,' Annie said irritably.

'Never mind, we can see them tomorrow, I expect.'

'I'm sure we will.' My uncle. I could never tell what his attitude was; whether he was ironical, whether he was pleased or stoical or what.

'And they're quite nice people.'

'That's because they're interesting. More than this stupid fish. Can anyone get these bones out?' Annie put down her knife, and looked plaintive. 'Please?'

'Annie, it's time you learned to do it for yourself.'

'Is it?' Annie appealed. I smiled at her; she stuck her tongue out, surreptitiously. 'In fact, I can do it. Anyone can do a normal fish. God knows what kind of a fish this is.' She took to stabbing it pathetically, and came out with one of her innocently calculated goadings. 'I should think that they got this fish from that sewage outlet. There's hundreds of fish there.

18

That would be the best place to get them from, wouldn't it?'

My aunt poked discreetly at her fish.

'No, I shouldn't think so for a minute.' My uncle played: 'But anything's possible these days. Pass your plate over then.'

'Your daughter's got a horrible imagination.'

'I'm not really his daughter, so that's all right.'

My uncle scalped the flesh away from the backbone. He handed Annie her plate. 'There we are, now let's finish eating. Quietly. With some behaviour.'

It was empty in the bar, the main hubbub would descend from the dining-room later on. We sat at a corner table, the waiter brought us coffee and brandy, Annie had a *crème de menthe*.

'So what are you two up to this evening?'

'I'm quite tired.'

'That's boring,' Annie scowled. 'If those other two were here, we could have gone dancing.'

'You two can go dancing. Philip and I are going to walk down to the village. They could take the car into Palma, couldn't they?'

'Yes, if they want to. As long as they're not back too late.'

'Who wants to dance with their brother? God!'

'I should have thought that it would have been rather nice. And there will be other people in the nightclub. Martin can look after you.'

'God!'

'Well who wants to dance with you?' I retaliated.

'Billy might, or his friend; someone interesting.'

'Oh yes, and then he'll put you in the movies.'

'That's quite likely.'

'Yes, of course it is, Annie.' My uncle sipped brandy and pretended.

'Not yet,' my aunt ordered.

'Except that I wouldn't want to be in films anyway.'

'You're not really that type of girl, pet, are you?'

'No. Of course, I might be. Later on. But I must finish school and do some training first.'

Sickening. I rolled my eyes up at Annie. The little greaser. She tried not to laugh. Her eyes sparkled with the effort. 'How are you getting on with your reading?' she hooted out; my uncle and aunt were disconcerted. 'Whoops!' She gurgled with laughter and put the *crème de menthe* back on the table.

'You shouldn't drink it all at once,' my aunt admonished.

'No,' I agreed. 'It's *very* strong.'

'He's so mental!' Annie lathered. 'You are, you know!'

'Calm down, you two.'

'Yes.' Annie couldn't handle overmuch mischief; she wanted it to end, she swallowed her laughter, she looked hard at the table.

'So what have you decided?' my uncle asked.

'Oh we'll stay here and be boring.'

'I'll give you some money for the bar.'

Not that Annie would drink anything much. We played at being a married couple for a while, without convincing each other; I drank a beer and she drank a Martini. There wasn't much fun in being a married couple, we couldn't quite sprawl around with the necessary distance between each other. We couldn't gaze into each other's eyes because that was mental. And anyway – as Annie said – if you were part of a married couple you just wanted desperately to talk to someone else. Annie decided that Philip and Jane had a different kind of marriage. I supposed so.

It didn't look as though there were going to be any storms out at sea, so we went to bed early. I had a nightmare about a train going over the edge of a viaduct, a bit like the end of *The Bridge on the River Kwai* except that it seemed more like Wales. I'd had the nightmare before. The train was always empty and the grey water was deep. The first time, I had been looking out of the carriage window. Then I was sitting on the roof of the fifth carriage. Now I was leaning against the parapet of the viaduct while the train plunged past me, though it was still going to take me in its slipstream. I had the dream about once a year; it had stopped scaring me. I knew that I would never hit the water.

There were never any stations in the dream. When I looked in a dream-book we had at home, there was a section on stations. A station was a woman; one could draw up at the platform or one could hurtle through. Very helpful. It annoyed me that after four years of collecting train numbers from Euston to Rugby to Plymouth to York, I still couldn't manage to squeeze a station into my unconscious – be it a wonderfully

mature and pillared Rugby or a new, sleek, plate-glass halt like
Hampton-in-Arden.

3

Annie was irritable in the morning. It was the mid-point of
our holiday, one week in, one week to go. Maybe that depressed her; or maybe she had suffered too much sun yesterday.
She looked around and wasn't satisfied with what she saw. It
was decided that we would cram into the Seat 500 and go
somewhere before the day became too hot.

We drove up the hill out of the hotel car-park and headed
north-west. Even in the morning, the air that came in through the
open windows was flat and dusty and had no smell to it. The
land was an overall brown colour. There were bits of green,
short trees with widespread roots. We decided to look for a
beach south of Camp de Mar. We couldn't see it, but you could
tell that it was there from the trickle of people with towels over
their shoulders who were all walking in the same direction.

There wasn't much to make the best of; just a mess of
grey-white sand, concrete shelters and changing rooms behind
them. People were busy with oil, as though greasing a machine
before applying it to the day's work; flicking through the order
book, one batch of suntan. Groups of happy exhibitionists
limbered up for netball, volleyball and soccer; rubbing their
hands athletically, exhorting each other, diving around in spec-
tacular fashion, male flamboyance in front of warm-oiled, indifferent women. There were not many strutters, though one
or two made it clear that they were pretty much a product of
God's blueprint.

'No chance of finding any crabs here,' my uncle said.

'No.' When I was younger, it used to be one of the best
times of my life: in Devon, scrambling over the rocks, peering
down at the tiny creatures, asking my uncle to poke in there
with his stick, tempting a pair of snapping claws. He managed
to invent a horde of characters. We didn't now have much
contact on that level, the onus was on growing up. He felt
himself to be a solitary man. I didn't understand why we
weren't close, but I adhered to my respect for him.

'We could look at the shops,' Annie suggested, 'and then we could be back in time for lunch.'

I wondered if my uncle was hurt. I think that he took us with a pinch of salt. Sometimes he snapped out a bitterly angry remark when it seemed to him that we were behaving thoughtlessly. He once said to me that life was more to be put up with than enjoyed.

We stopped to browse through the displays of leather bags and shoes and belts, but he wouldn't be lured into making any rash offers. I stood with him while my aunt and Annie went through their observations and their ferreting. I knew that they wouldn't buy anything, even the shopkeepers knew that they wouldn't buy anything; but my aunt brandished a polite stubbornness, a refusal to be hurried.

'I might go off and look for a newspaper,' my uncle said.

'I might too.'

'Don't you think you need another pair of trousers?' my aunt asked.

'Not really.'

'Well, now that Pop is here ... '

'I don't want another pair of trousers. Shall we meet you back at the car?'

'Oh yes, all right then, half an hour.'

'Super,' Annie said.

I caught up with my uncle. We might have a lot to say. We didn't.

'Are they all right?'

'Yes. I said we'd meet them back at the car in half an hour.'

My uncle checked his watch. We both bought newspapers and sat out in the open near the car, reading them. We made each other nervous. I knew that I was incapable. There was a loony paragraph in my newspaper about how it had rained frogs in Scunthorpe. In his newspaper there was a long article on the possibilities of peace in the Middle East.

'Pop, what do you think about university?'

'I don't think it's a very good idea for you, but I think that you want to go, don't you?'

'Yes.'

'That's all right. You must let me know if there's anything I can do for you. I expect it's changed since my day.'

He turned to the next page of his newspaper and began to

skim. He skimmed the page twice. I was interrupting him. I thought of telling him about the frogs in Scunthorpe; but probably that sort of thing happened every now and then, probably it wasn't important. He was glad when the other two arrived.

'It rained frogs in Scunthorpe the other day,' I said as the car got close to the hotel.

'Ugh, don't!' Annie said crossly.

'I expect that's the sort of thing they put in the papers to sell them,' my aunt quietened Annie. 'You never want to believe anything you read.'

'It happens sometimes,' my uncle agreed with me, 'the wind picks them up and puts them down somewhere else.'

Something had happened. We saw half a dozen people hobble into the dining-room. They had stepped on sea-urchins. It was an incident. Severe warning notices were plastered up in Annie's head.

After lunch we went to have a look at these sea-urchins. They had decided to occupy the step-ladder which led down from the rocks into the sea; they waved harmlessly at us from the lap of the water, five of them at the surface, although they were clustered into black tufts lower down. A poisonous doormat.

'You can still use the pool.' My uncle returned to his chair.

'Stupid things! Who would make a thing like that?' Annie demanded. 'And why do they come here? Of all the places they could go. Now we have to sit by the pool all afternoon.'

'So what?'

Annie had never minded sitting by the pool as far as I could remember.

'So nothing, that's all.' Annie shuddered. 'Just look at them.'

'The raft's empty,' I said. The hotel kept a raft which was moored some fifty yards out to sea. It was usually occupied by one group or another, and you couldn't really swim out there unless you wanted to meet people.

'Who wants to die of poison?'

'You could jump in.'

'And jump out, I suppose.'

'They're all on the left-hand side of the step.'

'They're not.'

'You wouldn't have to use the bottom steps; if you put your foot *there*, and pulled yourself up by the rail,' I considered.

Annie didn't bother with the practicality, she was tempted by defiance. She switched on her long-suffering brown eyes. She had another query.

'How do you know that the sea's not full of them? If you're so clever.'

'Because the ones that float around get eaten by the sharks.'

'Don't! You know that puts me off, it puts me right off.'

'They're *aren't* any sharks.'

'*I* know that, but I think about them.'

'Have you got your bikini on underneath?'

'Yes. Shall we go?'

'Yes.'

'What shall we say to *them*?'

'Nothing.'

'All right.'

'Come on then.'

'They look as if they're going to sleep anyway,' Annie surveyed the chairs. 'Be careful then.'

I stood on the lowest step above the waterline and pushed myself away into the sea. The water was immediately deep so there was no fear of touching the bottom with your feet.

'Did you get bitten?'

'No.'

'Are there any more of those things?'

'Wait a minute.' I ducked under the water and kept my eyes open. The water was clear, the sea-urchins were intent on the ladder and the surrounding rock face. 'It's okay. It's easy if you push yourself away from the step.'

'Promise?'

'Promise.'

Annie lunged, and came up like a drunken walrus. She fussed with spitting and choking and rubbing her eyes. If we hung around too long we might get pushed against the rocks by the wallow of the sea; but I didn't tell her that. Nor did I tell her that from out here you couldn't be sure which step the sea-urchins were on, unless you looked for them from under the water, which you couldn't do if you were trying to climb out.

'Not too fast,' she said.

We swam out slowly and easily. It was more than fifty yards. The sea was a bit greasy as we turtled along.

24

There weren't any urchins clinging to the raft. I gave Annie a hand up and we lay there, getting back our breath and listening to the soft flop of the sea against the side of the wooden platform.

It was like being shipwrecked; the way the raft rose and fell, that feeling of being personally examined by the sun, no creams and no sunglasses and no books or interruptions. It was pointless to moan about the heat. Annie lay on her stomach, frowning slightly. I rolled off the edge of the raft to cool down. Annie splashed water over her shoulders or sat with her feet dangling in the sea. 'I don't know if I like it being so quiet.'

'Why not?'

'The others might all disappear.'

'Why should they?'

Annie shrugged and sulked. And she kicked water at me. I grabbed hold of her ankle and pulled her off the raft. When she surfaced, her eyes flashed. 'You'll never have a girlfriend.' She swam off round the platform.

I hoisted myself out of the water and sat watching her as she continued her circuit. She stayed very close to the raft.

'Do you think they know we're here?' she asked when she was sitting beside me. She was worried. I didn't know whether to joke or not. There was no one standing near the hotel step-ladder.

'We couldn't really be anywhere else. Of course they know.'

Annie brightened. 'I suppose we haven't been here very long.'

'Only about half an hour.'

'We could stay here for another half an hour and then swim back. I don't want to stay out here until it gets dark or anything.'

'I don't either.'

It wasn't at all a long way to the shore. Annie relaxed and lay flat on her back. There wouldn't be any currents or anything. I sat on the edge of the raft and looked at the shore. I saw my uncle. I waved. I told Annie. Annie shielded her eyes and waved. He waved back. He held up Annie's towel.

I was nervous. My uncle seemed to be in charge of the sea-urchins. Maybe they had multiplied while we had been out here. Annie was a game swimmer, but maybe she was tired.

My uncle watched. We swam back.

There wasn't any other place to land.

We trod water six feet from the ladder. Annie looked up at my uncle for instructions.

'I don't know how you're going to do this,' he stipulated. 'Can you see the sea-urchins from where you are?'

'No,' Annie worried. She looked to me for an answer.

'They're not all on the steps. If Annie swims forward and holds on to the rail, I'll swim underneath her and put her feet in the right places.'

My uncle looked annoyed.

'Come on, Annie,' I whispered, 'or it'll be a big incident.'

'Hi. Are you stuck down there?' Bill asked, smiling and serious at the same time.

'They've got themselves into a bit of a mess,' my uncle said.

Bill was all for trying to make himself useful. He offered to dive in.

'When she's got her foot on the steps, she'll just need a hand up, to pull her out of the water,' I said. Bill got himself ready and my uncle followed suit.

'I'm starting,' Annie warned.

She lay along the water. I went underneath and took her ankle and guided it forward to the step. She was almost sitting on top of me for a moment, I saw my chest pushed down towards the black spikes; but then they must have got hold of her and she was drawn up.

I managed it okay.

'I don't know why you chose today of all days to swim out there,' my uncle said.

'Because *I* wanted to,' Annie rallied. 'Anyway, it's nice when there's no one else there.'

My 'sorry' got lost in the procession back to the chairs. My aunt greeted us without flurry; Donald thought that sea-urchins were just terrible. Annie was pleased to be back. She was pleased that we had done it, though. Billy made everything a lot less stuffy. 'No more swimming to the raft, hey Annie?' and the bold laugh.

'*I* wouldn't go out there,' Donald complained, 'and don't you let these two young people talk you into any madness either, Billy.' He looked away shyly, as though the whole world was outrageous and he was hopelessly unable to cope with it; which was funny. My aunt laughed; Billy did his 'Oh

Donald ... ' and rolled his eyes at us all. My uncle lay back in his chair.

We had an hour of sun to go. There were people splashing in the pool. Billy and Donald played a lot off my aunt. I listened and watched. They were more direct than the usual holiday people and so they had been accepted by now as part of the family. My aunt and Donald would be serious about New York, she would ask questions and suggest about their world, their pace of life. Billy plunged into an answer and made her laugh; Donald was more serious. My aunt drew him out and then Billy would play light with him. They disagreed, Billy joked and Donald complained: 'Well Billy, you know *that* isn't true ... ' and then the brash laugh from Billy, my aunt soothing the conversation along with one of her cure-all observations about life or holidays or show-business. Sometimes she chided Billy, like slapping him lightly on the wrist as though he was a peculiarly attractive child whom Donald couldn't manage. Billy probably thought that he was making an impression. Donald seemed to worry about him, when he was allowed to. And Billy was quite aware of himself; sometimes he just shut himself off as though he knew that he was a mixed blessing, and all the conversation petered out with a comment on how nice it was with the sun and all, and we all lay back on our chairs.

'I think I'll do some reading.' I stood up quickly and felt stupid. I thought that at least Annie would make a joke, but she didn't. My aunt was disappointed, Billy was polite. I went up to my room.

It said on the back cover: 'There were six of them in the heist out on the coast. Three went down, then the other two crossed Parker up and ran with the loot. That was stupid because Parker could kill a man in seconds flat with his bare hands. From being the hunted, he now became The Hunter. He cut his way through the syndicates; he beat his way past the gangland bosses. And finally – point blank – came the inevitable execution of a sentence that had been set the day the others got too smart.' When Parker had fucked a woman, I stopped reading.

I sat on the balcony and watched other people's wives, lying on their recliners. Laura was too young for me. She wouldn't know what to do.

Billy and Donald, my aunt, my uncle and Annie all came in from the pool. It was the pale grey time of day; the wives stalked across the tiles and went through a door three floors below me.

One husband and one wife were staying in the room next to mine. I heard them come in. Our balconies were separated by a smoked-glass panel. She washed her swimsuit and hung it over the balcony rail; she then went into the shower. They left their room an hour later, after having appeared on the balcony in fresh, casual clothes.

The pale grey concrete acted like blotting paper to the water that was oozing out of her costume. In the morning it would be dry and slightly stiff, with a smattering of white concrete dust where it had touched the balcony. After breakfast, she would come upstairs, brush the dust from her costume and stand naked in the room before putting it on. The end of her fine blonde hair was cut in a straight line. She washed it every night. She liked to smile at me if we were laying out our costumes at the same time. She might well have had a pale grey carpet in the lounge of their flat in Copenhagen. She and her husband talked quietly in Danish. I didn't like him, with his serious beard. When would they make love? At midday there were sometimes technical journals left on the seat of a balcony chair. His or hers? What influence would that have? Did it all go smoothly? Quiet people at school were often interested in engineering.

The sun left the sea alone; the air darkened quickly. The same people sat out by the pool, looking different in their fresh, casual clothes. I could hardly follow the wives through from their swimsuits, or decide which was more alive, the half-naked or the clothed.

Someone switched on the underwater lights round the edge of the pool. The husbands and the wives sat with drinks. Women looked distanced and beautiful, as though they had prepared themselves for an entirely pleasurable endurance test. It was their time. The men were anxious, the women moved as little as possible. Presumably they remembered how they looked from the mirror in the bedrooms. There was a lot of intelligence in creating these self-contained structures.

Her bathing costume was still damp. I wondered if she thought about that, what she felt about pulling a damp, cold

28

costume up over her legs and the damp cold against her dry stomach. If she felt the same way about it as I did; I hated it. Her physical structure was somewhat different. But with breasts it couldn't be pleasant. I saw her down by the pool, one of a group of four; she was warm now, and dry. The ends of her freshly washed hair were on a level, she knew this. It wasn't important to her; this hemline was often uneven during the day. But in the evening she was sociable; and her exactitude took the edge off sociability. Her husband drank whisky. Was he the engineer? Was she the engineer? Or did they have a rule that on holiday they would both read the journals recommended by her hairdresser? While her costume dried.

'Come in.'

Annie was worried. 'Don't worry,' she said to me, after she had shut the door.

'Why?'

'Pop wasn't really cross with you. You know how he gets. There's nothing to be upset about; just ignore it.' Annie was concerned. I wondered if I was upset.

'I was more tired than upset; I just felt like being on my own.'

'Why?' Annie worried again. Whenever she was perplexed she got worried; childish, instant worry.

'Those two are a bit much, Billy and Donald.'

'Oh I know. Jane's exhausted. It's because they're American. They're nice though. We're sitting and having a drink. We can't even get away to change for dinner.' Annie flopped down on the bed. 'Do you think it *is* because they're American?'

'Of course not. Do you still fancy him?'

'Not really. We think they're *peculiar* anyway.' Annie looked sternly, not sure of the significance. Peculiar meant homosexual. 'What do *you* think?'

'I don't know. What do you think?'

'I think they're funny. Do you think they kiss each other?' She was wide-eyed, and there again she was ready to peal with laughter. I laughed and she laughed. 'I didn't think you were in a bad mood,' she said.

'I'm not in a bad mood.'

'Will you come and have a drink then? We could get changed quickly and then we could take over while Jane gets changed.

We decided that we should take it in turns. Do you think there'll be a storm tonight?' She was bristling with excitement.

'Are you drunk, Annie?'

'I've had *three* Martinis!' Annie shone. I laughed with her. 'He doesn't even ask Pop, he just buys my drink with the others.'

'Don't drink too fast.'

'I could drink hundreds of Martinis, they don't do anything,' Annie rippled. 'Will you wait for me here?'

I said that I would. I closed the door behind her. 'And don't be long,' she called.

I changed. She came to collect me. I don't know what I was expecting to find in the bar, but it was much as normal. My aunt and uncle were sitting alone. Annie was crestfallen.

'Where is everybody?'

'They went into dinner.'

'Oh.'

'I expect they were hungry.'

Annie sat and fidgeted. I suggested that we should go on into the dining-room, there wasn't much point in waiting.

'We could have asked them to sit with us at dinner, but probably another time,' my aunt said.

'I don't think that we want to start all that,' my uncle decreed.

'We could sit with them.'

'Billy said that he would see you later on. He asked us, you know.'

'Anyway, they're half-way through their meal by now.'

It was better that they didn't take to eating with us. Meals were such a solemn affair. They would get very bored.

We stood up to leave the bar. Annie and I were to go ahead and eat on our own. My uncle took me to one side.

'We're going out after dinner, Jane and I. Bill asked us if we minded if he spent the evening with you. Apparently Donald likes to go out.'

'With the Danes.'

'I don't know. Anyway, just keep an eye on your sister. You know what I mean.' He didn't look at me directly.

I passed the next two hours wondering about this keeping of an eye; what it meant, how it could be done.

'How do you feel about men?' I asked Annie during our

meal together. Annie looked blank. 'What do you want to do this evening?' I asked her. How far would Annie go? Not very far. *He* might though.

'Let's see what Billy wants to do.'

They didn't come over to our table on their way out. Donald waved and Billy mouthed a silent hi. He hadn't bothered to change for dinner; Donald had knotted a lurid scarf round his neck.

We eventually found Billy out by the pool. I thought that he had wandered off, but Annie persisted in looking for him. I saw him first and said nothing; even when Annie noticed him I hesitated. He sat in the shadows, smoking a cigarette; he looked as though he were sulking, his mouth hung down, he looked bitter. Nobody looked bitter on holiday. He was too personal. Annie said that of course he was waiting for us and come on.

We sat by him and he was very reserved. He smiled to welcome us but we were young and didn't really matter. Annie immediately felt sorry for him, she put herself into a timid silence. It usually drew people out. Billy was very polite. He asked us if we had eaten well, and if we had found the sun too strong during the afternoon. He was dulled in some way or other.

Annie and I sat respectfully. Behind and above us was the clatter and very little chatter of the dining-room. Probably our aunt and uncle were in there. We looked out at the sea, Billy faced the golden blue of the pool. I thought about going upstairs but Annie would be disappointed. I asked if anybody wanted to drink something. Two soft drinks and a beer. Billy let it drop that he had taken his pill, and he didn't mix it with alcohol. Annie asked if he was sick from the hotel food.

'Hell no, I'm not sick,' Billy laughed. It was almost a poke at Annie's naivety; he squeezed her forearm to apologise. 'I just get a little tense and I have to learn to control this tension. I'm learning all right!' His laugh was quiet and gutty. 'Every now and then I need a little help from the medication. I get too excited.'

'What about?' I asked.

'Meeting you both, being here, getting to know you.'

'*I'd* need a pill for that!' Annie said.

Billy laughed. 'Come on, Annie ... '

'It's probably Europe, you always have to practise for it,' I announced, without having any idea what I meant. I hadn't been anywhere else.

'I make mistakes,' Billy said, 'people look at me as though I'm crazy.'

'They don't,' Annie defended him.

'Yes, they do. Sometimes,' I argued. 'Look at how everybody told you to keep quiet when you said that God often talked to you.'

'That was probably a bit mental.' Annie tightened her lips and didn't catch my eye. I wished I hadn't said it.

'I think that's wonderful, you have a gift and I think you should be very proud of it.' Billy leaned forward and looked sincerely at Annie; she didn't know what to do. 'And we don't have to talk about it. Some people have that gift. Would you believe that Donald goes to church every Sunday ... he'll go out and get drunk tonight with his Danes and he'll get up tomorrow at nine in the morning and he'll crash round the bedroom with a hangover looking for his glasses. And when he's got me out of bed and we've found his glasses, he'll go and look for a church ... ' Billy sat back and guffawed. 'I tell you that it's the last time we check into a room together. You should be there in the morning! You should see the way he gets out of bed; he doesn't know where he is. If you really want to take in a good show ... ' He kept on and on, until Annie and I were hurting with laughter, and then he stopped and then just the thought of the two of them in the same room kept Annie giggling. Billy started again; and there was Donald bumbling and moaning and searching every surface with one hand and clutching his head with the other. 'Don't, that's enough, don't,' Annie pleaded.

Billy wanted to continue; I asked him not to, because Annie might be sick; and he said that they'd never made a pill that could keep him calm and thank God – if you couldn't have a little excitement, what was the point in going on living?

'How long have you ... ?' Annie dried.

'Known Donald? A long time, a long time. Too damn long. I can't shake him off. Sixteen, seventeen, eighteen years. And the first time I saw him I thought what the hell is that? He's a great friend. Seriously. What are you laughing at? I mean it. Oh come on now ... what's so funny about that?'

'She thinks it's strange.' I steel-eyed Annie.

'He is the kindest man you could ever run into. He's a remarkable man. He's looked after me through everything. The whole trip; relationships, training, ups and downs. And there are downs. We don't want to get into that. Don't you ever laugh at that man; he is a rare human being.' We sat rebuked. Billy allowed this and then he broke it. 'Oh brother, Billy, there you go again! I didn't mean to upset you both. He's what we call an angel. If you go out there, you need someone like him and I love him for it. I love the way he is. I feel very deeply for him. Hell, you're young and I know what you're thinking; we're not lovers, if that means anything to either of you. I wouldn't expect that it does yet. If we were lovers the whole hotel would know about it, I can promise you that. I wouldn't hide it away. I couldn't. I'd have to talk about it. Don't tell me you didn't notice that Billy had a big mouth. I think I'll shut it and let us look at the sea for a while.'

He took a cigarette out of his packet and stood to turn his chair to face the sea. Somehow he had lost himself, and the air was full of nervousness.

He possibly needed some help but we didn't know what to do. We were isolated. He didn't want to look at the sea, except that he didn't want to look at us. Maybe we had disturbed him from the pill, and he needed to get his energy back. Annie and I were nervous for him.

'I like you both very much,' he said, not looking at us, but holding his cigarette unlit.

'We like you too,' Annie answered.

'Yes,' I said.

We watched the sea until Annie got cold without admitting it, and past that until the dining-room people washed up against our backs.

'Well what do we do now?' Billy asked. 'You tell me.'

'We usually go upstairs. We sit on the balcony and play cards.'

'You can watch the storms out at sea.'

'It sounds great. I'll buy a bottle of wine. Do I get invited?'

'Oh you are invited, Billy.'

'Yes.'

'That's just fine. I'll meet you at the party.' He was up and active.

'There's only three of us,' Annie said.

'The three best people. All right? Don't you forget it.'

I gave him my room number.

'I suppose that it *is* fine,' Annie pondered as we went up in the lift. 'They won't get angry, will they? As long as it's not in my room.'

'I don't know.'

'And he's so lonely.' Annie sighed. 'He must have been in love with this Natasha. It's sad, things like that.'

'What Natasha?'

'You don't notice anything important ever.'

'I do. Bring another chair from your room. And bring a glass.'

'I only want a sip of wine.'

We arranged the balcony. 'For entertaining,' Annie said. Even the cards were laid out properly, and the lighting got changed. I put my clothes in the wardrobe.

Billy arrived. He looked a lot younger. He had done himself up in a dark-blue shirt and black trousers. He joked and made fun and the room might have been full of people. At the same time, he was amazingly courteous. He lost five years and made us five years older; we talked as though we lived next door to him, about New York and life and the other people in the hotel, who might be interesting, who did what, who walked absurdly, why everybody was married. He asked Annie what she wanted to do with her life and he helped Annie to answer instead of just making out that she was a kid sister.

So Annie asked him some questions and became star-struck when Natasha was *the* Natasha Stewart and his nightclub was the most successful happening in New York, a lot of famous names. She was suspicious, and not prepared to make a fool of herself. She let it pass over her head in the very sophisticated way she sometimes had, I don't know where it came from.

It depressed Billy because of Natasha. Each time he said Natasha he missed us; we were like two young spaniels at his feet in front of this fire, and we didn't know anything about love, and we couldn't imagine Natasha being called anything but Natasha Stewart.

You could fall in love with Natasha Stewart, at a distance. Several people at school had pictures of her. But loving Natasha was something else. I thought so, anyway; it didn't seem to confuse Annie. There was more confusion in Billy, as though he had an object very close to him and an object far away from him – and his eyes moved quickly between the two in case he lost either of them. He couldn't focus.

I practised with the end of my finger and the swimming costume on the next balcony.

We were good listeners, but we couldn't help much. Falling in love was not something gentle, apparently.

So we watched the storms. Far away on the horizon they flashed soundlessly like a series of faulty neon lights. They never came close to us. Billy fell quiet, he smoked cigarettes. I worried in case his face would go slack, as it had been earlier in the evening. He wasn't an ordinary man. Annie and I always watched the storms as though we were safely locked out of a mad dance hall. We liked it this way. For Billy, if the storms weren't in and around him, they just didn't matter. We were kids and we were inadequate. He didn't play cards, he didn't drink wine. Wine bottle and cards were untouched; the sheet lightning fluttered pathetically.

Annie stood up and said that she was tired and going to bed. She kissed Billy good-night and slipped away. I envied her. I would have to be older. I poured a glass of wine for myself; Billy didn't want a drink.

Later, I felt that I could probably stay on the balcony here with him for a long time, when he was quiet and relaxed and there was no noise from the poolside, no noise from the people next door; light-headed thoughts and imaginations could come and go in the semi-darkness.

'You have a great gift,' Billy said, putting his arm across.

'No.' I started.

'You just don't know it yet. Don't fall in love with an actress; have an affair but don't fall in love.'

'No,' I agreed, vaguely man of the world. It was the darkness, it wasn't me. It had nothing to do with me. I could move in the darkness. I could watch things, I knew nothing.

'You're very lucky that you can take so much for granted.' Billy spoke with some bitterness, which I watched fall back upon himself; I was even glad that it did so. 'You have to hand it to the younger generation, they know how to look after themselves. They're nobody's fool.'

35

'Why should they be?' I demanded.

'They *will* be, babe; but I still love them for it. Our generation struggled out of nowhere and wherever we go we drag nowhere with us. Let me tell you, it doesn't shock me that no one wants it. You get on with what you believe in.'

'That's not true, is it?'

This prospect of a vast vacuum, as much in him as for me. You don't want someone older than you to talk about emptiness.

'The hell it's true ... ' Billy's reassuring gut laugh. 'We have this thing in America called the Movement; have you heard of it? It's a lot of silly kids with a lot of energy who think they're going to change everything. And I love them for it. They have so much energy and they're so sure of themselves. They say: I don't like it, change it. They'll work at it and they'll change it. You can't help but love them. They don't go to college, they hang around on the streets. They want to know. They want to know why. Do you think I know why? I've been in the business since I was fifteen, I was the youngest person ever accepted at the Actors' Studio, I didn't have time to think why. Why was a dumb question. I don't know what to say to them. You ask me why ... '

I didn't. I don't. I was bored. He smoked a whole cigarette. I wondered if he was a good actor. I didn't think I could fall in love with an actress.

Billy told me a story:

'We had this little girl in her first big show, appearing with Lauren Bacall on Broadway. Lauren Bacall. I'll take you to meet her when you come over, she's a great lady. And this cute little actress only had one small scene and all she had to do was cry. We're on final rehearsals and it comes to her time to cry and she can't do it. The director says what's the problem. She doesn't know. It's backing up at twenty thousand dollars a day, that's what it costs to rehearse. And she says: I don't understand why; I can't do it because I don't understand why ... '

I nodded, ignorantly sympathetic.

'You have to meet Lauren, that lady is a diamond. She was in the wings. She walked on to the stage. Leave this to me, she growls. And she got hold of the little girl's arm and marched her out of the theatre. She got her out there on the street and

36

she turned her round and she showed her the lights on the front of the theatre. The name of the play, and in twenty-foot lights underneath it 'STARRING LAUREN BACALL'. Lauren said, "That's why you cry when you're told to, honey." We walked her back inside, she cried every night and she got noticed and she'll make it.'

'Maybe she didn't want to make it.'

'Bullshit! Everyone wants to make it. Everyone.'

'In America.'

'Everywhere. Maybe you don't think you do; most people don't, think it or make it. But *you* do. You.'

'Maybe it's a bit different ... '

'Yeah, I think it must be. With the – what's that book? – *The History of Western Thought* that you carry around. You'll cry one day.'

I hated his intrusion, the effect of power, the American way; the indication that his honesty presumed my dishonesty.

'If you don't think it's any of my business,' he said, 'you should tell me to keep my mouth shut.'

Sitting on a hotel balcony in Mallorca, after midnight, as though the jewelled carpet of Broadway lay at our feet on the other side of the railings. When all there was was the sea. And there wasn't any business. Jewels were rubbish that women wore. Pale grey *was*.

'Let's go for a walk.'

'Hell now, calm down.'

Not in this room with him. It was too naked. 'No; let's go.'

'Sure.' He took his cigarettes in one hand and gripped my arm with the other. 'We'll make it. I didn't mean to frighten you.'

'No,' I agreed dumbly. I don't think I cared what happened as long as I could find refuge in it. It surprised me when we were on our way, walking normally towards the lift along the corridor. Billy was walking beside me, tired amber eyes. I looked along the corridor for an ashtray, he had a drooping grey carcass on the end of his cigarette stub.

'What time is it?' he asked.

'I don't know. Why?' I pushed the button for the lift and stood looking at the dark-brown doors.

'I should stop off and take a pill.'

'Why?'

'I have the medication once every four hours.' His cigarette ash dropped down to the carpet.

'You don't need it, do you?'

'What do you know? You don't know what might happen.'

'Nothing's going to happen.'

'Do you know what hypertension is?'

'Yes,' I lied; but hypertension couldn't be that stunning, for him or even for Lauren Bacall, whoever she was.

'And that's why we're going to sit out by the sea, huh? Okay, that's all right by me. Okay. I have it under control. Do you think Donald might be back?'

'I don't know. If he is, he'll be drunk, won't he?' Where was the lift, everything was falling to pieces.

'You're right. How do you so often get to be right, dammit ... ' Billy smiled boyish-hesitant. A bell chinged and the lift arrived. It brought us the two well-manicured engineers who slept next door to me. He had a vile, neat, wiry beard. His wife smiled with impeccable, warm grace. Billy didn't face her. He waited for them to get out of the way; he glanced at them in a cock-eyed loop.

'What do you think of them?' I asked as we descended.

'Who?' he slurred.

'Those two who came up in the lift?'

'I'm sorry, I'm afraid I didn't notice them. Were they friends of yours?'

'No.'

'Don't play any games, please, Martin.'

I manoeuvred him through the bar and out to a chair at the far end of the pool. I didn't know if he was acting or what. I fetched a glass of iced water and we sat in some defeated silence.

'Do you want to go to bed?' I didn't want to observe him. I wondered if my uncle and aunt had been in the bar and had seen us.

'It's early, isn't it? I'm very grateful for your contact and friendship. I would like you to understand that. You should go to bed if you're tired.'

'I'm fine.'

I didn't like to ask him how he felt. He had such dramatic changes. I wasn't sure whether it was intentional, and I didn't

38

know what he was other than the effect he had; we both seemed to be at the mercy of this effect. I didn't know why it was all so important, or why I was not lost in coyness, or why I used it. With him, I could remain shallow and pretend that it was deep. It would cost him a lot to touch me because I would watch him do it and he would have to accept that I wouldn't get involved; his anger would only rebound on him. I was innocent. He flattered me, I took it shamelessly, he was too much for me. I even enjoyed being confused by myself. I rubbed the pad of my first finger over the smooth white skin on my instep. It was immaculate.

'What will you do?' Billy asked. I didn't want him to be interested, I wasn't interested.

'I don't know. Look at everything else; none of it cares. It's all right on its own, it's harmless. I don't want to interfere with it. I don't see why it has to be personal.'

'I guess that's the way we like it.'

'In America?'

'No, dammit, in *living*. I bet you spend your time looking at that sterile blonde's swimsuit.'

He pierced me again. His mouth flopped open but his voice was hard and mechanical. 'And you giving me all that come-on ... I bet you enjoy it. Let me tell you, I don't sleep with men and not with boys. And you don't either; you may want to, who cares? But I don't sneak around. You'd better know that. Then we needn't waste any time playing games that hurt. I get hurt, and I don't like it, not when it's done coldly. If you think you've hurt me, you're wrong. You haven't even got near me. All that innocent boy crap. There are people who do it a lot better than you do. They have to, they make a living out of it. You wouldn't last two days. You'd be wasting your intelligence. I keep waiting for you to tell me something I don't know, or show me something I don't know. Maybe about yourself. It's in you.'

'What?'

'You're the one who's got to live with it; you figure it out for yourself.'

Billy was looking at the sea. He lit a cigarette. In the glare of the match I suppose he saw me looking at him. We were the only people out there, the pool lights were switched off. There was some noise from the town but the hotel was quiet.

The barman had collected all the glasses from around the pool. Only the bar area was lit up behind us.

'It could be anything,' he said. And then: 'I like the way we argue. Up and down. I think we should go to bed before that poor bastard in the bar locks us out.'

Billy put his arm round me as we walked back inside.

'I got by without my medication.'

'Billy ... '

'Hell, I know.' He gripped my shoulder. 'We're making it. I'll see you tomorrow.'

4

'There's this peculiar postcard under the door.'

'Leave it.'

'All right, all right ... ' Annie hung there for a minute and then went out. She didn't shut the door as quietly as she might have done. The thought that something was wrong made me wake up. I took the card.

Thank you – I shall think of you so often – I feel very deeply for you both. In time to come may we have many more evenings as late last night – I miss you – I love you

Billy

By the pool we had four red chairs and two green chairs. What colour chairs did we have yesterday?

'Hi, hello there ... ' Billy and Donald chorused.

Annie cast a dismissive eye.

In his world he must go through talks like that every night. He had written a love letter. I only wanted to be alone with him. He didn't look at me. I looked everywhere else.

'You must be hungry,' my uncle said.

'I am. We stayed up late last night.'

'We covered the world pretty well,' Billy laughed.

'Did you manage to change it, Billy?' Donald asked. He was a bit skittish, with his hangover.

'Did we? I don't think we did. We will though.'

'I don't think I'd worry about that,' my aunt said. 'People

have been trying to change it for years, and you'll never change human nature. It's not what you know, it's who you know.' She adjusted her sun hat.

'Donald didn't manage to make it to church,' Billy teased.

'What a shame.' My aunt and Donald fell to talking about church. My uncle never went, my aunt went when it was convenient. A year ago, Annie had suffered some mysterious disease which had left her bedridden for long weeks. My aunt stopped going to church services. She had faith in Annie and me. If God messed with us, then God wasn't picking the right number out of the barrel.

The sea-urchins had gone. Billy and Annie and I went into the sea. There were two other people on the raft, but since they didn't want to be disturbed they swam back to the rocks. Billy lay and coughed, Annie poked fun at him. Light dazzled off the surface of the water.

'What else is there to do?' Billy asked Annie.

'*I* want to go dancing.'

'Well we'll go.'

'*You* could ask the girl in the white bikini,' Annie smiled maliciously at me. 'She probably isn't as horrible as she looks. And she fancies you.'

'Shut up, Annie.'

'Maybe she's mental. She keeps looking at you.'

'She doesn't.'

'He never notices anything.'

Billy laughed at me. I hated Annie. She was trying to be twenty-five and lolling in the bikini with the tits and the joking eyes, making a fool of herself. All because she didn't stay up last night. Now of course she knew about the world.

'We'll take that girl along anyway,' Billy encompassed her easily. 'She looks kind of bored with her parents.'

'Who wouldn't be?' Annie rolled her eyes in sophisticated agreement.

'You don't mean that,' Billy's look settled on her, 'if you ever strayed too far from home you'd rush back.'

'You would,' I insisted.

'I might not. Anyway, it doesn't mean that I can't pretend that I wouldn't. So there!' Annie held on to my arm and tried to drag me towards the edge of the raft.

'Damn right!' Billy leapt to his feet to help her. I was shunted

41

into the water. Annie jumped in on top of me. We wrestled in a frustrated anger, until Annie suddenly stopped. I came up to the surface, prepared to push her under, but she was immobile, she was looking at the raft.

We watched together from the sea as Billy staggered back. His face was nervous. He held one hand up to his chest, fingers clutching at the skin. His face went pale and slack, his legs gave way. He looked at us. His eyes were preoccupied and yet trusting. His eyes slid up and he lurched backwards, collapsing off the end of the raft into the sea. The water ker-flumped as it took his body. Annie held on to my shoulder.

'Is it ... '

'Annie, he's only acting.'

'How do you know?'

'He's too young to have a heart attack.'

'They do in America. Go and see. Do something!' she urged in panic.

The quickest way was to swim under the raft. I ducked down and opened my eyes to look for his body. I saw him swimming round the corner.

Annie laughed and joked. She got on with Billy, but she never trusted him again.

I ate lunch.

I pleaded the need to work. I needed to study. I was irritably certain that I had to read the book. All right, I'd sit and have a coffee first.

I'm going now. Yes, I'll see you later and yes we'll go dancing. I'm going now. See you later.

I suppose that there is a vacuum. The book is full, dense. Even comprehensible when I want it to be. As the pages build up on the left-hand side of the spine, so it becomes more dense on the left-hand side of the spine. I ought to have this increasing density in my mind. Somehow my head should be leaning to one side with the weight of filed ideas, there should be a whole index down one side of my head. But it's only in my hands, the weight of pages passing from right to left, the book leaning.

The room is stunningly empty. The book should be cross-indexed, like the mileage chart accompanying a road map: Beauty, God, Imagination, Perception, Reality, Will, etc. along the top of the page; and Beauty, God, Imagination, Perception, Reality, Will, etc. down the side of the page. So you could . match up, for instance, Will and Beauty; trace Will in from the left until it meets Beauty coming down from the top – there is a box marked 310; turn to page 310 for seventeen one-sentence statements on the relationship between Will and Beauty. Pick out whichever of the statements appeal to you and throw them at each other. Like cock-fighting.

I was lying on the bed, and that parable in the Bible about the three people with the talents started to annoy me. Two of the people, the ones with the most talents, go out and flash their talents around. They get a pat on the back from God. And the bloke who buries his one talent – the poor bastard was only given one talent to start with – he buries it and God promptly harangues him and gives his talent to the big wheeler-dealer, the one who plays the game. Maybe the bloke with one talent liked to sit on his front doorstep and watch the ebb and flow of the world, he didn't want anything to do with God and those bloody talents. And for that he got flung into utter darkness.

The room is stunningly empty. There is a vacuum. Warm air, rich golden light, blue sky, books, swimming costume, benign smiles – are pegged around the walls. I want desperately to fall in love.

At four o'clock, my aunt knocked on the door.
'How's it going?'
'Not so bad.'
'Are you all right?'
'Yes. It's quite difficult, trying to do it.'
She occupied herself with arranging pieces of my clothing. I wished that she wouldn't do this, it gave out a feeling of suspense. As though she had something important to say and hoped to slip this importance into the natural course of events. I watched from the bed as she folded a shirt and put a pair of trousers over a hanger. 'There.'
She smiled warmly. I knew that she wanted to put me in a good mood, that she wanted to have a chat. She sat on the bed.
'Friends?'
'Friends.'
'I know we are. Is Annie annoying you?'

43

'Not really.'

'What is it then?'

They unnerved me, these questions. There was only ever half an answer at best, and that was always faltering in the face of such sympathy. There was never any answer. In the old days we would have had a bit of reassurance before I ran off to throw earth bombs at Annie.

'I don't know.'

'I expect we're just down in the dumps,' she remarked, her eyes seeking to beguile my sense of humour. I didn't wish to be so distant, but I was.

A gynaecologist once said on TV that having a baby was like taking your top lip and pulling it up and back over your head. I imagined it helplessly. My uncle had been in the war. Somewhere there were some atrocious photographs of him, how he had been when he returned from the Japanese camp. Everything was rightly hidden.

My aunt stood up. 'You and Annie and Billy are apparently going to eat early, so you can go dancing ... '

'Do you mind?' I demanded, standing up with her. It shocked her.

'Mind? No, of course I don't mind. Your lives are your own. Yours is. Annie will have to wait a bit longer.'

'And you don't mind?'

'It's something we accept. You know you've always got a home.' She looked at me.

'I'm not going anywhere, am I?'

'No, I suppose not.' She smiled. 'I don't know why I said it. I think you're restless, I don't think it has anything to do with university. You'll travel, I suppose. And you'll always have a home. Pop feels the same way about this, you know.'

'I never know what he feels.'

'Don't you really? I think you do, you know.'

'No.'

'I think you do. I think we're all right, aren't we?'

'Of course we are.' I kissed her cheek.

'That's better. Now then ... ' she looked around the room. 'What are you going to wear this evening?'

'I was thinking that I wanted to fall in love.'

'Oh.' She looked at what I had in the wardrobe. 'With anyone in particular?'

44

'No.' I relapsed into gloom, then we laughed at me.

'I expect it'll happen sooner or later. Now; what about this shirt?'

'No!'

'I'm going, I know I'm getting in the way. It's nice to have a little chat. I can see you're all right.'

'Yes.'

'Goodbye then.'

'Goodbye.' Our eyes twinkled at this severity. 'See you later.'

'Yes.'

She is passing me on.

What to say? To Laura. Never mind, dance again. Everybody was here to pick someone up. We certainly weren't. Perhaps this confused Laura. She said that she thought Billy and Annie and I had known each other for a long time. Perhaps that was the way Billy whooped us all along, the chatter and the laughing in the car, playing the fool with each other, the harmless way in which she was invited to join the gang. Her long dark hair still shone. She had it pinned back from her face. It showed off her high forehead and then hung like a curtain down the back of her lemon dress. Yes, she would like a Coke. Yes, she would like to dance.

When she danced, she looked at her shoulderblades, first one, and then - shake the head and the body - the other. She came from Nottingham. Brown shoulderblades. I looked at my knees. I came from outside Birmingham. White trousers, thunka-thunk music. She thought that she had heard of the Pink Floyd. Had I seen *The Family Way* with Hayley Mills? Unfortunately not. In Nottingham it was on in one of those double cinemas and the other cinema was showing *The Battle of the Bulge*. Aha. Thunka-thunk. She must just go to the ladies' room. Okay.

'How's it going?' Annie demanded from across the table.

'Okay.'

'She fancies you.'

'How do you know?'

'I can tell.'

'How's it going with you?'

'Billy's a wonderful dancer.'

He was. He'd danced professionally in New York. It was a

it flamboyant. It was to do with 'interpretation' and sweat. Laura, on the other hand, didn't perspire. Billy was dancing now, on his own; Annie was knackered. Laura was walking across the middle of the dance-floor. I thought about stirring a bowl of cold suet. I looked at Annie. Annie registered mental. I stood up while Laura sat down.

Billy asked Laura to dance. Laura went off to keep an eye on her shoulderblades.

'I don't think she's my type,' I said to Annie.

'She's not anybody's type. I told you that she was more boring than I was, but you wouldn't believe me.'

'Annie, do you think she's in love with her body?'

'What a silly thing to say.' Annie was considerably put out. 'How stupid.'

'Well why does she keep looking at her shoulders?'

'So that her bra strap doesn't show, idiot! God!'

'Yours doesn't show.'

'That's because I pinned it.'

'Where?'

'I'm not going to tell you. You don't ask those things.'

'I don't see why not.'

The music changed to Zorba the Greek. 'Come on!' Annie scrambled.

It was dreadful. Billy took charge of the line and knew the steps. We did it three or four times, all this bowing and stepping and bending. I had my hand on one of Laura's sacred shoulders. Laura didn't mind.

She didn't mind a bit of a clinch during the next slushy number. We were probably getting on okay. I think she was not averse to being kissed, but she was a bit tense. Her bra strap was probably on her mind. Annie's bag was always full of spare junk; this was no time to be inconsiderate.

'Would you like a safety-pin?' I murmured.

'No, thank you. I usually stick to Coca-Cola the first time I go out with anybody.' She smiled dutifully.

'Yes.' Were all girls as moronic as Annie?

'I'd never even heard of a screwdriver until your friend told me what it was.' We loosened our holds and gyrated politely.

'What is a screwdriver?' I said to her ear as it came within hailing distance of my mouth.

'Vodka and orange juice. What do they put in a safety-pin?'

46

'Oh, beer and *crème de menthe.*'

'I'll remember that. They have interesting drinks, don't they?'

She didn't mind my arm round her on the way back to the car, and through the hotel foyer to the lift. But when the four of us sat on the balcony, I was pleased to have my arm back.

When the three of us sat on the balcony, the two of them laughed about it.

'You certainly picked a cold fish,' Billy grinned. 'I don't know who she thought she was but she certainly thought she was someone.'

'She was probably in a mood,' I said.

'Oh hell ... she was stuck up.'

'She'll get married in two years,' I said.

'Why?'

I didn't know why; it occurred to me. But she would.

'She'll be a nagger, you can tell that. How dreadful,' Annie shivered. I brought her my sweater. 'You know what I'd like? I'd like some tea.'

'Annie ... '

'I can't help it. I would. It's not nagging, it's different.'

'In that case, we'll get some tea. Why not?' Billy laughed. He picked up the phone and ordered. He called to us. 'Let me interrupt Donald, otherwise he'll sit there all night over his papers waiting for me to come in.'

It was strange, sitting on the balcony with Annie, hearing Billy talk to Donald, Billy's half of it. It was very serious. Billy didn't ask about papers or business; he murmured, almost crooned.

'Yeah ... yeah, I was a little down. You were down too? Uh-huh ... sure you were ... I know how it is ... yeah ... did you talk with Linda? ... she's a darling ... she is ... just a party ... they're fine ... sure, why don't you ... sitting around, making out ... uh-huh ... of course, you won't, Donald, don't be an asshole ... okay ... we're not going anywhere ... uh-huh ... sure they do ... oh and why don't you call the desk and have them bring you some sandwiches ... they will ... that's fine, we'll see you. Three eleven. We'll be here ... '

'I invited Donald, he's feeling a little down.'

'We'll cheer him up, won't we?' Annie, engulfed by sweater, smiled excitedly.

47

We were up until four, covering the world again. With Donald there, Billy became more pliant; he seemed almost grateful to be childish. At times he'd cajole, at times he'd be humble. I talked irritably and stupidly. Annie and Donald preferred to remain cautious. I didn't really know what I was talking about; bits of politics, staleness, resentment. Annie got angry. Donald acted as though it was none of his business. Billy prised. I had a feeling of tremendous claustrophobia, I was even sick of the sound of my own voice, almost a despair at being self-centred at the same time as being hollow. I saw Annie as being closed, Donald closed, Billy playing open/closed, open/closed, and doing it easily.

It wasn't the same with the four of us. We had to sip politely. Donald was too likeable and I knew Annie; like I knew that she was annoyed with me now and a bit worried. I sat still. Billy's hand snaked across and gripped my wrist momentarily.

The engineers had made a point of shutting their balcony door, it was late enough to have to be quiet. Billy and Donald started their act, with Donald raising his eyebrows and undercutting when Billy left a space for him. We had to swallow our laughter. Annie bit her lip and dug her mouth into the sweater, but then she had to go inside and laugh into a towel. You couldn't perturb Donald, he acted as though he didn't know what the fuss was about. He did a better impersonation of himself than Billy did. He'd be over-meticulous, over-chiding; you didn't know whether it was real or not, this businessman seeming to be totally lost in the world, his 'Oh my!' assertion of ineptitude in the face of things, whatever 'things' were. He did drink a lot of vodka, which seemed to melt him. I suppose that Annie was by far the oldest of us all, given this clowning by which Billy and Donald deferred to her; as though nothing should touch her. Annie was no slouch. She rescued us from stagnating over vitality. And we didn't talk about Natasha. Billy had Emmys and Tonys but they were funny too, we didn't know what they were and Billy didn't care.

Four o'clock; and we decided to borrow the car to go across the island.

'Not today,' Annie pleaded.

'In six hours' time? That *is* a *little* too much,' Donald decided for himself. 'It's time for bed, Billy.'

'Right now, I can take anything. I haven't felt so good in a long time.'

'It doesn't mean you'll feel good tomorrow.' Donald smiled at Annie and me.

'Don't bullshit me, Don!' Billy whiplashed across the table.

'*I'm* sorry.'

'Time for bed. I'm going anyway. It's very late.' Annie moved out of the way, she laughed for us all. 'Good-night, everybody,' and she yawned.

'Good-night, darling.' Billy looked from his chair. 'You sleep beautifully.'

'I will.'

'Good-night, Annie.'

'Good-night, Donald, and thank you.'

'But it's your party.'

'If I keep saying good-night, I'll never go.'

'Go then. Sleep well.'

'I will.' She meandered off across the room and blew a kiss from the door.

'That's one sweet kid.' Donald stood, not knowing what to do. I was confused and tired, Billy sat slumped.

'She sure is.'

Donald looked at the debris on the table; empty coffee pot, shreds of sandwich, cups and spoons and glasses. He put his thumbs in his pockets and stood like a boy of thirteen, glancing uneasily through his spectacles.

'Well ... are you coming, Billy? It's been a long day. We could use the sleep.'

'Yes, I'm coming.' In anger, lips tight, Billy sat.

'So ... ' Donald dithered.

'I'm going to bed.' I went into the bathroom and washed. It took me a long time to wash. Billy and Donald were arguing in low voices. I wished that I had the power to dispel anger, like heroines who step out of gleaming enamelled bathrooms in black lace negligees open to the thigh.

Donald tapped on the bathroom door; he thanked me for the party, I thanked him cheerily. I didn't open the door.

When I came out of the bathroom, Billy was standing foot-loose by the wardrobe. I went to the dressing-table and took the money out of my pockets. The silence was one long live electric cable laid out on the carpet.

'I can't talk any more, Billy. I'm exhausted.'

'No, Martin, we can't talk any more.'

Again, before the dressing-table, I have that feeling of weakness, the not-knowing how to act or what to live up to. Billy no longer has his presence, his provocation; he is confused. We need a chaperone.

I keep my eyes on the mirror reflection of myself, not wanting to be responsible for anything.

'Good-night,' Billy mumbled. He kissed me on the cheek. 'Take care.'

'And you; yes.'

He went quickly.

Lying on the bed in confusion, almost dismay. Whether I have done wrong in doing nothing, what could have been done.

'Too many late nights.'

My uncle had taken to draping the newspaper over his head for the latter part of those long afternoons by the pool.

'That's it; too much talking about the world. If you read about it during the daytime and talk about it at night, that's much too much. This is your holiday; for heaven's sake, enjoy it. If they want to be up until all hours of the night, let them. Don't let yourself get involved.' My aunt wriggled her shoulders as if shaking off a wrap. She had smoked a cigarette, which was unusual for her before six o'clock. Annie had been to breakfast, had yawned and dozed her way through the dangerous midday glare, and had been packed off to bed after lunch. I had passed her in the corridor, on my way from sleep to food.

Billy was on the far side of the pool, his back to the sun. Donald leafed through his business papers. Billy occasionally passed a remark, he sheltered firmly behind his sunglasses. He went inside before the sun disappeared.

I welcomed my pale grey light and the strange way in which it accentuated the few sounds of dusk – a scooter bleating its way up the coast road, the splashes of an efficient swimmer in the pool, laughter from a balcony, somebody's radio. The dark arrived too soon.

I passed Billy in the foyer, the glasses still covering his eyes. The way he moved, he seemed to be feeling for the space immediately next to him; his whole spirit sagged.

'Kind of a bad day for me. Don't worry.'

'I'm sorry.'

'Don't be. I just have to take it slow and easy.'

'Do you still want to go tomorrow, in the car?'

'Can we do that?'

'I'll ask.'

'Don't ... create any problems for yourself. If it happens, it happens. I should know better. Enjoy your dinner.'

He made a sudden movement with his hand, down by his waist, as if snatching some part of himself away from me, protecting me. Nervous. He frightened me. I didn't know how much of it was acted, or if that mattered; he *was* an actor. Even in swaying towards the dining-room, it was Billy.

5

Annie is a magnificent wheedler. Supreme. She isn't at all a whiner. Her art of suggestion takes for granted the *fait accompli*.

'If we took the car and went out for the day, do you think that the hotel would give us a picnic lunch, Pop? We do have to pay for lunch anyway, don't we? So they should do, it's only fair.' And then Annie sat back to watch for the result. Admittedly, we had done some groundwork. My aunt knew of the plan. Probably my uncle knew as well.

'I should think they would, if you asked them.'

'I mean *if* we took the car.'

'Yes. And I suppose that you do want to take the car?' My uncle smiled.

'We don't know about that,' Annie said, 'we'd have to ask you about it first.'

'And where do you think you might go?'

'I'd like to drive across the island,' I said.

'And what does Billy think about this? I take it you want to go with them?'

'It would probably do him good, I don't think he's very well. And they can't get out because they haven't got a car.'

'You might find some tricky roads.'

'I know.'

51

'As long as you know. It wouldn't be a good idea to drink a bottle of wine and head off on some wild binge.'

'No.'

'I think that's all right then.'

'Oh thank you.' Annie gleamed.

'And as long as you look after your sister,' my aunt added.

We were waved out of the car-park at the start of a brilliant day, Billy at the front with me, Annie and Donald wedged into the back of the Seat 500. We hammered along the coast road and turned north. We climbed. The Seat tutted obstinately.

Going uphill, it was similar to that first slow haul on a roller-coaster. Once or twice I wondered if we were going backwards. We willed the car forward until it became so ridiculous as to arouse our fondness. From the driver's seat I had the leisure to scrutinise each individual flower in an approaching clump. Every time we rounded a corner, it was as though someone had handed over a different photograph. Hills, half-derelict olive groves, gnarled trees grovelling with age. One ancient tree stumbled forward like a sea-lion, balancing a kinetic spray of silver-grey leaves on the end of its nose. Billy saw none of it; he turned in his seat and kept the party going in the back.

And then we went downhill, which engrossed everybody. Billy sat up straight, rocks and flowers whizzed past us, Billy pulled his sunglasses down over his eyes, I laughed.

'Do you know how to control this thing?' he demanded.

'We seem to be going *very* fast,' Donald called.

'Sixty,' I said.

'Do you want one of your tablets, Billy?' Donald had their bag on his knees.

'No,' I said. 'We can go slower.'

'Then we'll never get there,' Billy laughed. 'You keep going; I don't need a pill.'

'Where *are* we going?' Annie queried.

And then we got there, all of a sudden. Back at the deep-blue sea, streaked with turquoise currents. Too fast.

I grumbled to Billy; he thought that we might turn back inland, or we could go on through to the next town and stroll around. There was a sudden upheaval in the back of the car; Donald flapped violently.

'Do you want to kill us?' Billy laughed.

'What is it, Donald?'

He squirmed and twisted and grunted.

'Donald ... ' Annie giggled. 'What's wrong?'

'It's a bee ... some kind of ... a wasp ... '

'Where?' Billy teased him. 'There's no wasp, Don!'

'We're on the edge of a cliff,' I said.

'Calm down. It's not there.'

'Well where the hell is it, Billy?' Donald twisted and bounced like a caged pig. There was nowhere he could move to. He lunged his neck forward as though the wasp might have disappeared down inside the collar of his shirt. Annie and Billy were spellbound with frozen laughter. Donald tried to stand up in the back of the car, as though the wasp was inside his trousers. The car was straining at the seams with panic. 'I've got to get out, look – I have to get out, will you stop this car ... ' He swung his arms wildly, his eyes were bulbous with fear, his glasses tilted to one side on the end of his nose.

Billy watched him like a child watches its first acrobat. Annie became frightened, Donald was suddenly filling the car.

The road straightened and I stopped. Donald pushed Billy out of the door and then stood by the side of the car, shaking hysterically.

'Where is it, is it in your shirt, is it in the back of your shirt?' Billy was malevolently amused.

'Is it?' Donald plunged his chest forward, with his arms held back.

'Is it there? Where is it? Take your shirt off.'

Donald held the shirt tail away from his back. Billy shook the shirt.

'There's nothing here; did you see it fly away?'

'No.'

'Well, is it in your pants? Take them off,' Billy urged.

'It doesn't feel as though it's in my pants, Billy.' Donald glared.

'It couldn't get into his trousers, he's wearing a belt.'

'It must be still in the car.'

I searched first the back and then the front of the car; ashtrays, map pockets, the joins in the seats, under the seats, behind the pedals, everywhere.

'How would it get into the car?' Billy snorted.

'How do *I* know? It was in there already; or it blew in the window ... '

'Did you hear it buzzing?' Billy was merciless; Donald stood half-naked in the middle of the road, brushing feebly at parts of himself.

'I heard something.'

'And you felt it?'

'You bet I felt it.'

Billy stood behind him, a broad grin on his face.

'I don't think it's in the car,' I said. 'I've looked everywhere. It must have flown out.'

'I certainly hope so.' Donald inspected his shirt carefully before putting it on and buttoning it up. Billy was over-solicitous, rolling his eyes with amusement at Annie and me.

'Perhaps Donald should sit in the front,' Annie suggested.

He did so. He was much happier; he occasionally switched his head from side to side as if to make sure that nothing was crawling up out of the depths of the car. Billy kept the joke going, too long. I was annoyed. It didn't matter whether the wasp had existed or not, did it? Annie was neurotically scared of insects anyway, so she didn't have anything much to be superior about.

I drove the car. I asked Donald about his electronics business. But he wanted to keep it a secret. As though it was insubstantial. As though the world of business had very little value when set beside Billy's world. Billy's world was exciting; *his* wasn't. It didn't surprise him.

I asked him if he could give me a job, if I went to America. He was at a loss. He didn't know. The company wasn't very interesting. I wouldn't enjoy it.

Billy said that hell if I came to America, he'd show me around, introduce me to people, I'd have a great time, East and West Coasts. Donald agreed with him.

We drove through Deya; we agreed that Deya was beautiful. We would come back to Deya for a coffee.

We went to the countryside to eat our picnic. We spilled out of our white metal box and camped under a tree; food, bodies and the contents of Don's bag littering the dusty grass. We ate, and looked at the car standing solemnly under the hot sun and we didn't feel like packing ourselves up again.

'What do you reckon, Donald?' Billy asked. He was

sprawled out like a dark-brown otter. Donald was propped against the trunk of the tree, reading his guidebook. He gazed into the middle distance and warned us about ants. Ants were in his guidebook. There wasn't much other wildlife. Presumably therefore, ants assumed the proportion of elephants; thus his concern for the middle distance. I mused. Annie soaked.

'Do you want me to read you about this area?'

'Sure.'

'Well ... ' Donald peered at the print. 'People have been living in Deya for five thousand years. Human bones and flint blades dating from 3984 BC substantiate this theory. Daggers, pottery and bones have been discovered in the natural burial caves – '

'Don't they do anything else here besides make bones?'

'Well, do you want to know, Billy?' Donald flushed angrily.

'Sure. Do you want me to stand in the corner? Bones!'

'Go on, Donald.'

'We'll take a rain check on the bones, I guess.' Donald flipped the page. 'It doesn't say that much about Deya.'

'Oh come on ... '

'These, I guess, are olive trees,' Donald looked around, got his bearings, and returned to the print-out. 'They're kind of old. Deya is situated on the side of a steep hill, the instability factor is controlled by supporting arches which span the village streets.'

'What does it mean?' Annie nudged Billy.

'Darling, I was never any good at school because I never listened. I think it means that they lean the houses together so they don't fall down on the bones.'

'They build arches across the street, didn't we see that when we came through?'

'You were sitting up front, Don; we didn't see that much. Is there anything else?'

'No. It just says that a famous artist is buried in Deya.'

'It's those damn bones again. We've hit the bone capital of the world!'

'You'd think they would have set up a glue factory.'

'Why? Why glue?' Billy rolled on to his side and lifted his sunglasses, looking at me.

'Bones make glue.'

'Don't kid me.'

'They make glue out of bones,' I insisted.

'Did you hear that, Don? He's kidding me.'

'I'm not.'

'*I* don't know how they make glue.'

'I'll tell you; no one's going to make glue out of my bones. You'll promise me that!'

We laughed.

'I want you to promise me,' Billy went on, 'is that too much to ask you, dammit?' He eyed Donald venomously. He was only restless. I laughed. His eyes fixed on me. 'Do you want your body to end up that way!'

'It's only for animals, isn't it?' Annie interjected.

'Can you feel it? Do you accept it!' he kept at me, staring. 'I don't know if you accept everything.'

Baked, brown houses with red, tiled roofs and small, square windows. These houses clung on to the opposite hillside, clustered together as if they had dribbled reluctantly out of some hidden crater. Like wax which had sagged over the rim of a candle and trickled into hard, knobbly goitres. Pinned under the sharp sun. I glanced at Annie. She raised both her eyebrows, ultra fed-up.

In Deya, we left Billy and Donald to have a coffee. Annie let out a deep breath. We set off light-footed down the street away from them.

'They're a bit much sometimes,' Annie said. 'You don't have any time to notice anything but them. It's stupid.'

Annie jumped her attention from window to window. In front of her, the shops started to open.

'What do you want to buy?' I asked.

'Nothing.' She laughed, that conspiratorial flash of exuberance. 'I just think that we should leave them to stew in their own juice. Donald moans so much, and Billy is so ... personal the whole time. It really annoys me. The next time, I'm going to ask him what *he* does and what *he* believes in and why doesn't he change *his* whole life. You shouldn't let him get away with it. It makes me really angry. I wouldn't ever go to America. Darling and angel and baby! And why wouldn't Donald give you a job in his sound company, or whatever it is. Pop wouldn't find any of *them* a job, you can be sure of that!'

'But Annie, they're different.'

'They think they are; oh, you can tell that all right. Just don't you get involved, that's all!'

It was so much like our aunt; I laughed. Annie smiled. 'You know what I mean,' she said, with retrieved sternness.

'Annie ... '

'Sometimes I worry about you, Martin. I never know if you know what you're doing.'

'What am I doing?'

'Anyway, we're going home soon.'

'Bossy.' I teased her, this kid sister.

'Am I? I'm not. You don't mind, do you?'

'No.'

'Good. Look. That's nice ... ' Annie crossed to the other side of the street. I followed her slim figure. I had forgotten that we were supposed to be shopping. 'It's pretty; don't you think?'

'The dress?' I supposed.

'The shirt. The dress is horrible.'

Annie went off into some daydream about the shirt. She looked especially childish, standing in front of the shop window, her knees slightly turned together and her old red rubber flip-flops, one heel raised an inch as if she was dawdling expectantly. A large and empty string bag dangled from one hand.

'I'm going to the next shop,' I said.

'Okay.'

And further. Down the street, there was a man laying out his tools on the bench beside his stool. Bits of dark-brown tree lay on the bench, twisted and knobbed into grotesque shapes. I looked through them. I picked up one monstrous aberration; about two feet long, it looked like a hunchbacked lizard, dragging itself out of a trap which had closed on the lower half of its body. The torso was stretched, the muscles along the back rose rigid with effort. Its front feet clawed desperately and its neck sank before the open mouth gaped in a hideous scream.

'How much?' My left hand fiddled inside my pocket.

Four or five teeth missing, the man shook his head. 'Ven conmigo.' He pushed aside a fly curtain and beckoned me out of the street into the front room of his house.

His finished products were smoothed wooden monks; some with candle holders fixed to the top of their heads, others standing unburdened, about eight inches tall. There were at least two hundred of them, solemn, with their arms crossed, looking towards the window. They were very emaciated, and they had oriental eyes and goatee beards. It was impossible to imagine them lying down, there wasn't an ounce of serenity in them; the wood was tight and ribbed. They would wait there in the gloom until someone built them a cathedral.

I paid for two, one with his candle-holder, one on his own. The man wrapped them carefully in brown paper.

Out in the street, he sat on his stool, picked up the crippled lizard and started to work. When Annie arrived, he wanted to show her his room; but when he realised that we were together, he considered that he had already achieved his quota of sales. He cut the lizard away from its trap.

'What did you buy?' Annie asked.

'I'll show you tonight.'

We strolled back up the street and turned left. Donald was taking photographs of the buildings while Billy guarded his bag. We were required to stand in a line with Billy; we were then preserved on celluloid. The four of us should be together. Annie persuaded a boutique owner to take the shot. We stood in line. At Billy's suggestion we all raised our right legs and rested our arms along each other's shoulders. A click and we were again preserved; myself embarrassed, Annie smiling sweetly, Donald with his leg held as high as a trotting pony, Billy lording it, open-shirted, with an exhilarated, snarling grin, nostrils flared.

'Perhaps she was just upset.' My aunt tried to calm us down. The 'she' was Laura; a question of hurt feelings and confused intentions, or the conjuring of a snub out of boredom. Hadn't we asked her if she wanted to go with us? There wasn't any room in the car. We could have squeezed her in somehow. Not likely. She would have enjoyed it. She didn't enjoy anything.

'Silly cow.' Annie scraped the top off her crème caramel.

'If you didn't ask her, that's an end to it. We rather thought you had asked her. That's all.' My uncle wiped his mouth with his napkin. He had the endearing habit of fiddling with cutlery, which infuriated my aunt and delighted Annie.

'What are they then?'

'This one holds candles.'

'What does the other one do?'

'Nothing much.'

'I suppose they just keep each other company. They're a bit serious.'

'That's how they should be.'

I told Annie the story of what had happened to a friend of mine when he was hitch-hiking through northern Spain. It got dark and he was left miles out in the countryside, on the edge of a vast plateau. He stood there for hours. There were no cars. The only thing that interrupted the flatness was a huge barn or building, about five miles from the road. When it was really dark, he started walking towards the building, thinking that he would sleep there and go on the next day. He walked for miles, it was midnight when he finally reached the building. He went inside. It was a huge, empty church. He went to sleep on a pew. Much later on, he was woken by the bobbing light of candles. More than a hundred cowled monks were walking in procession up the aisle. There was a lot of chanting, and then there was silence. Then he saw three nuns, all dressed in white, almost asleep, or drugged. These nuns were put into three niches in the wall and then they were walled up alive. Six monks had bricks and cement, they built the wall up in front of the nuns. In silence. He hid. He was scared as hell. They didn't see him. The procession came back down the aisle. He waited until morning and then got a lift to Barcelona. He went to the British Consul. They told him not to say anything and they flew him straight back to London.

'Are you *sure*?' Annie looked at me out of the corner of her eye. 'This friend of yours, is he batty?'

'No, he isn't. I saw the consular stamp in his passport.'

'Well; why did you have to tell me that just before we go to bed? What happened to the nuns?'

'They probably took them out.'

'Of course they did.' Annie decided that she had been deceived. She was cross. 'I hope you weren't thinking of giving me one of those wooden things, those monks.'

'No, I wasn't.'

She picked at her toenail. She said suddenly: 'Are you glad we're going home?'

'So so.'

'I expect you'll miss Billy. He likes you. You should write

to him. I shouldn't worry what *they* think. I'm quite happy for you. Really.' She looked up. How could she ever get used to having such long hair. She never picked at it, she never had that affected way of running her fingers through it or sweeping it back. 'I like him. Honestly.'

'Annie, what are you on about?'

'Billy. And why do *you* like him?'

'I don't know if I do. I mean, he's open. And he doesn't really care what happens. It's a change, that's all.'

'I suppose you're lonely; I mean with all of us, we're not really the same thing. It's nice for you to have a friend.'

She sat on the bed and thought about it, for both of us. She looked so unready, it was hard to tell which of the two of us was more confused.

6

It was our last full day; Billy and Donald had another week before they flew back to New York. I had slept heavily. At nine o'clock I had woken up and had put myself back to sleep for another two hours.

I resuscitated the last reverie. Policemen were bouncing through a shopping precinct on their heads.

Suddenly I was in a dream which centred around a blonde-haired woman of about forty. I was staying in the house of a farm worker, sparsely furnished, a garland of roses at the base of the television. There was a man leaning at the foot of the bed, making telephone calls. We went to see *her*. She had invited all her boyfriends singly, but they all met. Most of them dispersed in anger, on horseback or walking. They seemed to be members of a hunt, in black or red riding jackets; they strode confidently.

She wanted to talk. I was amazed at her house; it seemed to be a 1930s 'Georgian' mansion, a mixture of brick and stone but with a lot of glass. To the right, and adjoining it, was a sculpture workshop – she made heads, *very* large heads.

Besides the eerie telephonist, it appeared that she had an owner.

I left the room with her dog. She wanted to talk. The three

of us walked down a track with fields on both sides. She and I talked in French. She was dressed in a light red shirt and a black flounced skirt, red, buckled shoes with high heels. She loved showing off her legs. We enjoyed looking at her legs. I wondered if she was a whore and how much that mattered. Her hair was piled up carelessly on top of her head, her lips sticked redly, there was a slight gap between her front teeth. There was very little attractive about her except for her aura.

We were back in the farm worker's front room. She called to me from the bedroom. The eerie telephonist had already told me that I would be her lover. He went, and her owner – whom I never saw – went also. She seemed very uncertain, nervously distant. She was ugly: but she was sensational. She sat on the floor at the foot of the iron bed, her right elbow resting on the mattress; she was elegantly irritated by her thoughts. I watched her from the door.

I awoke, still dazed, with a prickly feeling around my eyes. The hot, white air was backed up against the balcony door. I half-expected to find her sitting in the shade and looking out over the countryside, not the sea. I had enjoyed talking to her even though I couldn't speak much French. We had a wonderful understanding. But the room was empty, the sunlight was listless, the balcony was concrete and on the other side of the frosted glass was a stiff, dry swimsuit which signified the unimportant break in a Nordic woman's bronzing habits.

Around the pool there was a shambles of desultory conversation which indicated that the holiday was as good as over. We all made brief points, the conversation didn't wander anywhere. Positions were staked out. My aunt kept a firm hold over England, when Billy tried to share it with her. 'Quite pleased to get back' was the agreed attitude, and 'I suppose that it won't really have anything to do with you' was the underlying apologetic statement. It was horrible. I swung between anger and gloom.

In deference to constant, laboured reminders about packing, I went back upstairs after lunch and put the *History of Western Philosophy* into my suitcase. The better half of my packing was done.

I was fond of the room, that it was impersonal and not decorated, that it had a lock on the door and large windows. Mostly that there were unknown people living on each side of me. And they were only there for a time, so it was as much as they could do to fill up their own rooms; they contained themselves, they couldn't move sideways; they could look out of the windows and they could only expand by jumping over the balcony and disappearing. Such a one-way process would be acknowledged by the engineers, who would have no need to test it. The swimming costume would in any case mark her boundary, a red flag warning her of the abyss.

They hadn't been in the dining-room and they hadn't been at the pool. They either had a car, or they were making love, or they were suffering from food poisoning. They weren't talking. They were perhaps looking through their magazines, he was reflecting on the skill of her hairdresser, she was considering whether or not she could renovate the central-heating system in their Copenhagen flat, if she could find the time for such a project, and the mistake in their priorities re the fitting of the ash-grey carpet. I knew that *he* wouldn't have figured that out; he was too dumb. She probably married him because he was a house-trained animal. His name was Glergbrot and she was called Finsewendel, after the flossy texture of her pubic hair and the tiny platinum stalks scattered over her stomach from seeds thrown carelessly.

Her swimming costume was as stiff as a plank. If there was a wind it would have banged to and fro like the clichéd shutter on the front of the clichéd empty house. If she was leaving tomorrow she would have to fold it like corrugated cardboard and compress it into her suitcase, next to the cotton and silk and chiffon and whatever. One thing that was strange, with her being an engineer, was that she didn't have a special drawer of clothes for going away on holiday. Summer clothes, yes – she obviously didn't turn up in ribbed tights, cord skirt and quilted, yoghourt-coloured jacket. But she wore nothing that proclaimed holiday, yes, here it is, my saved-up holiday glam togs. Conceivably, she went swimming in her Copenhagen lunch break. The acquisition of a new swimming costume would be annual, but it wouldn't necessarily be at the beginning of each June. I would like to work in her office, to see how she moved round the side of her desk or her drawing-board. Or at her home. Someone, sooner or later, would drop a fillet of cigarette ash on the carpet. Her husband would mottle himself with ill-repressed anger and take upon himself some of the guilt. Forced to notice this event, she would remark on the stupid design of their ashtrays. She would never be unfaithful to him, but when he crumbled she would choose to live on her own. She would buy another carpet, the same colour. She wouldn't let me have the swimsuit if I asked for it, but she would understand my request.

I swam to the raft.

From the level of the sea, the rock shelf climbed like a scaled, reptilian foot, damp-dark from the water and then sun-baked pink oyster. On the top of the foot was the white concrete block of the swimming-pool surround, an empty diving-board. And the hotel behind it, seven floors, railings along the balconies, green curtains in the windows. It had been placed on the sandstone after the trees had been cleared.

It was still warm on the raft when the hotel and the swimming-pool and the sandstone were in shadow. From out at sea, they were swamped by black rather than grey. The sun would soon fail to reach the raft. Already the water was chopped by the evening breeze.

'What's Donald doing?'

'He's going out with his Danes. He said that he'd see you in the morning.'

'I think I'm going up to bed,' Annie said.

'All right, darling, you sleep peacefully.' Billy stood up to kiss her good-night.

'Don't you two stay up for very long.' Annie gave me a warm kiss, a smile which was both sad and yet encouraging.

My aunt and uncle had already gone upstairs. To bed early, and the holiday company bus would call for us at ten o'clock to take us to the airport; we should have a good night's sleep.

When we had sat in the bar, Billy and Annie and I, we had all leaned forward towards the table between us, as though something was going to happen on this table; with our elbows on our knees, as though we were going to discuss a plan. But we couldn't think of anything to say. We had all reserved this moment and then it was like sitting in a waiting-room. Billy watched us with a careful screen of irony across his eyes; it gave me the feeling that I always had during those ten minutes before going into a room to sit an exam, that closed-off nervousness in front of the huge, silent wall of facts which I had inside me. I was programmed; I didn't want anyone to say anything. When I saw the questions, I would know which bricks to pull out of the wall in order to build the answer I knew they wanted. After ten years of male-segregated schooling, I was asked to write on the treatment of women in *Paradise Lost*, *King Lear* and *The Winter's Tale*; my answer had scored me a place in an all-male Cambridge college.

Annie had looked at the other people in the bar. She had finished her drink and had gone to bed.

'Shall we go and sit on the balcony?' I said to Billy.

'Sure.'

Without sunglasses and, I think, without drugs, he affected his stoned amble; and then he gave it up, he became serious. On the balcony, as we talked about packing, his braying laugh shattered the night. He sent down for coffee and beer, he had a surprising sympathy for Laura when I was rudely dismissive, he said that it wasn't the way to bring the world together, that she had no confidence, and if you didn't have any confidence you found it difficult to be generous. I asked him: was it all a matter of giving and giving and giving?

'It's not as bad as that,' Billy laughed, 'that's more of a feeling you have when you can't see what you're getting back.'

'Then you should be on your own.'

'I hate that. That's hell. Anything's better than that. I don't believe in it. You shouldn't believe in it at your age. The whole world is full of different, interesting, loving people. If you don't notice them then you're missing a lot. You can kill yourself that way.'

'Like who?'

'Pardon me?'

'These loving people.'

'Anyone.'

'Not *anyone*.'

'Why not, dammit! You think you're special?'

'*You* are.'

It stopped him for a moment. I think that he knew he was special, but being told so was perhaps commonplace and even cold. People probably used it as a convenient label when they didn't want to think about him. He wanted to be thought about. I had never used the word before, except for things,

64

like 'special key' or 'special paintbrush'. I didn't mean that sort of empty function. I didn't want to mean it that way. Or perhaps I did.

He considered me, perhaps there was a language difference. Perhaps there was a huge difference between a white Marks & Spencer shirt and a green shirt that was open three buttons at the neck and chest, with a gold chain resting against the mat of black hair.

'I want to know what you're going to do, and then I want to know when you're coming over to the States. So we can get it fixed up.' He put his coffee cup on the table and opened a battered pocket book.

'I'm at university for three years.'

'We'll see.'

'What would I do if I came to America?' I asked angrily.

'You'd do it. In America, you have to do it or you sink. I don't think it matters what you do. Right now, you can't afford to do nothing.'

'University isn't nothing.'

'I think it is. If you're a scientist then you've got a lot to learn. If you're an artist, you're wasting your time.'

'I'm not an artist.'

'I don't see what else you can be. If you're not bored then you're scared; you, do you realise that? Unless you're one of those people who don't live. You have a very easy way of putting people down with your eyes, I don't know if you know that. You did it to Laura and you did it to me the first time we met. I can't live like that. I have to have people; screwed-up, wonderful people. Open people. People who I hate and love and people who love and hate Billy Maffett, because they know how I am. Those kind of people who you don't expect to make it to your funeral.' He finished with a wild, raucous laugh; a fatuous defiance which shocked me the moment before I laughed with him. That kind of careless laughter at doing something dangerous when you're drunk; knowing you can't fail to get away with it. 'You know,' he said, 'I don't care if you turn out to be an artist or not.'

'Good.'

'You're lying.' His smile ended suddenly. He leaned forward in his chair. 'Sooner or later you'll get stuck with it. You want to make sure that you give it everything you can give. And you don't want to give a damn what anyone else thinks, or says, or feels. Because every son of a bitch in there is waiting for you to crack so that he or she can climb over you to get to the top.'

'Were you at the top, Billy?'

'Sure.'

'And you didn't like it?'

'I loved it. You know that song – "All of Me" – is that a Peggy Lee number? You don't know. What the hell *do* you know? That song says it. I loved every moment of it, and I still do. I am hard skinned. I'm going to survive right through it all. You can bet your last dollar on that.'

I had written my address in his book, and he now copied down a New York address on a piece of hotel stationery.

'I'd better let you get some sleep.'

'No, I'm not tired.'

'You tell me when you want me to go. Here. It's not too far from the Park, up on the West Side. Where do you live in England? Near London?'

'Not really; it's in the centre.'

'Uh-huh. I'm going to leave you.' Billy stood up.

'Billy, what pills do you take?'

'Nothing too serious, you don't want to worry about that.'

'Okay then.'

'You and your sister are pretty much alike.'

'What about your sister?'

'Our family wasn't that tight. Are you going to get to bed now?'

'Sooner or later.'

'You should do.' He laughed.

'Have you got a job when you go home?'

'If there's anything around, I'll always want to do it. I get bored sitting on my butt. I admire your ability to sit there for three years; you don't want to pay any attention to what I said. I couldn't sit there. I've given you a lot of rough talking, haven't I?'

'I don't know.'

'Too much?'

'No.'

I was standing next to him, almost in tears. I thought only about fighting down the feeling. I was dazed towards every-

66

thing else; avoiding his eyes, sensing the touch of his lips on my cheek and his promise to see me in the morning, his body walking away and the click of the bedroom door behind him.

And then, when he wasn't there; and the whole of it was uncontrollably stupid, clothes had to be put into the suitcase, two at a time if they were folded to start with, two clothes, one article if it had to be folded at a time in a blur. Fighting it down. With no way out, nothing to be done about it. Sensing that it was a safe place, I lay on the bed. I turned off the lights and took off my clothes and lay under the blanket; and slept; and fought through the dreams.

Until Annie touched me.

'You can't look like that. I'll tell them you're having breakfast in your room. Don't worry. I'll organise it. You'll have to get up in an hour. I'll wake you. Go back to sleep immediately.'

It would be a mistake to invite those dreams, the swirling gargoyles lunging upwards through my own vertigo. It was unpleasant to lie down. I sat up and then I went to the bathroom and was sick, a choked slime of substanceless bile and finally a pure exhaustion. My back was too long, the bone too rubbery. But not sleep, not now.

In films, people trusted in a shower at this point.

My kid sister carried a cup of tea and a bread roll. She said that I looked better. She put her arm round me. Well, we've got to get ready to go. If you have something to eat then you'll feel better.

There was a pile of suitcases in the hotel foyer. My uncle and aunt were sitting opposite them in their travelling clothes.

'He's *been* sick,' Annie announced efficiently, 'but he's feeling better.'

I smiled at my aunt. 'Oh dear,' she smiled bravely. I had the feeling that they didn't believe a word of it, or that they were maintaining that it was out of their hands. I had no wish to sit in the hotel lobby. I felt that I might be sick again.

'I think I'll go outside.'

'Get a bit of fresh air,' my uncle said. 'Don't go too far; the bus will be here in a minute or two.'

'In ten minutes,' Annie contradicted.

'I expect it's just a bit of nerves,' my aunt said. My uncle tweaked at the crease in his trousers, and agreed.

Just then Billy and Donald came out of the dining-room. I didn't want this. I walked towards the plate-glass doors. I heard Donald start his 'Well it certainly is sad that you're going like this ... ' and as I stepped outside into the sun, Billy was at my elbow.

He took my arm.

'I just want to get round the corner – '

'Sure.'

We walked almost briskly, nervously, in silence.

'Come on now ... slow down ... we don't have very far to go.'

'No,' I said.

'I wanted to apologise to you for running out on you last night, leaving the room like that.' He nursed my arm.

'Billy, I bought you this.'

Since leaving the bedroom I had held the monk rigidly in my right hand, now I offered it to him at the very end of my fingers. Small wooden thing, not so important, his brown eyes wondered.

'I love you.' Over his shoulder, in his shoulder. I didn't know how to kiss him, how you could do that, and he held me tightly. I clenched the monk. I watched the tears, imagining how I looked and not wanting to be seen. Babe ... babe ... I love you too ... A long time on his shoulder, on the shirt.

'Come on now, let's walk a little.'

Strangely still in the morning. The road was tarmacked, without verges. It went straight from soft, yielding black into pink dust. I could have gone on and on walking away with that strange, exhausted relief.

'Come on; where *have* you been?' My uncle's eyes darted. He shook hands quickly with Donald and Billy, and I followed him on to the bus. I sat next to Annie, welling tears. Billy didn't wait; he walked back into the hotel.

'Don't worry,' Annie said, 'you'll see him again.'

The doors of the bus schlunked together. The driver had time to make up. On the way to the airport, we ran over a pig.

68

7

It really didn't happen. In any case, what was it? What had or had not happened? Nothing.

A deep sadness and a sense of futility. And no one noticed. Rather as if I had made a fool of myself. Had dropped a pile of plates which hadn't hit the floor. I looked down and they were always there, about to crash, about to smash. But they stayed three inches above the floor.

At night I would sometimes cry. I would try to cry when I went to bed but I couldn't. I lay in a rage of frustration and non-comprehension. Why was there no one there to love? And obviously: how could I *love* if there was no one there to love? I would wake up crying at two or three o'clock in the morning.

Of all the people who crossed my mind, the Danish woman lingered – with her artificial severity, her composure. She was gracious. She allowed me my own perspective. I held long conversations with her. Her smile had always been an item on the agenda, in that hour before the hotel dinner. I talked with her in her Copenhagen flat, and the corners of her mouth showed a warm amusement. I caught her sometimes a little embarrassed. I noticed her ankles and her shoulders, her hair touched her shoulders. She liked music and hated dancing. We both liked the smell of chlorine on her swimming costume which lay over the drying-rail in the bathroom. I asked her what purpose her husband served. Apparently he stopped her falling in love. Again, she was amused. And so we lived to- gether, without ever talking about love. With both of us it was the same. She lightly caressed an object that was still warm from my touch; I stroked something that had just been in contact with her.

When Billy crossed my mind, he went very fast. My eyes didn't follow him, he terrified me. He disappeared.

My uncle worked, my aunt shopped and cleaned and cooked, Annie went out to talk to girlfriends or to go to parties. I slept until midday. Mostly I remember our empty hallway, with its green carpet and dark brown wall-panelling.

And then Billy telephoned. One late afternoon. I was sitting on the stairs, the phone was four paces across the hallway on a dark-oak table. I heard myself simply giving him directions, he was in London. Our conversation ended quickly. I wasn't sure what had happened.

I saw every connection and no possibility.

'Who was that?' my aunt called.

'It was Billy.' I walked into the kitchen and stood with an arm on the fridge. The house was too small, it wasn't grand, people didn't often come for dinner, my aunt liked to make a special effort for those who did. It was hopeless.

'Billy?' My aunt knew; she was immediately as unsure as I was. She stood facing the sink, looking out of the window at the garden. My uncle had a gift for roses.

'He's in London and he's coming up here.'

'Oh, that's nice. He does get around. Where will he stay?'

'I suppose he'll have to stay in a hotel.'

'Yes, I should think so. I should think he'd want to. Is this on business?'

'I don't know. I don't think so.'

'Well I don't think we can have him here.'

'No.'

'And I'm sure your uncle wouldn't agree to it.'

'No. Well, I think I'll have a bath.'

I didn't want to look at my aunt. I suppose that I was a bit ashamed, both of her and for her and of how I would be with Billy. We were all suddenly representatives. Billy wouldn't understand. I would fail him. It was a mess. It was ridiculous. It didn't fit us. I searched the floor.

'You're still rather young, you know.' She had turned and was looking at me. She was holding a wet, skinless potato and the potato peeler. Why should my aunt have to peel potatoes? Why *should* she?

'I know.'

From the bathroom, I heard my uncle come in. When he arrived home from work he would sit in his car in the drive for several minutes listening to the radio, and then he would open the front door of the house and put down his briefcase, take off his coat. Thus the evening started.

The bath was always too hot. It reduced me to a light-headed faintness. I delayed my recovery. I didn't want to enter into the discussion about Billy, I couldn't imagine pleading. There would be no argument.

They had discussed it.

'And what time will he be here?' my uncle asked.

'I suppose about three hours from when he telephoned.'

'Well he'd better have something to eat with us and you can fix him up with a room at the Victoria.'

'Okay.'

'Will you go and pick Annie up?' my aunt asked.

'Yes.'

I telephoned the Victoria, a small-town hotel; I took the car and went to fetch Annie.

'Oh God,' said Annie, 'he won't like it here.'

'Do you think it's terrible that we won't have him to stay?'

'No, it's a very good thing. Do you mind, though?'

'I don't know.'

'I know how you feel. Don't worry. We'll just have to think of things to do.'

'Like what?'

'Well there's a party on Saturday, and then you can take him to Stratford. Do you want me around or would you rather be on your own?'

He handled it so well. He looked exhausted, as though he hadn't slept for several days. I collected him from the station, we kissed. He sat next to me in the car. I drove slowly. He slumped. A huge weight seemed to settle through him. His eyes were swollen, his head sagged. 'It's been a bad time.' He smiled as if he was thinking of an old friend.

As we turned into the driveway, he lit a cigarette and held my arm for a moment. And then as the car stopped and my aunt opened the front door, he was out and 'Hi, so good to see you,' with a small present. My aunt was sure he'd like a bath, he complied, he joked with Annie, he was courteous to my uncle, he let himself be manoeuvred along the well-worn line of preparation for dinner. I was proud of him.

Upstairs, I showed him my room, showed him the bathroom. He took it all in. I wanted to look at his eyes as he was looking at other things, I wanted glimpses of him. And he laughed loudly as though we were together in this plot.

Hesitantly, trying to support both sides, I explained to him about the hotel. I knew that he was hurt. It was true that we were expecting a relative any day. He guessed that he should have called previously, how kind of Philip and Jane to receive him, he didn't want to be an inconvenience. His spirit sagged. 'Things are crazy,' he said, 'my schedule got changed; I thought why the hell not.' I fell in love with his back, the whole incongruity of having him in my bedroom where there wasn't the space to swing a cat and there wasn't any balcony; the complete and necessary way he destroyed the years-old atmosphere in that room. I no longer felt any attachment to it.

He couldn't know all this, because I was frozen.

At dinner we talked about Donald, sea-urchins and wasps. We couldn't talk in the same way. There seemed to be an unwillingness to laugh. I felt very scared for him. I couldn't understand why he let himself in for so much, why he allowed himself to try so hard. He asked for a cup of coffee between each course and smoked a cigarette. His laughter became more nervous, almost authoritarian. Though my uncle and he laughed together at things I didn't find funny, nevertheless I knew that he was being treated warily. I could never make my uncle laugh.

I noticed that Annie was anxious. She had a way of sitting with her hands together between her knees, which brought her shoulders forward protectively. My aunt sat with her arms crossed, rather shy, pretending that her sole function was with the plates and the gauging of the moment when they should be gathered. My uncle leaned back in his chair. In fact, all of us stayed carefully away from the table; except for Billy. I saw that the English have a lot of cruelty in the way they watch, in the way that they want to make someone feel that his attempts to be friendly are having only an average impact.

Billy struggled, he was held politely at a distance. I thought then that he would fall to pieces, that this was more or less what everybody wanted. He began to look drained and nervous. I prayed for him to keep going.

The family washed the dishes and cleared the table. I was left with Billy, sitting silently. Though he pretended, in the most piercing way, to be entitled to his exhaustion, he was more sapped by regret. He wanted nothing so much as to get away; he was abjectly lonely.

In the same way that we had watched him entertain, we sat in the lounge and watched him disintegrate; and when that was too embarrassing we watched the news on television with claims that we never watched much television. He had his ashtray and his cup of coffee. It was as though we were waiting for him to upset the coffee on to the carpet so that we could be solicitous – a lesson for him in mechanics. His hand trembled from time to time, and his eyes occasionally closed in a slow, mad fashion; though this latter, Annie told me afterwards, only happened when he thought that I was looking at him.

Why did all this go on?

His mouth shocked me into fear and desire, repulsion and need. Here there was distance. I watched him swallow coffee, I watched him draw in and exhale cigarette smoke, I hung on that beautiful, filthy mouth. All of this was so obscene, here amongst the soft furnishings and the four bright identical sidelights which protruded from the walls like sets of small antlers. So I couldn't be alone with him. I sat with everyone else and was nervous.

Annie went to bed first. In one enviably easy and significant gesture, knowing full well the capabilities of her innocence, she kissed him good-night and said that she would see him tomorrow.

I was to drive him to the hotel. My uncle and aunt said how nice it was to see him. He thanked them for the dinner. My uncle reminded me that the garage doors should be locked up for the night on my return. I collected Billy's suitcase from my room.

In the car, Billy said: 'I guess I'm a bit much', and I was silent, unable to comfort this truth.

When we were to turn right into the hotel yard, across the oncoming traffic, I couldn't trust my judgment. I waited and waited. The gaps between cars were long. I couldn't do it. Billy wasn't a driver. He took a long time to realise.

'What's wrong?' he asked very quietly.

No. Nothing could be wrong. I cut through the traffic very precisely. Rather suddenly. There was no danger to us from any other car. I was the danger. I wanted to leave him.

The hotel, built in the seventeenth century, had been modernised. It had been a coach stop and was now two large bars and a restaurant, with a few surviving bedrooms on the first floor. After we had waited for fifteen minutes, a girl came to sit behind her desk and she registered Billy. We took his suitcase up to the bedroom. He wished to sit over a pot of coffee. Room service existed only to tidy up after the guests had departed in the morning. In any case, the room was chilly and inhospitable.

We returned downstairs and asked politely for some coffee. A vile barman informed us that it was closing time.

The small bedroom was like a coffin. I left him sitting on the bed; I said that I would collect him tomorrow.

'You have to get out of here,' he said. 'Promise yourself. If you can't do that, then promise me.'

My aunt had stayed up, hoping to talk, to smooth it all over. I couldn't do that. I went to my bedroom and stayed awake until dawn, punched by nerves, my eyes painfully dry. I lay with the smell of my sweat. I hated Billy. I stumbled into sleep as I was listening to the sound of my uncle's morning wash.

'You're a great help.' Annie sat on the bed, watching me.

'It's not my fault, Annie.'

'Jane said that you were tired. Well, we're all sitting downstairs quite happily without you. You could come down some time if it's not too much to ask. Lunchtime maybe? Or some time in the afternoon? I'll run the bath for you, that'll make it easier. God! Brothers! I don't know how you get away with it. Billy sends his love.'

'How is he?'

'Fine. He slept well.' Annie drew the curtains. 'He telephoned us about ten o'clock and we went to pick him up. I should think he's getting a bit bored. Of course he's only really interested when he's talking to me. But then I'm quite interesting really. Probably only the intelligent people realise this. Most people don't know what they're missing out on.'

He was quite self-satisfied in the lounge downstairs.

In the evening we went out to see some friends of Annie's. I paraded a flamboyant cynicism in front of him. He seemed to be sad that he was having no effect on me; I was exuberant.

'When do you think you're heading back to the States?' I asked him late Friday night as I drove him to the hotel.

'Hell, I don't know,' he muttered. 'What's happening tomorrow?'

74

'My aunt's got us tickets for *Hamlet* in the afternoon. There's this boring party later on. We could take it or leave it.'

I swung off the road into the hotel yard and parked in front of the glass swing-doors. He sat for a moment and thought, and he stepped briskly out of the car. I locked the doors and joined him, prepared for whatever might or might not be going on in the hotel. For some reason I thought that there would be a party, that we would carve our way into it easily. I held open the glass door for him. He walked through as though he was arriving home, he was indifferent. Inside, he slowed our pace and said: 'You know, I think I've lost a lot of the respect I had for you. You won't make it. Good-night now.' He walked off down the royal-blue carpet.

I watched him go. He rounded the corner at the end of the corridor. I thought that he would wait there at the bottom of the stairs and that we would laugh or we would talk seriously. I strolled down the corridor, the stairs were empty. I went on through the hotel, the bars were locked and there was no party. I walked back through the bright lounge where the cushions were all plumped up for the next day. The hotel was quiet and empty, the reception desk cleared except for a black pen in a black, weighted holder. I stole a glass ashtray from one of the lounge tables and walked with it to the swing door. I left it inside the door. He could make you feel full or empty.

He was the totally charming guest at lunch the next day. This time he did it effortlessly, as though providing a short, tasteful glimpse of himself. Lunch was a collection of people purring happily. Sunlight dappled the dining-room carpet, red roast beef oozed thin blood and then slid off the end of the carving knife. Playful exclamations about the strength of the horseradish, warm smiles stretched over white teeth, much agreement.

It led to an invitation for Sunday lunch – but he would be gone on an early train to London. What a shame. Well, any time you're in England, Billy. Thank you, you're very kind, you're wonderful. Give our kindest regards to Donald. I will.

The Royal Shakespeare Theatre at Stratford-upon-Avon is a massive redbrick building which has been deposited on the river-bank, a building in harmony with the burgher spirit of a market town. The inhabitants of Stratford-upon-Avon are content with their disdain for the local industrial city of Birmingham and its *nouveau riche* suburbs; they are occasionally perturbed by the Shakespeare Coffee Bar. They attend their theatre with pride and remember *Henry V*s and *Hamlet*s and *Julius Caesar*s. Actors visit for the season and are sometimes invited for lunch. Coaches arrive with tourists, a Hilton has been built, also on the river-bank. Opinion differs as to the architectural merits of the Hilton.

Stratford houses a large number of people whose companies make money in Birmingham. At the end of the day, these people drive back to Stratford, where there is cultural experience. Other bosses live in small Warwickshire villages because they like the community atmosphere, which is occasionally found in the local pub on Sunday lunchtimes. Cultural experience and community atmosphere are reassuring.

In Shakespeare, groups of menials occasionally clump across the stage with the odd nod at each other and one line each. But most Characters have Human Nature. Where would we be without human nature? My aunt suspects that we would be in Russia.

I wondered what side he was on, when he put up so many sides after a quick rehearsal. On the road to Stratford it was like driving a very important person. I settled for this. He made comments on the greenery of the landscape, the Tudor-beamed houses, the age of the villages, the cheerful family atmosphere on the pavements.

'Come on; don't sulk.' He put his hand on mine when I stopped at a red light. 'I forget how young you are. I wish I'd known as much when I was your age.'

'I don't know anything.'

'Don't kid me.'

'I don't know where I am from one moment to the next.' The light turned green. I stalled the car.

'Nor the hell do I,' Billy grinned complacently, 'it's a great gift. You've got nothing to lose.'

From the car behind us a horn blared. Billy threw open the car door and stood with his hand on the roof. 'What's eating you, you goddam sonofabitch! Go fuck yourself!'

In front of the old black-timbered shops, the families turned in shock.

'Now run like hell!' Billy slammed shut his door. When we pulled off, the driver behind us stalled. The light turned red again. Billy laughed.

'Do you want to go in for the second half?' I asked him.

'No. Do you?'

'No.'

We walked along the terrace which overlooked the river. The swans were well-fed and sedate, heavily mascaraed around the eyes. They taxied through the water in the sunlight. Reaching back for bits of their plumage, they were teapots. Starling Billy with directorial tread, turning to grasp the rail: 'Hamlet's a closet person, I haven't got the time for him.'

'That's what the play's about.'

'Sure. And look at the actors. None of those actors cares if there's anyone else on the stage. They talk at each other, they're not building anything up. I don't know whether that's because they're lazy actors or if they just can't crawl out from underneath Shakespeare. That's kind of a disappointment. We have a lot of respect for England.'

'Why?'

'We need to have respect. I love that about America. But *no one* in that audience felt anything. You think Hamlet felt anything? It looked to me as though he thought that one feeling might bring the house down in so much applause that it would disrupt the show! That holding back and waiting, the English reserve. You've got to replace it with something else, dammit. I don't know what's there and what isn't there. I get the feeling there might not be anything. How do you manage to live off that? Do you want to be a thinker?'

I wasn't there until the final word. I was looking at him, surprised at what I saw. I knew the anger and the clenched creativity, although it still frightened me. But I saw a strange lack of conviction and a lonely dislike of trust. Perhaps a wound. Perhaps he was a failure, which made him spiteful. Was it a failing, to have an extreme sensitivity that seals you off from being sensitive towards anyone else? And which of us did *that* afflict? And at least he was a violent hater of the failure in himself. And did I want to be a thinker?

'Yes.' Or anything. A thinker? What? I burst into laughter. A duck stuck its arse in the air and nibbled the depths. Billy grinned broadly as though it was the end of his performance and he was unsure about the value of its reception. An attendant came out on to the terrace and asked us to keep quieter during the second half of *Hamlet*.

'I'm sorry. I don't even know what he's laughing at,' Billy smiled.

'Let's go.' I linked an arm through his and dragged him off; through the tea-rooms, past the marble staircase, across the foyer and down the steps. Leaving the Royal Shakespeare Theatre is always such a joyful moment.

'Do you feel that England is a plot?' I asked him on the way out of Stratford.

'Yeah,' he laughed. 'No, I think that there's a lot of covering up which everybody presumes is in the interests of society and so they don't bother about it. They talk about socialism – well they did in London when I was there; I don't imagine your uncle wastes his time talking about it – anyhow they talk about it as though it would be a solution. I think that it would be like acting with someone who doesn't give anything to the show, someone who sits around after rehearsals and talks about sharing to a crowd of wiped-out performers who've already given everything they've got. People like that make good dictators. These frozen people. They don't like making contact. That makes *me* nervous. Politicians make me nervous, politicians and thinkers who have ideas about people.' He slung an arm over my shoulder, he looked with pleasure at the Warwickshire greenery. 'On the East Coast it would all be burned up by now. You know Donald and I bought two trees for our penthouse terrace. I can't figure out which is going to kill them first, the city pollution or the dog.'

'You've got a dog?'

'Sure. Rusty. You'll meet him when you come over.' He had his head turned easily towards the side window, he took it for granted that sooner or later I would be with him in America.

'What are you like at home?'

'Oh, pretty much of a tyrant. You'll have to get used to it, or you'll move on. Don't expect too much. You'll move on anyway, I can only give you a start. Hell …'

'Thanks. And I like Donald.'

'Yeah, I know what you mean; six days and I miss him too. I'll call him tonight from the hotel. We have a great relationship.'

'Give him my love.'

'He'll get so embarrassed.'

I didn't know what a relationship was; what I was or was not missing. I pinned it on my idea of women; a girl or a woman would at some point be an answer. She would even ask the questions, but not too many.

'We should go back to the hotel and take a coffee,' Billy announced. 'Otherwise your family might be hurt that we didn't manage to stick with *Hamlet*.'

'Yes, they would.'

'You'd better not tell them at college either.' He pinched my shoulder affectionately. The teasing was now more respectful than possessive; his barb was either blunted or else bedded securely inside me. With his encouragement, I let my own enthusiasm run wild. I told him of my love for the characters in books, the years over which you could watch them: Anna Karenina, Birkin hopping from foot to foot, the Cannery Row troupe, Ada. The people whom writers loved in books, that supposedly unseen love. Bugger the skilful dissection or the clever positioning. But characters who are written about with so much generosity that they appear generous themselves, they stream off the page and fill the room. People with whom writers make you fall in love.

Billy might not have listened; he was a small figure in the distance. From the look on his face, as I pleaded finally with him, I wondered if I was mental. I was banging the palm of my hand on the rim of the steering wheel. 'I'm sorry,' I said, 'but it's different. It's just that when you ask me why, that's why. And at the same time I don't know. I *don't* know.' And I am so inarticulate.

'That's great. You don't want to worry about it. That's great. You see, we talk about the same thing.' Billy smiled. 'And you do your three years, you finish them; and then we'll see each other. We'll keep in contact, dammit. We will.'

The force and the persuasion were there; Billy became restless, and then he seemed depressed. 'Three years for me is a long time these days. I don't know why that is. I can't think in blocks of three years. I don't know what I'll be doing next week. But if we have to think of three years then we will.'

'Will you be there?'

'Yes. I promise you.' He laughed as though divesting himself of our seriousness. 'It's good for me to promise. It convinces me that I *will* be there. Yeah. I'll be there.'

'Good.'

'And you damn well better have something to show me.' His voice hardened. He looked out of the window at the hotel car-park. 'So we're back at the funeral parlour. I can't imagine they're going to serve us any coffee, do you?'

That was in a way the end of it. There was a deal. Only time had to be killed. Having coffee was more like the being married which Annie and I had attempted at the bar in Mallorca. Billy and I had very little to say, we might have been tired of each other. The coffee appeared on a tray, we drank it and smoked a cigarette. I ate a sandwich. Billy looked around the hotel lounge, watching the way hotel staff behaved, watching bodies; waiting to be polite in a conversation, should one arrive.

'Can you bring me a clean shirt from your home?' he asked, clearing his throat and lighting another cigarette.

'Yes, certainly.' I looked at the clock over the bar.

'And maybe a pair of pants. I don't know. What do you think?'

'It's only a normal party; sitting around and dancing. No one will be very dressed up. It doesn't matter how you arrive.'

'It matters to *me*, babe. I'm not going to show up as if I thought these people were nobody; or as if I was nobody. They've been kind enough to invite me. If I sell myself, I don't sell myself short. Is that all right by you?' His voice was prodigal with contempt. 'The deal is that you don't *not* care. That's the way it always is with me and I thought you were the same way.'

His uncomfortable stage again; in a Midland suburban hotel lounge, brightly lit for travelling reps. The barman in a red jacket cutting slices of lemon, one other tea-tray on a table at the other end of the room.

'That's the only way you'll ever manage to create anything.' Billy, on his way out, squeezed my shoulder.

80

He whirled Annie at the party. We danced and we left, just before midnight. Annie said goodbye to him outside the hotel; I said, 'See you soon,' on a Birmingham New Street platform next morning.

'Yes, not goodbye,' Billy leaned out of the carriage window, 'I don't make it on goodbyes.'

'No.'

'I don't usually make it much on promises. This one's there.'

'I know.'

'And I don't write too well.'

'Okay.'

'You work hard.'

'You too.' There were no other lovers on the early Sunday-morning train. He looked back until his carriage reached the signal light at the end of the platform; I stood with my hands in my coat pockets. Neither of us waved.

8

Cambridge. A student in the room beneath mine would spend an hour each day lying face downwards on the college lawn and would then come inside to play loud rock music, leaving his door open in an attempt to attract friends. He spoke nine languages.

I formed up behind a plywood cannon and chanted 'Bang! Bang! Bang!' at a smug, dumpy Conservative Home Secretary. I rooted for the Angry Brigade, let loose a hail of tomatoes at the Communist Party and sat in nervous dismay at the sterility of the student life that cradled me. But I wouldn't leave. I laughed firstly at the University, then at my friends and finally at my own jokes.

It might not have been like this if I hadn't met Billy. Cambridge would have been straightforward. But Billy got in the way.

For the time being, I lived in a brittle bedsit. I hammered up a plywood partition between myself and the rest of the world. I was dependent on an empty cleverness, which I couldn't quite master. I drugged myself into silence; I was not so much deformed as blunted by this protracted childishness. Outside the

University everything was concrete; but I had nothing to say to it, I didn't share any responsibility for it. I knew and felt that it was crumbling. So there was nothing more honest than to steal from it what I could.

I merely suppressed the love for Billy. Suppression was rife anyway. It became quite obvious that the sole stance one could not afford was to pose oneself as one might be. I surrendered Billy. I couldn't have done anything else. He sent me letters, I wrote to him. Neither of us wrote well. His letters were simple statements of how he was feeling; mine were short, clipped, officious stage directions to myself. He talked of love and friendship, not really what one talks about at Cambridge.

At the end of that first year, a student sat the Tragedy paper in a German war helmet to ward off the gods; and a Catholic priest lifted his cassock to kick an anarchist disruptor in the balls. The occupation of the Senate House was memorable for the number of demands made to world powers and the appalling acoustics of a local rock band. I sent Billy withering accounts, with my love tagged on at the end. I had an affair with a girl in which I presumed that my love was tagged on at the end. In the summer I could have gone to America, but I spent my time on Social Security searching through books for the love affairs I had had before.

And then I was driving my aunt's car past Stonehenge on the way back from a rock festival. I picked up a bloke who was standing on the side of the road. He placed his rucksack in the back seat and the two of us talked about music, man to man, man. He was a sincere, friendly American; he asked me if I had ever read the Bible, he talked about how he felt and Jesus. I dropped him at the first available town; he stepped off with a thank you, brother.

I arrived home and sent his pamphlet off to Billy, with a flippant letter which parodied Billy's own style of writing; the truth of friendship, new knowledge and moving forward, the pure gold of love.

Two weeks later, he sent a short note: 'I am writing this letter from Kennedy Airport. We don't have any problems with monuments in this country. I find your letters too depressing, maybe we shouldn't write for a while. Until you have grown up a little. We have enough problems over here without neat putdowns. If you have to go through that shit then at least do it on your own. Don't spread it around. Your friend, Billy. P.S. I am learning and teaching now. I got hit by a car. Forgive me.'

PART
2

Approaching Water: Billy

9

I've got nothing personal against California. They're not my kind of people. They can think about things for three weeks and they'll still give the job to someone they know out West – everybody expects it but you still have to wait for the smog to clear from the Los Angeles brain.

It's a great song and dance movie, I'm fit and I want it. I was born for it. And they worry that I'm too much of a dramatic actor. Screw them, I'll get it.

'You act like you don't want the job, Billy,' Donald warned me. 'You'll have to climb down from there some time.' Will I? Hell. If it's that tired old crap they want I'd rather spend the summer working with the kids at Cape Cod, *that's* the kind of energy you need for a great show, you don't need a timid energy that waits for permission from a line of executives behind a damn desk. Those kids hang around the theatre, working fourteen or fifteen hours a day – so enthusiastic that even the leading man wants to pick up a hammer and nail down the set. That's how I started in the Mid-west, looking in through the theatre door; I was there every day, annoying Donald into getting me up on stage. And I still annoy the hell out of him.

'I'll get that part, Donald.'

'Until then, you could pick up the coffee from Zabar's; you could at least do that, Billy.'

Donald and his dinner parties. Where does he think we are?

My sunglasses.

Why do all these kids worship the streets? If you're born on them, you can't wait to get off them.

Zabar's is a Donald store. It's an emporium, not a delicatessen. There's too much choice. The smell of coffee hangs like the smell of the stockyards. How the hell do I know what brand Donald wants!

'Can you charge this?' It's hard enough to think through the dope, but when you come up against Zabar's ...

Amsterdam. Sidewalk. You can't believe the number of people who have dogs. I don't want to work too often out there on the West Coast. This is my town.

His hand waving sideways, his fingers curled at the knuckle, waving me away, from behind his windshield, a mass of green up to my thigh, he can't see this? Lose him. Shit, you've done it again, Billy ...

'We can try to sue him, Billy. But the witnesses say that you stepped off the sidewalk.'

'And he hit me, Donald! *I'm* lying here; do you think he's suffering? How much damage did I do to his car? Do we *apologise* for that?'

Donald's eyes moved nervously. It's a scale that I get tired of, that I am deviant according to how much discomfort I cause Donald. What is this 'fairness'? You think the world works on fairness? Is that how we get this penthouse apartment with the walk-around balcony and the ten-block horizon? Fairness?

'Billy, if you can think it through and come up with a different picture, then we can go right ahead with a lawsuit.' He poured himself a drink. He has his faith but he doesn't put it in fairness without a couple of shots of vodka.

'I could be stuck in this apartment for weeks.'

'That's not official.'

'Sure, sure, it won't be that long.'

'Billy, this accident could zero the West Coast job. David called up last week and I had to lie to him.'

'So lie to him, I'll be there.'

'You could have been killed out on the street! I mean I didn't know what kind of shape you were in, I didn't see too much of you. Were you going through a bad period with Linda?'

'We're not getting along. It's only temporary.'

'Did she call today?'

'Sure she did. We talked for an hour this morning.'

'I wouldn't have asked you to go to Zabar's if I'd known you were down.'

'For Christ's sake, Donald, I was as high as a kite.'

That did it for him; dope kills his sympathy. It distressed him so much that he had to go through to the kitchen to check his Chicken Véronique.

'How was your dinner party anyway?'

'Well, we watched them knock you out at the hospital and

then we came back here; and we talked about how we could set up a schedule of discreet people who could give two or three hours of their time to sit and listen to your self-pity.'

'Did you find enough people?'

'There aren't that many people in show business who could keep their mouths shut.'

I wanted to be out of here, having a ball with Linda. Being flat on my back with a numb leg wasn't my idea of a good time. 'Am I in a bad way?'

'You're not in a bad way physically. You went into shock for a while. There's no permanent damage to the leg; you should be able to walk soon and you might be dancing by Christmas. But if I tell MGM that, they won't even consider you. They won't take that risk. I have to make certain that they don't hear about it.' Donald sat down. 'And suppose they want to see you again, in the shape you're in.'

'And what happens if the deal falls through?'

He spread his arms along the back of the couch, he looked as though I was pinning him to the wall.

'You can pick up an off-Broadway play in the fall, maybe we can take another pitch at the West Coast when you're fit.'

'Great.'

'We're out, Billy, if we lie to them. Can you imagine signing a contract for a male lead dancer in a musical and then sending them you on crutches?'

I laughed. Donald said: 'We'd never get looked at again. Never ever.'

'What do we do?' I asked him. 'Do we kill it?'

'If you stay here, someone will find out. We have to get you hidden away and delay them.'

'Can we do that with MGM?'

'I think that they won't accept it, but that's the only hope you've got. At least they're not going to get fixed on the idea that you're permanently damaged; they're not going to *see* you.'

Yeah. Damn it. Donald waited.

Damn it.

'So what do I do?'

'Well, I can arrange to take a vacation at the end of next week, and you should do the same. I can get someone to drive you upstate.'

'What am I supposed to do up there?'

'You don't have to do anything. You can rest for a couple of weeks. I'll fudge around on the negotiation. If it gets killed then you still have time to fly to the Cape to rehearse those kids. Will you still want to do that?'

'Yeah.'

'Okay, I'll find someone in the office to take care of Rusty. Don't let it get you down, Billy. Just stay away from everything.'

Diane is an old friend. I met her again after she had quit acting; we hadn't seen each other in four years. She told me that she ran some clinic or home for alcoholics and she asked me to drop by. I said: 'I don't need that much help, do I?' She said: 'One time in your life, Billy, you might be able to help someone else. You're a little older now.'

I got embarrassed the first time, up there at the Farm, watching those people try – people who are never going to make it. In the business you just have to turn away from people like that; sad, honest triers. If you hang around with that odour of failure it ends up asphyxiating you as well. These people were salesmen, housewives, secretaries, lower-level executives, decorators, people who got fired – every kind of normal alcoholic you want to get away from.

Diane was a saviour – but so what? You can waste your time with these people in America. If you waste your time, you sink. Problems are a point of social contact, no one takes them too seriously. If someone cracks, there's nothing you can do. They understand that. You haul yourself up or you drop. I live with that. I don't like a group which featherbeds itself.

'These people have got more guts than you'll ever have,' Diane told me.

We sat in chairs and the finger came round.

'My name is Dave. I am an alcoholic. I'm fifty-three, I have a wife and three kids. I should say that the kids have left home though our daughter lives with us sometimes. I started drinking eighteen years ago; I had a good job, my wife and I went down to Florida every second winter vacation ...'

'My name is Mary and I am an alcoholic. I am twenty-nine years old. Nobody else knows I am an alcoholic because I keep it hidden. This is hard for me. I am here because I'm tired of deceiving people. I'm down to getting out of bed early to sneak my garbage downstairs so the neighbours don't see the bottles ...'

'My name is Billy Maffett. I think that we should be in this thing together. It's hard to fight it when you're on your own. But I don't drink.'

They looked at Diane as though she had betrayed them. She broke the pause. 'I should say that Billy is a friend of mine – and if he doesn't drink, he does everything else. So you shouldn't feel that he or any of you is anyone special. You're all friends of mine.'

'Is Billy a doctor?'

'No, I'm an actor. We believe that there's nothing we can't do if we want to, and if we try hard enough. And if we treat ourselves honestly with the help of the people around us. I don't believe in failing.'

We got along fine, they were a great bunch of people. Over the next two years we held reunions in a Manhattan bar, a different bar each time because nobody made enough money out of 7-ups and Cokes. Two years is a long time.

In show business, if people are going down then at least they bullshit you that they're not. And something comes along which proves they're okay. I've been in it a long time with a lot of people. We came out of the nothing of the fifties. I know that nothing. It follows you. We pulled ourselves out of it, each one of us. The young people work together now, they don't know that fear of being nothing. So they can look out and they can change society. They're not fooled for a minute. They know when they're getting taken before the offer comes, they keep their sincerity and they work hard at it. We never had that. Every bit of advice we can give is part of the problem to them. I understand that. If you talk down to them you miss them. The kids do things naturally that we worked on for years. They do it and then they shelve it. Shrug it off. Because they've done it and they don't want to do it again. When we were young we took it and took it, just to try and get in there. They don't want to get in there; they look at the crap and they say, 'Screw it, that's not what we understand about being creative; I'll only sweat for what I believe in.'

We never had the time to realise that. If you didn't impress the big man then you didn't make it, and if you didn't make it then you went back home to the nothing.

91

This time will be my third visit to the Farm. It can't have been a farm in the real sense for two or three generations, I guess its money always came from New York and it was kind of a hobby. Diane has sold most of the land, she keeps a large area around the house as a recreation space but she doesn't have a swimming-pool or anything like that. You come up that long flat stretch towards the Catskills and the Farm is off on the other side of a rise, down a rocky track. Once you're there, you tend to stay around the house, people don't seem to go back over the rise unless they drive into town. They take walks in the other direction.

The house is pretty large, the top half of the barn next to it has been turned into guest rooms so that Diane can keep some upstairs space for herself and family. Downstairs in the main house it sometimes has a hostel atmosphere, maybe because the lounge is a professional meeting-room. But the big kitchen is a very strong, personal space that is hers; the two front rooms may be clean and open to everyone, and the yard may be wild, but that kitchen is indisputably hers.

'Hi, Billy!'

'Hi, darling.'

'We were waiting for you. How was your journey?'

'It was fine.'

'So, how's it been going?'

'Diane, my name is Billy Maffett and I got hit by a car. I can hardly walk, dammit!'

'Well, you can limp, can't you? We don't take anyone who can't limp.'

'Sure I can limp. The stick is just for show.'

'I'll bet! Come on inside and we'll see who's here.'

All of us ate supper together. I was determined to make the evening meeting; Diane told me to stay in the kitchen. I was too weak to fight her and the medication put me a long way from anywhere. Donald called from New York to give me the number of his hotel in Corfu. Diane stuck her head in at the door.

'Are you okay, Billy?'

'Sure I am.'

'We've got a runner.' A runner is someone up here on the retreat who can't stick the pace and heads for the nearest bar. He walks seven miles for his medication.

'Is there anything I can do?'

'Yes, I think you can sack out.'

The first night is a bad one. New York is never quiet. There's always someone awake, someone you can call who's starting something or who wants to talk over the late show. Just someone.

Up here, you listen to the dogs across the country. You open the curtain and there isn't even a lighted window. It could be that everyone who has ever meant anything has been chewed up by the blackness. The runner would be sitting in a bar, drinking greedily, fighting off those teeth. Three bars in the town; they'd have him back pretty quick unless he bought himself a pint of bourbon and walked off the side of the road someplace.

You lie in bed and listen, until even the dogs call it a day. It's only one a.m. Someone's calling on the phone. I can make the door, dammit. Someone's out there.

'Diane!' I whisper to her in the corridor. She has a worried face.

'Billy! What are you doing? You can't walk around out here without your shorts on, you know that.'

'Did they find him?'

'Yes they did; now you go to sleep, Billy.'

'I have to call Linda.'

'No you don't. You give me her number and I'll call her and tell her you're fine.'

'Can you do that?'

'I can lie with the best of them. Where's the number?'

'Do I look bad?'

'You look a little grey. Leave yourself alone for a couple of days. I have sleepers if you need them.'

'I have some.'

I heard the police bring the runner back. The doors are always open – the police hassle Diane but she refuses to lock them.

She was a fine actress but she never had the push. She must be in her late thirties, a beautiful woman, not in any slack sense. Her beauty was always under a stone. In the couple of movies she made, it showed up four or five times; when it wasn't written in. You sat there thinking: this isn't a bad movie, it's pretty good – and then suddenly because of her the movie was bullshit, she was more interesting. On the stage, she couldn't project anything but you found yourself watching her. She was too substantial. So people stayed clear of using her. She married a guy who was a writer and she disappeared; she had a couple of kids and he ...

Died? Left her? I never asked, she doesn't talk about herself.

She's someone of whom you could never say 'She didn't make it'. You had the feeling that the business missed out, the business was too small for her.

Some show types do this charity thing out of duty, or that chic earth-mother posturing. Or because, having quit the stage, they still need the audience. With Diane, it was more like theatrical management, mixed with a stylish calculation. Her husband was gone, her kids grew up and were moving around; and so the space needed booking. No one told her what to do. And it's just the Farm, it's a home.

I have her younger son's room. There's an old football schedule still tacked on the wall. Some of her guests sleep two to a room in the house, the others have rooms in the barn.

Sunday evenings she dresses up and you do the same. That gives these people some kind of respect which maybe they've forgotten. She doesn't dress as if it's a première, she doesn't smile artificially, she may wear a light perfume; she doesn't look stunning, she looks good. And these people are aware that they're eating with class, they're talking with a classy person. Most of them have been through a week of confused shit. A lot of confession. These bozos can often only associate pride or self-confidence with being juiced. Alcohol gives them the class they don't have. Sunday evenings, Diane gives them the class. Straight down the line and they rise to it. There's a whole lot of darkness outside this house.

The next day, the runner clouds the atmosphere. Everybody feels a sense of failure and the runner feels his responsibility for this. After lunch they go out walking and I sit in the chair next to him. Harry.

I am living in that hazy world of painkillers and Harry is sunk in on himself. He is a big man in a plaid shirt, a member of the Teamsters. He and his wife don't see the kids any more because the kids have gotten hooked on the protest against the war, too much hanging around with college people. Harry doesn't feel so much about the war except that we're in there and so we damn well fight to win without pulling the feet away from the boys doing the dirty work. His brother has a fine boy out in Saigon.

That's not why he drinks; he's always enjoyed a night out on the town with the guys. Up here was just a holiday while his wife went to look after her mother.

He knows everyone is kind of pissed at him; he answers it with a dumb, childish grin, he rubs down the side of his face as if he was trying to sandpaper his jawbone. Ten years in the truck and your liver and kidneys were screwed up anyhow from the vibration. The union was working at it. Things could be a hell of a lot better if people worked for changes like that, instead of love and peace and a lot of communist screwing around. He was in Korea. He knew.

There's something fundamental about those people. You can't say it isn't good. It's American. Even the way they deceive themselves is aggressively optimistic. I like the contact with them. I'm only half-way there anyhow, with all this medication. Get rid of this stick and cool off on the medication before it totals my brain. Doctors give you anything to keep you quiet.

This meeting-room is depressing if you're on your own. Like a clean battlefield which is used regularly. Television in the corner.

I spend five years in love with a penthouse apartment and now I miss the traffic. Stuck here with one leg. Down to looking at the trees.

'Diane?'

'Hi, lover, what can I get you?'

'Nothing.'

'Okay ... so let me put you in the kitchen. We just got back and there'll be a whole crowd in here. I want to *talk* to you, Billy ... I never seem to have the time.'

She cupped her chin in the palm of her hand and we talked about the mortification and the excitement of New York, the energy coming up off the sidewalks and the small theatre houses, the thousand plans and the million quirks, the people who fall flat on their faces and the people who claw their way through. Pam and Andy got on with the cooking. They're nice kids – young and quiet, a bit puritan I guess. Hell, this is for Diane and me. I don't care if they aren't interested.

She has a few grey hairs, but the lines around her mouth float easily when she laughs at the craziness. 'You know, Billy, I feel good. I thought, forty – that's *it*! But forty is great!' She over-reached slightly. She pulled a True out of the pack and lit it. She became the seemly mother. 'How did you make out with Harry?'

'Just fine. He had a hangover, I was phased on painkillers. We got along better than we might have done for a hardhat and a pinko actor.'

'Don't you find it strange?' Diane blew her smoke across the room.

'Babe, there's nothing left that isn't strange.'

I pitched at her for a quick laugh. It was way off the plate. She inclined her head hospitably, the shower of ash-blonde hair fell away from her face. She looked at Andy, who was out on a limb with the package of frozen clams.

'The scissors are in the drawer to your left, Andy.'

'Thank you, ma'am.'

He didn't take to being helped with something unfamiliar. A kid of twenty-five. Diane said: 'We can talk later.'

'Sure, sure we can.'

'Don't mind us,' Pam called.

I wondered why Diane was so reserved. Guarded conversation wasn't her style. Her house was open.

She was tight. She walked over to the stove; it wasn't her walk. It was the walk of a woman who was trying to clear out a frustration by contradicting her style.

She tasted the sauce. She rested her hands on Pam and Andy. 'Good.' She nodded at them, mock-solemn. We all laughed at her act.

'Hold it, Diane!'

'What's happening, Billy?' She folded her arms and looked across the room. Our old challenge. We've played it on and off over the years.

'What colour are your eyes?'

'Green eyes. Which leg is injured, right or left or left or right?'

'Dammit, Diane, I don't know right from left, you can't use that one again.'

The green eyes laughed. She said: 'That's the advantage in growing older. You learn how to keep the sons of bitches down.'

The evening session was no session. People weren't sure whether Harry should be a problem, whether he should disrupt their group development. Everyone was hurting to say: 'Don't worry, and let's have this thing out of the way, you know and we know, and let's forget about it.'

So they fetched cards for poker, or listened to music on the stereo, making sure that no one got left out. There was a feeling of letting it lie and waiting to start again. Someone had dropped, so they all had to even out on a new level.

Diane wanted me to get to know everybody, so I did that until it was too tiring. I said good-night. It seemed as though I immediately disappeared into the mattress, without requiring any precaution.

Kind of dumb. Some time in the morning when it's grave black, I need a pill.

The shock of waking; the sweats. No, I remember this pain. This pain was here before. Somehow it must mean that the leg is getting better, this is just a price for the movie part.

For a hundred years of ten minutes the pain sticks.

I can't pull through pain. Screw the movie, I just want to lose myself. I daren't move in case some part of my leg ups the volume level. I want a barrier between me and the leg; every time my breath has finished jerking its way out I seem to be closer to the leg. The pulse hammers the pain. This isn't going to make any difference to whether I get the job or not, I don't have any say in that.

And the pill unpeels the pain, strand by long smooth strand.

10

A week later, we had our clique; the two of us, the non-walkers, Diane and I. I felt better, the leg had calmed down. I was getting used to the countryside. We sat out back in the sun, tanning our skin and drinking iced tea. Diane had put herself on vacation – she dug a swimsuit out of a cupboard. I rated myself as over-weight; Diane decided she was fleshy. We wore sunglasses while we checked out these submissions. She was a little more full, and comfortable with it.

'I'd forgotten how good it is to be on your own.' Diane pulled off her glasses and dropped them by the side of the chair.

'Uh-huh,' I agreed with her. I laughed; she opened her left eye and smiled.

'I thought I wouldn't get away with it.'

'Darling, you are one wonderful picture of contentment. Don't let me disturb you.'

If I stayed up here for six months then I could maybe lie back with my eyes closed and let it happen. But my eyes switch like a horse's tail, away from her, to the trees, across a pond, to a fence post, to a car, to her foot, to her eyes.

Whereas her eyes are steady. She suspects that behind the sunglasses I am looking at her.

'Do you worry about yourself, Billy?'

'Not unless I'm asked to, professionally.'

'I suppose that worrying about yourself is a luxury.'

'That's because you take up your time worrying about everybody else around here.'

She went off at a tangent; she said: 'I keep forgetting that we trained together. I did a middle-aged woman for you when you were eighteen.'

'I fell in love with you. You know, you looked older than you do now. You must have played up on the age. "You're taking the easy label, Diane!"' I imitated Rykov's contemptuous growl.

'Was I scared of that man!'

'Who the hell wasn't? If I ever have to reach for fear, I go back to being in front of him. Nothing else touches me.'

'It doesn't,' Diane considered. 'He certainly killed fear.'

I thought playfully of moving up here, not for the first time. We shared a lot, we usually had a good time together.

Diane's eyes moved over the pond and the fenceposts, she established her property; she was understanding towards trespassers but she knew that they were all drifting and she didn't want any deadweight, that was the feeling she gave me.

'I'll make us some coffee,' she said. 'Can you get yourself over there in the shade?'

'Yes I can.'

She walked quickly over the grass to the house. She lifted her hair away from the nape of her neck. She was great to look at. A lot of women are vulnerable from the back, they don't like being looked at from behind. Diane's back matches the strong expression in her eyes. When she reached the door, she met Andy and she dealt with Andy's laconic appreciation.

The leg was better. On the tenth day out of the city, I could live without a stick. I felt a bolt of pain sometimes, which gave me an instant sweat. It was like catching sight of someone through a window. By the end of the day he was knocking on the door. But I was down to a painkiller in the morning and another one with the sleeper at night, after I'd called up Linda.

She came back over the grass with the coffee on a tray, in blue jeans and a shirt, her hair tied back; something of the Sunday-evening Diane, something that encouraged you to take your eyes off her to check that the chairs were arranged okay.

'He's only a kid.' She had no persistent sympathy for Andy. 'These days I react drowsily. I have this cloud of maturity. And then I appear through it and they all find me a little sudden. The word gets around: "Diane's wired up; stay clear." '

She smiled at my laugh; as though it was a well-turned joke and she was down to watching its reaction on other people. I never know with Diane. A disdain comes over her, a super-cilious resignation that other people aren't on the same wave-length. It accuses us of neglecting her.

'You must get tired of the people here.' I poured the coffee and left her cup steaming on the tray.

'I don't think I should like Harry, or people such as Harry.'

'There's no reason why you should. You're not guilty about it, are you?'

'Come on, Billy, you can do better than that.' Her eyes were tracered with sarcasm. 'I'm old enough to get a kick out of hating some of the people who come up here, some of the crummy people who pretend they're sick when they want something to hang on to.'

'Sure.' Not my line, baby.

'It's not personal, Billy.' Her eyes appealed. When she re-laxed I felt as though she had just filed away an image of me, like a camera. 'I use Harry the same way I could use anyone.' I stared at her mouth for a full minute, the seriousness over her lips, her right hand off somewhere drawing a pattern of explanation. And then I started to pick up on what she was saying, I made some nonsense out of it. '… Robby and John. Robby has. He's the eldest.'

'Yeah.'

'Are you listening, Billy?'

'Sure I am.'

'Robby said that he no longer wanted to be a part of this country. And if they go to Canada to avoid the draft, then they won't be able to get back across the border. I sat there and I thought, well, shit, my sons are going. You prepare yourself, but it doesn't work.'

'Yeah.'

Diane looked at me. 'Is that all you can say? Can you do any concentrating with your medication?'

'I was a bit lost there for a while. What did *you* say? To Robby?'

'I told him that I thought he'd made the right decision. What else could I say? He was serious about it, and he was so lost.' Diane shook her head slowly. 'It's not college Marxism, or the rah-rah idealism that's around at the moment. It's a painful decision. And it's like some … deep betrayal of faith. For all of us. Do you know what's *happening* to this country? We don't *have* a society any more. We don't.'

'Okay.'

Yes, it would kill Diane; that solid liberal faith. Wake up, babe. It's the same bullshit on both sides. It's American – that kind of perplexed, ham-fisted innocence.

'This country was never built to take society. People change their friends every five years.'

'I suppose,' she said wryly, 'that as an intelligent man you know how to deal with feelings of impotence.'

'No,' I grinned at her, 'Linda deals with it. And Mary-Sue, and Cindy, and Barbara-Ann. I work like a nut and pray. Donald buys me kelp tablets.'

I kept her laughing with the story of Donald's relationship with God, about the hangover Sunday in Mallorca, about Europe and its society. We got away from America. I told her of my promise to survive and a lousy hotel in England.

'That's going to test us,' Diane claimed, 'when England goes Communist.'

'They're not going to have a revolution in England, Diane; they're too lazy.'

'Perhaps they won't need one,' she mused. 'If they do, it will be against us and the people we pay to look after American interests.' She was started up again.

'Come on! We're not all that bad!'

'That's the way it is everywhere else.'

'Not in England, darling.'

When we stood up to go inside, her hand touched mine as though she wanted to show some gratitude. I checked to see if I'd left my cigarettes under the recliner. They were there. I took her arm for the twenty-yard limp to the house.

'Your kids will be fine,' I told her. 'They've got each other. My big move was pure instinct, at sixteen. And I made out okay. Anyhow, the war won't go on.'

She won't crack, not Diane. Something would have to be very wrong with the future of this country, and the future is hopeful. It's the present that's blocking us.

'Maybe they're better off out of it,' Diane shrugged. 'Johnny travels up and down this state, and he says that the government are rehabilitating the old war-time internment camps.'

'What?'

'We don't want to know, do we? That's what it's down to. Nobody wants to feel part of the sickness.' She waited for me to open the screen-door on the porch.

It's the kind of crap that doesn't wash with me. Internal moral conflict. Diane succeeds in depressing me. Nothing personal – but who needs it?

At the evening meeting, she offered plain guidance like a blanket. Alcoholics were children, and children must not challenge her. They should be brought up well. She was sparing with herself, as though pointing out that 'Life will not always be me, here are a few helping rules. Number one: have respect for each other.' She might as well have said: 'You are tiresome, go to bed.'

She doesn't really want to talk. And it isn't part of her act to encourage me to go looking for her.

She hasn't lost any faith. It's not the faith which has come unstuck; it's the bargain, or the social deal, that she thought was there. She hates the thought that she might be alone in having faith. When I was a kid, I learned fast. I learned to use every trick in the book to get what I wanted, even to get what I didn't want, to get gifts, to get people to feel for me. Any people, even people I wasn't interested in. Come out of yourself! What for? Come out of yourself for me, if you can't come out for anything else!

Hard work; people are dumb. They're scared and conceited. They don't give a damn about anyone else. Sympathy is pretty much calculated; you don't get your share of it unless you calculate back.

Vietnam? Hell, the Vietnam war has given more people more great parties in this country than anything since prohibition. Young people are letting go; screw a career, screw watching television, let's smoke a little pot and go to bed with each other, talk about the anti-war committee.

I said to Diane: 'Do your sons give you a hard time?' She said: 'They don't expect their mother to pick up a gun. I drive into the city for the peace marches, it's like going out on a date with two fine young men. I feel that I'm acting in a Jimmy Stewart movie. I feel decent, responsible, conscientious. And irrelevant. That's our relationship with the administration.'

She turned, and she added: 'And this is mother doing her thing. The boys come up here to help out for a month over the summer. But it's not their bag; they're against and they're alternative. They want to build something else. They don't want to mop up the trash.'

I thought about it in bed that night. I've met those kids, there's nothing special in them. Idealism and frustration are pretty much interchangeable, they can put to sleep the threat of hard work. Diane, do you think people are going to say, 'There goes a woman with misgivings, we appreciate that'? Are they, hell! They'll say, 'There goes a woman who wants to carry the can, maybe I can talk her into carrying my can.' That's not a badge which lets you lay down the law in America, babe. If you live well, people respect you; if you're only half-alive, they'll step around you.

'Who are you going out with?'

She leaned against the stove, her legs crossed at the calf. Her face was a bit red from the sun. 'Maybe you're right.'

I laughed. 'Who is he?'

'He's a psychologist in Boston.' She added: 'Not *my* analyst.'
'And? Come on, Diane!'
'That's enough,' she said. 'That's all there is; no big scene.'
Verboten.

So we operate.

I talk to Linda on the phone. We listen to the minute details of each other's day, how many cups of coffee, who called at what time, deflections of mood, what moods our friends are in, what feeling we draw out of our contact with other people, our own experiences that might refer to or substantiate some pattern. These long murmurs which keep us both up there on top of the weather-vane, which give us our position. We won't get lost. We have an even surface. We're in this together.

I wrote to Martin in England, telling him about this hope that is all around us now. We've gone through the 'letting it all hang out' and 'whatever turns you on'; that kind of tolerance which we thought was positive but which was only indifferent. We're in there now and we're working at something good, each person in their own way, working on themselves. Your life is a straight line, you lose it sometimes and then you climb back to it. I'm getting there.

11

On Saturday, Diane's younger son Johnny arrived. Diane hugged him, but he was at the stage where he didn't like being hugged. He was falling out of love with his mother, she had set herself not to hang on to him – so he was a mess of vindictive feelings about desertion. I watched him and he looked like a nervous rapist when he was near Diane. She had to accept it and pretend that it didn't exist.

I moved into the room next to her so that Johnny could take his old room.

Diane in a frock. She walked with a brisk self-assurance that she didn't feel, hoping that this would kill her son's predacity.

One weird picture. Harry, Diane and Johnny standing on the porch late Saturday afternoon. Loyalty changing hands.

Diane supporting Johnny, Johnny forming some cynical alliance with Harry, Harry respectfully supporting Diane. When Diane hated Harry and Harry hated John and John hated almost everything.

John took himself off, probably to smoke a joint in his room. Diane was left suddenly next to Harry. I put an arm round her waist and we walked to the pond.

'Johnny will pull out of it,' Diane hoped, kicking lightly at the grasses. I squeezed her. She dropped her shoulders and the muscles in her belly.

'He will because he'll have to. It can get lonely.'

'Don't start me worrying, Billy. He has plenty of friends. It's when I catch that cold analysis and dislike in his eyes; that flips me.'

'That's an act.'

'You think so? I know I have the right to say "Look, buster, I spent eighteen years of my life changing your diapers and putting you through school, you parasite." And you know what I'd get then? I'd get a wounded animal. That's a little more painful.'

We sat by the pond, she lay on her back with her legs drawn up, one leg crossed over the other. She kicked off her shoes, smoked a cigarette.

'You know why I want this man in Boston, Billy? I want to be loved. It's very calculated. He won't know it's happening, and I don't think I care about that.'

I could see only her legs and her arm through the grass, and coils of grey cigarette smoke.

'He'll be very lucky.'

'Yes,' Diane agreed flatly. 'You know, I think I could love anybody within a certain wide type. I'm through with loving everybody. It worked for a while. You get it back in bits and pieces; some surprising pieces that really come through to you. I don't have the dishonesty to knock that. You come to love yourself again. Now I make sure that I have plenty of time to love myself. When I was married, my husband made me feel so wonderful that I thought I was a shit. It wasn't even important when he went, that was just the period at the end of the sentence. And with the Farm I've never been too much bothered who was around.'

'Is that going to end?'

'I don't think so. It's one of my habits. Diane and her bozos, Diane and her Sunday dinners. It could be Diane and a few psychiatric patients. Alcoholics are falling off pretty far down the list these days, they're way behind acid heads and war veterans.'

She sat up. She bunched her dress round her thighs and rested her chin on her knees for a minute. She smiled. 'I've been earnest for a long time, Billy, and it just doesn't help anything. Now it's becoming fashionable to be earnest, and I have to work at it.'

Someone was anxious to know whether the meeting was open or closed. Harry and I left the room and went to sit in the kitchen.

'Would you ever admit that you were an alcoholic, Harry?'

'I would if I thought that I couldn't go to work. It hasn't gotten to that point. I can feel rough; I've never hit a bad slide though. This visit is kind of useful for taking a check on myself. These are different people from the guys I'm used to being with.'

'The pacifists?' I laughed.

'Diane won't change me and I won't change her,' Harry grinned. 'I know what I believe in.'

'What do you think of the kids who say no?'

'I think they're shit scared and I think they're cowards. Nobody gets anything without fighting for it. That's something you have to face up to, huh? You look like a fighter. You don't find reasons for hiding yourself away. That's selling out on your country. We keep a lot of people safe. We're a big country, we're going places. If anyone doesn't like the system they should go and live in Russia, we don't want them here.'

'How about Canada, man?' Johnny had come in and was leaning against the door-frame.

'That country is one hell of a lot of nothing.' Harry checked him out. 'They wouldn't get by without us. Canada is a poor man's United States.'

'Johnny, what is this crazy story about the internment camps in this state?' I wanted to know.

'They're everywhere, man; the government's building prison camps all over the country.'

He came off the door-frame and walked restlessly across the

kitchen as though we'd disturbed him by dragging him into society. His eyes roved around; he sealed himself off behind a flop of hair, his badge.

'Who're they building them for?' Harry grunted.

'Anyone who gets in the way of the administration, man, anyone they don't like. War protesters, blacks, heads who don't choose to get off on alcohol ...'

'Have you seen them?'

'I know about them. And the FBI lists.'

'Oh hell, those guys always have lists. You scared the shit out of your mother, you know that?'

'What the fuck does *she* care?'

'Because you're her son.'

'Yeah, but let's not get all personal about it. She has this trip of being personal. It's unreal.'

Johnny shook his bored, stoned head and smirked at the straights. 'Wow,' he added, contemptuously.

'Do you smoke a lot of pot?' I asked him. He glanced at Harry.

'Some. You want to be my uncle, Billy?'

'No way.'

'So what is it with you guys? You want me to go live in Russia?'

He sauntered out of the kitchen. 'You can't talk to them,' Harry said, 'they don't give a shit.'

'It's the kid's home, Harry.'

'He doesn't treat it too good. She doesn't have anyone to whip his ass into line.'

'Diane doesn't operate that way. No one whipped you into line when you went out to get juiced.'

Diane came through to make coffee.

'How's it going in there?' Harry asked.

'O-kay! You can go back now if you want to.'

Diane wanted Harry out of her kitchen. She moved around him with a nervous arrogance. Diane wanted everything smooth.

We went with her eighteen cups of coffee. We walked into the meeting-room which was hazy with cigarette smoke, although someone had opened the glass door on to the porch. I sugared a coffee.

'Someone's calling you from Europe, Billy,' Pam shouted from the door.

Up again. 'Okay, I'll take it.'

'Take it in my room, Billy.'

Diane's tidy bedroom, now ordered so that you could see the furniture: lightweight furniture, a thin-legged chair, a desk full of letters and papers which were squeezed into unlabelled compartments. On the top was a photograph of a man which could have been taken without him knowing it. He had been stopped in the corridor by a student, he had an expression of immediately applying himself to the student's problem although his energy was related to the pile of books and papers under his arm. On the table by her bed, there was a framed photograph of her two sons, aged maybe ten and eleven. I picked up the phone.

'Hey, Donald ...'

'Billy, is that you?' His voice searched as if he was lost in thick fog.

'Sure it is. How are you doing? Do you have any news from MGM?'

'Just great ... over here, two-thirty ...'

I pointed the static at the ceiling, and when the static died away I locked with Donald's thin, curling voice: '... how you were making out, in heaven's name.'

'I'm okay.'

'Can you speak a little *louder*, Billy? The line isn't so good ... Billy? ... Are you there? ... Holy – '

'Did you hear from LA?'

'We went partying with some people. You sound a little down.'

How much the hell louder did he want me to shout!

The man in the photograph on Diane's desk, his seriousness had me pissed at him. A guy with an easy answer and maybe always the right answer. Solid ambition, two or three faces, one of them a listening face; a sophisticated, withering intelligence for smart remarks in bed. I don't want her to love that guy.

'Donald, you just caught me when I was down.'

'Why do you think that is, Billy?'

'I don't know. Maybe there's too many fucking normal people here. Is there any news from LA?'

'... sun on the island ...'

'Yeah?'

'... flying in Thursday and I'll have ...'

'Donald, I'll see you later! Okay? Donald? Hey! Thanks a bunch!'

He'd gone. I might as well kill the cacophony.

He'd had a few drinks, he was crisp and vacationed, he'd had his sun and drink and horsing around on the edge of some group or other, one more guidebook for the apartment. He buys guidebooks to take the edge off his guilt over vacations, the same as at dinner parties we have to spend an hour talking over some boring subject.

I feel transitory, kind of shallow. You pick up the phone and all you get is a blockage. I wish we had talked longer. He doesn't know anything about MGM. He knows as much about MGM as I do about this leg. Fuck it.

Come on! We're fine!

This is a great room. Diane's room. I don't know how she does it. A lot of old and new familiar things. She makes things familiar.

She came in; Diane, inquisitive, holding a cigarette. Pleased, though the green eyes don't sparkle and the lips are a little tight by the end of the day. She asked: 'Have they got to you?'

'I guess that I *am* sitting this one out.'

'Is Donald all right?'

'I think so. He sends his love. We agreed that you're wonderful.'

She nodded approvingly, amused, pursing her lips to exhale the rest of the smoke.

'You know, darling, it strikes me that there's nothing in this room to smash.' I watched her.

She looked around and smiled. 'You mean there's nothing left to smash.'

Okay. 'Yeah, that's what I mean.'

'Do you think that it's too arranged?' she asked, narrowing her eyes, as if it mattered.

'It suits you; it's comfortable.'

'I feel that.' She moved away from my chair. She could be wilful; but the way she knew about herself would check it. She had lived by herself for a long time.

I escorted her to the bedroom door; she was first through it.

Following her down the corridor, I had one of those moments of sexual dalliance. I watched the way in which she might fuck; it was a turn-on, because of her frustration and her boredom with her own self-control. And her selfishness; strong selfishness, human. But the sterility of knowing what to take and how much to take, that cold independence – where's the fun in that?

At the top of the stairs, she looked over her shoulder at me, her eyes sly-angry with disdain.

'I'm tagging along,' I said; liking her as an object, not caring that much about her.

Downstairs, Johnny was spare and I was spare; Diane hustled us out to the porch with a couple of bug-exterminator lights to kill off whatever might crawl through the screens. The half-dozen people left in the meeting-room didn't bid to follow us. Johnny walked as though he had a heavy iron girder strapped across his shoulders; he sat morosely until he became aware that Diane wouldn't acknowledge it.

She played hostess with a lot of skill; casual conversation about journalism with enough mistakes for Johnny to correct and enough interchange between submission and shrewd criticism to allow him to get his feet on the ground. I started off thinking that it was funny, and then I got interested. I had this vision of Diane squirming uncomfortably, after the way she had prodded us outside. As she sat there she looked at her own legs with a complacency that was frankly sexual, almost a compensation to herself, like a man enjoys shaving with a wet razor. And then she shelved her legs, and for a while she showed us her face – her mouth and her neck in the light which came through the window from the meeting-room. It became the effortless art of drawing the two of us together in front of her. I can't really say. Enrolling male desire is about as complicated as picking up a can of beans at a supermarket.

'Are you all right, Billy?' Diane touches my arm.

'I'll go make us some coffee.' I don't want her to look at me.

I made the coffee and went back to the porch.

'Where's Johnny?'

'He's gone upstairs to smoke. One paper.' Diane raised a finger from the arm of her chair. As if to shed herself of some sensation or other, she arranged her chair so that she sat with her back to the wall, looking out through the screens into the darkness. She tilted her head back and meditated. I kissed her.

It was a mistake. Her lips were cold. I ran my hand down her hair and clasped her shoulder, and went to my chair.

She stretched out her arm and I held the hand. She said: 'You're a very warm man.' And then she said: 'The last time I went to bed with a man was two years ago and it was a disaster. I suppose it wasn't serious. That's where I went just now, back there. When you're sixteen, seventeen, your resilience carries you through. But you lose that. And then when it goes wrong, it's not ... I can't just walk away from it.' She stared at me. I didn't know what I was supposed to live down to.

I said: 'Yeah, maybe not.'

She's right, we are that old. I felt old; it depressed me.

The mosquitoes don't stand too much chance. Some rich people have those ultra-violet lights on their porches, the whole evening is punctuated by crackles as the bugs explode. Diane gazes through the screen. We're still holding hands, she makes no move when Johnny joins us, she might be tired. He sits on the other side of her, cross-legged; he doesn't care when she ruffles his hair and tugs at it; he fends off her weak punch.

'*I* found something out,' she announced.

'Yeah? What did *you* find out?' Johnny mimicked her.

'I found out that the something-or-other sea-shrimp swims over to a certain beach in California once a year, on a full moon. And each of the males lays sixty-four females, and each of the females gets herself laid sixty-four times. The males die of exhaustion and fall to the sea-bed while the females float down on top of their bodies and die while they are producing their eggs. What do you think of that?'

'It sounds pretty much like California.'

'It solves the problem of the generation gap,' Diane pointed out.

'Poor old lady.'

'Not me.' We were in a line; Diane and Johnny didn't need to touch hands.

'Billy, do you think I should go to Canada? I know that Mom ... Diane ... is sort of split.'

Diane closed her hand, in encouragement. What did Diane want me to say?

I said: 'If you think you can make out better in Canada, then you should go. That's why I'd go. You're only one person

110

and you're not going to make much of a ripple at the Pentagon. I don't know what the hell we're going to do to stop that war. Maybe we should all go to Canada.'

Whatever I said was dumb, I don't know anything about moral principles or family arrangements. It was a misplaced compliment for the kid to ask me. The war doesn't knock at my door, I guess. I can't rationalise it through. I don't believe anyone in this country knows what America is, they just fly flags or burn flags because they need some form of identity and they like the razzmatazz. 'You should take a vacation up in Canada and find out if you like it. You're the one who's going to have to stick with it. Hell, get out there and take a look.'

'That's the tradition in this country.' Diane gave it a dubious value.

'That's what I like about it, wrong or right. You can go out there and find yourself.'

Diane stirred uneasily. 'You know, there's more bullshit talked about finding yourself than there is about any other subject. I don't know what it is that makes people think that they *have* a self. The self is a very sacred cow in this country. And finding yourself comes down to avoiding yourself, the way we do it. The amount of spiritual need in this country is disgusting and I think it's a dangerous sham, it's phoney. I don't believe America is that empty.'

'Mom, you spend too much time talking from experience.' Johnny picked at his bare feet.

'I do?'

'Sure you do. I like it sometimes. I guess you're sort of a conservative.'

'Thanks a bunch, honey.'

'You don't get fooled by anything much.'

'I don't want *you* to get fooled.'

'I know. It feels kind of inevitable though.' Johnny was philosophically solemn about it, nodding at the floor.

'You shouldn't worry about getting fooled,' I interrupted, 'it's the only way you'll ever learn anything. If you go around thinking that you might always be tricked, you'll stop yourself from ever doing anything.'

We sat in silence, listening to the bugs. I smoked a cigarette. Strange how in England, people offer around their cigarettes, and watch each other's gestures. It's an actor's country. In America we like to get something out of each other. So maybe we do end up confused, because we try more.

Johnny went to bed. The screen door cluttered shut behind him.

Diane and I should go to bed together now for the peace of it. Not sit here with our thoughts sucked up by the night, our eyes picking out the disconnected movements of the darkness. 'You smoke too many cigarettes, Billy.' She lights one as well. She smirks. 'I think that we have a runner.'

'Who?'

'I'll stack it on Harry. I haven't seen him in the last couple of hours.'

'He might be going through some changes up here.'

'Nothing he won't shake off.' Diane switched her head and reached out to pull the ashtray nearer to her side of the table. Her formulas depressed me.

'Johnny's a nice kid. You don't have anything to worry about.'

'He's so naïve. Something swallows him up and spits him out, and he gets hurt and he wonders why. I wasn't thinking about him. I was thinking: what makes it so much easier for *you* to say, "Don't worry about being fooled, go take a vacation, see how you find it"? Why don't *I* say that? He's been playing with this move for six months and I've done nothing but turn it into a big decision for him.'

'Darling, I say what *I'd* do.'

'You may be more honest. I get lumbered with being supportive.'

'You have to arrange your life around him more than I do.'

'Why?' She posed with the cigarette.

'That's you. You're open to change; you live through other people and – '

'Do I?' She froze.

'Who doesn't? People who live off themselves are insane. I spend my whole leisure and my whole career living off other people's characters and their energy. I'd be dead without them, Diane. You're dynamite on loving the people you want to love. Sometimes I wonder if you know that.' Diane was fishing for compliments. There were typical reasons for her to be unsure and worried. But both of us are pretty selfish. 'With your guy lined up in Boston, you can't wait to get rid of the two of them, can you?' I laughed.

'That's –' Diane's eyes were hard and alarmed and knife-edged. 'Even for you that's too much.' We rolled our hatred around at the back of the throat like a glob of loogy.

Harry came through the outer screen-door. Diane immediately stood up. The screen-door closed quietly, Harry rubbed the back of his neck. 'Where the hell have you been, Harry?' Diane held out her arms to him.

'It's not what you think, Diane. I was out leaning on the fence.'

He ducked his eyes towards me. Diane's arms dropped hopelessly to her hips. He said, 'I'm sorry, Diane. I didn't mean to have you worried. I should have been a little more aware. I'll just sneak on through. No hard feelings, huh?'

He reached and shook her hand.

'Night, Billy.'

'Night, Harry.'

Diane stood straight, with her hands on her hips. He went, she stayed still. She tapped the toe of her right foot on the wooden porch, she looked down and brought the foot in next to its sister. She looked at the porch corner-post. Her face was hidden but the light caught the full deep blush on her neck.

12

There is no midday meal on Sunday. Pam and Andy leave a spread of salad in the dining-room. The house was quiet so I didn't know whether the others were still in bed or if they were out somewhere. They might even have taken themselves off to church.

I didn't have anything to say to Johnny; that would be dealing with his whole life, for Chrissakes. I lay in bed in the early morning, thinking what I could say, responsibilities and all that crap; it was like bouncing a tennis ball off a wall. The harder I threw it, the faster I had to move to catch it.

I ate a sandwich and walked out into a still Sunday. I thought that I might test the leg. Taking the leg for a walk; like not being alone.

Several famous show business and TV people had houses up here; expansive deep-green lawns and large, shampooed dogs. There was no sign of people, nobody on the roads, nobody going in or out of the houses. Maybe it wasn't the season, or maybe they all went to a late-night party.

I had no clean pants. I knew some of these people, in the city, even worked with them. I don't like calling on people. I don't like their homes and the way they guard whatever relationship they have at the time. Their dogs sniffed at me from the ends of the driveways. Some of the dogs were friendly, others poked their heads forward and barked themselves off their front feet. Not one of them came further than the gateposts.

One movie director I knew used to have his chauffeur call round the day before a party, and each of his guests had to hand over a piece of clothing so his dogs had the smell.

Rusty may be a sleaze but at least he's human. The apartment in New York has been burgled twice over his happily wagging tail. The second guy left a note – 'Cute pooch.' Donald wanted to give the note to the police department for a handwriting analysis. What the hell; we don't have anything of *value* in that apartment other than Rusty. Oh yeah, there's Donald's alarm-clock!

The Tony and the Emmy are with my family. I couldn't live with any of those awards. We're free of all that. We're going forward. We're not tied to that old game. There's so much energy in this country. People aren't allowing themselves to get structured, the younger people are moving sideways to help each other, so we can all move forward together. We have to get in on this new spirit, crash through ourselves. Diane can be kind of paranoid. It must have something to do with living in this rich area. Tell Linda how it looks. We're fine in the city; city people. I would die in Canada.

'Johnny said to say goodbye.'

'Shit, Diane, I didn't mean to miss him. He must have left early.'

'He doesn't like driving in traffic.'

Clink. Sunday-evening dinner.

Diane was adrift. This Sunday evening, the formalities were

spread around her like leaves on a sidewalk. Her voice burst out occasionally, she was abstracted from the questions she posed.

Eight of the group were leaving the next day, nobody wanted to part on sour terms. They wanted addresses and telephone numbers and contact.

When we sat in the meeting-room over our coffee and generalities, Diane encouraged her guests to stay in touch with each other, she passed herself around like a leisured hostess. It was like a cocktail party. An older woman called Evelyn held a simple court over by the window. I sat in the chair next to her, amused by her poking motherliness. We had ourselves a double act, the old and the invalid.

'People will think there's something wrong with you. Now why don't you chase out Diane?' Evelyn suggested firmly. I hadn't noticed that Diane had gone out of the room.

I looked for her in her bedroom, but it was empty. I collected my address book and went down to the kitchen. Pam and Andy had cleared away the dishes and Diane was in there alone, racking the herbs and the salt and so on.

'Hi.'

'Hi.' She was standing still, straight as a board, a long block of exclusive Diane, absorbed, edgy. She filled the room and yet she was unapproachable.

'Do you want to talk?' I asked her from the door.

'No. I'm not going to move you back into Johnny's room. We only have five people coming tomorrow and they can go in the barn.'

'Sure. Diane, I'm sorry if I hurt you last night.'

'You didn't; so don't worry about it.'

'Okay.' I couldn't think of anything else to say. Diane spoke.

'I'm going to say goodbye to the others and then I'm going to bed.'

'Sure. I'll probably stay up for a while.' I invited Diane but she stood waiting for me to go out of the kitchen first so that she could kill the lights.

I felt ridiculous with this goddam address book. It seemed like the time for exchanging addresses was over.

I have two or three hundred addresses in this book. Brando. Warren. Jane. Natasha.

Diane talked to people, her eyes alight, dishonestly; she

stitched together their plans for leaving. The first people started to go to bed.

I got a screw of pain from the leg so I went upstairs for a pill. I might have phoned Linda, but I sat in front of Diane's desk and liked her room for ten minutes before I felt like an intruder in front of the unmade bed and the beginnings of this week's intimate mess. She had a few clothes over a chair, a jacket on the floor and a book half-way down the mattress. I don't read many books. I don't read enough books. Who the hell has the time?

I shouldn't be in here. We wouldn't go anywhere.

The ache in my leg hasn't gone, those pills aren't strong enough.

I stopped off in my room. I closed the door and took another painkiller. I couldn't stick that room. I heard Diane come down the corridor.

'Sleep well, babe.'

'Night, Billy.'

She closed her door.

Yeah, I have a book too. It's no cure.

I stayed in bed with my own kind of hangover. In the afternoon I took off for a long walk. I punished that leg along the roads and it stood up pretty good. The time of the leg is over, but I guess it's too late for Hollywood. When I left the Farm, Pam and Andy were affectionately cleaning the main house. In New York, when you have your apartment cleaned, you call up some outfit; they send over an employee and he or she bugs the hell out of you by being friendly the whole time, a constant hassle of friendly questions. Donald wanted a regular house-boy, we tried that for a year until I heard Donald talking at one of his dinner parties about our 'good relationship' with the houseboy; and I really didn't want another dog around the apartment, didn't want a 'relationship' with some guy who arrived once a week with a brush and bucket. I told Donald that unless we freewheeled with the houseboys I'd invite Cae-sar – or whatever his goddam name was – over to every dinner party we had; let him out of the trap. We're not that emotion-ally bankrupt. Screw relationships.

I had this plan of making it as far as the town but I sat twenty feet in from the road and thought about Diane.

116

She made the introductions and told everybody how the house was organised. The five new people had arrived and she already had their names and occupations in her memory. She explained to the group that I was Billy, I was a longtime friend of hers, I had had a fight with an automobile 'which he didn't win, but he'll be back there and I hope some of you will get the chance of talking to him.' Her hands were very silent for Diane, and though her eyes were energetic they darted about over a dark sleeplessness in her face.

Evelyn took the chair and described herself and her submission to alcohol until she quit in her fifties. She was a minister's wife, she talked with a simplicity that cut through the usual humble evasions. Hers was a life of depression and fear, a totally unreasonable depression which stunned the room into respect. We shared her experience and there was a long pause after she had finished speaking.

The group would come to sit in a circle, but tonight the chairs were drawn up in two lines to face Diane and Evelyn. It was like watching Diane on stage, her same withheld appearance which intrigued you although she made no attempt to direct your attention towards her. It wasn't her looks; the long oval face and those green eyes and the body's trained composure. It wasn't that. It was the feeling you had that both you and she were being duped by her air of placid melancholy. But that was natural to her. She didn't adopt it.

So you ended up being irritated with her. Because you thought: does she accept this? Is this how she likes to see herself in the mirror? Or is the mirror how she sees the world? As a man you want to take away the mirror, solve a simple problem for her, make her laugh.

She waited for any response to Evelyn, and when no one spoke up she said that one of the most important aims of the Farm was to encourage self-expression, and that being a part of a group should encourage a deeper awareness.

'My name is Doug' – and by the tone of his voice he obviously disliked Diane's presidency – 'I am an alcoholic. I got a lot of hope from your chair, Evelyn. I'd like to say that one member can tell me more about myself than a whole group or group discussion.'

'There is no set format here, Doug,' Diane snapped. She

117

leaned forward. And then maybe she was tired, she dried up, both embarrassed at her own sense of authority and annoyed at the check on it. For a second her eyes floundered in irritation, and then the blank unworldly expression returned.

'This is my second week here. As you'll find out,' Evelyn suggested in her gentle manner, 'almost everything around Diane and her house is open to you and I'm sure that goes for the question of having a chair. I must say that I don't think that it does any of us too much good if we separate off into little cliques with our problems. I'm just too old to come to a dating club and I don't want to get left out. I'm not going to let you sneak off with each other.'

I caught Diane's eye and we laughed along with everyone else.

'This is not a gloomy house and none of us is old or sick or holing up in the lobby of a hospital. I've said my – ' Evelyn was drowned by the outbreak of laughter and applause.

The meeting disintegrated. I watched Diane smile and talk and negotiate her way to the door.

'I didn't know you had this potential, Evelyn,' I told her as she sat down next to me.

'Billy, two or three times a week I have to sit quiet as a mouse in church while my husband tells us all what to do. And I don't tell him, but he isn't the best speaker in the world. I have some life cooped up in me!' She had an irresistible delight in herself. 'We all have to take a share, you know. It isn't fair on Diane. That poor girl! And all the men round here grumble and moan like little children. I thought that you came up here to help her out, but you don't want to, do you, Billy? Well, that's your business.' I was shocked. Evelyn was high on success. With a grand flourish she turned to Doug; she soothed him and poked him and handed him on to the group next to us. 'And now here's the coffee,' she observed, as Diane and Andy carried in the trays.

'Can I get you some coffee, Evelyn?' I stood up.

'Thank you, Billy. I'll save your chair.'

'I won't sneak off.'

'You won't, I know that. You're a good boy.'

I came up behind Diane, stood while she was arranging cookies on a plate. Bending forward, she seemed to be confined within a pyramid shape, a tough point of energy in her head,

118

rigid lines bunched up around her shoulders, the lower half of her body weak and scattered and out of touch. She was aware of the people around her, she censured them, she shied away from Andy's lackadaisical presence next to her. She was standing guard over herself.

'Hi.' I bent over with her.

'Hi, Billy,' she said.

'Why don't we get out of here tomorrow?'

'Why?' She straightened up, eyes not curious, a kind of cold question.

'Why not? Let everybody take their own responsibilities.'

A pair of hands reached round me to take two cups from the trays. Diane watched them go. 'I have to go out tomorrow to the supermarket. If you don't mind coming with me, you can take over one of Andy's chores.'

'I can handle it.'

'That's one arrangement which has worked out,' she said with a light, self-pitying sarcasm. She picked up one of the trays and took it down the far end of the room. That had me pissed. Three guys were standing and talking, maybe about her; they each had a phoney smile when they took a cup of coffee from the tray as she served them. I carried two cups away to Evelyn.

'Diane has a man, you know.' I stirred my coffee. 'She has a photograph of him in the bedroom.'

'This Michael? I don't think he exists.' Evelyn was unruffled, slightly indignant. I laughed at her.

'I think he does. Come on, Evelyn, I've known Diane a long time and she isn't a screwball.'

'She certainly isn't. I mean to say that for all the good he does her, he might as well not exist. She's confused. And where is he? She deserves more than that. Isn't she beautiful?' Evelyn held out her hand for Diane to take, an absent-minded Diane, a little of the mock-waif and some more of the unwilling daughter. 'Sit here, honey.'

'Well, Evelyn, I'm bushed.' Diane sat down. 'Do you think they're all okay?' Despite herself, her eyes searched after reassurance.

'We're fine.'

Diane lit a cigarette. 'You know, I think tomorrow I'll get up and I'll take the car and drive out for the day.'

119

'I think you should do that.'

Evelyn's encouragement appeared to bounce off Diane, but the permission nestled down snug somewhere inside her. Evelyn started talking about the porch windows and how good it was to have a porch, the beautiful ornamental bowl in the hallway and how difficult it was to stop yourself filling a house with objects; Diane saying that she preferred a house full of people as long as she had her own private hideaway.

I sat on the outside. When I was a kid and I was off school, sick but not bed-sick, I sometimes sat like this when the woman next door called on my mother and they talked and sooner or later I would stand up and do my act. Mainly out of the fear that they were pleased to forget about me; their strange exclusive intimacy, their never getting anywhere, their lack of plans; and the feeling that they didn't really like each other, they just lived across the way and they wouldn't ever live anywhere else. The little man stood up and took their minds off these things; and finally they waved him goodbye with a kind of pride and a kind of indifferent acceptance, because he wanted to make it.

I found myself looking at Diane, unable slowly to believe that we were pretty much of the same generation and we were both down to making empty arrangements with our love lives.

When she stood up, she said good-night and she went. At the door she turned and she mouthed something quickly across. I stood up but she had already closed the door behind her.

'What did she want?' I asked Evelyn.

'I think she said "Thank you", didn't she?'

'To me?'

'Well it wouldn't be to me, dear. We understand it.'

Diane was up earlier than I was; by the time I came downstairs she had most of the group breakfasted and they were lounging in the meeting-room. She stood over a list; she checked cupboards, she suggested and took suggestions from members of the group, she carried her pen.

Over my head. She and Pam went through the freezers, Andy took himself out of the way to attend to a broken screen which suddenly needed fixing.

'Bring your towel, Billy,' Diane called from the door. I

grinned at Pam but she was right there with Diane. This was serious, this was the way things were run.

'Okay?' Diane sat behind the wheel of the station wagon. She banged the ball of her hand against the fuel gauge. 'I thought they fixed this. I just hope we have enough gas to get us to the Exxon station.'

'Sure we do.' I lit a cigarette. She made me kind of nervy. She noticed this and smiled to herself.

'If I give everyone too much time they all get ideas about what we could eat and I get an order for eleven different brands of cigarette. No way. I do it on a clean break. Anyhow, I thought we might go up to Tangle Creek.'

'Sure, whatever you like.'

I watched the way she shifted the car into drive and how we progressed out on to the road. I have this fear of automobiles. I had it before the accident. When I'm in an automobile I use the time to talk to myself. People who drive are off on their own trip. I respect that. I regularly look at the levers and the pedals. No other passenger seems to do this; they all travel like animals in the back of a truck, laughing and rooting around for jokes. Except dogs. I noticed the way Rusty handles it. Dogs check out the levers every once in a while as though they have a vested interest in the machinery. And they wonder about the driver's fault potential. It figures. You can see a hell of a lot of dead dogs laid out on the side of the road.

'Are you missing anyone, Billy?'

'Me? No.'

'I should have woken you earlier. You don't like being driven?'

'I don't drive, so it's always been that way.'

I just wanted her to pay attention to the machinery, you know. She has her shoes kicked off and, next to her list, her red cotton skirt is bunched up around her thighs; down amongst the pedals it's working okay, like climbing around in a bedroom; and up above the waist it's like an office.

Pretty country.

'The country is beautiful,' I said to her.

'Spring and fall are more alive. The fall is my time. Light green has never made a big impact with me.'

'So do we have a plan?'

'I always have a plan, you know that. I go to the wall for a plan,' she mocked herself.

'What is it?'

'We drive another forty minutes up to the Creek, we buy lunch, we lie out in the sun and on the way home we get the chores done. That okay?'

'It sounds okay.'

'The Creek's quiet during the week. I haven't been doing too much for you, Billy, since you've been up here.'

'When I arrived up here I couldn't do anything anyway.'

She agreed, she didn't say anything. She balanced it off; we were evens. She concentrated on her driving. A long, straight road with sprawling curves, forest on both sides of the road, those trees with thin grey-white trunks. In high summer they still looked bleak and ungenerous under a blue sky. Yeah, we were evens; really just independent.

I glanced at her. There is an impossibility of belonging with her. As sure as the guy in the photograph is real; and he is, whatever their relationship might be.

'Wasn't that look a little severe?' Diane watched ahead through the windscreen. 'We don't have too far to go. What do you want to eat?'

'What do they have?'

'Pizza, sandwiches, hot dogs; that kind of cuisine.'

'Ham on rye with a pickle.'

'And a milkshake?' she quizzed. 'It's that sort of day. Let's be high school about it.'

'Sure. I'll be the one-legged quarterback. All right, I'll take a pineapple and passionfruit. You?'

'I'll have chocolate.'

We stopped at an Exxon station. The guy filled us up and filled himself up on Diane's legs. 'Asshole,' Diane murmured, when the window was closed and she was sliding her credit card into her wallet.

'Isn't that being touchy?'

'Wasn't *he* being touchy?'

'What happened to high school?' I reminded her.

'Yea, team!' We waited on the edge of the filling station for some cars to go by. 'Hell, I don't care,' she said.

She drove us another ten miles through the country. She pointed out a broken-down railroad station, a few shacks, and then we came to some very neat white-painted houses with fences and gardens and flowers, and the whole town was white, even McDonald's had obliged with the white paint.

'Is this Tangle Creek?'

'Yes.'

'You said it was quiet. This looks more like Niagara Falls.'

Diane laughed and wound her window down. We cruised, looking for the milkshake parlour. There were a lot of cars, a few expensive craft shops and that kind of check-pants, fat-assed tourist who pretends not to be searching for something to buy.

'These people are gross. I hope they realise it.'

'You're being snobbish,' I teased her.

'If we get to my favourite hideaway and we find any of them up there, I'll turn downright mean.' She was serious.

When she opened her door at the milkshake parlour, it was like she didn't want to let the 'us' out of the car. She swept off to buy our lunch, she ordered, the server missed his slot for platitudes. And the whole way out of town Diane protected 'us' with an ironic account of her adolescent grapples. She entertained us. She used a lot of flat mouth and eyebrow. She picked me up.

And then she took the car off the road and up some track, we bucked around for a couple of minutes, she killed the engine and it was quiet. Livid green silence.

Diane rested her knees on the rim of the steering-wheel, her feet dangling, her head laid against the back of the seat. I looked out of the rear window. 'We shook them off.'

'Good.' She had her right hand floating lonely; I took it and squeezed it, she squeezed back. It was childish. Her eyes wandered over the roof covering. 'Okay,' she said, 'we have work to do.'

'It's not some kind of a trek, is it?'

'Uh-huh.' She reached for her shoes and opened the door. 'We go through the trees, over that way; and we find the creek.'

She carried a straw bag with our towels and the lunch, I took two mattresses, following her around the trees. It was bear and snake country.

'I never see any,' Diane said. 'And down at the water they don't even have mosquitoes.'

The air began to cool, you could smell the water. Diane

sauntered ahead through a thin veil of sound, which misted her image for me. Losing her personality.

I have a strange feeling about water, a weakness. It dissolves me, I go kind of crazy trying to keep my head above it. I find it unnerving; not wanting to be lost with the mass, I feel as though I'm a series of bright drops hanging in the air, frivolous and frantic, a haphazard chain of brief moments, light sparkling. I have to turn my head to see where I'm coming from.

In front of me, Diane was sturdy. Relaxed and light-hearted, but physically sturdy; a creature of the earth. She trod, not confused like I was. Sure of herself. There was no coyness in her movement and no friendliness. I might as well not have been there.

We came out on the edge of the creek. It wasn't large, it didn't flow dangerously, it didn't explode with noise. It swirled down from some jagged rocks to our left and it dropped maybe five feet over a ten-yard stretch, and then in front of us it was wider and calmer, maybe fifteen feet wide, moving ignorantly through and away, pitted with sliding whirlpools and air-bubbles.

I stood there beside Diane, blown away. The movement of the water had some nightmare to it.

I laughed and whooped. I had to have some reaction. I laughed and whooped. Diane smiled: as though it had all spent the last millennium rehearsing for her. I put the mattresses on the bank and lit a cigarette, then I rubbed my hand up and down her back. It was like rubbing a horse. Diane didn't give an inch. I never rubbed a horse in my life. Diane's eyes caressed the stretch of water like a favourite body.

'Okay,' she murmured. She turned to her right and moved off a couple of paces, picking her way back into the greenery.

'Where do we make the camp-site?'

I didn't want to move alongside this water.

'There it is.' She pointed downstream.

Like a full head of long silver-grey hair, the water parted at the top of a brow of rock. And it streamed round the sides of the huge smooth whitestone which lay in the middle there.

'There's another rock in the middle of the channel. You can't see it. We jump across from the bank.'

'No way, baby. No way am I jumping across anywhere. You've got to be kidding. I won't do it, Diane.'

'You don't know if your insurance covers it?'

'Damn right.'

'Chicken.'

'Whichever way you want it, darling.'

'You can't drown, Billy. You might get your feet wet, that's all.'

'We could stay here on the bank.'

'With the snakes?'

'Come on ... I have this paranoia about water, okay?'

I unfolded one of the mattresses. I put the cigarette down in the grass. Diane looked at me from up there.

'For real?' she smiled.

'Hell, you go out there if you want to.'

'Do you get it with the ocean as well?'

'Not if it's calm, like a pool or something. I don't know. I get confused by this. It wires me up. I can't handle it, that's all.'

She gave me one long mean look, and she walked away with the other mattress.

I watched Diane settle on top of the rock. Like the summit of some mountain, bare and bleak. On which she lay, possessing it.

I was down there among the mosquitoes and bugs, and some kind of genetic deviation with a bulbous, hairy body whose wings could hardly hold it up, and it buzzed around like a military transport aircraft, full of poison and short hops. Sooner or later its repulsive interest would brush up against my skin. Furry and twitching. It wasn't as scared as I was.

I got across to the rock.

I don't know whether it was the relief, or Diane, or the brown skin on her shoulders and the smoothness of that skin – but the rock was familiar. It was secure and taken for granted. She herself lay still, saying nothing, soaking up the sun.

I lay beside her, pricked by the creek spray.

I smoked cigarettes.

I looked round the shape of the rock, saw all this water going past and always more of it.

Diane reached out and pulled some of the water in on her chest and neck. She left her hand dangling back in the current.

I reached in my side and pulled out some water. That was enough for me.

125

But Diane bathed. She slipped down the slope at the back end of the rock, she took off the blue and green costume and she lay in the calm backwater pool next to where she had put our milkshakes. Below the horizon of the rock. I lost sight of her.

She came out naked on the slope of the rock, rubbing puny goosepimpled breasts with a towel, small diamonds clinging to the thick black mat of pubic hair; somebody's mistress, white-sided, moving across a window. She turned her back on me to pull up her costume.

'You don't have to wear that, Diane.'

She continued, covering her ass and her hips and then, folding the costume down, she sat on the mattress.

'Dumb, isn't it?' she said. 'What you can't ignore.'

'Sure.'

She pinned her hair back and she lay down.

When I moved on to her, she wrapped her arms over me. I didn't disturb her. Her eyes looked past my head, up at the sky; she dug her chin into my lips and arched her back slightly.

'Do you want to take the costume off again?'

'No, Billy, I won't. Let's leave things the way they are.'

'Are you hung up?'

'Is that how you see me?' she asked contemptuously.

'I'm very turned on.'

'You're nervous. Just relax.'

'You're kidding.'

She watched me for a moment, blank-eyed as a dead fish; but green eyes and ash-blonde hair, and maybe careless reluctance.

She wound her legs over mine, pinning me. I watched out for my leg.

'Does that hurt?' She relaxed her legs, as if in apology.

I said: 'No.' I sucked and chewed on a large brown nipple in my mouth, Diane closed her eyes and tilted her shoulders from side to side gently.

I pulled back and looked at her but she had her eyes closed. I looked at the rock and the creek. Her pelvis reproached me. She opened her eyes then, they were hospitable and easy; when I was a kid it was green eyes are greedy eyes. Hers were supercilious.

I reached my hand down and jerked at the costume which was tying her up in this protection. No. She stopped that. She serried us.

She started to jostle herself forwards. I gave way to this game, sliding on top of her, rubbing. She took my head, requisitioned my mouth for her nipple, one hand stroking my hair. Her other fingers scratched and played and grated on my back, while our two layers of material scraped together what we had in warmth. When I saw it, her face was mottled red, pinpoints forming clouds, her mouth clenched. While her forehead frowned, somewhere perplexed.

We all have our loads to dump. I got free of my pants, I left her costume where it was. The tops of her thighs clamped me and we screwed that way, she humped in good, short, steady jerks. Diane keeps her own programme locked away behind the steady flesh and the teethmarks on her lips. Her eyelids stay closed and the lines on her brow flutter; her own fingers rub and pinch her nipples. We bring each other up to shine like a couple of old lamps.

She wetted her lips, lightly, and I wanted that mouth, something resentful, like knocking a screwdriver up into that brain. So I pulled away and up out of the aridity and crawled up her body; she blocked my hips with her thighs, her hands fled down and they stopped me, they throttled my hard and they manipulated and they worked like a maniac until they squeezed the sperm out somewhere over her breasts.

I know a bit less about Diane.

My sperm, dammit.

She rolled me gently away so that we lay side by side on our backs, each smoking a cigarette. She stared off somewhere and then closed her eyes. Splotched come dried like glue on the skin above her tangled costume, the nipples were swollen and red, the mouth full-heavy with casualness. She wanted it to happen.

She acted as though she had just told her best friend's secret to a stranger.

I stacked my cigarette ash in a pile. Then, being naked, I stuck my finger in it and rubbed it around until all that was left was a discoloration on the stone.

I went down the rock to wash. That water was cold! I left a foot in it and wiped myself down with a towel.

'How do you lie in that cold water?'

Diane didn't answer. I went over to her with the milkshakes. She lay with her eyes closed, I put on my shorts and crouched beside her. 'Diane?' She opened one eye. I put every trick I knew into my own eyes. I kissed through her. She had an arm round me, she stretched out her legs. 'Are you sore?'

'At you or at myself?' She propped herself up, folding her right arm under her head. I noticed her armpit, white and with grizzly hairpoints, the skin lines on her neck. 'I have to get back in training with lovers.'

'What do you mean?' I asked.

'Perhaps I'm a cold person.'

'You're one of the warmest people I know.'

'But we know each other pretty well.'

She wasn't content; though she kissed me, it was only perfunctory. She picked on the milkshakes, she wrapped her hand round one of the cartons and remarked that maybe they were too warm. She wiped down the carton when I thought that she might wipe down her own body. She was practical, sitting with her legs curled under her stained body, the costume twisted; and she held this carton as though she was cleaning up some kid before he went off to school. She took the straw, jabbed it through the lid, and tasted.

'That's not good.' She stood up and took the two shakes back to the water. Then she paid some attention to herself; modestly, I turned my eyes away.

She lay down naked opposite me, smoking a cigarette. I looked a long time for her eyes but she had them shut.

We ate lunch, pushed ourselves through the milkshakes, felt sticky and gross and sugared in the sun. Diane reached into her basket and pulled out a bottle of mineral water, which got rid of the sugar.

She started to give us some order. She sat upright in one of those lotus positions which I can't take too seriously. Nude housewife with swollen genitals goes pure on rock in middle of New York State. But she looked better and a big part of that was knowing she looked better; she had that same brazen pride that had fitted her on our walk from the car, it adorned the pleasure she felt in her own spirit, as she sat on that rock, strong-backed. I had a sense of my own redundancy, but this was how she wanted me to be – a small

128

cruelty for having stripped her down so carelessly. We both hated gratitude.

The light bounced off the bank behind her, leaving a perspex green, flat and hard against the white torso. She absorbed the sun, her eyes wandered over to the trees behind me, on their guard, summarising us and our surroundings. A statement of her own discipline and her superiority over the fumbling water and the fumbled sex and the bedraggled green undergrowth. Above us, the creek gushed down through jagged teeth and we sat like two thick-skinned frogs on our white rock.

'How long did you stay up Sunday night?' she inquired.

'Pretty late.'

'I worried about you.'

'I got a little spaced on the painkillers. Harry saw me up the stairs.'

'I heard the noise. Be careful, Billy, you can only indulge yourself *so* far.'

She let it drop behind a screen of silence. She lowered herself down from her lotus, the sun devoted itself to her back and her legs.

'We missed out that evening,' I suggested to the back of her head.

'You know, I felt that we might get involved when Donald called to say you were coming up here. I didn't want to get involved. I still don't. But I didn't think about it; that's where I went wrong.'

I wanted to say something like 'Come on, Diane, this is all so serious, laugh, get a little joyful about it.' It? Herself. Whatever.

'Then you were here, and I did think about it,' she said, 'and it triggered off a whole series of feelings about deprivation. Getting thrown, why not? But I know why not. I have sex with people because I want something. I've had periods of sleeping around, like a restlessness. It was mostly selfish, and it didn't touch me. Women who whine get on my nerves. When you arrived, do you know how *sick* you looked?' She turned her head to threaten me.

'I manage to fool most people.'

'You're no older, are you Billy? No more sense. Here I am, world! Come get it!'

'Do you feel guilty about us screwing?'

'We didn't. And why should I?' She lay like a slug.

'I'm in a pretty bad time; okay, sure. Yeah. Sure. What do you want me to say! I'm not working, I was waiting to do a movie but I've screwed it up. I'm not married, I don't have any children, I don't reckon on moving out to Long Island or Connecticut; I'm down, I'm nothing. Okay?' Diane was beneficent, or she made herself beneficent – flowing out, concerned, gracious; whatever the hell beneficent means. I hate that. 'Is that all right by you? I don't care. You win, darling! Whatever you like. I just take it as it comes. I can't deal with a lot of distance, babe; that's too cold for me.'

She had to take an inventory. I can pull any trick that's going, even honesty. I'm stronger than Diane is, because I'm still in the business where it's all out in the open.

She went over to the water, cupped some of it over her back. Another bimbo, starting to lose her body, unable to get off any longer on the mystery-fragility ticket, her butt spread, lining up a guy in Boston who wouldn't mind her self-inflictions. He might take notes.

Asshole.

She had the imprint of the mattress stamped rude-red on her butt; she straightened up and gave me that look, that I was interfering again.

'We're brawling, you know?'

'I could kick you in the leg, you know that?' She reached up to let her hair out. I went over and held her waist.

'Are you angry?'

'I do have two sons, Billy. I don't want another one. It's not the kind of relationship I want any longer.'

'How?'

'I was thinking about that severe look that you gave me in the car. And I ... think *what is that?*' She looked at a tree in her exasperation. 'Or what does he want, what does he expect? And why? What right do you have ... not to respect distance. Okay, honesty, okay. Even your own honesty would come back and knock you flat if it ever caught up with you.'

I was slow; I wasn't looking at her because I was listening.

'Poor man's hatred of beauty,' I mumbled. I looked at her because she was quiet; and I saw that she hadn't got what she had played for, her body was tense and her belly held in, her legs weak.

She replied: 'It's mean-spirited, that hatred. And I feel it. You see that?'

'Wanting you?'

She considered me quickly.

She rubbed my back in speculation; she was silent, looking over my shoulder. She relaxed. Her belly swelled in against my own.

Why did I use that?

She put the litter in her basket, dressed herself last of all, handed the mattresses across the water to me. When we sauntered back through the trees I still carried the rush of water in my head.

I liked hearing her talk, to have that quick flow of Diane; her leaning to and fro against me and the pleasure in her voice, the carefree irony and the tenderness. As we got to the car, her hand squeezed my back and the gentle lilt overlaid the sound of the creek in my mind: '… and you're not going to stay, Billy, are you?'

The green eyes flit light-heartedly across mine. She is very close and this kiss surprises me with its warmth, frailty and decision. Then her hand on the trunk of the station wagon.

She opened the door of the trunk and started to arrange the inside. She reached a hand back to take the mattresses from me.

Too much sun, too long at the megamarket, too long unpacking and storing. Diane changed her clothes and people involved her in their clamor. They all suddenly wanted to settle in quick, perhaps they wanted to compensate for the nit-picking last night. Diane was back in position, she liked it and she liked to pass the session giving it away again.

I went upstairs to take a call from Linda.

We didn't talk very well. Linda seemed to be in the middle of some crazy attempt to write a series of proved equations on a blackboard, leaving out every alternate symbol. I was supposed to fill in. When that failed she went into a New York mood, and I didn't really have much to contribute. I heard her. She complained, she speculated, she invited, she informed, she joked, laughed, was bored. We arranged to meet for dinner on Thursday.

The bedroom was dead without Diane. The skirt, sweatshirt and costume in a heap on the floor with some other clothes. I went downstairs to hang around and Diane was just shutting the door to the meeting-room. She stood with her hands behind her back holding the door-handle.

'No great shakes tonight,' she murmured derisively.

'That makes two of us.'

'See me home?'

'Sure.'

She let my hand drop to go upstairs ahead of me, then she took my hand again in the corridor. Her door was ajar and she pushed it open with her foot; I had left the light on, she looked across at the desk as though she wondered what world it came from, or maybe she wondered about my telephone call. Anyhow, the photograph was still there. And Diane was lazy about going on into the room. We stood like two clumsy sacks. She rested her weight on one leg, her other foot bent back against the door-frame.

'I could spend,' she sighed, 'maybe an hour, leaning here. Half-asleep. What time is it?'

Neither of us wore a watch. 'Well,' she said. 'Let's say good-night.'

We kissed fondly.

'Night, Billy.'

'Night.'

She crossed her arms. She watched me go back inside my room, she tapped her heel against the door-frame. A couple of minutes later I heard her close her door.

The corridor was more friendly than the corridor of that hotel in England, and my room was more friendly. But I could have had the same feeling about both of them. I don't like having the same feeling twice over. That's the kind of unknown pattern I can do without. I don't worry about loneliness. I'm not alone. What the hell are we doing?

13

We shuffled the deck for most of that Wednesday. Revisiting the semi-wilderness out back, Diane's tranquil neutrality, shirt

132

and jeans while I went for the sun. Two pairs of sunglasses diverting the glare.

We talked on and off about nothing. Reclined. We had some formality about ourselves which I couldn't dislodge, so we suffered for it. Most of the others went out walking. Andy took Pam to see a movie, and Evelyn sat reading in the meeting-room. I felt like having her with us, making the offer since our own generosity wasn't with each other. But Diane said no. 'I don't like being treated like a kid. Sometimes she's a help, but more often she's just sticking her nose in.'

Diane didn't say this with any malice. She said it with that clinical dissection of character that women sometimes display when they state their relationships. They're right, but it's too much for me.

'Evelyn's rooting for you.'

'I can root for myself. People have always made the big mistake with me of thinking that I need bringing out. They end up getting it wrong. You mean she's rooting for us.' Diane's face was expressionless. 'At that age you have to find some intrigue. Do you think that one of us owes the other something?'

'I missed you last night.'

'And maybe I'll miss you tomorrow night. You didn't think about that?'

'That's not a good excuse.'

'It's a good enough excuse for me. I have to go start the supper.'

'Great.' I stood up with her, she held her sunglasses in her hand. It pissed me that she looked at me sadly. There isn't any vanity left in me. I don't want anyone to be hurt.

We walked towards the porch. 'Can I come back here after I've finished at Cape Cod?'

'You know you can, Billy.'

'Should I?'

'Yes.' Carefree, and then she hesitated. 'Don't make it a leading question. Are you going to come and be useless in the kitchen?'

I loved her for the way she only hinted at her own losses. She pretended to go through the rigmarole of figuring me out, but she was never unsettled. I don't know what to do with people who are right about themselves.

In the kitchen, she was friendly but she didn't want to be diverted. Her preparation was almost dreamy; she allotted me my chores, we worked separately. I thought that you never had to doctor vegetables; but Diane hadn't got her vegetables from the supermarket. Some of them were dirty and twisted, she liked a mess on the table, she liked wiping the table down. She had an aloof respect for the food, this old-fashioned style which was slightly mad and definitely uneconomical against the amount of energy she used.

I can't see her. I can, and I can see around her. I watch for her, every one of those expressions on her face. I have nothing to say. Any impression of her that I have had over the last few days has been about as useful, and as immediately disposable, as a plastic cup. There's an endless line of them in the dispenser. I don't know anything about her. She's all over her body and all over the room, the kitchen is suffused with her. And yet ... *she* isn't. Isn't tangible. Like she is at the moment looking at herself in the same way I'm looking at her. 'You don't like eggplant?' she asks.

'Sure I like eggplant; is that what it is?'

'Don't be vulnerable, it scares me.' She had come across nervously; I was nervous, I don't know, one time when I couldn't face her. Just at that moment, Pam came in and said, 'Are we late?' and Diane had her hand over mine, she answered, 'No, how was the movie?', pressing my hand.

'Shall we finish up in here?' Pam asked.

'No, it's under control. I'll need you in an hour.' Diane moved, leaving me at the end of her fingers. 'One hour and I want to get out of these clothes. You could do a little mixing with the group tonight.'

'That's no problem.'

'Well, Billy's going tomorrow and I want to spend some time with him.'

'You are? That's a drag. Sure, we can take the group. They're an easy bunch.'

'How's Andy?'

'He's in tune with things,' Pam laughed. As she went through the kitchen, Diane and she seemed to exchange their pleasures.

'That's a sweet girl,' I said.

Diane turned, looking negligently for something to worry

about, something to check up on; acting. 'Yes, she is. She doesn't let anything get to her. She's different to the vacant chicks Johnny brings home. I think he serves them up on me – that kind of soft, spacy little girl. It's like bringing home his dirty shirts. We sit, and we have to talk very slowly and seriously … otherwise we're going to tread … on the flowers … on the moon. You know? I think it's called senility. Anyhow they all seem to worship their grandparents.'

We found ourselves looking at each other. We suddenly couldn't care less, we were ridiculous.

'Does he have anyone steady?'

'They're interchangeable, that's steady. They're just kids. Sometimes I think that if they're going to put themselves through all this questioning now, then in five or six years they're going to be glad to be simple cynics, they won't have any energy left. If it doesn't work out, they'll just feel betrayed.'

'We had some pretty dippy stuff which we didn't end up taking seriously.'

'Well I hope they don't take it too seriously. I try to pin Johnny down but he doesn't want to know. Where was I? Yes, and the girls all have patience. I never hear them when they're making love; no one giving or taking. I get a certain pride out of knowing that people are enjoying themselves; you know?' She raised an ironic eyebrow.

She went with a smile from the freezer to the sink, she looked out of the window and up at the ceiling. Tongue in cheek and she was jubilant, with her sleeves pushed up to the elbow, with the crazy slump of her hips against the sink, with the faucet streaming water over her hands. I don't know why she is how she is, or why she changes.

She turned to half-face me; her hands on the edge of the sink, her mouth loosely assembled. Her eyes caressed inquisitively. 'Do I take a shower before dinner or after?'

'Both.'

Her mouth tumbled into a lovemaking.

I took a shower; I dressed up, Diane laughed at me before we ate dinner. In the meeting-room she kept quiet and polite, she eased the group into a relaxed exchange. She set herself to talk to Evelyn, a little oozy and plain; I slipped away as Pam was edging in to replace her. I couldn't keep from grinning, Diane was so beautifully dishonest.

Upstairs in her room, the photograph was missing. If she had had more time, she would have arranged the covers on the bed, folding one side down to welcome us both. It was for her.

Donald called, I laughed him into laughing about himself, and so he became uneasy and came out with the information quicker than he might have done; he didn't really extend into Diane's room. I undressed and lay on her bed, waiting for her. I started to read her book. It was too serious for me, Eastern religion and transactional psychology, a whole lot of step-by-step precise crap papered over with yoga positions that I used to fantasise someone like Diane being found in when I wanted to jerk off after school.

We did those same positions sometimes at the Studio. She had been ambitious in her training, as though she feared laziness; she was tall and slim, often surprisingly inflexible. It annoyed her to be looked at.

It was tough at the Studio; being stripped down isn't easy. Rykov shredded us inside a minute, right after the show when we were raw. Sometimes in the mornings she would arrive in a fog of suffering, as if she'd replayed it all in her solitude that night. Sometimes there was a startled guilt. Any inquiries were brushed aside, she wouldn't let anyone interfere. If you playfully put an arm around her, she was offended and she was cold; her investigation of herself seemed to be more than anyone else could manage and she made us feel that we were just carelessly indulgent, letting bits of ourselves fall out all over the place.

We were all floating on open sincerity, crazy exploration. Nobody's feet touched ground. She took lovers occasionally and for short periods, though nothing in her would have told you what was going on. Another actor would hang around her for a while, which only seemed to surprise and irritate her. Someone once said that he felt he had made Diane's filing cabinet – but that was his own mentality, she was too private to be malicious and she wasn't a girl who accumulated anything other than the results of her own experience of herself. Looking round the bedroom I wondered if that space was mystical, or just empty. This book of hers described how you might fill it – throwing cords across the void.

136

I was naked in her bed; she stood with her back to me, finding something to do with the desk. She was unsure. She walked across to shut the door, and walked back and looked over the desk. It was too forlorn to be a ritual.

I joined her. She looked down my body, that I was naked; she went over to the windows to pull across the drapes, then she strolled to the center of the room, her eyes down as though she was looking at the front of her legs and their own nakedness. She picked up those clothes of hers that were lying on the rug and she put them over the chair. All of this in a silence. She watched me finish lighting a cigarette and she put her hands on my shoulders, standing in front of me.

'What are you thinking?'

'Nothing. I'm not thinking,' she stated.

'You're not sure about it.'

'I am. And I'm the one who knows. I'm going to make a fire; you're not warm enough, are you?' She tapped her fingers along my shoulder, her eyes followed them and came back mischievous to me.

'I am. Well ...'

'You're not wearing that many clothes.' The eyes laughed.

'I feel that way.'

She grinned. 'I thought so. I might like Mexico too, but this isn't it. How about a blanket?'

'Anything.'

She stopped half-way across the room to peel off her sneakers; she found me a blanket out of a cupboard. I noticed the fireplace for the first time. Once I had the blanket around me Diane knelt in front of the chimney and opened the vent. She went to another cupboard for wood and firelighters. I never made a fire in my life. Diane had it figured out, setting it and lighting it and looking at it start.

'This is what I do in the winter. Stay up here, light a fire. Bed, kitchen, chores and fire. For a week at a time.' She tilted her head to watch the flames. 'When it's quieter.'

'So what do you do?'

'Nothing.'

'Bullshit.'

'I read.'

She crouched, rocked back on her heels and stood up. Part of an exercise.

She carried a bedlamp and left it by the side of the rug, she switched off the main light and the desk lamp.

She brought over an armful of pillows and cushions. I settled on the rug in front of the fire. Donald sometimes makes a fire in the penthouse if we have invited people, and it goes pretty well on its own with no one noticing it too much. This kind of countryside intensity disturbs me – the lights down low, flames reeling.

Diane crouched again, she arranged her dress. She checked the fire and made it efficient, she tipped the smaller wood into the center, she rested the logs diagonally so that they leaned up against the back of the grate. One log rolled off center. She reached into the fire, hauled it out and put it back where she wanted it without burning herself. I sat in the blanket, not saying anything, assisting at this ceremony. I needed an ashtray; I didn't want to push the ash forward past her into the fireplace.

Her hands arranged, her hair swayed easily. I glanced at my half of her face, the flames picking her out in small snatches, her eye considerate and intent on the fire.

There seemed to be this vast open space, around and behind us, back into the stretch of the room. We were in a rosy hollow, the bed was a huge flat plateau above us, and she was absorbed in her reactions to the fire.

She caught herself. She stood up and leaned against the wall, her eyes skipped over me. She looked around the room and she swung her body away from the wall. She cleared her throat. She laughed shortly. 'Maybe it's all a bit much, this room.' She stepped past me with a flourish of hemline and went to her desk, putting two folders into a drawer.

'Should you be at the meeting?'

'No.' She looked back in surprise. 'I don't have to be there all the time. Why?'

'You're restless, darling.'

'Mm-hmm.' She pulled open another drawer and took out a bottle of wine. 'I looked through all my wardrobe before dinner and I couldn't think what I'd like to wear.'

'I only have a blanket.'

'You look all right.'

'So do you, you look great.'

She brought over the bottle of wine, she went through to the bathroom for two glasses. That stone-cold bathroom light hit

138

me and slammed the firelight up against the wall. She left the light on and sat next to me. She poured the wine.

'That bathroom light is a little bright.'

'And there's no music?'

'Diane …' I complained. I took her hand and she came over easily. She took off her dress, and the rest of her clothes were *very* sexy: a black brassière and shiny black pants which she wanted to keep wearing on her way to the bathroom light and back again. She fixed the radio by the bed.

'It's a long time since I've been in a home.'

'It's as long a time since anybody else has been in here like this with me.' Diane drank, we sat with me facing her side, looking at her shoulder and breasts. 'The kids and I used to sit round in front of the fire.'

'In those underclothes?' I laughed.

'Is something wrong with them?' Coy sarcasm.

She let me feel my way around her ear, she turned and we broke away through fondness. She sipped her drink and unwrapped herself from the blanket, crawling forward to mess with the fire.

'How do you know when to do that?'

'Just habit. If I let it burn too low the new logs take time to pick up. These logs are still damp. The stack outside will be dry by thanksgiving.' Her tail towards me, that long full woman. I nudged in behind her, mounted over her back; she closed her thighs on me. 'I knew you'd do that,' she murmured, watching the fire.

'Don't tell me you didn't encourage it.'

'I didn't say that.'

'Is this how you'd like to make love?'

'No.'

She knelt up, I was obliged to kneel behind her. With the fingers of her right hand, she stroked the tip of her cock, poking its head through the small triangular window at her groin. Her neck returned to be kissed.

She took away her fingers, clasped our arms around her stomach. 'It's warm, isn't it?'

'Sure.'

'How do you feel?'

'Diane, isn't that a dumb New York question?'

'Yep.'

'I feel loving.'

'I was kneeling there thinking "Put it inside me, slowly."
Wanting it without any mystery, or you.'

'Sometimes that's how it is.'

'Then you asked me.'

She was alert, suddenly; I felt it run down the center of her
neck. 'Can you hear that tree creaking outside?'

'What?'

'No. Listen.' She tapped my arm.

'Yeah.' I couldn't hear anything.

I smoked a cigarette.

The room was warm, the music on its own; tracks that I
knew from parties.

I laughed loudly. 'Do you reckon they're all in bed yet?'

'Most of them. Thank God,' Diane snorted.

'You *like* problems, you know that.'

'Yes, but not always the people who have them.'

She lay alongside me, her body facing me. Her head propped
up on one hand so that she could look over her waist at the
fire. Forgetful. While I looked at her. I got bored with this. She
pretended not to pay attention when I filleted the silk off her.
She rolled back and I lay on top of her, pushed in. She moved
a cushion. She arranged her head and she clasped her arms
round my neck. She lowered her legs.

Rocking up and down the cushions, she grunted softly.
Calves tensed, heels planted. She enjoyed it. She came back
down the cushions, wanted it in her as far as I could go.

Her lips opened and closed like a child trying to mumble its
first words.

Mah, mah, mah, mah.

Give it to her. The method works. She falls apart from the
inside, her arms unwind. Her fingers start playing along my
back. Eyes open, drugged and heavy, laced with greed.

Huh? Huh? she injected. Huh? Huh? Blood high in her
cheeks, hair frothing up around the top of her head.

She felt it all. Tight as a pipe leading underground. Anything
that moved she felt. Cold too.

Covered with a thin cold oil, that's all I feel. I don't see her,
I see the black of my own eyelids and I feel that cool allure.
Always cool on me, beckoning me up. I can't hold on, not
with that.

140

Diane lifts me on to my arms. Like struts. We switch to automatic.

Her right hand scurries down to the space between us. She encourages herself.

We are now each on our own.

Diane's eyes are determined.

I am far along the process, I glaze over her selfish annoyance. She is at the top end of a corridor, she breaks forward, she tries to catch me. I can do nothing, babe.

I look back along the corridor and there is no one there. She pulls me out, twitching and welling, on to the long white-tiled stretch of her belly. Efficient and practical. And I do care for her somewhere, I do.

More than the hand stroking the back of my neck, than the comfort it gives. My name is Billy Maffett and I believe that we're in this together, fuck it. I hate this.

We would try again. I started to tell her what it was like, making love with her, and why; how beautifully cool. I whispered to her. About being inside her.

She let me finish. She was at her most beautiful. She was heavy and relaxed. One finger tangled in the hair of my chest.

She said that she was fertile. That she knew this at the moment. And yet she didn't wear anything and she didn't take any pills.

'You're not that careless.'

'No I'm not. I've done all the work before. If I had another child it would be a luxury. I would choose it.'

She thought with her chin on her hand.

'Didn't you choose it the last time?'

'I was in love the last time.' She rolled over and sat up. He crossed her mind. She looked down at her body, dissolving him. Perhaps because I was in the room.

She liked her body, it was well-known to her. A friend. She sat with her legs half drawn-up, greeting it. She had a beautiful heavy stomach which got left out, she leaned forward and rubbed her legs like a man rubs his dog when he is absent-mindedly affectionate. When she looked at me and saw that I was watching her, she looked at my body quickly, uncertain whether we should go to bed or not, if we were finished.

'Come back, Diane.'

'I have to put some more wood on the fire.'

She stepped keenly across me, leaning for a piece of wood.

'Do you know that you have beautiful legs?' I grinned.

'Yes.'

She finished what she was doing. We made ourselves comfortable and kissed and held for a long time, smoochy. I stroked her legs. She smiled at my possession, looking down at them.

'They're the reason I moved up here. When I ... do you want to know this?'

'Sure.' I was pressing her knees.

'When I was twelve.' She commanded attention. 'I couldn't walk for a time. I couldn't stand up. And during the winter in the city my knees swelled with arthritis on cold damp days. So we came up here.' She dropped the subject abruptly.

'I didn't know it was protective, I thought it was narcissistic.'

'I'm sure that it is by now,' she laughed, as glad as I was to be out of the history. But irritated; in the way she uncoiled and got to her feet like someone lurching up on stilts. She stood by my side. I couldn't see her face. I saw a forest of hair with heavy brown lips sagging over the cool; she took this away. She walked across the room and half-opened the drapes. She dropped more wood on the fire. She placed it with her foot.

'Diane, stop arranging.'

'Billy, shut it.'

'What would you like?'

'Anything. Another glass of wine.'

She got the bottle herself, poured us both a glass. And she lay looking at the fire. Night closed in between us.

'I'd like a back rub,' she asked.

'Sure.' I touched her shoulders.

Scratched and rubbed her back at her pleasure. Around and around. Her back swayed and did the searching. Her flesh was like emulsion; smooth, thick ripples spread away from my nails. Clean nails. Makes a change. Part of the shower. I was clean. She murmured her pleasure, held my hand for a while and then turned her head away. I fell in with the fire, following the yellow marionettes. Tracing them on to her body while she lay white and still.

As the fire died down, I thought she was asleep. I stopped, and I felt her eyes open.

She lifted up off the cushion and kissed me. I lay back in the shade of her. To pay off her debt, she started to rub my back. But it wasn't our style. She wasn't interested. I got off my ass and went down on her. I'm a good lover.

Diane has a slow passion, she isn't easily tempted. Tense and ponderous, and tense. She straightens with the weight and it lifts off her.

Much later, in bed, I see her back and her hair and the bridge of her nose. She wants us to be even. She wants me to open my legs wide so that she doesn't hurt the bad leg. Then she kneels and closes her eyes and ignores me, goes to relieve me, what I have, steadily and monotonously. Her head rises and falls, the muscles along the small of her back stiffen and capsize, her head falls and rises.

Is held for a moment, and bobs. We believe that there's nothing we can't do if we want to, and if we try hard enough. There is something terrifying about this machine age. Everyone is fervent; America wants pleasuring. I love her shape, the fullness of the pampered white body, the pathetic control she exercises. I can desire her from behind as she leans forward on her knees over the other body. Not a piercing. I can see that she is desirable but I can't touch her. And I want to *be* with someone.

But the sensation arrives. Someone inside me is cleaning a swollen chimney with a wire brush. Diane lick-tickles the stack with feathers. I see the blade of her nose and two swathes of hair, the chimney belches and her head stays still, a lump in her throat rises and falls, rises and falls, rises and falls. I go to sleep knowing only that I must act, I must be with someone, I must act.

Diane watched him for a moment, watched that simple glassy-eyed stupor and his eyes roll away from her. She held the hand he offered because the palm was white and it was open – childish and affectionate.

She was uncomfortable. Kneeling seemed to stretch the skin on her knees, her back ached. She glanced across at the fire. It was mostly burned away, the ridges of two logs balanced on the red embers of their bellies. Billy was asleep. She left his hand, quietly crawled away down the bed and stood at the end. She stretched her back, precise and poised. With the taste and texture of Billy still in her mouth, she picked up the wine-glasses and took them through to the bathroom. She didn't need to turn on the light; and she didn't want to disturb him. She rinsed out her mouth.

She turned and saw him from the door, his hand gone back to rest on his thigh. In one moment of pleasure she recognised that she wasn't attached to him, and then with all her guilty heart she wished him everything. She honed it down to wishing him luck. Sincerely.

She smiled.

She lifted an eyebrow at herself. She wasn't hard. What was she? She felt like a cantaloupe, pips and goo. She liked making love with a man, she had forgotten about that. Billy was tender and sensitive to her pleasure.

She came from the bathroom and put a cover over him, she put the cap on the wine. Running her tongue along her teeth, she took the wine bottle again, rebuked herself, and went back to the bathroom for a glass.

She took her wine to the mantelpiece and with a poker broke the logs down so that they would burn. The smaller wood took flame briefly, the fire glowed. Diane absorbed the glow on her pelvis and stomach.

She thought how and where Michael would find her; she knew how he would find her, how she was.

Where, bothered her. At the same time as it was exciting. She held her right foot out towards the fire; when she caught herself dreaming at it, she wriggled her toes; she was entertaining herself; she rebuked herself lazily, remembering the remark about narcissism. Canada, or Boston, or here. She didn't have the taste or the interest for a commuting relationship.

She felt strongly that the Farm could go. Not strongly; but if the Farm wasn't her interest then the Farm would fall apart. It was already falling apart. She was bored with it.

She had been guilty about that, the influence of her boredom. It had come to a pitch, and now she simply disliked the Farm. It was finished for her.

Canada? Michael wouldn't want her children, and they

144

wouldn't want her breathing down their necks – she knew this proudly, without any particular sorrow – and she didn't want them that close. Anyhow, Canada was cold.

Boston was too much him. He felt that.

They hadn't talked about it. She felt the same way about the Farm; it was too much her. They hadn't talked about anything. For one time in her life, Diane had been content to go through all the rigmarole of being ... what? Flirted with, pestered, suggested to, invited to share trivialities? Seduced. She smiled. Though it hadn't come to that.

With some amusement, she thought that she had been practising. Recently. And tonight.

She edged that sharpness out of reach.

Billy was attractive. Billy wasn't a fool. She'd helped him enough over the years. She remembered that a friend of hers had once told her that Billy was a great person to go to bed with. At the time she hadn't even been interested; that friend went to bed with a lot of men and they were all great people.

Anyway, it was fun. Billy and she were friends. And love. Well, lovers. It had been on the cards for years.

'And love. Well, love.' *He* was amusing about that. It had made her laugh. In Boston. She'd never laughed before in Boston. Outside the Massachusetts Institute of Technology. Michael was watching the demonstration, she was participating – rigorously. Or maybe it was the other way round: he participating, she watching – rigorously. She saw the same sadness in him about hopeless duty and the coldness he felt from duty. It angered her to have her sincerity undermined. In the same way that her husband had undermined it a long time ago.

Patterns no longer bothered her. Diane sipped at the wine. She looked down at her crimson belly.

She would trim her pubic hair; now, while she thought about it. Tangled straggles; a nothing. But Billy was in the room, the scissors were under a pile of papers she had pushed into the desk when she had arranged the room, she should have put the damn scissors in the bathroom cabinet.

She scratched and fluffed out the hair evenly. She didn't like people in her room of a necessity. That would have to be figured out. A lot of rooms anyway. Or one each and then space for the ballgame.

Michael had said: 'America will be much more fascist than it is now. There's no individuality coming up. In the youth movement, masses of people swill to and fro with ideas like slop in the bilge of a boat. If you're alone these days, you're rated as a cripple. "Weird, man." And they gawp.' He had made her laugh. 'And love. Well, love. Some of them say "I love you, man" to their girlfriends. Chicks. It's all a kind of anaesthetic dismissal; being instead of thinking.'

And she had found herself cutting him off, resenting his voice, wanting herself to be with him, saying, 'I hope that those girls can see through being a chick. Otherwise they're not going to have anything to do with men when they grow up, and I think that's a pity.'

Diane put the guard in front of the fire, mouthwashed and lay on the bed. She pulled the covers up and sought Billy's arms around her. She hugged him.

In his dreams, Billy was falling towards a lake of stagnant water. Shaking himself free of the nets. He felt her lips. He awoke later and saw Diane curled up with her white back turned towards him.

14

'It's done you a power of good, Mr Maffett,' George observed, spinning the wheel of the car. These chauffeurs drive with two fingers. The cars have power steering, George tells me, power brakes, automatic speed control – driving isn't what it used to be. Being a passenger is pretty much the same, from the back seat.

George didn't really give a damn about the countryside. He had his light-grey peaked hat on when he arrived, he kept it on when he was with Diane. We were a dozen miles from Diane.

'Why don't you take off that hat, George?'

'Thank you, Mr Maffett.'

'Billy.'

'I'll stick to Mr Maffett, if you don't mind, sir.'

After six years.

'Hell, I don't mind. How's Mr Douglas?'

146

'He's in good shape. I went to fetch him in from Kennedy.'

'How's the city?'

'Hotter than the kitchen and you pay for it straight down the line.'

New Yorkers love to talk about New York. There's nothing like it. George wisecracked and grouched. The Sanitation Department, the hookers, the shows, City Hall, Brooklyn. I laughed. New Yorkers are resilient. We get by, we keep coming back for more. Call Linda, call around, get out there. I'd been away a long time.

And that town was dirty and baked and beautiful. I felt it coming off the sidewalk, the one big pulse. That great hustle. You plug into the grid. Song and dance. Leg? What the hell leg!

Linda and I ate in our favourite restaurant with some of our friends, we slept in her niche, argued crazily, made the next arrangement.

And then Donald.

I asked him and he said that he was waiting for a call from LA. It wasn't dead yet, that was all he knew.

We both knew that even if it wasn't dead, it certainly wasn't kicking. His lines were a little straightened out after the vacation, and if I thought about it I was pretty clear. He sat there worrying about some sound system for the White House, having to go down to Washington, installing it, getting hold of the right tapes – 'Who can I trust to supervise the job? This system is complicated, Billy. Those people down there aren't running some rock concert.' He scratched Rusty. As if he was doing it all for Rusty.

'Those people are the same as anyone else.'

'They're bigger.'

'They're still people.'

'Well, they're running a bigger operation. They're running the country.'

I laughed. Donald smiled dimly. He really doesn't get off on iconoclasm. He poured himself a vodka. I offend him, he loves it. But he's watching me.

'I called the lawyers today, Charlie thinks he can make something out of the accident.'

'Drop it. I had a pretty good time upstate.'

He was glad of the diversion. 'How *was* Diane? With that

Farm?' He's never been able to wrap up Diane. The word
'farm' disgusts him, he's put himself a safe distance from the
Mid-west. But Donald isn't really interested in people and
Diane is only interested in *some* people. Donald is polite with
her and about her.

'She's fine. She has some big thing going with a guy in
Boston.'

'What kind of big?' He wasn't interested. He went through
to the kitchen. I wasn't interested either. I don't know. Diane
and I have different sets of values. Diane has a set of values.
We've had an affair. We've always had something; too far
apart ever to do anything about it. This time we did something
about it. Dumb. She was right too. We don't want to love each
other.

'What kind of big?'

'You know how it is with her. If there is anything, it's big.
Like the White House.' I stood up irritably and walked through
to my room. Donald watched me again.

I called Diane. Our conversation kangarooed. Maybe she
was busy and I should be busy, making arrangements, nothing
to do with either of us. She gives us distance. Hell, it's only
the truth; we don't need to want each other.

I called Carol at the Cape and that was all set up, I got the
names of the plays we would be working on with the kids. I
won't see Diane afterwards. I ate dinner with Donald.

He just started annoying me with the way he watched me
and the way he went on about the job in Washington.

'Bringing home the bucks.'

'Well, you know,' he said, 'we have to think of those times
when acting jobs aren't regular.'

'What the hell do you mean? We're not busted, are we?'

'No.'

'So?'

He shied away, looking from side to side.

'Why don't you come out with it?'

'I have to pull you out of the movie, Billy. They want to
start scheduling it. You can't do it.'

Yeah, I know that, but he looked away sadly. Maybe he
thought I was taking it hard.

'If I can fuck, I can dance, dammit.'

He was surprised; he put one and one together and didn't

148

want to see the two. He doesn't want to know that much about me, there are some ways in which he doesn't want to leave the Mid-west.

'If everyone in Hollywood thinks like that, maybe they'll do a lot more musicals. We'll get another chance.'

'When?'

'You don't have to find work. Financially. You don't have to find work anyway. People are calling.'

'But not the right people.'

'I don't know who the right people are, Billy,' he pleaded. 'Not any longer. Do you have any ideas? It's changed. Some people put a script together … '

'We have to get off our asses and get in there.'

He fell to worrying and being tired. He looked across the room at the dirty dishes, he made a move towards them.

'Leave the dishes! We pay someone to do the dishes.'

He *was* tired. Lovable. Sick of Billy Maffett. His glasses sunk down on his nose and his arms hanging loosely. Never really at home anywhere. I don't know how he makes it through this world on his sympathy. I apologised.

'We'll try. Like we always do.'

'Maybe I won't see you in the morning. I might have to take the early shuttle down to Washington to sort this thing out.'

'Sure. Is it that big a job?'

He stood by the door; gratified, tempted. I guess I don't give him very much. Acting is such a lousy, self-involved business. We treat our friends like shit. We keep them alive.

' …·it's complicated enough, my God! All the hocus-pocus those Secret Service people throw around you. The technicality is about 10 per cent of the job – '

'You bill them extra for it.'

'I don't like to do that. We have to have *some* national security, for heaven's sakes.'

'You mean that if you bill them too much they'll look into your tax records,' I laughed.

'You think so?' Donald blanched.

'They don't touch old patriotic Americans.' I put an arm round him, jested him. He looked suspicious.

'I'm glad you're not too depressed about the West Coast.'

'I knew it wasn't going to happen.'

'Okay. Well, you have some mail, you know. On the table. Something from England. Will you go up to the Cape?'

'Yes I will; some time next week.' I picked up the letter.

'That soon?'

'The kids start the week after that; I should do some preparation.'

'I hope to see you before then.' Donald came back out of his room, worried.

'Sure. Why don't you come up there one weekend?'

'I might do that if I can get away.'

He wouldn't. I smiled across at him. 'I'll be around here or over at Linda's in the next few days.'

'Okay.' He looked dubious. He looked as if he didn't expect too much from life. I opened the letter from Martin. Through the open door of his bedroom, Donald was going about packing his travelling case. All our lives were in cases: we moved in and out and around this apartment like a couple of transitories. We've always done that; aren't we sick of it?

'She's a sweet girl,' Donald said. I looked up. He was trying to get rid of my hanging out by his door. 'Linda.'

'She's a doll.'

'She is. I'm sorry about the movie though.'

I went down the corridor. We have our own bathrooms, back to back between the bedrooms, soundproofed bedrooms. The kitchen, the dining-room and the lounge are on the other side of the apartment. It's a great apartment. The landlord does nothing to it; neither of us does anything to it. Why should we? He'd only raise the rent.

The rooms are soundproofed because I like to go wild sometimes at night; Donald doesn't. There isn't much in my room. If Linda and I sleep together, we sleep at her place. My room is good for listening to music and moving. It's a good rehearsal space: an old couch bed and a bookcase, a reading lamp and a parquet floor. The sound system.

I've been in the pits in this room. And we've had some great highs, great parties. It's just a space. At the side of the bed is that old wooden monk, Martin's present in Majorca. That monk's depression is tough! I had it in the lounge until a friend of ours told me that Donald hated it. I could have trashed it, but now it's by the side of the bed; I've gotten used to it.

Each time I get a letter from Martin, I sit here and try to

150

read it. I never understand the damn letters. They are pretty empty letters. I don't know. They hide. Linda said one night that they were the letters of a paranoid schizophrenic. Do the hell I know? Or care? Maybe that makes six of us. Whenever I see something English reviewed in the *New York Times*, I write back, that's all.

I put on that one track Linda gave me. Paula King. I shut the door. I want volume. Loud. A whole lot. Let's get out of it.

'When you want me, tell me. When you need my love, I'll come. You only have to tell me, I know you never failed me, I'll take you on home ... '

She sings. She wails and pumps and sings.

'Won't leave you, babe, oh my own sweet love ... '

We're going! Bend! And up!

'I know you have to go and chase your dreams ... but when you need my hands that touch you so softly, and my love that understands you so well, just bring yourself ... '

Break! And, turn!

> 'No one else can do it for me!
> No one else gets through to me!
> Nobody holds me
> Like you do ... '

Again.

I'm too stiff and the leg's too stiff.

First time out. It'll come.

Again.

Like jerking a skeleton around.

Again. Sweat! I'm not going down, not that easily, not without a fight.

Better.

Again. Wash that sound. Slide, turn, pirouette, stretch. Dance you sonofabitch! 'No one else can do it for me! No one else gets through to me! Nobody holds me ... '

Again.

Wait for it. Bend. Slide. Turn! And ... up, sway, roll ... 'No one else can ... ' Down. Turn!

Again.

Again.

Take it easy. That's enough for the leg.

I work on my back and stomach muscles, and I take a shower.

Lying on the bed. The letter comes with a printed sheet about the Bible and, as I read it, about humility. Martin's letter.

I don't like insults.

Donald is in the next room, praying for everyone. I am praying for work, Linda and I are praying for our relationship. Diane's praying for her kids. Everyone's working for themselves. Are you alive to anything, Martin?

Yeah, I like humility; I respect it, nothing changes without you changing. I get humility, I don't rip it off, I know that it's something valuable to build on. You don't go into humility keeping all your exits closed; you don't fill the auditorium that way. Don't you deride humility. You could be more honest in deriding giving. What the hell do you know, Martin?

I find your letters too depressing. If you have to go through that shit then at least do it on your own. Don't spread it around.

On airline notepaper from Kennedy.

Coasting

15

Six months later, in February, Billy and Martin had their affair.

In February. Martin made the mistake of thinking that he was bored, that it was boredom which sucked in at his face like a polythene bag. He was writing a thesis on Hobbes and Defoe and Fear and Capitalism and Individual Isolation. In February. When England is unbearably grey and futureless, whatever the government.

And then Hobbes was finished and Martin was terrified at all the correct meanness of English customs. He called Billy; he had only three minutes.

'Sure,' Billy laughed. 'Sure. Great.'

'Will you be there?'

'I'm always somewhere, you know that.'

'But will you be there?'

'I'll wait a week.' And he did. The phone call lasted only one minute and thirty-seven seconds.

When Martin arrived in New York, Billy was pleased to see him. He was nervous and he didn't ask Martin about anything. Nothing at all. His eyes dosed Martin. Martin looked around and hardly at Billy. They were to fly on to Los Angeles in three days and money didn't matter. Martin was frightened and then not so. He loved Billy's smell, Billy's holding. His lips and his back and his not understanding, Billy's gift of himself, his ability to love.

Billy had had a great time up there on the Cape, teaching and encouraging and kicking those kids. It worked out that he didn't have time to go back down to Diane's; she was dry-cold on the telephone, Billy guessed that she was wrapped up with her man in Boston, making her move. So it was thanks for the memory and to hell with involvement.

He did a play in the fall. He couldn't make it any better than it was so it was either a lousy play or he was a lousy actor. Good notices took them through a couple of months. Donald came most nights when he was in town, they had great parties. Billy was back in, he didn't want to do nothing again.

When Martin called, Billy was about to go back to the West Coast Actors' Studio; he was a student, Martin was a student, perhaps they could share it.

He wanted to go back to the Studio to work on himself. There were no credentials for acting, you just had to be a type of loose, open individual who didn't give a damn about security and wanted to change. Fear came when you looked around and saw that along with everyone else, slowly and inevitably, you didn't want to change.

Billy needed to change. After Diane, and surely not because of Diane, he had been hardening. He pushed himself towards the West Coast, and as part of the chaos he welcomed Martin.

Martin arrived in New York, and Billy thought that Martin was mad. Or high as a kite. But he wasn't high, he was un- natural. Out of that thin, long, straitjacket of a body his eyes flicked about, condemning everything from a gaping innocence. Billy wanted to go in there but the responsibility scared him. He knew a lot of people who looked for love, but never from such an empty insularity.

Martin read books without noticing them. He lived in a luxury of patience – being with Billy occasionally, feeling for his anxiety, flirting with Billy and listening to his laughter. Billy would soon become sick of him, he knew, but that wasn't important; Martin wanted only to live off Billy for a little time, live off some belief and faith. Billy was very tender about things he didn't understand. Sometimes he laughed easily and he'd know that it was too easy and he'd say 'Oh hell' and go to make a telephone call.

On their last night together in New York, before flying to Los Angeles, Martin asked him about the Actors' Course. It had always been 'we' and the great time 'we'd' have doing it together. Martin wondered if Billy would be hurt if he didn't want to.

'It's there, it's open!' Billy exclaimed; he laughed. 'It's not for you. I know that.'

'How do you know?' Martin was hurt.

'*You* do. You couldn't handle it.'

He put on a record and danced. Martin could never have lived in a room like Billy's. The room was bare and waited for Billy to create himself in it, and then the room would be created. Some people had a contrived, neurotic, spartan-bare room with placed objects to which they had a very concealed attachment, objects which they had bought and which helped them feel. Billy's room had a corner-chaos of things he had bought. And then the rest of the room had occasional objects given by people; they weren't mementoes, he treated them cautiously, as though they were the people themselves sitting in his room. He would leave the small wooden monk alone on the bedside table with a great deal more respect than he would treat Martin. He wouldn't touch it.

'Shall I come with you then?' Martin asked.

'Sure.'

His timidity always angered Billy.

Billy was going to spend the night before leaving town with Linda. He went over there and ate dinner and told her about Martin. She condescended, jealous and uptight. He'd never seen Linda tight; she didn't have any reason for that snide bitterness.

'I am not going out with any creepy gays, Billy. I'm not going to be a fag hag.'

'Hey … '

'No, you hey! I put up with a lot. You know? From you. And I take it. But not this. It comes down to being retarded, doesn't it? Isn't it pathetic?'

'That's pretty straight – '

'Straight or not, I don't care.'

'I *will* go, dammit.'

'Too right you will.'

About one time in each six months she acted as though someone left open the door of her cage. There are probably gay zoo-keepers in the city by now; Billy wasn't one of them. Who put these labels around anyway? Village people. He wasn't looking for one of those tight little love affairs, not with Linda.

155

Martin sat up late, reading. He lit a fire in the sitting-room fireplace. Donald arrived from Los Angeles. He was gracious, he asked about England, about Martin's parents, about college. 'This is quite a surprise.' And all of it a dream, coming and going, filling Martin. 'You'll have a ball on the West Coast,' Donald said, and he seemed thankful that he wasn't invited. Perhaps he was glad to have Billy going away, or glad that the arranging was done. Martin tried to ask him, but he was tired; he went to bed.

Billy came back tense. He treated Martin with affectionate indifference; he prowled, he threw things into a suitcase, putting the suitcase down on the opposite sofa, going into his bedroom, fetching things, not knowing what he was doing. It was all so young and out of control and of its own male rhythm that Martin didn't have the feeling of being unwanted.

'Let me call Linda.'

'Donald's back.'

'He *is*? He's keeping a little quiet, isn't he? Hey, Donald!'

'Oh *God*,' came from the bedroom, and Billy guffawed and went in there and talked; half an hour later Martin heard a telephone being put down. 'Is there anything *else* I can do for you?' Donald's self-mocking sarcasm and Billy's comforted laugh.

Billy came back into the sitting-room and put his finger to his lips, a broad grin of excitement.

'Are you ready?' he hissed.

'What?'

'Anything. Let's get out of here.'

'Let's go for a walk.'

'Are you crazy? You'll get us mugged. Okay, let's go for a walk.'

'Through the park.'

'Around the side of the park; that's my limit.' Billy held up the palms of his hands. He fetched his coat.

At the bottom end of the park. It was simply a hugeness of light and dark and piercing cold. Great, bland monoliths were shuffled up to peer over the park, haughty with glaring electricity. Over the concrete swamp Billy and Martin scuttered, steam flouncing out of subway grills away down the avenue, battered yellow cabs tanking people home, other cabs new laundered with the occasional crumple, smoked-glass royal

156

limousines lifting prow-first off the stop lights. A siren flailed its tentacles through from downtown. No one else walked. Billy spurred up their cock-eyed amble, chilled as hell, they both were, with not even the benefit of a mad scheme.

'Have we gone far enough?' Martin asked.

'We get half-way up the other side.'

Billy lurched his chin out over his coat lapels and put it back again.

Quarter-way. They turned for home. Two coffees for Billy, a coffee and a brandy for Martin; in the corner bar.

Billy was known. Remarks and conversation and jokes were pitched over by half a dozen late drinkers. Billy batted out the brash replies. His eyes soared round the bar, following his voice; his look perched on the half-dozen and sprang away with a morsel of each. 'Take it easy, Billy', 'Be seeing you', they called when Billy went out. 'You too,' he waved.

Martin laughed in the elevator.

'You're mad,' Billy grinned, 'dragging me out round the park.'

Standing and looking out of the lounge window, with the penthouse view going east, Billy said, 'Great people. You like it?'

'Yes.'

'It's beautiful, isn't it?'

With the snow on the roofs, and lights, and the black dent of the park and the thousands of people somewhere. Billy rubbed the glass again, taking off the condensation with the sleeve of his coat. He smoked. 'All creative people,' he muttered.

'Are they? Not all of them.'

'Yeah ... '

'Not like you anyway.' Martin put his hand on Billy's shoulder, wishing to woo him, wanting to stop this melancholy. He touched his neck. His hand fell back; he was frightened, not knowing of what.

'Are you *doing* anything?' Billy said, with some beguiling laziness which didn't quite cover his disgust.

'Not really. Of course I am.'

'You're not. You're dead.'

Billy's head turned and his eyes landed on Martin as they had done on the people at the bar. Statement eyes, clinical; toying. Martin looked for his lips, they might help him through. Billy noticed that and turned away.

'Why?' Martin asked.

'I don't know. Everyone gets screwed up at times. You need too much love, I can't give it to you.'

'I don't want you to.'

'What the hell are we talking about then? We're going to LA tomorrow.' He shrugged. He walked over to his case, looked down at it and flipped it shut.

'You're hard, Martin, you know?'

'So are you, aren't you?'

He came slowly across the room. 'Don't cry,' he murmured, and he held Martin. In bed, much later on, he told Martin: 'If you become an actor, you cry so many times you wonder where it comes from. You don't learn it. I don't like to know any longer where it comes from.'

Los Angeles. It had been a long time since Billy had stood up there and given everything and had Rykov say, 'What are you doing?', 'What do you base that on?' 'Don't you feel anything?' Or faced Rykov's indifference. In front of everybody in the small theatre. An audience of actors, observing.

'You've spent too much time being a star, Billy; you've forgotten the rest of the people. You remember what it's like to have a mother? Or how people spit at you, how you feel when you're lost? When you're nothing? Try being nothing for a day. Wake up the next morning and still be nothing. When you know that, come back. Don't waste our time. Understudy!' he ordered, 'get up there and be that character. *You'll* do,' he pointed at someone.

Rykov used to hammer Diane; she would get her insides dragged out. She went white, the blood sucked out of her. She stood it bitterly, Billy remembered. In the break, someone would go to her to try and lift her. Because you thought that anyone would be cringing by now. She would smile disdainfully: 'I came here to learn about myself.' She disliked sympathy. Back on stage the next run-through was terrible, everybody trying to feed her. Rykov would cut it short. 'Leave her alone! Stop defending yourselves.' And the following run-through was a mess, because no one knew where he or she was. 'Good,' Rykov grouched; 'next scene.'

Never mind Diane. There were thirty or forty in that class, they had all been through a hard, great time and a lot of them now carried very famous names.

Billy knew that the old man would take it out on him at the

start of the course. He caught him by his car, someone else was driving.

'Shall I come in tomorrow?'

'You will. You know, I saw you in a play last fall.'

'I didn't know that. Why didn't you say hello?'

'I didn't want to meet any actors. As I remember, you were sloppy.'

'Yes? It wasn't that good a play. I didn't have much feel for it.'

'It wasn't a good play. What you forget is that writers only ever have it half worked out and actors shouldn't have it worked out at all.'

'You're right.'

'You were too clever.'

'Maybe that's getting older.'

'Forget about old age. You're not a bad actor, Billy. Are you making any money?'

'Some.'

'Everyone else is. They make money and they quit to become lousy directors.'

Rykov was driven away. Billy didn't know if he was driven away pensive or if he didn't give a damn. He didn't offer Billy a ride. California was stone cold without people like Rykov. Nothing County.

Green. Walk. Down De Long.

Billy had Martin clogging up his nothing. A kid. We've all been plaintive. Billy hated nothing. You fight to get out of it. Nothing is underneath. Forget that, and you drop into being automatic, clinging – to Linda, Donald. Diane? Rykov was right; it was time to be alone and to carve it open.

Billy told Martin. He didn't think that Martin understood – Martin didn't register, it had no impact on him in sunny LA, on his vacation.

'Okay,' Martin said, formally. He uncrossed his legs. It seemed as though his acceptance was immediate, which Billy couldn't take from him, a cold acceptance.

'I have to be on my own.'

'That's all right, Billy.'

'How the hell do *you* know?'

'I've done it for a year.' Martin left the room.

Billy put music on the sound system and waited. He went to Martin's room, to find him lying on his stomach on the bed.

'You don't really care, do you?' Billy suggested.

'It's up to you.'

'Come on ... '

'I just don't have anything to say. Sorry.' His arm curled round Billy's back, and he looked up at Billy without a single thought in his mind, absorbing Billy. Billy hated that.

'You love me, don't you?'

'Yes.' Martin's eyes twisted away.

'Or need me?'

'I don't know. That's stupid. You talked about need when we were in New York.'

'I don't remember.'

'You don't remember anything,' Martin smiled.

'You know, I nearly lost my girlfriend in New York because we slept together.'

'Sorry.' His mouth hardened into guilt, but his eyes wouldn't have it. 'It won't happen again.'

'Because you don't want it to?'

Martin only wanted Billy to stop asking him questions. 'Yes,' he said.

'Will you be all right?'

'Yes. Fuck it. Yes!' He got up off the bed and walked up and down the room, touching objects occasionally. 'Fifteen days. Then we fly back. Fifteen days. Right. That's fine. Fourteen if I meet you here the night before.'

'Don't be so distant.'

'Sorry.'

The room was tight with agitation.

'Babe ... '

'I understand.'

'We love each other.'

'I know.' Martin dismissed Billy with a flicked smile. He looked away at the corner floorboard. Billy thought: what the hell ... a bag of nothing, a bag of suffering, a bag of love and useless guilt – how many more bags does anyone want me to carry ...

Then Martin surprised him. Martin said, 'Yes, I know.' He did, this time. With conviction, out of himself. Touching Billy afterwards with his hand and with that isolated seriousness. It was like Diane after the break; Billy couldn't act off it, it was too definite.

160

16

California. Martin left Billy.

It was in the evening and he was standing on the side of a road looking out over the ocean, confused between the thick smell of mosses and redwoods and the sight of a fat tube of pale grey fog which cushioned the dying sun from the water. A car stopped. Martin was joined by a small bearded Jew from New York and a thin girl with a scar on her forehead. The three of them stood quietly and watched the waves rolling the dusk inshore. His boots kicked bits of stone and her arms were crossed under her breasts against the chill. They offered Martin a ride to San Francisco; they talked in the dark car.

They arrived in San Francisco late and went up to the Presidio for a joint, passed crucially between cold fingers; then downhill to the apartment where they sat yawning over tea. Martin was told to sleep in the room down the corridor. He took his case and pushed open the door, fighting to be noiseless as his eyes picked out a spread of black and a ruffle of blonde. Hair on the mattress on the floor. The room was dark and there were breathings of sleep. He placed his case against the wall and went back into the corridor, but his guide was gone and there was no apparent light switch.

There was space on the mattress. Out of his case, Martin took a thin sleeping bag. He put the bag on the nearside of the mattress, he spread it out and undressed and eased himself down inside. Lying on his back with his arms crossed under his head, he slowly investigated the details of the room as they materialised out of the swirling dark. He picked out the rectangle of his case, over near the door. After concentrating on it for a while, and playing with various possibilities, he was satisfied that however deep his sleep he would awaken if the case was moved.

There was a glass partition, ill-covered with an Indian sheet; a picture rail went round the walls, elevating slightly to get over the door. Just to the left, there were clothes thrown over a cupboard, or it might be some sort of a packing case. Behind Martin's head was the rough edge of a spare pillow. He moved it down to prop up his head. The clothes were all of a type, sexless except for a long skirt. He was glad that Billy existed.

There was a bunch of flowers on the window sill above, in a vase; trinkets of jewellery and a few pots of cosmetics. Most of the floor space was taken up by the mattress and the three people lying on it. He didn't know if Billy would be sleeping alone.

Martin lifted his head. He could see very little of the blonde, small enough to have to be female. There were ringlets of hair reaching towards him as she slept, not more than eighteen inches away, on her side, one arm out over the covers and a smooth left shoulder rising and falling gently as she breathed. She was facing a cascade of black hair that swept down over the pillow. The owner of this hair was as if laid out in death; on his back, the length of him filling the mattress, his two feet surfacing near the wall. This being had no qualms about sleep, hair groomed away from his face and unshaven stubble; he was as if offered to the ceiling, his spiritual pose countered by a hoarse grating from his open mouth, as the air jerked in and out of his throat. Martin lowered himself down to the pillow. Lying on his side, he closed his eyes.

The body next to him stirred and turned over. Martin settled. The sleeping bag was drawn into his chest but was as far from his back as a stiff blanket would have been. He thought about being removed from Billy; of not being away from Billy at all, Billy's gift. And when a hand rested on his shoulder, he thought at first that it was the air, and then he knew that it was a hand.

The hand moved down Martin's shoulder and brushed away the hair from the back of his neck, moving indifferently in sleep. The atmosphere in the room seemed to change from impassivity to a lazy playfulness. Martin rolled on to his back, and the hand slid on to his chest. The breath, eddying, was very female. His blood streamed down his body.

'I'm not asleep and neither are you,' her voice whispered in his ear. Martin turned to face her. The blonde hair swung away from her eyes for a moment and she was very childishly beautiful. A nose that hinted into an upswing and a mouth of wry amusement. She laid her head against his shoulder, kissing it speculatively, and her hand ran down his stomach.

'What about *him*?' Martin asked.

'Mmm?'

'Him. Beside you.'

'He's asleep.' She didn't care. 'Can't you get out of the sleeping bag?' She helped Martin. There is very little grace involved in getting out of a sleeping bag.

They lay and talked; they made love and went to sleep entwined.

Morning. It tumbled in with the sound of congas from another room. Martin awoke. He remembered and wanted reminding; the girl was on her back a little further away. He reached for her and found her finger pre-empting him, mixing her drowsiness with pleasure.

'Hey,' she stretched both her arms over her head, her eyes heavy with langour, fine lashes flitting to the day.

'Hey,' Martin murmured.

'Hey,' grunted another, the owner of the second finger.

The girl laughed, came awake; she brought her arms down and hugged her lovers round the neck. The unshaven face and some large brown eyes dawned over her breasts at Martin.

'Mornin'. Franco.'

'Martin.'

The girl laughed. 'And Sharon.' She threw off the blanket, disengaged, and kissed the two hands. She opened the curtain. The fog slunk close to the window; Martin's case was still there. Franco played very good guitar, for days on end. That was Franco. Sharon was Sharon. So what was Billy?

What is Billy?

He is quiet on the flight back to New York. Pale and exhausted, as if he has just parted from a lover not knowing when they would meet again. He is often shy in company and the plane is full of company. His reactions to the hostess are automatic and minimal.

And Martin?

Worries. Is afflicted by his detachment from everything and everyone. As if there might be a hundred lovers and they will never take enough of him.

They sit like two adults stricken with childhood. Each gives the other an appalling sense of isolation, too severe to ignore. They are lovers only because neither of them has the slightest idea of what that means, while both of them have a huge, futile capacity for love.

Over the next thirty months, they didn't keep in contact. Billy hung around in New York and Los Angeles, he was reclaimed by Linda and taught himself to rely on her. He learned tact. Tact dogged his heels in a series of straight lines and right angles – dishonesty had far more rules than honesty. He fought not to hate. Something at a safe distance had to take the blame and the rage. Diane as object, preened for Boston; he imagined her choosing to have this relationship and then the two of them choosing other interesting people, describing these people to each other, drawing the lines. He had her again, violently, in his talons, many times, in black and white, hacking her into portions – 'don't stop don't stop don't stop' – Diane as object, all used up and shrinking away somewhere between his rioting brow and Linda's closed eyes.

So far down that long, cold passage that he once called the Farm, not knowing what to say; he imagined Diane in a white uniform and didn't know whether she would sign him in. Her voice, a voice like hers – 'Diane's in Europe, Billy' – and the how-are-you going on and on with Pam, the not wanting to have any news of Diane, that trek away again and the cheerful wave. Tact. A kid with a toy trumpet.

Then it sickened him, it shamed him. That he only went to Diane when he needed help, when he was down, when he couldn't walk.

Over the next year, Billy cajoled and scared a hundred kids through acting courses, prising them open scrupulously and affectionately with a hard faith which they found difficult to take. He didn't know that. It wouldn't have made any difference if he had known because he would have refused any other way. And perhaps he was rewarded. He got a break and landed a large part in a Hollywood movie.

That same summer, at the end of the University term, Martin worked on a building site with a crew of five bricklayers and two young hoddies. Each Thursday at noon, they were paid in cash. Martin watched as the crew played blind brag at lunchtime. The hoddies started with sixty pounds cash; in an hour each of them would lose thirty pounds. At the end of one of these sessions, a bricklayer asked him: 'Who do you vote for then?'

Martin, who had never bothered to vote in his life, said: 'Conservative.'

164

The bricklayer encouraged him. 'At least you're not a class traitor.'

Martin walked home and buried his sixty pounds. He knew that Billy wouldn't be interested.

Holding the Mirror: Diane

17

I am guilty.
I believe in duty.
I am proud.
'I am all right.'
I am controlled.

The only thing that bothered me was that Billy might come back to the Farm when he had finished on the Cape. I felt sure that he wouldn't, that I had done enough to discourage him. If he over-rode this discouragement then I could take him seriously. I wasn't committed to Michael; in the days after Billy's departure, I was alarmed at the whole idea of becoming thus attached. There is no one like Billy for scattering plans, nobody who is so infuriatingly and generously selfish, nobody more naïve. The youngness is contagious but it's something he needs for himself. I am always in two minds about accepting it from him.

I suppose that I resent the fact that whenever he comes to the Farm, even with an injured leg, he brightens the place up. And he knows me, he knows how to get round me, he has the right answers - or if he doesn't have the right answers, he has the blind force to make me think twice and his answers seem to work as well as my own. It is hopeless to feel subverted by a child, to feel angry and ashamed at myself; but then wanting him is akin to the exasperation of not wanting myself.

Why not admit to that? Is it impossible not to feel guilty about one's own malaise?

Billy would be uncontrollable. Which, although I envy it, I couldn't live with. I couldn't arrange myself around it. Anyway, Billy is Billy. After eight years we make love, his hand lies open against his leg. And no. No.

He doesn't call up, and when he does call up he is either guilty or evasive or lying in his partner's bed, and he calls up as though he is worried that he might have left the downstairs light on and would I please turn it off.

No. I will not have that ... I won't have it left. That *easiness*. Nothing comes of that, it's great and it's stupid and he's a friend who came to bed because everyone goes to bed with each other nowadays, and he isn't different to anyone else.

In fact, Billy is a part of those lingering old times. Those days when I was scared and depressed, about everything – love, acting, my sexuality – when I was scared of excitement and depressed at my own refuges. Billy comes from that time.

I got out of that, on my own and very successfully. I fought my way free of that.

I married a man who didn't pester me or my home, who assumed that I would grow out of my fear, who alternated between being warmly amused by me and idolising me craftily as a way around me into the cosy, rough-edged solitude of his own thoughts. *He* was contagious. A man, as they say, with a past. An interesting man, quite capable of being father, brother, lover or husband as long as I made it clear which one of the four I wanted. And he made me laugh. I was genuinely lucky in what I merited.

He died at the right time. I could go on living off the self which I had developed independently. And by then there was also the routine; the children and the Farm. The Farm was a base, it is a base still, although by now I take it for granted. It was chaos at first, but people liked the children and helped us. The boys have grown up with a healthier perspective on the human race than I had. I have no reason to be insecure. I have every possible right to feel smug.

Damn Billy.

He didn't arrive. I spent six months carrying my affair with Michael shoulder-high and out of reach of the friends, associates and Boston camp-followers with whom Michael surrounded himself. And then we went to London for a year. We took a split-level apartment in Chelsea on an exchange with a don at the London School of Economics who transferred to Michael's house in Cambridge.

So I am loved. I have my own way, which is one thing, and I have Michael. I can describe it all in terms of trust and partnership, and then I can say that we are both almost childishly delighted at the surprising gift of being in love. I am a winner, and I don't care about it.

I laugh a lot. One of the things Michael and I have in common is people, we have both worked with people, on people. And we're both a bit sick of people. We have never been allowed to be playful and selfish and we have never done anything to the hilt, so now we love to the hilt.

'I've never met anyone quite like you,' Michael said.

I've never met myself as I am at the moment.

So there isn't any other way besides plunging forward, which for me is new. Every now and then I wonder – what do I think about him? And I wonder about myself. What do I feel for him? Recognition? I don't know.

I feel that it's right. It's right for me. After the period of being wary, of not wanting to waste myself, of kindling our enthusiasm. And it was very easy to arrange our sabbatical in London; he would work with an English colleague to establish a center for sensory research and I would take a course in Art History.

We're good for each other. My practicality makes him reflect, he is more airy.

He is very clear; he is ambitious about his work. He and his colleagues in Boston had started with an investigation of mystic states. They had induced conditions of aloneness and detachment from physical response, which they hoped would allow the subconscious comparative freedom of reaction towards the higher states of being. Seeing godhead. In a mirror. And thereby understanding the prerequisites for a balanced mind. We took it as a running joke at the expense of philosophy.

It *is* right. He is affectionate, witty, committed, and not dependent on me. He is lively enough to prick me out of my brooding, warm enough to douse my anxiety. I have what I want.

What do I feel about him.

I don't know, it's fall, I miss the Farm, London makes me suspicious, the way the English sneak into winter. I have a feeling of unreasonable melancholy and resentment. Diane has given too much, the world owes Diane more, Michael owes Diane more. He is too close and yet not close enough.

I don't, suddenly, want him. I don't want his proximity, I don't want his papers about his interesting work scattered over the chesterfield. I'm relieved to see him every evening, and I'm immediately restless with him and the way he manages to exchange one academic chamber for another.

171

It's unfair of me.

We no longer find anything to laugh about together. The English in the pub have a jovial, half-drunken, stupid laughter at their own willed, secure absurdity; which I hate. Michael laughs with them. I don't laugh and he's embarrassed; we walk home – home! – and there's nothing.

Which he accepts. Of course. He is kind. He is respectful. I have contempt for myself. I can't bring myself to love; a horrible, dishonest feeling of guilt lingers beside me and talks its way into bed.

I trail around with him to a series of London Christmas parties. He wants to play with London now that our playful days are over. I start to scheme so that he doesn't give me the wrong present for my birthday. Playing games, wiring him up. It's stupid and dangerous because we are so far from home and we can't afford not to support each other, I know, but I do it, and I will it; I feel for him sadly, but scornfully.

We function, I suppose; we meet faithfully. We undertook this year and this relationship and I won't go back on it. If we didn't stay together, Michael would feel himself as unjustified as I would. However bitter it is, we will go through with this strange war.

But *I* am doing the feeling, all of it, and examining myself, alone in my room with my Art History course. Downstairs there is one other still life with smile, Michael, half an eye on the muted television, not really interested in it or in the folder on the arm of his chair. He smiles and I smile. The only thing to do is to go on through to the kitchen and make a mug of coffee, carry it carefully back upstairs to my room. I am well aware of silently screaming at him – 'This coffee is important!' – but instead I have my act of carrying it very carefully so as not to spill it of course; is it my fault that I just won't give, that I'm relieved and yet stifled at leaving him there behind glass, an image of understanding?

I was in front of the television and Michael was leafing through his papers. Both of us were aware of the tension. He left the sitting-room. I went upstairs to talk to him, to fetch a book, anything; and I saw him masturbating in the bathroom.

I was shocked; I covered myself with disdain. I went into

172

my room and fingered the books, insulted, absorbed in my hurt, nervous. I sat firmly on the bed, fighting off the feeling of weakness, not sure what was going to happen. I felt that I had interrupted something, perhaps I had come upstairs on purpose, to be coy, to challenge. I didn't know what to do. I heard him go through to his room and I undressed.

He refused to take me. I sat naked on his floor, without identity. He told me that I was a coward. He told me to fetch a mirror, to make myself up, if that was what I wanted. That hurt.

I hung on the edge of my nerves, asphyxiated by desire and terrified that I would be rendered inadequate by him or by his boredom with me, that he would leave me with myself.

He rubbed me, not softly; he led my hands away. A strange luxury of abandonment settled over me. I weakened gratefully, my cheek against the carpet, waiting for his intention, on all fours, my stomach churning; only worried that I would defecate, he would see me defecate. Finding myself delineated quickly and suddenly by the pain and by his detachment, my prevarication was exhausted and I cried out at the unravelling of my pride.

I loved so easily after that night, the severe years dissolved. He helped me to cry.

And then, abruptly, he was tired of me.

I asked to join him at the center, but he told me to wait. He seemed to have lost his perspective on his work, to be unsure of what he was doing. At Easter, although I wanted to rent a cottage in the English countryside, I encouraged him to fly back to the States. He talked precariously of funding and programs; I accepted that he was strained and homesick and in search of his balance.

In the fortnight while Michael was away, I had an affair with a student from my course; as two individuals we solved a small problem for each other. I discharged him painlessly when Michael returned.

We didn't talk about staying in London, neither of us was much concerned one way or the other. But the cutback to the States was much too swift. I spent a month in Boston and then went back to the Farm. If, during that month, Michael had asked me to marry him, I would probably have said yes and I would have shut the door on everything else. But the ensuing weekend visits were a poor solution, Michael and I only managed to talk ourselves into irritation.

I assured Robby and John that they had much better winter up in Montreal with their girlfriends; Michael and I occasionally had the Farm to ourselves. I showed him my containment. I stood off from him and enjoyed the fear that this would probably kill our relationship.

Pam arrived back from Florida having left Andy on an extended vacation; the two of us partied and gossiped and laughed and slept together against the cold. We became very close. We defied everything, everyone. We didn't miss men. Did we? Only momentarily. And even then I didn't call Michael; I called Billy, but Billy was away.

When asked, I went off to Boston for a weekend. Michael was assiduous in his attentions but I wasn't touched, I felt too much in control. I expected his anger rather than an attitude of calculation and dry wit. I couldn't believe how ponderous he was. I don't think that he had missed me, I think that he was scared of me, or scared of the respect he had for me. He didn't want to get involved. Perhaps he wanted to get lost in involvement. The warmth of his parting embrace repulsed me; and then, later, I wondered about my behaviour.

Back at the Farm, I lost myself in hosting the first of the weekend reunion groups. I demanded of myself that I return to square one – things were to be as they had been, I would deal with my feelings; the holiday was over. There was no disillusionment.

But the Farm couldn't bear the weight of my application, there wasn't enough to do. My sympathies were becoming patterned and automatic, I had lost the ability to disarm people. Something had to happen.

Michael calls – can he stay at the Farm, he has something to discuss.

I expected some pressure from him, which I would deserve. Or some bitterness at my recent behaviour – perhaps a volley of sniping at the spotlit showgirl Diane whose demise is only a matter of course; we could play at that. We could play at being lovers, I decided, for both our sakes.

' – I'd rather stick with what I *was* saying, Diane, I don't want to get drawn into us or our relationship.'

'That's fine.'

He was weak and pompous, only human; and I was dressed to kill, which he must notice.

'At the Center,' he said, 'we've been drawn into the position of working for either the leisure industry or for the government. Our research is being fed on to governments all over the Western world so that they can build sensory deprivation cells for people whom the State can't handle. Political people. Unbalanced scientific idealists, or freedom fighters. On the West Coast an executive can come home with business pressures, take ten minutes in a suspension tank and lose his tension. A Marxist Leninist in Germany is put in a deprivation cell and loses his or her mind. Which is worse? The mass marketing of a technique for dissolving worry comes very close to the mass opiating of moral responsibility, and there's a hell of a lot of difference between all this and helping individuals. Which was where we started.'

'Do you feel that you've lost your authority, is that the problem?'

'Maybe.' He was disconcerted. He wanted to talk about principles and we were back to talking about him.

'You were bound to lose that authority.'

'I tell myself that I can't feel guilty or *responsible* ... for what happens outside the researchers I deal with.'

'Of course you can't.'

I was, despite myself, manoeuvred into feeling rather tawdry and shallow, even into walking across the room away from him as though I was considering the problem, his problem, deeply.

All right. I felt sorry for him.

But why did we never talk about this before? It was too late now.

For old times' sake we made love – perhaps that was why he was here and why I lured him across the room; simply to make love and to enjoy ourselves. Americans do have a constitutional right to happiness. I wasn't involved, and in him there was a different anger; we dispelled certain pretences without entailing others, I thought.

I was up long before he was, when the house was cold; only the kitchen was steeped in a drowsy, hungover warmth which

175

made almost anything worth while. I went back to him with his breakfast.

I lay and watched him eat, with a wretched nostalgia for his body. I realised that my fingers were absent-mindedly piano playing against his ribs.

'I'm sorry.' I smiled.

'I'd like you to join me at the Center.'

He was watching me very seriously. It was sad and annoying and much too dramatic.

'Why?'

'Why not?' He was vigilant. 'What else are you doing with yourself?'

'I have a lot to do here.'

'Yes. I'm sorry. I didn't mean it that way. You might like to get acquainted with the place and the type of work we do, and then maybe consider getting involved.'

But I had thought about this eighteen months ago.

'You see, a lot of our subjects are women. Our group is all male. I'd like a woman in on the team.'

'I don't want to be a token woman and I don't want to work for the government. You should know me better than that.'

'Well, then, we could think about setting ourselves up independently.'

'Oh Michael, this is crazy. We have split up, you know. We both know. And I love you but I'm not *in* love with you. Is that hard?'

'No.'

'Even if we get along and we sleep with each other sometimes, like now ... there *is* a difference, for me. I've probably played a lot of games recently ... '

'None of them has been definitive.'

'I know that.'

'And I'm not trying to define you.'

'What are you trying to do?'

'I asked you what you were doing with yourself.'

'It's not your affair.'

I reached over him for my gown. I arranged the breakfast tray and carried it across the room. He came to stand beside me. 'I'm sorry if I was presumptuous.'

'Don't get cold. Put some clothes on.'

'Do you dislike the presumption? Women have a habit of disliking it and yet resenting it when it's not offered.'

'Do they.'

'What else can I say that's entirely wrong?'

I didn't want him to keep talking, moving in and out of me as though I was predictable.

'Yes, I accept that we've split up.' He talked from the bathroom; I looked out of the window at the snow, at the line of the frost along tree-branches, dainty skeletons around a mostly empty house. 'I don't think that's any reason for us not to try something. Not love or being in love. Maybe more of a contract.'

I thought of Marlon Brando in *The Godfather*, and I smiled. At least Michael was more Marlon Brando than Al Pacino. Billy had been up for the part Al Pacino played, but he was too physically sensual. Billy. Would I have had any part of this conversation with Billy without both of us laughing at our pretensions –

'Yes,' I called absent-mindedly to the bathroom. A pause.

'Yes what?' Michael came back.

'What?' I wondered. 'Contract,' I said firmly.

'I'd like you to take a two months' course. We can pay you two hundred dollars a week, and you will have your own apartment provided for you with all the utilities. But you must stay in Cambridge while you do the course.'

He was drying his hands like a surgeon. I noticed this; it's the sort of mannerism I would always have noticed, it must be new for him. And he was very impersonal now, no doubt feeling that he had revealed too much of himself. It was fair enough. We should get out of my room.

'Why don't we go walking?'

'Yes, it's beautiful country.' He looked at the window.

'I'll get dressed.'

'I'll wait for you downstairs.'

'Go into the kitchen, Michael, it's the only warm room in the house. Pam and I don't use the central heating when we're here on our own.'

'I'll fix us a cup of coffee.'

Before he went, he looked around my room to check that he didn't leave anything behind.

Once we were out walking in the open, I was determined

that we would enjoy ourselves. He elaborated on his offer – it was more of an offer than a contract, with no strings, and no expectations other than the lightest of hopes that we might find a future which would seduce us both by accident. 'It's stupid to go any further because one of the effects of the course is to loosen the subject from any bonds. So let's forget what I said this morning, it wasn't a very intelligent way of trying to reach you.'

I liked him then, I liked him very much. And? I was flattered by his offer. Not quite flattered enough to want to be stupid or to be overwhelmed; warmed towards acknowledging a vacancy inside myself but at the same time feeling much the same way as I would feel towards any casting director. A little suspicious, excited. Because, after all, it would be a challenge to work with and to learn from those people. What else *was* I doing with myself?

Knowing my own feelings and my own position now, Michael accepts what we are. He *is* intelligent, and an expert at preserving himself, finally – I glance at him and his smile in the warm February sun. There is something rootless about his hopes, he is as glad to be free of our love as I am. Perhaps love isn't that important. I stop him. 'I don't want, in any way, to take advantage of you.'

'No.'

'Will I?'

'I don't think so. Only if you don't take yourself seriously. That's a bit vague,' he laughed. 'I would say that whatever happens over the next four months, I would expect you then to tell me what you feel about the future.'

'I would owe you *my* side.'

'Yes, I think so. So that we don't waste our time misunderstanding each other. Don't you think?'

I did think. I saw also that he wanted to get married, to marry someone, which was very exposed. I thought that he would not marry me, and I was in an objective way happy for him. He would certainly find someone else.

He said that he would like me to come to Boston mid-way through May; he kissed me formally, he held my hand, and he left.

I brooded over my decision for two days, knowing underneath that I would go if only because it was the best offer on hand. If I thought about it for much longer, I would lose the decision in a welter of self-indulgent complacency; as if I had already completed the experience and was weary of it.

I called Michael on the Wednesday and said that yes, I would come, and could he advance the course to March? He would call me back.

I told Pam before receiving his agreement. Pam was more worried about me than for the Farm; Pam disapproved of scientists fiddling with anyone, she wanted me to protect myself. I concluded the formalities on the kitchen phone. Pam laughed.

At the beginning of March, I moved to a two-room apartment in Cambridge.

I had called in at the Lancaster Gate house in London where Michael had worked but I hadn't been very inquisitive. The Cambridge Center, perhaps simply because it was larger, seemed more impersonal and better oiled. Sympathy came as a matter of course, an upmarket extension of 'Have a nice day'. I appreciated the stumbling sincerity of the Farm.

I said nothing of this to Michael. He had adjusted to this climate; he had become part of a speciality. I didn't want to provoke him, I didn't want us to become close in any accidental way. So as not to let him down and perhaps to justify myself, I imagined and I planned from the program Michael had suggested how we might organise a center – graphing out structures and activities, relating the Farm to Michael's description of his techniques. That first week, when I was free to settle in, I reorganised the entire establishment, leaving Michael and me very firmly in a deposit account, well out of our reach.

And on the second Monday morning, I walked down to the Center to begin my course.

Diane applies herself with a prim enthusiasm. Two sessions of encounter groups each day and she has the answers. Once or twice the deck tilts but she is always able to congratulate herself on the way she rights the balance. She honestly thinks that she is getting somewhere, she is interested in the opinions of others on herself.

And then she was bored. We were delving into our discoveries, people were droning on about problems, poring over emotional minutiae, everybody was waiting to be interviewed, like flabby strippers jostling in an audition line. Even the occasional cracks and collapses were tedious and stage-managed. Each evening it was like coming out of an examination class, the students jabbered excitedly to each other about where we thought we 'were', the little egos bobbed to the surface. We were all going to pass, there was no threat. The men paraded their emotional development – 'Look, I can show my feelings!' – in front of the women; the women, being in a self-conscious majority, clustered frivolously or strode like determined girl scouts over the terrain. I tried hard not to make any friends.

I became aggressive and noticed the aggression in others. Sympathetic response ran dry and was ousted by snide cynicisms from people who looked around the room, sure of general encouragement. The subject became the victim, often chose to become the victim.

Towards the end of the second week the structures were relaxed, the framework of time and tribe started to vanish. We were whetted by different guides, we were plunged into different groups, I found that I couldn't remember if I had told the same story twice to the same person, or if the story was the same in the telling, or if I was telling the truth. On several occasions I was rebuked, I was given very little time for reflection now, I clung on, waiting for the weekend.

We don't get a weekend. We are worked on and harried until we loathe and love each other, and that is gone, quickly, and a new set of proponents appear, as anxious as I am to build up a relationship, we, people to stand together, to discover each other immediately, we tell each other everything, blurting. I lose track of it, reeled in towards the immediacy, with the adrenalin and the need to go on.

Michael is around; he takes me home sometimes. I have no desire for him or for anybody. I talk to him, not conscious of his meaning. I could take anybody to bed, no desire but I wouldn't care about having sex if it was part of a conversation.

'You're going through a lot of stress,' he tells me. I agree and talk on, about stress, about anything. I awake, find him sleeping in a chair, and hate him.

We are given two days' rest. Most of us home in on the Center. Our guides anticipate us.

I want to go *through*, there must be some peace. I am empty and depressed, uncertain of the value of what I have exposed, of me.

We talk only to the therapists now. In the group, our reactions are very simple, often speechless. I share the feeling of letdown with the other subjects, there are a lot of tears. I am assigned to another therapist, Tom, and together we sift through Diane, everything is identified for me, exhumed and laid bare and still for me to dissect. I prod like a child. We build Diane up, piece by piece. I don't know if this is what I want, this establishment, this unconvincing equilibrium, but I am grateful.

'You have these aspects pretty much under control, I feel.'
I agree cautiously.
'No?' Tom searched. Such a kind face.
'The control is there now, that's all I can say about it.'
'That's right, that's possibly the only thing you *could* say about it. If you had taken it for granted then we might agree that you were refusing to acknowledge yourself. I think you can go on. Michael and I want to take you on to the suspension tank when you're well rested.'
'I'm game.'
'Do you know about it?'
'Only from the outside.'
'Uh-huh. Well, you lie in a sealed tank of water which is kept at body temperature; you are immune to external sensation. This kind of detachment can put you under stress after a while but we'll be monitoring your reactions. You might just be euphoric. But if it becomes unpleasant, or we register what we call an anxiety spiral, we'll come and get you. You'll find that it clears out a lot of the residue; after that, where you go is up to you. I could bore you for hours about sensory process controls and regressions, but we'll start slowly and it's really just a sensation of floating above yourself. Michael and I will bring you down to earth.'
'When does this start?'
'We'd like you to take a week just following your normal life pattern, and if during that time there's anything you want to talk to us about, any part of yourself that doesn't seem to fit, then you should come and talk about it. I'd like to see you

three or four times during the week anyway to make sure you haven't gotten lost.'

In the void of the suspension tank, Diane hung. Back behind the plate-glass window they watched their instruments, they had an audio link with her. Diane said nothing. When they asked her if she was all right, she said yes.

Inside the tank, apprehension. My mother. The irregular pump of the heart, the pain. My mother's reluctance and fear. The ambivalence towards the foetus, unwanted, expelled. I, the baby, blinded by light, hands clenched in panic. I, somewhere, years later, throttled by the sorrow for myself which pumped mechanically from the gut. This black bile of conscience, my evasion of love. They came to get me out.

For two months, twenty-four hours a day, at the Center or in the apartment, I was on tap. I lost thirty pounds and was haggard. All points of reference had crystallised and dissolved.

Exhausted, I found only a pure self to come home to, the last of the snow lying in patches. Back at the Farm, people surprised me; I saw them clearly, their vivid colours. I received them until I felt pressured by them, their wanting to fathom me. I wouldn't allow this. I wasn't defensive about it; there was a vibrant energy in me which they could neither subvert nor possess.

Nobody understood. I couldn't talk about it. I wrote about it; when I re-read what I wrote I trembled. There would be no one to understand it, it was closed, I would have to accept that. But I wanted to make some testament to ensure by the act that I wouldn't forget, however much I might want to forget. I couldn't possibly send the letter to my sons, they would think that I was mad. So I sent it to Billy.

Bored Children

18

In the old room which Martin occupied at the University during his final year, a student had hung himself in the thirties. Probably near the sofa. The carpet looked newish; they must have changed the carpet.

Martin went down to lunch in the Old Hall. The sun streamed through those tall religious windows and many students fled in silence from the impossibility of mingling disciplines. Martin ate the thin soup that had to be good, *had* to be good, because he was staring at the plate so hard and desperately in order to avoid those trapped eyes next to him.

And then, to nudge sudden fear, the priest, in a sports jacket, appeared, smiling, with a group of disciples. The priest sat down next to Martin and charited a well-meaning concern for Martin's health.

Martin's effort to pull his eyes out of the soup, to show no panic at the interruption. Telling the priest quickly of the ghost which breathed late at night - over in the corner near the heating pipes - its friendliness, the most human sound in the University, it stopped the darkness thinking - and someone else *had* heard it as well so Martin *was* proven sane and just threatened by people only, now would the priest keep himself to himself and get on with his meal. Thank God, some divinity student fell to considering the problem in meaningless terms, which obviated the necessity of paying any further attention to the priest.

So, of course, his friendship with the ghost was all over the next Saturday morning, when Martin went to open the door and then slept in a neighbour's room, while a posse of *cognoscenti*, clad in their habits, put the old student out of his misery of the place. It was no surprise that the Bursar came too, jangling the small change in his pocket; no fucker could get out of that University without paying dearly.

Martin felt the cold.

He sat in a room with his Tutor, bookcases leaning over them from every wall, complete cultures gathering dust, and the most concern that was ever shown to any man stood in twelve volumes and *he* was called the Wolf Man. An old servant stumbled from the kitchens, across the lawn in the courtyard in the sunlit afternoon. He brought a silver tray of tea and manicured sandwiches, which he placed under the photograph of Wittgenstein. It was the sunlight which was horrible; the most grotesque.

Martin's affair with his Tutor.

People's affairs with Martin, like draughts down a long empty corridor, with Martin chasing to close doors. Black cats appeared to watch him from the top of a staircase.

Afterwards, in a house on the West Coast of Ireland, a woman's soul gaped at him silently and her body threw itself out of his bedroom window, night after night. Martin, drunk, watched the thin prickle of hair rise up the back of his neck, night after night, made the sign of the Cross on the wall above his bed, fought off the woman. Across the river, past the sick bloody spume of rhododendrons, at the end of a main street of drinking rooms, the priest told him of sadistic English ancestors, the ruined purity of Ireland, it would cost money to have the house exorcised. It wasn't Martin's house. He chose instead the sweet mercy of Hoffmann-La Roche, through the National Health Service.

When the accumulation of death crept up to his shoulders, he cashed his savings, and he went back to New York, kill or cure.

It was two years since they had seen each other. Longer. Billy was subdued on the phone. The keys to the penthouse were left with the janitor downstairs.

With the summer of New York locked outside the windows, with Rusty slumped on a sofa cushion, Martin waited.

The dog was old. The apartment was tidy, chilled and dark. Without an ember.

Rusty slithered off the sofa and waddled lamely to the terrace door; Martin escorted him. They were caught by the sun. Martin, tired and thin. Rusty, a bundle of indifference. Martin urged the dog forward. Rusty flummoxed down the step and picked his way across the terrace. In spite of the sun, Martin was cold. Rusty returned in a slow procession and clambered back inside the room. Martin closed the door. The top of the city was aghast with sunlight, pummelling his eyes. He turned his back on the city and went down the corridor to Billy's room.

He was amused. He wanted to be, so he was amused by the childishness of the messy room, by the pulse of Billy condensed within the four walls. By the bedclothes over the floor, ashtrays half-full, cigarette butts, record covers and records, towels and shirts.

And then he was nervous. Vomit stains on the floor and in the bathroom; tight-screwed balls of underwear; the pungent, rancid smell of sexuality.

All Billy's objects, his people, were close together on the small bedside table at the head of the pillow, like a desperately closeted altar; all very close together, one centre, the monk incidentally a part of it. Also on the table, in a large space, a decanter of whisky and a glass. There were three books under the bed in a neatly squared-off pile. Martin looked to his left; all the books in the bookcase had their spines facing the wall, they weighed outwards, heavy and blank.

He took a blanket from Billy's floor.

Donald's room was exactly as it had been two years ago.

On the sofa in the lounge Martin wrapped himself in the blanket and tried to doze.

When he heard the elevator stop and the key being put in the lock, he quickly folded the blanket and went out into the hallway. Donald was surprised by him. Quickly, Martin re-counted the phone call, his arrival, the collecting of the keys, the janitor, the agreeable mood of the janitor. Donald locked the door again from the inside.

'I'm glad that worked *out*. I don't like to leave the keys with him too often. You can't trust *anyone*. You should know how to fix these locks. The bar goes into the floor down here and then slides across.'

'Yes.' Martin leant forward to look carefully at the bar. Donald stood back beside his small business case. They still hadn't caught each other's eye. Martin stayed a long time, looking at the bar attachment; until Donald started through to the lounge.

'So how was your flight?'

'It was okay. It's nice to see you again, Donald.' Martin shook his hand.

'My, it's been a long time.' Donald sat down and stroked Rusty. 'How long is it since you were here?'

'Two years.' Martin sat opposite.

'That's right.'

'I was here in the winter.'

'When you and Billy went to Los Angeles.'

'Yes, how is he?'

'Billy? Oh, he's fine. He's going strong; he'll tell you about it. It's begun to work out for him, I guess. Well, my God, it *has* been a long time.'

Donald stretched both arms out along the back of the sofa, turned his head from side to side and turned it back to look at Rusty.

'It has.'

Silence. Martin looked at his hands in his lap and then at Donald's hands.

'So do you have any plans, are you over here on business or – '

'Not really.'

'Just touring around?'

'Trying to emigrate.'

'My *God*. How are your aunt and uncle, and your sister?'

'They're fine. They send their love.'

'We had a great time that summer.'

'Did you go back ever?'

'I went back there last year. I stayed in the same hotel.'

'With Billy?'

'No, Billy was working; I took off on my own.'

'With the Danes?' Martin beamed.

'You know, I couldn't find a single Danish person on the island.'

Silence.

Donald stood up and walked stiffly out to the kitchen.

'Are you doing anything tonight, Donald?'

'No, I don't think so. I'm a little beat.'

Martin wondered about eating; he wondered anxiously why he was here. Where Billy was. Why Billy.

'Do you drink nowadays?'

'Yes.'

'Well we have vodka, or Scotch, or bourbon.'

'Can I have a vodka?'

'Sure you can. Do you like it with a mixer?'

'Yes please.'

'We only have tonic, I hope that's okay. Did Billy call?'

'No.'

'Well, he's in town, I think. Do you have Linda's number?'

'I don't know Linda.'

'He's over at her apartment more than he is here. Cheers – is that right?'

'Yes. Good health.'

Large, strong vodka and tonic. No arrangement, nothing.

Martin stood up and took his English money out of his right-hand pocket. He opened his case and put the money down one side.

'How's business, Donald?'

'It doesn't seem to be a very good time; the market's depressed.'

'Too much confusion about the war.'

'I guess so. The US doesn't seem to be winning, and it's been going on for a long time, Martin. That's un-American, for heaven's sakes. Even the older people are bored with it.' Donald raised both eyebrows innocently.

'They should knock it on the head.' Martin took a mouthful of vodka.

'They certainly seem to be trying to do that. I don't know if it's going to work. It doesn't make us very popular out there.'

The Vietnam War.

Sitting there with a formless hatred that could be ridiculous, a vodka, a nervousness and an aimlessness, Martin looked for any light in Donald's eyes but there was none.

'I'm going to take a shower and then we'll send out for something to eat.'

'Can I make a phone call?'

'Sure.'

Martin crouched over the telephone. Franco's father gave him another number.

'Franco? It's Martin.'

Those two years ago, Franco had flown back east to New York the same night Martin left for London. It was a simple coincidence; Franco was bored with California. Billy and Martin were in the middle of a snarling argument about nothing, arguing only because they didn't know if they would meet again and they wanted to leave an impression on each other. As usual, their argument pivoted around Martin's lack of interest in himself. Franco's call interrupted them. Franco said that he didn't figure he'd ever go to Europe, and he'd see Martin the next time round, enjoy the journey, ride the good times. Martin and Billy left the apartment together and picked up a cab to Kennedy. Martin promised Billy that he wouldn't come back until he had something. Billy laughed, hugged him violently, and was gone.

'Are you still there, Franco?'

'Yeah ... '

'You sound a bit vacant.'

'Hmm ... well ... how's England?'

'Okay. I'm in New York.'

'No kidding. This is kind of crazy on the telephone. What do you need?'

Martin laughed. 'Somewhere to stay for a while.'

'No sweat.'

'Can I call you later, when I know what I'm doing?'

'Yep.'

'What do *you* need?'

'Well ... ' Franco drawled theatrically, 'what do I need ... ' Martin heard a girl laugh. 'I don't need much. Maybe a fresh bottle of whisky.'

When Billy called, he spoke only to Donald; and Donald came out of his bedroom to pass the message on to Martin. 'He's in a bar on the lower East side, he's a little tired. He suggested that the two of you meet up there.'

'Shall I keep these keys?'

'I guess so. I might be asleep when you come in, and Billy's hours are kind of irregular right now.'

Donald, pink and refreshed, wrote down the name of the bar.

In the cab, many fragments plummeted through Martin's

mind, memories of Billy, visions of Billy stampeding him towards Billy. The cab bucketed downtown, the back seat lit up in searching flashes; Martin liked riding in cabs, he reminded himself, the movie of the streets, his own feeling of control, that safety in glancing out of the darkness at the swiftly unwinding reel behind each window. The intangibility spread through him.

'Hello Billy.'

'Hi.'

The intangibility vanished. Billy made as if to stand up, a drained smile; his eyes retreated painfully, like a dying creature.

They sat on opposite sides of the table, away from the bar. Billy's right hand shook as he lifted his coffee. Billy was poisoned, deep grease lines down each side of his nose, he was in an unhealthy sweat, his clothes rank and smeared, his face yellow-grey under the suntan, hair lank. He was a long way from Martin; his eyelids fell forward, his mouth hanging loosely; a long way from anyone. Billy garbled. Or maybe it was Martin, too recoiled to pick out the words.

' ... so I ... we ... got to ... damn thing ... '

'Do you want anything, Billy?'

'Yeah, I'll have a coffee.' Billy grinned sicklily.

'Or to eat.'

'You go right ahead, babe. I'm fine.' Billy slobbered at his coffee cup, coughed and wiped away a string of viscous drool. He went into his pocket for a handkerchief, he stood up and wiped his shirt front. 'Hell I *am* sorry. I know I should have said that a long time ago. I know.'

'What?' Martin asked.

'At your family's fucking house.' And he sat, and smiled at Martin. Billy said again – 'Hell, I'm sorry.'

'That's okay.'

Billy slurped loudly at the coffee, mocking him. 'How are they? Are they still alive?'

'They're fine; they send their best wishes and so does Annie.'

'They always were so kind.' Billy weaved along the narrow ledge of irony.

Martin stared at the table, sticky with Billy's slopped coffee. When he looked up, Billy was staring out of the window.

Martin took a sandwich. He choked on its dryness. Billy regarded him, amused.

'What are you doing then?' Martin asked.

'Living,' he jabbed. Then he sank back complacently on the bench seat. 'Living through the pipedream.'

'Oh, that's why you're smoking cigarettes.'

'You're damn clever, aren't you?' he rolled his eyes. The coffee cup tinkled and clattered against the saucer. The eyelids sank, and opened.

'I *loved* you, you know?' Martin reached fearfully. Not wanting the past tense, hating it and the slip of his confessional tongue.

'You didn't. You might have loved the effect I had on you.' Then he seemed moved, by himself. Billy held all the power, he always had held all the power. 'You've changed.'

'Yes? I haven't.'

'Only assholes don't change. For shit's sake, take it.'

'What do you mean?'

'It's a lie. I'm spinning you a line. Everything else is gone, you've all I've got left. God damn you, stop shoving your rotten soul in my lap. Another one.'

The drugged drawling clouded his words. Martin grasped between lie and line, not understanding these riddles.

'Take everything you can get your hands on,' Billy said clearly. He shivered and closed his eyes. Martin wondered if he should take him back to the apartment. The difference was that in New York no one stared or got uneasy, so maybe Billy was normal, with this filth and sagging mouth, cigarette after cigarette, coffee after coffee, just another extremity.

From the bar, it looked as though Martin was in love with Billy; his look stroked the hair from Billy's forehead, hung on Billy's cable body. The bartender, who had half a mind on asking Billy to move out, saw Billy open his eyes and start to speak, and Martin's entranced addiction to Billy's eyes until the words seemed to catch up and split the love cleanly apart. When Billy looked at him, Martin held the beautiful amber eyes with their bloodshot sadness; and Billy sneered.

'What are you trying to do, accuse me?' The voice slithered over the table. 'Don't play the wise guy with me. I've learned more about life than you'll ever know. Just because you've read a lot of highbrow junk, don't think you can fool me.

190

You're only an overgrown kid. Mama's baby and Papa's pet.'
Martin looked away. Billy's lips betrayed nothing. 'The family
White Hope. You've been getting a swelled head lately. About
nothing. About a few poems in a hick town newspaper ... '

Martin had shut himself off. He patted his pockets, feeling
for the keys: the only thing to do was to leave, like a refugee.
He said, 'Yes,' to nothing in particular. He glanced at Billy,
saw Billy calm and detached and stubbing out his cigarette.
They both stood up to go, Billy's light stumble towards the
door, Martin following. He pulled open the door for Billy.

'I haven't got any poems,' he said, embarrassed. Billy
squeezed his waist.

'Poets are dead, sweetheart. That's a speech from a play by
Eugene O'Neill.' Billy looked around him, he yawned. 'Can
you get into the apartment?'

'Yes. Donald gave me a set of keys. Should I stay, Billy?' He
looked at that hard ball of other-life.

'You do what you want to do.'

'Okay. Are you coming back?'

'Sure I will. I'll see you tomorrow.' A brief kiss.

Billy ambled away and turned the corner; Martin went back
into the bar and, with the same loneliness, drank a beer. At
the apartment he took cushions from the lounge and lay on
Billy's floor. He failed in his effort to wait up for Billy.

Billy came in at dawn. He desperately wanted music and he
wanted love. He was fighting.

He went past Martin's body and back into the lounge. The
huge ball rolled over in his stomach; breathing deeply, Billy
brought on the tears. But he was still fighting. He thought
through Linda and Donald and the whore he had just been
talking with – he needed none of them.

In the character of Jamie, no one existed; that was damaged.
Just the booze and the guilt and the fear of this empty need to
be loved which overtook him. Needed it all.

But still fighting. It was a great, black, honest pit of a play
– the men crawling round the sides of the gaping mother;
incapable. No more love, not enough love. All need.

He wanted out of it, he wanted to drop it.

Diane wrote him a letter like that and he wanted to drop
everything and go to try and get lost in her.

Curl around and hang on to yourself.

Billy rolled across the couch and stayed half-conscious with his exhaustion. When Donald woke him, Billy snapped back; they argued, and Billy went off to sleep on his bed.

Martin was reading when Donald came home from work. Billy was still asleep. The vodka reappeared.

'Which play is Billy doing?'

'He's doing ... ' Donald looked at the books, 'that one, *Long Day's Journey into Night*, and the moon play. That would be Billy's bigger part. They have some great people lined up.' Donald gave a list of names which meant nothing to Martin.

'Why aren't you pleased, Donald?'

'Well ... Billy just finished a musical out on the West Coast, and he kind of leapt into this. It's been very much a personal choice for him. I hope it's a good one and *then* I'll be pleased for him.'

'Is it a good time for me to be here?'

'It may not be a good time for Billy, if he feels split between seeing you and doing his research. He takes it very seriously.' Donald was in an expansive mood, father talking about favourite child, almost a snub. 'This is an important production for him, you know how Billy is about the classics. And they're making a whole festival out of these O'Neill plays.'

'He hated *Hamlet*,' Martin remembered.

'He has a *great* respect for that kind of theatre. Have you read it? How is it?'

'It's depressing.'

'Oh my God, aren't they all?' Donald raised his eyebrows. Martin laughed. 'I hope they manage to get an audience. Billy is playing Jamie and Jamie is the link character; if he dives, the whole world will know about it. I didn't want him to take it. That film will start him off again when it comes out, he was a great leading man; we could just sit here and wait for the calls. But he wants to put himself on the line, playing an alcoholic.' Donald, bewildered and stranded. Martin sat respectfully, flicking through the books he had taken from under Billy's bed. Donald looked at his watch. 'I have to wake him. We're going to a party tonight.'

'Can I come?'

'Sure. He'll expect you to come.'

After swearing and shouting and showering, Billy was assembled. Cleaned up and authoritative he came into the lounge, eyes puffed but friendly.

'Hello, how are *you*?' He squeezed Martin's hand.

'Great.' Martin stood up stiffly.

'Good.' Billy moved away, another Billy, also removed, also acting, reaching for a cigarette, sitting easily on the couch opposite Martin, eyes dappled with amusement, the leading man, mocking Donald's delay in the shower – 'Anyone would think he was going to *meet* somebody. Come on, Donald! Get yourself in line!' His eyes settled on Martin and the books.

'I took them from under your bed.'

'Did you read them?'

'I read two of them.'

'They're good.'

'I know.'

'We get together the end of July and go on in September.'

'You're looking forward to it.'

'Damn right. Did you study him?'

'No.'

'Because he's Irish? Or because he's a little raw?'

'Because there was a lot to study.'

'And you got through it.'

'Yes.'

'So you've got your degree and you're finished.'

'Yes, I suppose so.'

'Well, now you start.'

'Yes.'

'That's great, Martin. Don't throw it away. You didn't invite me to the ceremony.'

'You wouldn't have come, would you?'

'I certainly would. I would have come. I might even have been in England at that time. I was in London.'

'You didn't get in touch.'

'You had things to go through on your own, didn't you? We understood that. Hey, come on, Don!' he shouted across the room, and then he found something else to do. 'You're turning into a slob, Rusty. Rusty has started to live up to his name.' He patted the dog and it flopped over on to its back. When

Donald came into the room, the dog was finished with. 'Right! Let's go!'

'Now just a minute, Billy,' Donald complained, 'let's not rush at this thing. Do we have *keys*?'

'We do.' Billy was laughing and putting on his sunglasses.

'I don't know how you can see anything in those glasses, Billy.'

'I have them so that nothing sees me, you clown.'

The three of them sat in the back of the cab, Billy's arm over Martin, Donald outraged by the streetlife – 'My God, *look* at that person' – Billy's rattling gut-laugh, they were high, they were coasting through a lighted fairground.

'Babe, this is Martin; Martin, this beautiful girl is Linda.'

Linda hated Martin.

There was food on a table, music and drink. The party was on two floors. Billy moved shyly, often close to Linda. Martin guessed that she was a business woman, there was some arid energy about her. Billy effaced himself; Donald was always in a group, making others laugh.

Martin had two serious conversations. He danced with one of them. She had a tight red dress. He was attractive to women, she told him, and his accent was beautiful. Martin thanked her and got drunk. Billy drew people into Linda's orbit, people, Martin saw, to whom he didn't really want to talk. He leaned on Linda and she sheltered him. They hardly talked to each other. When they danced, Billy was minimal.

Martin and the girl tried to get to know each other; after half an hour they knew about her and she was impressed. Martin found her unbelievably unattractive. He told her that he was an engineer, and she was still interested. He told her that this was a lie; she was more interested. He told her that he was gay; that did it. When she went to pour herself a drink he followed her, which irritated her.

'Well, how's it going, Martin?' Donald was drunk and benevolent.

'Arrogant. Billy looks subdued.'

'Oh he is when he's with Linda.' Donald was in favour of her. 'That little girl keeps him together.'

'I thought you did that.'

Donald turned away, offended by Martin's prying; he found another group. Billy found Martin.

194

'I'm going to stay at Linda's place tonight, so you can take the bed.'

'I might leave tomorrow, Billy.'

Billy looked anxious; his hand strayed on to Martin's arm. 'Will you call me at Linda's tomorrow morning? Her number is in my book. I don't want to handle all this right now. I expected it but I didn't think about it. You know, these people bore me too; we should talk it over.'

'Billy, that's okay.'

'Goddam it, you're always saying that!'

'Sorry.'

'I thought we grew out of that. There's too many damn things happening. We'll get together later on.' He outdid himself in sagged exhaustion, he lifted his glasses. Linda appeared, to say good-night. Billy went with her. Martin went with Donald after whisky, drunkenly in love with the world; Donald talked him out of walking the last ten blocks. He hugged Donald in the hallway, Donald nodding his head like a toy pontiff.

They talked for an hour on the phone, Martin from Billy's bed, Billy from Linda's bed; they caught up, finally.

'Forget the anarchist part of it,' Billy said. 'I'm through with the Movement long since. I saw men didn't want to be saved from themselves, for that would mean they'd have to give up greed, and they'll never pay that price for liberty. So I said to the world, God bless all here, and may the best man win and die of gluttony! And I took a seat in the grandstand of philosophical detachment to fall asleep observing the cannibals doing their death dance.'

'That's O'Neill.'

'Yeah. I was going to send it to you.'

'I might have taken it personally.'

'I hoped that you would.'

'Why?'

'You might hate it and shout the bastards down. You know that an actor *does* nothing. An actor just *is*. In a way that everybody else isn't.'

'Is that still O'Neill?' Martin asked. There was a dead silence at the other end.

'No. Screw you.'

195

'Sorry.'

'That's okay.'

Martin waited. It was strange lying on Billy's bed with Billy out of the apartment. Billy, too, seemed devoid of substance.

'Listen,' Billy said, 'I have to do some research for this part.' He spoke very precisely. 'For the character. Out of New York. It will probably have to be out of New York for my own perspective. There's a woman called Diane who has er … a home for alcoholics. I want to take a look at that. We can go up there together.'

'When?'

'I don't know. In a few weeks. I'll fix it up.'

Martin hesitated. 'Is she like Linda?'

'No, she isn't. No. Leave your number.'

19

They could both handle scenes. Nothing shocked them, that's why the whole damn relationship was so stifling. If Billy pleaded, he would be allowed back. Linda organised her rituals.

Billy switched between fear of her and contempt for her. These emotions were no good to him. Anyhow, he wasn't sure that he was feeling them any longer. He noticed a voice and a lot of cosmetics and a charge account; a skill at preserving the façade which disgusted him.

'Hey, I'm sorry.'

'Are you?' she asked, without prejudice.

'I seem to poison everything.'

'You don't poison me.'

'I need the space, Linda! I need that space.'

'You have so much space, it's embarrassing, Billy.'

'It's a bad time.'

'It's always a bad time. Shit, forget it.' She took the coffee cups out to the machine. There was nothing in that apartment of hers that fitted Jamie, not the colour, not the books, not the decay, not the bottles, not the stories.

Women were obsessing Billy, and he resented that. Black, droning pits of women, women like hundreds of loudspeakers which hung from streetcorners and yapped and spittled.

He was frustrated by the plays; there was no way into them except through women. That whole deep self-pitying dirge of women and men with women. Women not wanting to be found out, women wanting to be understood.

'I'm not getting anywhere with the part,' he confided to Linda. 'I'm not getting there. There's nothing of that Jamie character in me. I'm *not* a fucking alcoholic. I'm *not* ashamed, I *don't* have any guilt – '

'How long is this going on?' Linda tidied the magazines.

'I have to get out of this, I have to get out of this right now. Do you understand?'

'I understand. I'm not going to sit around waiting for you to understand it.'

Billy walked round the room; Linda sat down, out of the way. She didn't want to watch him, didn't want to see him crawl.

' ... like a promise of peace in the soul's dark sadness, I can't get it. I don't know that in myself. That's no part of me ... ' Billy's tears went unnoticed by him. 'Screwing a whore on top of the mother's coffin. Jamie is sick. He can't be saved; I don't believe in that. I can't accept that ... '

'Change your beliefs.'

It had happened before, that intense insecurity in him as he searched through himself for a character. She knew better than to try to help him. The more she entered, the more lost they would both become. It had once excited her, this change, this nakedness. It had exhausted her, and there came a time when she simply realised that it was no longer significant for her. She pulled clear to save herself, she kept Billy at a distance; she knew that she was feeding him scraps. It seemed to her to be a waste of time that might go on indefinitely. She put a block on her compassion, and now it irritated her to be played off for meaningless sympathy. Without intending to, he made her feel sluggish and defensive. She was tired of having to perceive when he was in character or when he wanted a rest from it. If what he said meant anything. She found herself acting out her acceptance of him. In the mores of a New York relationship, both of them felt that the other side of the balance was a little light. Billy, she knew, had a hard time getting through to her; she didn't want to see him try, and Billy protested.

'You know, Diane and I spent a lot of time in bed, balling

each other. We forgot there was anything in between. With us, there wasn't anything in between, nothing in the way, no relationship.'

'You'd better go, Billy.' She was more disgusted by his self-denial than she was hurt by his small meanness. She flipped through a magazine.

'I didn't mean that,' he pleaded.

'Diane is a cold bitch.'

'Diane is my friend.'

'At one time I would have said that was a compliment to her.'

'I was lying, Linda.'

She looked across at him. 'You still are. I don't care. I know that you had an affair with Diane. You couldn't hide it. Nobody has a faithful man any more; they're out of fashion.'

'Linda, I don't have sneaky, private affairs.'

It decided her. 'Well, I do,' she told him. 'And right now, I am having an affair. I'm the one who wants the space.'

'Who the hell with?'

'That's not your business.'

Billy sat on a lurching sadness. 'What the fuck does it matter ... that's great.'

Everywhere he looked in the bar, there were whores; in every movement of each woman there was the attempt to sell herself – the need to sell herself to a watching man. Billy took it for granted without being sympathetic. He would have preferred to drink downtown; he had the habit now of enjoying the warmth of no-hopers, listening to the stories of the drunks and failures as they propped each other up. The one thing they all hated was home. Home separated them.

He hadn't seen his sister for a year, and he hadn't seen his parents for five years. His sister had problems. They loved each other; he kicked himself for not having seen her before the O'Neill thing started. Right now he didn't want to see anyone. He was interrupted; by a woman, chiding his thinking.

'I was thinking if my parents had any problems.'

'Not many people think about that.'

'I know why,' Billy laughed. She was taller than he was and she looked at him with the obvious opinion that she had intuition. Billy knew that one. He laughed inwardly, sarcastic at himself. Perhaps she did have great intuition, he didn't like her. Didn't dislike her; just didn't care about her. He played sensitive, with enough flattering irony to hook her. They had a few drinks and went to bed at her apartment. She saw him about three times a fortnight when they both wanted to bat hell out of something. He needed that character.

20

Franco drove Martin down the turnpike to New Jersey, with beer in brown paper bags and the tape deck needing a nudge in the spools. Sipping beer and grunting cynical remarks, Franco was fatter and smoking Camels under a greasy cap. No second gear, so they both took to cursing the car because there wasn't much else to say. Martin took the couch in a ground-floor apartment which Franco shared with John.

Franco had no money, he was shifting furniture for his father. John worked for the Davies Brush Company. It was reckoned on five seconds for each brush. John shaped handles. With Dexedrine, John did three and a half seconds and bonused fifteen dollars a week, averaging 4,305 brushes in an afternoon.

The apartment was compiled of leftovers from Franco's father, mainly a solid couch that faced the TV and a fridge that sheltered vats of tuna fish salad. In the evenings the three of them got drunk and watched TV. They didn't venture out into the summer.

Laird's Applejack was good with beer, not unpleasant with fish salad, and a salutary experience when taken with bread which peeled like blotting paper from the polythene pack.

After two weeks of old romantic movies, quiz shows and Watergate hearings, Martin irritably offered Franco the observation that John was a moron. Franco wasn't surprised.

'See, he was a junkie for two years, then he volunteered for the Methadone programme. You know the Methadone programme? It's run by the government. They drag the dudes off scag and they put 'em on Methadone, which isn't much different. John came off that four months ago.'

Franco blew smoke at the television, watching his boot.

'He got a job at the brush place. I feel kind of proud of him.'

He cocked his head to one side; his hand swung down and stubbed the cigarette under the pile of ash. Franco smiled, pushed his cap back and wiped beer from his stomach. His brown eyes floated slowly across. 'It's good to see you again. I don't do much any more. I dig to get juiced, watch TV, get fucked when there's no hassle with the girl.'

Martin wondered at this distant benevolence in Franco, how he sat there watching TV with the occasional 'Shit ... ' when something annoyed him, and the dry laugh like an old stager who knew it all. But Franco moved in a shroud of easy affection, he said as much: 'I'm easy,' he said, 'I've been travelling around, I was logging up in Canada. This just seems like the right place to be at the moment.'

The phone buzzed in the kitchen. Franco belched and shambled through to get it.

'The Kid's coming round,' he announced, 'we're going to get some songs down.' Franco picked up his beloved guitar. 'He's from California.' Franco shrugged indifferently. 'Maybe it's like it used to be out there.'

'Did you ever see Sharon again?'

'Yeah, I saw her in New York once. She was just another fucking middle-class lady once she got out of that Californian daydream. It's strange how we end up here together because of her body.' Franco chuckled. 'It wouldn't have been because of her head.'

'That's unfair.'

'Yeah, it is. Maybe.'

The Kid sped in, with a bag of grass, a girl he called Lady, a fiddle and a new electric guitar. There were jokes and parodies of old songs. Then Franco fell to gazing in concentration at his strings, tapping his foot, playing, smiling up at Martin occasionally, leaning over the guitar, balancing the Kid, filling in under the soars of the fiddle. And then he went out on his own, going a long way, challenging , smoothing, always holding it tightly.

The Kid put down the violin. He was strung off the face of the earth and he didn't like it. He rapped to Martin, wotcha mate and England, he had been lead violinist for the San

200

Francisco Youth Orchestra, this here was his old lady for the time being ...

Franco reached over his guitar for a whisky, the light dying from his eyes. Yeah, wearily, he supposed that the Kid should lead with the fiddle while he'd take rhythm, that's okay, he'd practise. They made some arrangements; the Kid and entourage left. Franco drank beer and watched TV in silence. He said later: 'Yeah, I'm proud of John. I'm teaching him to play the harp, that'll maybe give him an outlet. Last year I was playing with a guy called Ray. He was tight, that dude; he was good. He played eighty-eights. We got regular work in a bar. Then the son of a bitch walked off the subway platform in front of a train. I didn't figure him for a junkie. He could make good music. John was telling me that the junk in the city is cut with quinine. It fills your lungs with water; it's another Italian way of getting rid of you if you're not a good customer. You know, sometimes you go through those periods when it's just enough to be alive. If there's nothing happening, it's good.'

The Kid had a spare room in his wooden house, and a bed. Franco ran Martin and his luggage over there one afternoon with the canvas hood of the VW slung in the back and a new Mose Allison tape.

The Kid was sitting on the back porch and was delighted with his English lodger – liven up the place. He took a potshot with his BB gun at a cat on the garage roof, waving aside Lady's anger. He lit a pipe of grass and called over Butch who lived next door. Butch slid in with some slack black rhetoric to meet the English mate staying awhile; and then a guy called Glenn emerged from the basement to squat on the tarmac and lob a baseball at the garage doors.

That first afternoon went on to cricket and pipes; later, beers from Jake's Barn down the road past the Texaco station. Franco drifted off to see a girl, rich and adolescent. The sun plodded round the trees to the right. The Kid descended his fiddle, Butch cussed and hollered about his job, Lady brought down some cakes with exotic tea. They ate, blew and shunted a lot of dope; it seemed to Martin as though he had been there for centuries. Glenn hurled a swinger through the garage window; they shifted to the front porch to watch the Texaco station and the disused bowling alley with the Marlboro

201

billboard perched on top; the evening closed in with a visit from a flirty fat-bummed Jewess, Evie, in a sighing tank of a car. The Kid was itching to drive and they took off for some tyre-screech round the block. Martin looked at Lady; she chose to make a fuss of the dishes. They carried them upstairs.

She hoped he was going to like it here, the Kid was crazy at times. Outside, Butch hollered and cussed, the door of Glenn's basement clacked, the neon sign shone jerkily from over the bowling alley, the tall brown cowboy lighting another of those cigarettes.

The Kid flashed back; with a whirl of blond hair he threw himself into a chair, eyes drooling out of his head.

'Yes sir, I am wasted, yes sir, no shit I am wasted.'

Martin laughed, scuffed a dish, bumped an elbow into one of Lady's breasts.

'Watch out for them, yeah. My ol' Lady, she's got big, big boobs. Ain't that true?'

'Sunny,' she jibed him. He was up on his feet and moving towards them, Lady fending him off with a fork. The Kid retreated and slid out a large hunting knife.

'Sunny ... '

The Kid was poised, threatening her.

'You know, Englishman,' he lectured, 'you know how to use one of these here knives when you're up in the woods. You hold it like this, see. Y'see how I'm holding it. Y'keep the butt into your wrist, then you don't spin round. It'll take you more than one stick at a big grizzly bear. I'll bet they don't teach you that in fuckin' Trafalgar Circus. Now dig on how I stick my old Lady here.'

He crouched with the weight off his heels, long yellow hair motionless. Martin was too stoned not to enjoy it. Lady froze, with a soapy dish-brush near her navel, side-on to the threat. Water fell to the floor, dripping from the brush. Martin watched.

'Fuckin' boots ... ' murmured the Kid, easing them off slowly, changing the knife from right to left hand, and back again. The top half of his body swayed very little, his balance was perfect, his eyes never left her lest she get away.

'No,' Lady mumbled; her grey eyes appealed wider, her top lip switched with a nerve. The left boot clunked as it hit the floor.

'See, with wolves, mate, a knife's maybe not so good.'

He moved forward in a menacing dance-cum-shuffle. He

lunged. Lady lumbered back into the corner. The yellow hair steadied again, the body took up its balance.

'Come on, ya grizzly bitch ... '

'Sunny ... ' she pleaded. Martin settled back with a smile.

'Come on, Lady, where's ya balls,' he snarled, 'get on it, ya selfish bitch.'

'Sunny ... '

'You bin sleazing with Franco again, huh? Ain't ya?'

'No!'

Martin woke up and realised that she was close to tears.

'Sure you're a sleaze. You hang it out for whichever guy comes round here. She screw you, Englishman, when I was out getting gas? I bet she sure tried. She screws anyone when I step out of here. And it's all my money, this place. I pay the goddam cheques and she goes down on the first cock comes under the mat. You're a selfish bitch of a woman, Lady ... a real selfish bitch. Just like ya fuckin' selfish family, bunch of East Coast Jews ... '

She cringed, a bewildered heap of pain in the corner, the thin plastic brush poking up from her hands. She suffered the Kid, her head bent in silence. He had let the knife back to his side, body tense as he raved at her. He flicked his hair out of his face with a shake of his head.

He marched closer to her in his stockinged feet, shouting. As he reached her and jabbed at her arse with his foot she looked up and flung a tray of cat shit at his shirt, bursting into tears with 'Why don't you go fuck Evie!' as the sand and slime and dung stuck to his chest and spattered the floor. She ran for her life to the bedroom, stumbling, crying, throwing away the dish-brush. The cat litter settled.

The grey cat was hunched on the window ledge between pots of herbs. It, too, was watching. It saw Martin smoking a cigarette in the darkness of the kitchen corner. It saw the Kid rigid in posture, leaning forward to keep his shirt away from his chest. It stood up to stretch, first with the back legs extended and the tail up, then sliding forward like an ill-nailed rectangle. It yawned, a luxurious yawn of fangs and whiskers. It decided that events were concluded.

The Kid whirled round to the dresser, grabbed an air pistol and put one pellet into the cat and one pellet into the window-frame. The cat howled off. The Kid grinned.

He eased the pistol back on to the dresser and took off his shirt. Martin pushed across the cigarettes. The Kid sidled over to the table and sat in a wicker chair, bending down to pull on his beige hide boots.

'Yeah, I'm wasted man, English, mate ... whatever ya goddam name is. Fuckin' women. You can't do without the bitches. Sure as shit I could dig to get up Evie, man ... now I gotta roll a joint, go talk to her, take *her* the joint ... apologise. Sure as hell the cat's gonna crap in the bed tonight. Gotta buy a Jeep tomorrow. Got an Englishman, for Chrissake, blocking up my apartment ... shee-yit.' The Kid smiled at Martin. 'You like these boots? These are Frye boots. Y'get boots in England?'

'Spanish boots.'

The Kid paused with the cigarette papers. 'Y'read books?'

'Yes.'

'I figured it.' The Kid shook his head from side to side, reaching for the dope. 'Books get you nowhere. My old Lady, she's always reading books, sitting there, reading books, talking with that bitch Evie about books.' He was too stoned to manage the paper with the grass in it. He emptied the dope on to the table, cupped his hand and swept it wastelessly into a pipe.

'You figure you know more than me?' He was interested, there was something nakedly naïve in the question. Martin answered it carefully.

'Yes. I know more than you about books.'

The Kid liked it. 'Okay, this is where you sleep. In here.' He showed Martin to a small room off the kitchen. 'We can get a door in the morning. This here's the bathroom. My ol' Lady's got some kind of a disease,' he warned, 'so take a different towel. I gotta go buy a Jeep in the morning. They have Jeeps in England?'

'They have the same sort of thing.'

'Yeah? I gotta take this pipe in to my old Lady ... maybe screw her, you know? We could get over to Jake's Barn later for a beer.'

He went.

Martin sat on the bed with the last can of beer, he picked up a sweatshirt out of his case and lay back on the bed, tipping beer from a height down into his mouth. Not much wan light was being drawn through the window.

From the other side of the apartment came music and the

204

pleadings of the Kid. Outside, in the alleyway between the houses, Butch slammed a screen door, tirading about the Man, going to work. From the back, Glenn revved up a Volkswagen Camper and powered out between the houses; he halted to pick up Butch and then the Camper bounced up the ramp on to the road. From Butch's garden a young voice complained: 'I ain't no white motherfucker', and a woman scolded, calling the child in. The cat appeared at Martin's door, wary, bounding away at the clunk of boots coming out of the bedroom. There was a noise of boxes being pushed aside, a loud hum and the popping of feedback as a guitar was plugged into an amplifier. The noise was adjusted and replaced by a brute strummed holocaust. Two dinosaurs jerked up on hindlegs in a fast pounding. The guitar ceased.

The boots clunked into the kitchen, the freezer door opened. 'Shit.' The freezer door slammed, the Kid clunked into Martin's room, clouds of smoke pouring from the pipe in his hand. He coughed, and a fog came over the room.

'Ah ... ' he wheezed. He passed the pipe over. He stood in the middle of the barren room, one hand in his pocket. He walked over to the door and leant against a filing cabinet. He switched on the light.

'Y'know how you kill wolves?' he asserted.

Martin removed the pipe from his mouth. 'No.'

'Y'reckon climbing a tree, like in the movies?'

'I'd get a gun.'

The Kid adjusted his stance, curling one leg behind the other. He grinned. 'Hey, English, you never seen a wolf. See, mate, up in the north of California, they got forest like you never seen. You can get a long way from anywhere. Them wolves are thin, grey bastards, mean; nine of 'em in a pack. Always with a leader. When he gets killed, they have another leader. And y'don't climb up in a tree, mate, them wolves'll wait a week for you to freeze and drop down.'

He had swung away from his leaning post and was standing in the centre of the room, drawing nervously on a cigarette.

'So what do you do then?' Martin asked.

'Whaddaya do? Y'run like hell, till you slip and fall and you can feel the wolves getting closer, they don't make no sound, you can only hear the breath catching up on you ... ' Martin noticed that the possessed face had only one real eye, the deeper-grey left eye was glass and motionless. ' … yeah, you see I've only got the one eye. And this left arm's screwed to hell. I can still play guitar, maybe better than Franco.' He paused, staring.

'Yes,' said Martin neutrally. There was a moment's silence.

'Yeah … well … when the leader gets up to you, he'll leap, he'll go for your throat to get you on the ground.' The Kid had his left hand clutched round his throat, squeezing it tightly. 'Once he gets you on the ground, you're dead; there's no way you can stand up. Then the rest get on you with them teeth. The leader's always the fastest, he's the one to bring you down; the rest of the pack are dumb, like sharks, they just want blood and meat.' Martin nodded, the Kid was pleased. 'The only thing you can do, mate, is to watch for when the leader comes close on you.' He pulled out his knife. 'You turn, and as he leaps you crouch down, like this see? With your knife in both hands. You gotta use both your hands and ram the knife up in his belly … ' The knife powered up. 'You gotta stay away from the blood. If you have time, snap his front legs apart; stay away from his teeth. Get the knife back out of him and start running again.' The Kid straightened up after the battle. He wiped the knife and slid it back in his belt. 'The rest of the pack will stop and eat him. But you keep running. Cause when they finish, one young grey bastard'll take off after you again. The rest of them'll follow the new leader. You gotta turn round and kill him every now and then, and keep running. You don't hang out in some tree, mate, not up a tree,' he laughed, 'they'll wait a week and then they'll eat you.' He rolled with laughter. 'If y'with a woman, you let them eat her first.'

'Why?' Martin asked. The Kid shook his head with the laughter, hair flying across his stoned eye.

'You ever seen a woman run, mate? Huh? Women can't do it. It's a gas. Boobs flapping all over; they can't run!' He was bent double with laughter. He hauled himself up with his arms outstretched; he was suddenly serious, supplicating.

'Y'know how tender women are? Y'know? With that smooth skin, that fat butt. You seen the butt on my old lady? Yes sir, that's tender. I get back all strung out with the hassle of the city, and she's real tender. She starts with this love in her head and it spreads all over her body.'

Martin was deranging clothes in a suitcase while the Kid

sincered away. He didn't want to get involved, didn't want to become confidential with either of them, but he asked: 'Why do you give her a hard time then?'

'Man,' the Kid lifted his eye to the ceiling, 'she's full of crap!' Martin laughed. The Kid was helpless. 'But ... y'need a woman. *You* need a woman?'

'Sometimes.'

'You like getting laid?' He was suspicious.

'Yes.'

'Ain't much that beats getting laid, except getting stoned.'

'You can do both,' Martin suggested.

'I get so wasted, man, so wasted.' He crashed down on the bed like an upturned crab. The phone rang and he was up off the bed in a flash, answering it. He came back.

'It's that Italian, Franco. He wants to talk with you.'

Martin reached the phone and the Kid hung on his shoulder.

'Hey, Martin ... I was just checking the crazy bum hadn't killed you yet.'

'No.'

'You think you'll be able to settle in?'

'Yes.'

'You can't talk?'

'No.'

'Huh. Well, let me speak with him.'

Martin handed the phone over to the Kid. He went back into his room and unpacked a few clothes, checked the bed, put the case in a corner. The Kid joined him.

'My old lady's crashed out. You wanna come for a beer?'

'I think I'll take a bath and get some sleep.'

'Yeah? *I* could dig a beer.'

'Let's make it tomorrow; I'm tired.'

'Fuckin' English.'

'You said it.'

The Kid hovered until Martin disappeared to run the bath; but the room was empty when he came back for his towel. The Kid appeared again in the kitchen, looking through the freezer, telling Martin that if you came from San Francisco, you never said Frisco. Martin nodded. He wondered if he really wanted to stay in America. He missed Franco, their sense of humour, Franco's detachment. Half-way round the doorpost, he thought he might ask the Kid about heroism.

'How did you get to lose the eye?'

'I was in a car smash in Connecticut.'

Later that night, Martin felt the Kid steal in from the bar, bootless. The Kid checked that Martin was sleeping alone.

Settle in? There was no time. It was like a sideshow.

In the morning, Martin went with them when they drove across town to the relevant gas station.

There was the Jeep, painted up but no frills. It was rangy. The Kid liked it.

He started paying out for it when he first hit the sprung driving seat. The huge redneck mechanic with 'Body Shop' printed on his Chevron shirt thought the Kid was mad; but he was turning an easy buck, and, seeing as how the more he shook his head, the more in love the Kid fell, he threw in a couple of Wild Hippie remarks and sold the Kid a tow-cable attachment and a World War Two machine-gun mounting.

'Y'can go up mountains in a Jeep ... ' No trouble to the Kid, sitting in the front seat with the feel of the steering.

'Sure can,' intoned Body Shop.

'Steep fuckin' mountains,' admired the Kid.

'Big mothers,' chimed Body Shop.

'Real solid, huh?' whacked the Kid on the dash.

'Don't build automobiles like it.' Body Shop nervously glancing where the Kid kicked and slammed.

'You can even drive into New York on ten gallons of gas,' Lady dared to whisper.

'Fuckin' Jews, man ... and this dude's English, friend of mine, staying with us awhile.' The Kid introduced.

'Honor,' said Body Shop, wiping two square feet of bicep with a rag. 'Figure you'll take it? I got another customer coming over this morning.'

'Hell, man, that Jeep's mine. Let's have the money, Lady. In the purse ... she keeps her damn head in her purse. *My* eye, Lady, that's where we get the money.'

He paid.

The time of the Jeep. It was good while it lasted.

The Kid and Martin would get dressed up in Glenn's Vietnam gear and bowl off to the park on the Kid's dope, ripped from ear to ear, the Kid flashing the lights for civilians to pull over.

Lady insisted on accompanying them for the second week. The Kid didn't rate it, her doing her embroidery in the back. So like the Jeep wasn't built for this cruising crap, as he swung off the road into the park, across a flower-bed, through a crowd of geriatric adolescents who were playing with plastic Frisbees. The Jeep lurched, the Jeep accelerated, Lady getting thrown out on the first hill and hobbling up after them as the gearbox fell out on the second hill.

The Kid was heartbroken. He kissed off 900 dollars on the resell to a very concerned Body Shop, who shook his head, trying to keep a straight face.

But, the Kid figured, you lose an eye in an accident, you get the insurance money by accident, hear of a Jeep by accident … what the hell … who cares? On the way back from the garage, the Kid buys a pair of flash white shoes. He considers Lady's protests and he buys another pair of Frye boots for bad times.

And, seeing as how the Jeep's gone, he buys a large husky-dog.

'You have them dogs in England? Them dogs climb mountains like you've never heard of. You get stuck in the mountains, that dog'll find you, he'll keep on looking till he finds you. He'll sniff you out; he'll fight off the wolves too.'

For lack of wolves in downtown New Jersey, the dog fought everything else.

It got on real well with the Kid. Both of them strolling out every day, and the Kid impressing on Martin the extent of the dog's fidelity; proved by the gashes on friends met in the street. Franco, one time, caught coming out of a bar at three in the afternoon, brained the beast with a secondhand saxophone and had to take shelter in the nearest car as the titillated monster snarled after him. The Kid was blown out with admiration.

They lost friends. Glenn backed out of tackling the stairs after nearly losing an arm. Evie spent one very paranoid afternoon locked in the bathroom while they were out. Butch was convinced that the Kid was now working for the Police Department. That animal ruled.

After considering Martin's 'Lassie', the Kid called it 'Dog'.

'Dog's a real honest name, mate.'

Lady entrenched herself in the bedroom with the grey cat, Martin acquired a table and started writing a mish-mash of apocalyptic verse-drama, every word a hair-raiser. The only time the apartment settled was when Martin crushed up some old Valium into Dog's food or, at the other extreme, when the Kid rehearsed on electric fiddle. Martin and Lady could then sit with their legs curled under them in the corner nearest the door; Dog on the floor, tongue lolling over his fangs. The Kid would serenade them with a soaring rendition of the Pentagon Nerve Warfare Blues Suite.

Martin sometimes worked with Franco. Despite his father's attempts to organise him, Franco worked only according to mood. He didn't want to get too involved with his family. When he worked, he worked wholeheartedly – if the two of them worked for a week, they were offered jobs for the next month through word of mouth amongst the Italian community. At that point, Franco's interest tailed off. He'd go back to grappling with the saxophone. Martin sat around at the Kid's apartment.

'He's a lousy saxophone player,' the Kid grumbled scornfully, 'why the hell does he want to fool around with a fuckin' saxophone?'

It was a game with Franco. He was amazed by the instrument, by the hideous sounds he could pull out of it. He'd pat it appreciatively and grunt as if he'd just finished a large meal. He used it to tease the Kid and he used work to tease Martin; he was through with being an entertainer.

In the bars, acquaintances approached him for his affectionate calm. A greeting, a few remarks, and Franco tapped his foot, reached for his beer and grunted. Seen it all before. The interview was over.

'She's okay,' or 'he's okay,' Franco summed up.

Martin came out with a dismissive cynicism, stabbing any convenient back. Sometimes to Franco's warm chuckle. Sometimes not.

'You can sure pin people to the wall,' he said sourly.

'I suppose so.'

'Maybe it's a gift. Everyone's doing it. I guess it's the art of making a quick buck. Probably all right for words. But it's not good enough. You can't do it in music, although that motherfucking Sunny tries hard. There's no way. I'm through with all that crap. It's not my time.'

210

'When is?'

'It'll come round.'

If Dog was shut out of the kitchen Franco would arrive at the Kid's with his girlfriend Chestnut and a bottle. He and the Kid would try to rehearse their guitar act. They were not very ensemble, if only because the closed door separated them. Franco rhythmed haphazardly under the Kid's din, and occasionally lapsed into a solo. The electric guitar stopped. The Kid marched to the door, dragging it open.

'Are we going to play that way?'

Dog appeared at his thigh, interested party and support.

'No, man, no,' said Franco. 'I was just foolin' around ... '

'Yeah, I figured. It seems to be going real well otherwise.'

'Sure does.' Franco nodded.

'Whaddaya reckon to going through that slow number again?'

'Yep.'

The door closed, they heard the thump as Dog flopped down. Martin cleared his throat, Chestnut relaxed, Franco winked and rhythmed, cigarette plonked in guitar neck, Chestnut poured out the Daniel's.

Sometimes Martin would come into contact with the Kid's idea of Nature. Sometimes when the back porch was so peaceful that beers and even Butch got swallowed in silence, the Kid would clunk inside, pick up his lumber jacket, leave Lady cooking the meal and drive the four of them up to an old reservoir. He'd let Dog run wild within a radius of ten yards while he target-practised the posts on the wire fence.

Butch never came without a sixpack, never went anywhere without a beer and an intuitive thesaurus of high-pitched laughing cusses on the subject of the Man: him and this white man, him and that white supervisor, him jiving this white boss.

'That dumb nigger's *full* of jive.' The Kid whistled Dog back to the VW. Butch and Martin crammed into the back seats with the beer, Dog gobbled his tongue gracefully from the seat of luxury, the Kid promising him California. Dog pants at the couple in the back, Butch freezes, the Kid smiles in the mirror and they crawl up to the plateau overlooking New York.

They arrive. The Kid springs out, Dog leaps out, Martin squeezes out, the beer clanks out, Butch rolls out.

Butch starts up, gets into gear, jives on. At Martin. The two of them leaning on the car roof with the beer cans, each to his own pack of cigarettes.

There is a chill settling, a breeze bringing it home to the hillside. Butch runs out of steam, he reaches for a new can of beer. Across the dirt viewing-point, the Kid is sitting on a wall cross-legged, shoulders and head sagged into the lumber jacket, looking out across New York, his arm over Dog. Martin smoked a cigarette to warm himself. He finished it and ground the butt into the gravel. Butch got into the car, the door slammed shut, the music started mid-track. A beer can comes out of the window, falls and rolls hollowly away, Martin watches it bucking between the stones. It stops, rolls back a turn, stops. The Kid looked over his shoulder in irritable self-pity.

'Don't let that dumb nigger steal the car, huh? ... *mate*.'

Martin shrugged. Butch turned up the music. It thumped outside in a fug. The Kid turned back. Butch wound down the window, the music made a curious refusal to step outside. Butch shouts:

'Hey ... Ah say Hey! ... now jus' what sweetness is goin' down out there? ... Butch is figurin' mus' be somethin' sweet as we ain't movin'. Now what is happenin', Sunny?'

The Kid crunched back across the gravel. They drove down, silent except for the Kid informing Dog about the Golden West.

The car swung down the alleyway between the houses, echo booming back at them, Butch slapped the screen door closed behind him. The Kid bummed a cigarette and chinned the wheel, keeping the engine popping. Dog waited by the porch, sniffed at dirt; he condemned a withered flower, leg arched high over it. The Kid wasn't about to say anything so Martin got out of the car. He reckoned on making it about half-way to the porch steps; he managed to get one foot on them before the Kid wound down the car window and drawled, 'You wanna go to California?'

'Maybe tomorrow,' Martin said.

That night he could hear through the wall Lady crying, and he got up in the morning to find that the Kid had left early. The Kid came back with a small Japanese TV for the bedroom.

'Sarasota, Florida (AP) – "In keeping with Channel 40's policy for bringing you the latest in blood and guts and in living colour, you are going to see another first – attempted suicide."

'With that startling announcement Chris Chubbuck, thirty, shot herself in the head Monday as her morning talk show was being aired by television station WXLT-TV.

'Miss Chubbuck was taken to Sarasota Memorial Hospital, where she was listed in critical condition.

'Station officials and eyewitnesses said Miss Chubbuck was reading a news report about a shoot-out at a bar when mechanical trouble developed with a film clip.

'After a few seconds, Miss Chubbuck came back on and calmly read a statement announcing her planned suicide attempt.

'Then she reached into her shopping bag behind her desk, pulled out a .38 calibre revolver, fired a single shot and slumped forward.

'Michael Simmons, news director, said the screen went blank within seconds after the gunshot. The station continued broadcasting with public service programming.'

Martin was out of bed fast, throwing on a shirt, pulling up his jeans from the floor, the paper flapping after his right hand as he rounded the kitchen through the rehearsal box to where Lady was stitching a shawl and the Kid was sieving grass.

'Do we get Channel 40, WXLT?' Martin demanded.

'40?' The Kid was taken aback. 'Yeah, we get most all channels on this set. That's a good little TV, mate. But we don't have a 40 in this area.'

'What were you watching yesterday morning?'

'What time?' Lady asked.

'Seven.'

'Seven? I was fuckin' sleeping at seven. Who watches TV at seven?' The Kid was scornful.

'You would if you were awake; you don't do much else,' Lady stirred.

'This woman,' Martin cut their feuding short, 'put a bullet in her head on the news programme.'

'Yeah?' The Kid was interested.

'They might replay it maybe … ' Martin moved across to the red plastic portable.

'Yeah, put it on, change the channel. Sure as hell they won't show it, but the war's on at this time. Let's take a look at 13.' The Kid had been watching an old Korean Robert Mitchum. Martin swivelled the dial; they got some news via the Channel 13 personalities. The suicide wasn't featured. The War Report came on. There was a tactful silence on who was winning. Shots of helicopters landing, soldiers running, radio messages, pillars of smoke – a lot of commentary and sun-kissed eroticism from a carrier deck of strike aircraft. The war was boring, the movie was better. The Kid gave a rundown on aircraft; it seemed he had been a model-flying champion on the West Coast.

'Here, mate,' the Kid broke off, 'this little fox is Donna. She's a friend of my cousin, lives in Trenton.'

'Hi.' The voice came from by the dresser. Martin was kneeling about two feet from the TV; he stood up and said hello into the shadows.

'We could use some tea,' Lady suggested.

'Yeah.' The Kid didn't look up.

'Right.' Martin went into the kitchen. When he came back with the tea, Donna had moved to the mattress under the window. She was boyishly delicate.

'Where's Dog?' Martin asked. She had a nervous way of smoking a cigarette.

'I had to shut him in the back stairs.' The Kid smiled from his chair. Her eyes considered Martin warmly.

'He's some dog.' She was definite in her dislike; it was endearing, and it seemed to extend into the question of why Martin was living in such a place.

'You're not missing a leg?' Martin poured tea. She wasn't missing a leg. She had two beautiful legs, one curled under her, the other she stretched out to the toes for their inspection.

'No,' she said, mocking their appraisal.

'How's Trenton?' Martin asked.

'Pretty terrible.' She leaned back for her bag and another cigarette.

'Asshole of New Jersey,' the Kid announced.

'I just live there.' She smiled.

They talked for a while across the movie. She organised a women's group in Trenton. Martin had to go out to meet

Franco. When he got back she was gone, and the Kid was several pipes in favour of the new dope and Donna.

'Oh yeah ... she's a little fox ... a real looker ... she used to work the Playboy Club with my cousin, and *that* lady has to be one of the best-looking chicks I ever saw.'

'She's attractive,' Martin agreed.

'She's a slut.' Lady left the room. Her voice was slicing. Even the Kid turned in shock. She went away into the kitchen, the Kid stuck one finger up at her back. He bent to pass the pipe.

'She's jealous,' he tittered. 'Donna left her number, right here,' the Kid tapped his leather pouch, 'and my old lady nearly went through the roof.'

Later on Martin took the number from the pouch.

21

He was bored. It was idling into one of those heavy summers; no one was moving much any more. There was a claustrophobia settling in with the atmosphere. If you were rich, you left town; if you weren't you drifted into a humid stupor and your nerves rose to the surface. There were often fights in Jake's Barn, even Franco had brawled a couple of times. He didn't like the pride it put into him. He entered as a peacemaker and had to fight his way out. He was a good fighter, but he hated it.

The Kid had met up with some musicians who were forming a band in Newark. The band was all black but their agent reckoned it a novelty to use a white violinist up front. One of Franco's fights had been in the bar where he and the Kid were to play, so their booking had gone up in smoke. When the Newark offer came through, the Kid was interested. It got him out of the house and it provided some entertainment in the back yard.

Most weekday mornings at eleven, a big mauve Caddy would rear and sway along the alleyway to collect him; three silent, black-capped Negroes in the back, and a driver. The Kid would be waiting on the porch with his fiddle. One of the blacks would get out of the back seat, the Kid would sit in front with a black monolith each side of him as the Caddy took off up to Newark where the band practised.

Martin never missed it; he pretended to keep his eyes on the same tree-top over the garage. Butch's wife called in the children at ten-thirty, Martin brought down the tea at ten forty-five, the Kid smoked a cigarette at ten-fifty, the Caddy slid in at eleven. Doors slammed, tyres flared dust, and the Kid departed with his towering henchmen.

The dust came to earth reluctantly. Butch's wife pushed the children outside again, when the mean niggers had gone. Lady came down. A swing of the hinges, a bang as the door swung shut, and she barefooted softly over the porch steps to sit next to Martin in her long white night-dress and shawl. They would finish the tea.

Lady was fresh from sleep, washed and scoured before the day. Thick, black hair fell down her back, her breasts swung heavily as she reached forward for her cup. She was going back to bed, she said, there was nothing to do in this heat except lie around in bed. The cotton was thin. They were there together every morning, warm, with nothing to do. Martin maintained a meticulous English politeness.

But the breasts were there, every morning, white, just inside the night-dress; and the long, slim legs, the cotton nipping between them. It was tempting; she knew it. They talked a lot, even, finally, about books. Then that died away.

He decided that it was time to leave. He was only waiting for Billy, he didn't want to get involved in domestic drama and he was tired of the Kid. He mentioned it to Franco.

'I don't like being pinned down', Franco grumbled, 'and there isn't too much room at the apartment.'

'Are you going to stay around here?'

'Yep. Anywhere else is the same. Do you want to work next week?'

'What is it?'

'It's a bitch. It's laying a concrete floor. But the money's good. It takes your mind off everything.'

Franco pulled open the door to the bar and was greeted. Drinks emanated quietly and cheaply from the student cellist who served lunchtimes. The bar had the atmosphere of a lonely pool-hall; dark, cold, a central island lit up, stools around it.

In the middle of this island, Franco played guitar or piano three evenings a week to drunks and a hard core of a dozen people who liked his music. It was better than the last place. Franco didn't have to change his shirt.

They talked each other into laying the floor; they had a four-day holiday paddling in concrete; Franco did an impeccable job on the final glazing, which pleased him. They were duly asked if they wished to graduate from the garage to the porch. Franco hemmed and hawed, the wages went up; Martin knew that Franco would refuse the job so he told the boss that they had other work lined up.

'Hey, that's right,' Franco nodded, 'I forgot about that. Sorry we can't help you out.'

They walked off with two hundred dollars apiece. There was no point in being exasperated with Franco. He wasn't carelessly lazy, he wasn't chasing a good time. It just seemed that Franco had flipped a switch and turned himself off. Martin wasn't even sure if he was brooding.

'Do you ever want to get out of America?'

'Why?' He pondered and didn't give an answer. A little vacant; and yet he seemed solid enough. He was utterly sane, he missed nothing in people, he chopped out a good line in wit when he felt like it.

'Did you ever paint?' He seemed to have that sensibility; impressions went straight into him without meeting any breakwater.

'No. I used to mess around with it before I played music.'

Franco had asked Martin about New York and Billy. Martin hadn't told him very much. He promised himself never to introduce the two – they would clash and he would have to be disloyal one way or the other.

Martin awoke one morning, reached for a cigarette and smoked it; he stared at the ceiling, following a crack along to the wall. He called Trenton.

'Oh, you called ... ' Donna said.

'What do you mean?'

'I called Sunny's place for a week.'

'I'm still here.'

'The last time I called, she said you'd left. She thought you'd gone back to England.'

'What?'

'That's good we managed to contact. I'm doing nothing for a while, why don't you come down here? I've got a small apartment.'

'When were you thinking?'

'What's wrong with tonight?'

'Nothing. Do I get a train?'

'Yes. Take a cab from the station.' She gave him the address.

That wasn't difficult, Martin thought, that was easy. He wandered into the bathroom and smiled at himself in the mirror. He packed and left a note of thanks.

Trenton station was more concrete. Those who came off the train moved away from the station quickly. It was eight-thirty in the evening; Martin thought that he would walk some of the way. He walked out into the street, took one look at Trenton and hailed a cab. Trenton was how he imagined Dresden in 1946. It didn't seem to need people; it needed just a bit more destruction.

The cab-driver was bullet-proofed and kept his engine running. Martin looked over his shoulder as he pushed the bell. Donna came down to the door, fumbling with her bag.

'Hi.' She gave him a quick kiss.

'I'll get my case out of the cab; I wasn't sure if this was the right place.'

'I'll pay the cab; just come *with* me,' she insisted. She locked the door behind them and came out in bare feet. She took his arm. 'How are you?'

'Very well,' he answered.

She put his arm round her waist, they walked to the cab. He paid. The driver wound the window down, took the money and drove off without saying a word. Martin kissed the top of her head. 'This is a friendly area.' She took his arm again.

'It's all right,' she said, 'as long as you're careful. Anyway, it's good to see you.' Standing on the doorstep, she looked back and smiled at him with the suitcase. 'I thought you'd come.'

'I wasn't that obvious, was I?' He remembered the way he had looked at her as she sat in the lilac dress. And Lady's reaction.

'No. But *I* was.' She grinned.

Donna went up the stairs ahead of him. There were a lot of

218

stairs; she must have felt him looking at her because she kept turning round. She spoke in a commentary as they climbed. 'It's a small house, divided into apartments. My parents own it. I've separated off the top floor to live in.'

The door was double-locked and the stairway was badly lit. She had a hard time finding the keys. They were right on top of each other in the gloom. She swore with irritation. She managed to get the door open. She was annoyed and embarrassed, spending a lot of time replacing the keys in her bag, trying to shut the bag, being lumbered with it.

'Are all these locks necessary?' Martin asked tactlessly as they stood in the hallway.

'If you're a girl living alone they are. It's the way of life here.' She slammed the door behind them. Martin touched her shoulder.

'It's good to be here, Donna.'

She leaned back in his arms and rested a moment. 'Being a girl living alone in this part of the town is just scary. I get scared. I don't know why. Nothing's ever happened. Whenever I see anyone, they always tell me that I should be scared. So I am.' She was resigned. '*I* couldn't even get the door open and I had the keys ... ' She smiled back over her shoulder. 'Maybe now you're here I won't be so neurotic.'

She freed herself from him and walked into a room, hurling the bag on to a couch. 'I'll give you a set of keys. I'll be here for the next three days, after that I have to work daytimes.'

'Right.' He wondered at the speed of the arrangement and her trust. She stood seriously in the centre of the room and lectured him, one hand on a hip, involving herself in explaining the intricacies of the air-conditioner. Martin watched from near the door. He couldn't understand what all this was about, since he gathered that the machine didn't work; she was explaining it too beautifully for anything other than her gestures to hold his attention. He was fascinated by her. She grew aware of it, and wet her finger to rub a smudge off her knee. She continued with a pose, her body more tense. ' ... o-kay ... so that's this room ... it's always hot ... ' she put a finger on her bottom lip. 'I think I'll get the air-conditioner fixed this week, while I've got the time off work.' She considered him, looked straight at him.

'That seems a good idea.' Martin hurried out with it. 'Don't you think?' he asked as she looked. 'I'm not an expert on air-conditioners.' She stuck her hip out at him and laughed.

She showed him round the apartment. He followed clumsily. Donna was very official; he knew that by now she was teasing him but her control was impressive. It was incidental that there were two rooms, a bedroom and a sitting-room with a cooking area; also a shower cabinet.

At the end of the tour, she sat on the couch; Martin waited about three feet away. He talked about something; she interrupted him. 'What do you think of the apartment?'

'I'll take it.'

She smiled. 'I'm going to move soon, into a bigger apartment. You could take this one. My parents will need the rent money but they won't hassle you for it until you find a job. I was hoping that you would come with me though.'

This planning was way over Martin's head; he was taken aback by the speed and the insecurity. He fiddled with a toe of hers, half picking at the nail. The skin on her leg was tight and brown and the shorts folded over at the top of her thigh. Everything was fast. He couldn't get enough into her, get her legs out of the way enough. He came much too quickly for her.

She put her head on her elbow and waited. Martin stirred restlessly. After all the deliberate tension, it was badly concluded. She felt between her thighs, she noticed the semen on the couch.

'I'll go and wipe off.'

She got up and went, a small body quickly into the shower. Martin followed and sought a flannel. She wiped herself thoroughly and neutrally, wiped him with affection. They made love in the bedroom, slower this time.

Later, she stretched, showered and put on a white dress. She got together some food; he went through to the other room when she called. He ate naked; they didn't say much and listened to a record, smoking after the meal, she lying across him under his arm, half-asleep. When the record ended, she got up to change it.

A female folksinger protested, with aggressive words camouflaging trite chords. Donna grew restless. She moved his arm again and chose another record. On the way back, she opened the window and let a sleek black and white cat move into the room.

'I don't know if I should let her out,' Donna frowned.

'Why not?'

'She might get lost or go out into the road.'

'Cats aren't stupid. She won't want to be shut up,' he said. Donna lay back with her head on his chest and curled her legs up, the dress rucked around her thighs. He put his feet on the table and felt rich; he considered the domain. 'You know, I think you've got the most beautiful legs I've ever seen.'

'You think so?'

'Yes.'

She stretched the right leg out; she laid both of them down along the couch and turned on to her stomach to look at him. She smiled and yawned. He asked her not to take off the dress when they made it again.

In the morning, the dress was creased up around her shoulders and she lay asleep with her back towards him. The sun came through the window over the bed; it was already hot. The warm, animal smell whispered from both their bodies, Donna with her haunches tucked in against his groin. He aroused into consciousness against the crack of her, but didn't want to disturb her sleep. She shifted uncomfortably with the dress and struggled to turn over. He unbuttoned it. She murmured, she opened her eyes for a look, and snuggled in on his arm. She slept again. His chin ran along the top of her head.

He looked at the wall before him, his eyes fell down her back. She was perspiring slightly. Her skin was deep brown, not a bone showed, she was as flexible as an inner tube. She had one foot bent back. It was white on the sole, the skin hard from going without shoes, there were three fine lines on her heel. The rest of her skin was like the surface of a deep and very calm lake of varnish.

She was waking. Her mouth was dry. She swallowed quickly three or four times. She brought her hand up and coughed in at his chest, drawing her legs up. She rolled away on to her back, surrendering herself to several deep coughs and took a final one to make sure. She came back to Martin's arm, her small form tucked in against him. She murmured, glad not to go to work, glad of time and freedom, laziness. Her eyes toyed with a doze.

Martin had a mouthful of light-brown hair, sweet-smelling but still a mouthful; he pushed his chin over the top of her head. He dried the sweat off the pads of his fingers on to the sheet; she moved with the muscles of his arm. He shifted his hips to let her know that he wasn't going to sink into sleep again. The side of her mouth crept round her cheek in a smile, her fingers closed and squeezed.

Her body was waking, not moving as yet but Martin could see the awareness pouring into her skin. Her legs stirred. His hand went between her thighs; she closed her legs tight on it and trapped it, her fingers tightened and relaxed on him.

In a moment of extraordinary poise, she lifted her left leg straight as a slim arrow to point in the air. She held it rigid, the hollow in her hip, the foot in a perfect dancer's line, the pressure on his wrist gone. Stasis. Then the position was dissolved. Like a tensed girder with its own mass and momentum, the leg swung across his body and over his thigh, it bent and wound under him. She rolled him over and lowered herself slowly down on him. She wasn't very wet. She winced as she rested down on her pelvis.

She leaned forward and took her breath, gingerly lifting her hands off his hips. Her breath wavered its way out. He kissed her hand, it being close. She eased up and kissed him on the lips, legs shuffling along the sides of his waist; her arms cradled his head as they held the kiss. Her eyes closed. The tips of their tongues touched hesitantly. They circled. There was the rough on the top of the tongue and the fleshy underbelly. The corners of the lips, what part of the lips had a small wrinkle, a pinhead of dry skin.

Afterwards, they lay straggled over the bed. It was too hot to touch. Martin wiped channels of sweat from her skin. They were oblivious to most things for a while, then, out of the blue, Donna said, 'My breasts are too small', seemingly to the ceiling. The remark meandered over to Martin.

'What?' He traced a line across her diaphragm.

'They are; aren't they?'

'They're not large; they're lovely,' he said.

'Do you think so?'

'Yes.'

She flopped her head over towards him, tapped his shoulder. 'Don't you think it's too hot in here?'

'Is it always like this?'

'It is in summer. Unless you're at the ocean, it's always hot.

222

There's never any wind. The best thing to do is to stay in the shower.'

She sat on the edge of the bed for a moment, running her hands down her body, and she wandered light-headedly out of the door to the shower cabinet. She came back with the towel, half-dried herself, stood abstracted with her back to him. She looked like a waif. Martin kissed her shoulder on the way to the shower, she smiled too quickly. He soaked under the water; hot, cold, hot, cold.

She was still standing with the towel over her shoulder, a small naked body, pensive. She had pulled out the drawers that contained her clothes, and put them on the floor. The wardrobe doors were open. She had a large number of clothes.

'What are you going to wear?' She handed him the towel.

'Why do we have to wear anything?'

'So you won't get tired of seeing me naked.'

'It's too hot for clothes. Donna, you're very beautiful.'

She drifted round her apartment, smoking. She dug out a photograph album; they lay on the couch and flipped through it. Through her Teenage Princess days, her Miss New Jersey days, her Playboy Bunny days. She didn't photograph particularly well – only when she was caught off her guard, otherwise she had trouble with her smile. The best object shots were taken low down, the viewer travelling up her legs, which were unimpeachable in any setting. Her body hadn't changed in a dozen years. She had refused to go into pornography: 'They asked me to do it as though I was fifteen. Is that a thing with men?'

'Sometimes. It's not a fantasy of mine. I always think of the kind of nonsense you'd have to talk about with girls of fifteen.'

She laughed.

'What did you talk about when you were fifteen?' he asked.

'Men.'

'So who wants to talk about men? Anyway, I don't like that self-consciousness which fifteen-year-olds have with their bodies.'

She frowned. 'You don't think I use my body self-consciously?'

'Only when you want something.' They both laughed. 'You use it with a sense of purpose.'

'Is that bad?'

'Why should it be?'

Donna turned a page rather suddenly, and Martin wasn't quick enough to see the photo. He turned back. She was dressed up in a short skirt and black stockings, naked from the waist upwards except for a long bib which hung conveniently away from her to give the consumer a morsel of nipple. She was standing near a kitchen cooker, holding a saucepan and smiling at the camera. Martin chuckled; he found it hard to believe. Donna moved over and sat firmly at the other end of the couch. She read. Martin turned the pages of the album. She was bent over in the black Playboy outfit, the breasts built up, the lovely legs; or in a bathing suit with a sash from shoulder to thigh, one leg pushed forward.

She glanced across at him every now and then, smoked cigarette after cigarette, poking the stubs into the ashtray, lighting another. There was no story behind any of the photos. She said nothing.

'Do you think they're good shots?' she asked.

'I don't know. They're stereotyped. You're attractive. It's strange.'

Martin closed the folder and pushed it on to the table away from him. He felt tired, and lay across her lap. She was still distant; she read herself to the end of a chapter. She closed the book. He kissed her and she stretched out beside him. He dozed.

He must have slept because when he next felt like moving it was late afternoon. Martin lay and felt hot. The cat crawled round; he stroked it and pushed it away, collecting the book that had absorbed Donna. He found an interesting chapter.

Half an hour later, when he had forgotten about her, there was a movement near the door and Donna was standing there quietly in a full-length silk evening dress, not blatantly diaphanous until she framed herself more fully in the doorway. It was a peaceful blue-green. She had lightly coloured her eyes in the same tone and matt silver pendants hung from her ears. Martin looked, incredulous. She came closer and bent down in front of him.

'Did you sleep well?'

'I'm not sure I'm awake.'

'No, don't touch.' She took his hand down. 'I'm going to fix up some dinner.'

She moved away, with the most objective grace. Martin felt dirty; he scratched his hair. He tried conversation but she always agreed with him and moved softly inside her own image, delicate wrists. The dress was superbly cut. When she knelt to pick up an ashtray, he caught sight of a thin silver chain round her ankle. He went to have a shower, unsure of how to cope with the evening. A clean sweatshirt?

When he returned, he saw that she had cleared the couch and that the table was laid with wine and fruit. She didn't notice him. She was quite grave, cutting up melons, licking at her finger. She smiled at him. They were being introduced over again.

He watched from just beside her. She slipped past him with a bowl of salad which she placed on the table. She surveyed professionally.

'Would you like some wine?' he asked.

'Yes. Would you pour it out?'

'Of course.'

The bottle chinked against the glasses. He passed her a glass.

'Would you like to eat?' she said.

'Yes, it looks good.'

It seemed like a joke – he wanted to laugh or applaud – it wasn't a joke.

She moved behind the table and sat on the couch. He sat beside her. They got through melons and salad, talking about very little and drinking to pass the silences. She started talking of her family and all the shit connected with the nothing she had had in the years of the body, and she was striving now, 'striving' being the one time her hand tightened round the wine-glass. She recovered very quickly, fetched raspberries and turned down the lights in the room. Martin wanted to listen. She poured out more wine, but couldn't recommence. She twisted a bracelet round her wrist and pulled at the chain on her ankle.

Wednesday was the last day of her vacation. She woke early and told him that she didn't want to do any reading. She warned him that she was entertaining a women's group in the evening. She wanted to be kissed. She wound her legs over his back. They make this melancholy love for hours. She was lithe and devoted. If she sensed Martin waning or becoming automatic, she would twist and curl down with her mouth at him;

225

playing gently with her tongue, jutting her tail up for him, pausing restlessly.

About four o'clock, they sprawled in the shower together, kissing in steam. She wanted to shave him. She did; holding his prick up like a thoughtful snake-charmer, shuffling around in the water. Then he shaved her; with baited breath, like a surgeon. Pushing his flooded hair out of his eyes, trying to get her thighs further apart, terrified of cutting her. She lay back in the shower, her eyes closed, her pelvis thrown up on his thigh, her labia dark and swollen. The result aroused them both, they sloshed around in the water; she had the energy.

They flopped out of the shower and dried on the carpet. Donna's skin was a wet gleaming brown. They both slept.

She shook him. It was late. She had a coffee for him and a sandwich, which he ate on the floor of the corridor. She dressed in the bedroom; she was everybody's innocence in a pair of jeans and a shirt. He told her. She was hurt, not very. She laughed at him and pushed him into getting ready. She hustled him with a bag of laundry and the car keys, because he wouldn't like the women's meeting and it was probably best he shouldn't be there. The women had to get to know each other, and if a man was there they would all be blocked. She fetched him another sandwich and shifted all trace of him into the bedroom. Martin watched in a blur and wondered where her energy came from.

She walked him efficiently down the stairs with the coffee cup; at the front door she was sorry for a minute. Martin wasn't. One thing he didn't think he could face was a room full of women. He felt liberated with the laundry. She kissed him and closed the door.

Martin didn't move an inch. He stood on the doorstep with the bag of laundry. He sank down in a fog of exhaustion. He dully considered a plant in the excuse for a garden.

A woman brisked round the corner from the street and asked him, 'Is this the encounter group?'

'Yes.' Martin nodded weakly.

'I said is this the encounter group for women, here?'

'I said yes, the apartment at the top.'

Martin hauled himself to his feet. She backed away and opened her handbag. 'Young man, I've got a gas rape-evader and an alarm right here.' Martin ignored her and pushed the

226

bell for Donna. He heard the feet running downstairs, the door opened.

'What's wrong?' She looked at him. Martin grinned facetiously.

'This lady's got a gas rape-evader and an alarm. Maybe we can trade those grenades we keep in the freezer.'

Donna glared at him. She spoke to the woman. 'Hi, I'm Donna ... come on in.' They went into the house, Donna shut the door.

Martin found her car and after picking his way through the massive bunch of keys, he got the right one and sat inside. He looked through the window. He hadn't been out of the apartment for three days. There was the same heavy, humid airlessness in the street.

He would have to adjust the driving seat. He opened the car door to look for the lever. He noticed a tree some yards down the road. It looked plastic; he went to check it. It wasn't plastic but it wasn't tree as he knew it. He supposed that the climate was to blame. He went back to the car, sweating already.

He drove off, found a shop full of washing machines and got back inside two hours. He let himself in at the door. There was some fierce self-indulgence going down in the sitting-room. Everyone was trying to get a problem in edgeways.

He lay on the bed. Donna came through. 'We won't be long, darling.'

'I don't mind,' he said. She went to discuss, he to sleep. When he half woke up, Donna was naked and trying to get him out of his clothes. He fell asleep again.

She woke him at seven, lying on top of him, kissing his neck around from ear to ear. She was going to work in an hour, she was unhappy at leaving. They made love.

He lay on his front like a starfish, one arm bent under his face, while she showered. When she came back in, she clambered along the bed on all fours, growled at him and kissed him long and slowly. She slid off the bed and dressed in a short blue skirt and blouse; he watched her standing in front of the mirror. She was looking professionally at her eyes, rubbing a colour on the eyelids. She was worried that he didn't say anything; she adjusted her blouse, pulled at her skirt.

'You look fine.' Martin rolled on to his back.

'Uh-huh,' she shook her head. She pulled off the blouse, left it lying on the floor, and took a T-shirt out of the drawer. She stood in front of the mirror again.

'What time is it?'

'It's eight-fifteen.'

'I'm going to be late.' She rushed for her bag, balanced on one leg at a time while she struggled with her shoes. She kissed him quickly and was gone. Martin heard the car outside.

He flopped irritably in the heat, the air was heavy and didn't move. He flung limbs in various positions, trying to find an inch of sheet that was still cool. He gave up and took a shower, dried himself and felt the heat advancing again. He doused himself with water and moved about the apartment dripping.

There was three days' living to put into some kind of order. Dresses, jeans, pants, shirts scattered round the bedroom. Half the wardrobe had been worn for five minutes and discarded. The bedroom was alive without her. Martin collected armfuls of clothes and dumped them on the bed. Some of the dresses and shirts jogged his memory as if he had seen them years ago; and yet they represented maybe half an hour, cornered somewhere in the last three days. He pulled out the silk dress, a green T-shirt, the lilac dress; he folded them away. They were all well-made, well-fitting. Skirts and dresses all very short, remembering her legs. T-shirts small enough for a kid of twelve. She didn't own a bra. He stepped back to look at the hanging clothes. Sexy. He laughed. One of the last pieces of clothing was the crumpled pair of shorts that she had squeezed out of the first evening, the evening he had arrived. He picked them up. They were virtually weightless. She had worn no underclothes, he recalled with nostalgia. Three days.

He lobbed the shorts into a drawer, and started on last night's dishes, finishing about noon. The cat hung around his legs. He put his head under the shower, shook most of the water off but relied on his hair to irrigate his back underneath his shirt. He dressed, picked up the twenty bucks she had left him, locked all the doors and was out on the street.

His shirt stuck to his back. You could chew on the air. He thought of returning upstairs but shook himself out of it.

He walked light-headed in a slob brute amble, his mind clogged by the humidity. He walked under the trees towards the corner of the block. Running parallel to him on his left was a four-lane highway, hidden by shrubs. This was a natural boundary; when he reached the end of the block, he turned right, away from it. The street in front of him led to a cross-roads. Martin stopped to consider; it was definitely a black area. A gang of young kids looked at him, two thin teenagers in sunglasses peeled from the wall they were leaning on, no-ticed him and behaved as if they hadn't noticed him. Someone under a car kept an eye on him.

What with the heat, he felt three-quarters of the way to the grave anyway, so he kept going. It took his mind off his sweat-ing.

Everybody in the street knew he was there. After a hundred yards he had got over his unease and looked around at the houses. The women were inside. Young fathers or old sons leaned on porch railings not noticing him. Once or twice he nodded at eyes that accidentally crossed his own; there was no reaction. The only feedback was from an out of town pimp with New York plates on a pink Chevrolet with heart-shaped windows. He was leaning against it, immaculately dressed, picking his teeth with a silver toothpick; two girls in the back of the car. He grinned scornfully as Martin approached along the pavement. 'Nice car,' said Martin, without stopping. Apart from that, the street was full of black disdain fifty yards each side of the white intruder.

He reached the crossroads and waited for the lights to change. Large cars halted and revved on their lines; Martin took a couple of steps into the road. A green Impala jumped forward up against his legs. Two blacks inside regarded his next move, revving the engine. Martin put a hand out in query, the driver's window slid down.

'You doin' some damage, whiteboy?'

'I beg your pardon.' The driver turned and laughed at his sprawled passenger. The window slid up. Martin made the other side of the road before the lights changed.

He was coming to a typical downtown shopping area, not busy in the heat of the day. Blacks hung around against the walls, talking in groups. All the shop windows had wire-grid protection. One or two older blacks were drinking out of bot-tles in brown paper bags. Two police squad-cars were pulled into the kerb, and one was parked further up the road on the forecourt of the liquor store. The cops were sitting inside, hats tilted back, shifting and sweating with heat and boredom.

Each time a black woman came out of a shop, her escort would flop forward, walk with her to another shop, let her go in and lean back against the new wall, exchanging a few words with whoever else happened to be waiting there.

The heat had everyone sullen and on edge. Martin bought food, beer and fruit and headed home up the black avenue. He took the stairs in slow time, dumped the beer in the freezer and got rid of his clothes.

Donna returned at six-thirty. Martin heard the key in the lock, and the door open and close. She didn't come into the sitting-room; he looked for her in the corridor. She was leaning back against the door with her eyes closed and her hands behind her on the door where she had pushed it shut. She stayed like that when he kissed her. She accepted it passively; she didn't want to end it, she invited him to stay. She rubbed her leg against his, and closed her eyes again, saying nothing until she had kicked off her shoes.

'I'm glad you're here,' she said in his ear. 'I've been thinking about you in the car. Am I wet?' She put her arms round his neck.

'Yes.'

She lay on the bed after she had undressed. They fucked brutishly like the first evening.

'Do you love me?' she asked afterwards.

'No.' Honestly. Stupidly.

'So it's just my body.'

'No.' Martin got off the bed and lit one of her cigarettes. He walked over to the writing-desk.

'Are you gay?'

'I don't think so.'

'You don't have to worry about it.'

'I'm not worrying about it; I'm not worrying about anything.'

'You like making love with me,' she went on.

'We both do, don't we?'

She reached for the pillow and lay on top of it, hugging it with her head turned away. 'Do you think I'm intelligent?'

'Yes.'

'Not from those pictures you wouldn't.'

'I didn't ask to see them.'

'I'm not very intelligent; I know I'm not very intelligent. I'm just getting started and I'm going to stick with it.'

He held her and kissed her.

'What does that mean?' she asked.

'It's just some love, and admiration.'

'Do you think you're a male chauvinist?' She took the cigarette from him.

'It's not for me to say, is it?'

'But you don't think about it.'

'Not really.'

She inhaled; she looked for somewhere to flick the ash. Martin fetched an ashtray.

'Thank you.' She kept looking at him; it was tense. 'Do you want to say something?'

'I made up some food for us and I fed the cat.'

Donna smiled. 'What else did you do?'

'Lay around and cooked. I went out. Do you want a beer?'

'Can you get me one?'

He fetched the cold beer from the freezer. The first can was shaken up and spattered over them. She retrieved her T-shirt from the floor and wiped him down.

'It's strange without any hair,' she said.

'It's a bit naked.' He sipped the beer; she lay back again, obviously. 'I can't. Not so soon, Donna.'

She sat up, hunched forward in thought. Without looking up she said: 'I've never had an orgasm.' The room seemed very large and each word ran for a corner. 'I haven't.' Then she looked at him.

'Is that my fault?' he asked guiltily.

'No. Not with you. I don't mean with you.' She squeezed his hand. 'I mean never. Never.'

'It must be important to you.'

'It doesn't matter.'

'Maybe it does.'

'Not that much.'

He wondered.

'I love every moment of it; I do!' she insisted. 'I never get tired or bored. Do you get tired?'

'Why do you think I sleep so much?'

'You shut yourself off; I thought you got bored with me.'

'You're joking ... '

'You don't?'

'Not at all.' He looked at her in consternation.

'I'll get washed up then we can eat.' She scrambled off the bed with the can of beer, disappeared through the door. The shower started running. She poked her head back into the bedroom.

'Don't worry,' she said.

'I'm not.'

'I took tomorrow off from the shop. They don't need me, so I'm free until Monday.' She went, smiling.

'Okay, that's fine.' It occurred to Martin that they were going to stick with this problem of orgasm.

They did. Donna was tireless that night and the following day. It was a long haul, stupidly misdirected. She hung on him. On Saturday morning when she reached for him, he recoiled and turned over. They shared a sense of emptiness. He said: 'Let's go out.' She asked: 'What do you want to do?' He had no idea.

They went for a drive around the ugliest parts of the world, driving without saying much, driving nowhere indifferently. They came back to the apartment. Martin half-heartedly tinkered with her. He took a book into the sitting-room. Donna prowled restlessly with a cigarette.

In the evening they got dressed and went to a bar. Martin found himself talking to another girl, Donna watched angrily. They argued in the car; the night strained at the seams. In the morning they started to make love but they had no enthusiasm and broke away. They said nothing. Donna lay on her stomach. Martin passed a finger over her skin. She was completely unmarked. She had a perfectly even body, tanned from neck to toe, hairless, pliant, small; her shoulders melted into her back into her waist into her thighs with the same tight, smooth skin. Skin like a baby, body like a panther, with a glisten of sweat. If he didn't open his eyes, it was hard to tell which part of her his finger was travelling over. It was an unreal, perfect body. There was no reply to it. It.

Monday, after she had gone to work, he phoned Franco. There was no answer.

Martin tried to write. At one end of the bedroom was a small alcove. She had a bureau. Her papers were arranged. He had told her that he was writing something, so she arranged her papers to give him space. She wanted to write. She would be a better writer than he ever would. She thought that it was important to write. Martin was horrified – he had invented writing as an excuse to get away from her. She understood that he wanted to write and she respected this.

It was impossible. He resented it. He sat with images of her: a varnished deck, the curve of a bowl. Her body. He had no plot, no character. He wondered if he would have to take up poetry, and how Billy would react to that. He called the apartment and left his number with Donald.

The cat was on heat. She stood on his lap. Purring. Her tail swishing from side to side. The small vagina was moist and anguished. She strutted it up before him. Martin hurled her away, time after time; until, ignoring Donna's request, he shut her out of the window.

Donna came back from work tired; she lay sleek after her shower, coiled up on him. They made love, they ate, they slept. She went to work again.

They accepted each other silently. She had very few friends whom she trusted, so they didn't go out. She was nervous when she came back from work and each night they tried a frantic cure-all as soon as she came through the door.

They began to try to avoid each other. Once, when they headed for the shower at the same time, they both apologised and were unable to make a joke out of it. Sometimes they made love violently but more often they picked at each other with all the enthusiasm of two dishonest car mechanics.

On the following Sunday evening, she knelt beside the bed and told him that they would soon be moving into the new apartment together. He could see no point in it any longer. While he was tidying up on Monday morning, Billy called. Martin quickly packed his belongings and left. He found it impossible even to write a note; he put: 'I love you. I'm sorry.'

The sealed limousine left immediately. Billy had the energy to chainsmoke, Martin to stare out of the window at through-ways and bridges.

'We're going to see Diane,' Billy murmured. 'She has a home for alcoholics in New York State. We were once lovers, but you don't want to know any of that. We have two rooms. You have to get to know these people.' He stated this in a tired fashion, as if he, not having the stamina, wanted Martin to carry them through.

Martin looked across at Billy. It didn't appear that he was acting. Billy looked away from him out of the window. Martin felt love for him, of one husk for another. All this love knocking around, on its last legs.

'How's it been?' Martin asked.

'It's been interesting. Donald sends his regards. And you?'

'I met a nymphomaniac.' A huge sick pain swung through Martin, of feeling for her and shock at his own callousness.

'Congratulations,' said Billy, viciously.

They looked out of their respective windows.

PART
4

Groups of One

22

Poor old Farm. This was the first time that I had returned in spring, when it had dragged itself through the winter. Coming upon it from the outside, waterlogged and overgrown, last year's vegetation splayed limply. A half-dead, sombre green atmosphere, rubbed in mottled blacks and yellows. The house was a chilly, damp pumice colour. I think that I might easily have decided to sell. But places only die if you let them. I hauled the Farm back up out of winter.

The bedroom furniture was heavy with taste and memories; I had spent years being depressed in that room – queen spider going backwards and forwards along her web of late-night self-interrogation, rushing to spin over the weak points in herself. How archaic she was.

It would be wonderful simply to announce that you were selling your bedroom, to show people round and have them make offers, or to auction the whole set-piece as an entity, inclusive of the nightgown laid across the comforter and the set of lingerie over the rug. I would be open to interpretation, no doubt flattered, and would go to bed with the purchaser as a kind of Green Shield stamp. Provided of course that he was Buffalo Bill. Or anyone who had no intention of over-staying the distance and who could cart all this crap off with him into the sunrise. Men should be there to remove your love from you, not to install themselves like a pile of sand sliding off the back of a dump truck.

I bought a brass bed. It stands to one side of the room, remarkable for the number of clothes I can hang over the rail at the end and for the way that it dignifies mess. It swings the balance back from the heavy-curtained windows on the other side of the room.

We held a garage-sale party one weekend when we didn't have anyone staying. My old bedroom stuff went with the hoarded odds and ends from the barn, and the childish souvenirs which the boys had dumped before going up to Montreal.

After the garage-sale, I started to get invitations. To lunches, dinners and parties. I went to all of them without deliberation or distinction. I found myself accosted by a series of anxious, well-intentioned men, in kitchens or in driveways, advising me that we had a lot in common. I wasn't attracted to any of them. I suppose that I was more degraded by the attitudes of the women. One wife confided to me that a woman really only needed a man to protect her from other men. We laughed. It didn't take contact lenses to see that she was unfaithful and particularly disloyal to her own husband. I understood that in the property market I had a high commodity status.

The invitations came and I kept going out. When I was being escorted around someone's far-too-picturesque country home I saw the perfect dresser, junking itself loftily in an outhouse. A gaunt, walnut H; a mirror supported by two glass-doored cabinets over a marble-topped dressing table. We called it a dresser but there was no convincing name for it; I fell in love with a marvel of stuffy absurdity which I imagined standing against my bedroom wall.

Time and time again I return to my deserted room in a film of satisfaction, enjoying its strangeness. I light a fire, I bathe and I pad naked across the bare floorboards. I like walking into the room from the bathroom; the arranged bathroom with its oils and cosmetics, and the knotted planks of my bedroom, an armchair from downstairs in front of the fire, the coolly flickering formality of the brass bedstead. I know exactly that the dresser will have one hairbrush on the marble top, letters in the right-side glass cabinet.

I have a strange freedom. I would say that it was a lack of self-consciousness, if it wasn't simultaneously exactly the opposite. It is as though I am the most trivial person; I have a thousand mirror fragments of myself smiling in irony and yet I am invulnerable. I could stick my two fingers up my god-head's nose, and laugh.

There were no animals on the Farm, as far as Martin could see; just guests. Diane greeted them all-knowingly, all-warmly. Martin didn't trust it. On their way into the house, she seemed to be sure of Billy. It didn't matter much to Martin although he found it embarrassing. The path was dusty, with rock pushing through, and they walked up some steps to the door. Martin was behind them, she went first, Billy was half with her. She didn't give herself away to him as she did to the few other guests they passed. Billy talked about 'we', Martin and himself; Martin hung back. Why were they here? And supposed to be getting along fine.

'Yes.' Martin realised that he was standing with his hands behind his back, like the Duke of Kent, saying yes and wishing that they'd all carry on without him.

Lost a lot of weight, some kind of fierce artificiality about her.

Billy wanted a time when he could just put a hand on her shoulder and tell her that he loved her. It seemed as though every time he came back here, it was the same thing – that he'd wasted a lot of time and she had changed. Coming close again was a matter of chance. They were still no further than chance.

He is more attractive now, something inside him has given way; something in his life that he wants to be shrewd about but he won't put his finger on. I like this shyness.

Billy unpacks his bag and talks about the Farm. I tell him about our spring cleaning after I had finished in Boston. He starts immediately to fill that time with Los Angeles and Linda.

I set him in a chair in the office and set myself to listen to him. He rambles. I watch his confusion, the bursts of laughter and the sudden silences, the heavy clamp across his forehead as he strives for a contact which he doesn't really want.

I resent him. I have the infuriating feeling of being back exactly where I was three years ago, a pointlessly emotional woman, angry with herself, angry with the apparent deception practised so intently by everyone else, wanting attention, playing for it.

But Billy and I have always argued and got on each other's nerves. After dinner he talks to a guest, a man in his fifties, and they seem to get along. I feel as though I am losing control, hearing Billy talk about his phoney alcoholic problems. He is like the child who lived down the road from the house where I was raised; this child did everything and told me the most wonderful lies about his adventures and the people he met. At that age of seven, I was sure that I could never do anything as extraordinary. Billy is lying, Billy is charming and I want him to myself in a form of panic.

I don't really want him to follow me. I'd rather that he found my room on his own, that he simply put his head round the door and be struck by the difference.

'It's changed,' he says of my bedroom.
I list with agreement.

Her gestures have changed. She doesn't seem to have any gestures, not with her hands. I haven't seen the old quizzical irony
along the top of her eyes. She laughs very quickly and it de-
prives other people. She has destroyed her bedroom, I don't
know what to make of such a statement; it's become the room
of a thinker, very anchored, severe. Boston influence.

There is a huge difference between us, between everybody,
a terrible distance, cold; fuck the letter from her, carrying it
around.

She has that same leg bent forward, toe touching the floor,
foot flat against the wall. Like a kid thrown out of the school-
room.

After dinner on the third evening, Billy took the chair and
introduced himself as James Tyrone Junior, raised on the out-
skirts of the city, a chronic drinker and a pitiless whoremonger,
hating himself and his poison.

I glared at him, but I let him continue. We were so far apart,
we had had nothing to say to each other, we might as well
perform to each other. All of this I could see, and the stupidity
and the childishness, our stamping round in circles, our re-
fusals. Maybe it was up to us, finally, just to perform. I think
that it was the only thing he wanted to do, or that was worth
doing. He had very little contact with me, even Martin ... I
suppose that Martin and I did more together than either of us
did with Billy, although we were both aware of him.

I thought that Billy was showing off. There was *that*. Never
mind his blustering through the faults in his story. And then it
struck me that Billy skirted in a stark and terrifying way
around the figure of his own mother. At such moments his
concentration went and he was petrified before his own eva-
siveness, and we all sat desperate for him to rescue us. When
he was through, and there was that gaping silence, it was
obvious that he himself had attained no relief from the experience. He was mistrusted by the group; his problem wasn't
alcoholic, his problem was stuck to him.

I would, naturally, have gone to him when he came offstage;
he would have that need. But I had a duty to the group and if

Billy chose to play with the group then it was up to him to carry through his own responsibilities. I forced myself to ignore him. I plucked his story and tried to extract the experiences that could be held in common by the group. I lied. I knew that I was lying because the body of my feeling fell towards Billy. It depressed me. That there was more conviction in make-believe than there was in simplicity; and in what I was doing there was no conviction at all. Once I had got the group talking amongst themselves I could no longer sit in that room with my own despondency. I looked in on the kitchen and told Pam that I was going to bed. Upstairs I lay on the floor with my legs drawn up, my head resting on two books. I will not lose my freedom, I will not lose my freedom.

Billy didn't want to know if James Tyrone had been convincing. He realised immediately that Diane had retired upstairs and he went out into the night. Passing under trees – the sky pompous with lumps of cloud, a thin wind – Billy asked himself if he cared about anything or anyone. He ought to care; Linda, Donald, his family. They loomed up, these people.

So the hell what? He clawed at his face. He practised it, the clawing at the face, it was painless and could be effective, it could be used, it made no difference. He had never fought a part before. Searched, changed. Seized. Gone in crazy directions. He couldn't slip past this one.

Diane's light was out. Cold. Calm. Back inside. Along the dark hallway, and he stood outside the kitchen door.

' ... and Diane and Billy have been playing games for a long while.' Pam.

'Just leave them to get on with it.' Andy.

'It doesn't bug me if they do that, but I don't think it's right to carry it through in front of the other people here as though deceiving them just didn't matter. That's a big difference.'

Martin's 'I don't know him very well. Most of the time he acts anyway. I'm not sure if I know him at all.'

Martin played to them, with the attractive eyes, the mock confusion and the charming English accent, faithless to perfection.

The violence brandished Billy. He could have gone in there and said: We were lovers, you remember that? And why?

241

But the violence compacted into cold stone; it rested on Billy's gut and he lugged it off with him to bed. It was unlike Billy.

Most people were attracted to Diane, the clear green eyes with the flecks of white gold. She was warm and half-open, turning this warmth from person to person.

'She's very naked.' Pam sat opposite Martin, Andy had gone to bed. 'And yet she's very strong. It's a weird mixture.'

'Why doesn't she get married?'

'Why should she? She has ... a guy in Boston. And Billy. She *will* get married though, that's my guess.'

'To Billy?'

'Billy's not that type of guy. I don't know. She's very single-minded and Billy jumps around like a jack-rabbit. Like tonight. They haven't seen each other in a long time and she was really happy when he asked if you both could come up here. Then they act like it's the other person's fault that they haven't got it together. Maybe you should ask her.'

Billy was up and about early in the morning, draped in his depression. He wanted to find Diane but nobody had seen her, she was apparently in her room, perhaps lying in. No, this wasn't unusual, according to Pam. Pam had awoken with last night's anger intact; James Tyrone was in the doghouse.

Diane, at lunch, supported her. 'You're up here to take a vacation, Billy, so just relax.'

Billy tried. He had only the lightest touch on other people, he couldn't seem to grip them. It saddened him. They were real enough; he was in a dream. He felt like an invalid, swollen in some part of himself, needing surgery.

He called Linda a couple of times. The first time, there was obviously someone else in her apartment. Billy was strangely lifted by this call – they had a deliberately cheerful talk, they were sophisticates.

But the second call was damaging. They didn't have much to say. Billy didn't want to talk about his role – he was no longer capable of intellectualising it; it was a dull, confused feeling – and so he floundered into talking about their relationship. He found it hard to concentrate. Linda was devastatingly practical. Right down to her concern for his welfare. Her capability terrified him. He discovered that he was assuring himself that he was all right. She consigned him to Diane.

He didn't dispel her misconception. At one time, Billy would have insisted on her guilt, she wouldn't have got off the hook so easily; but he didn't trust himself.

I had known Billy since the Actors' Studio. I knew that he swung wildly between his exuberance and his bitterness. But I had never seen him so without faith. He walked, ate, was polite and kept himself to himself.

I saw him patrolling the road, he had twice approached the track leading down to the Farm and had turned back. When I went out to join him, he was suspicious. I wanted him to talk, to burst out in some anger. But he wouldn't. He spoke of his unfairness in relying on Linda. Without any apparent feeling, he even mentioned our affair. I looked for some plea in him but there was nothing, he wanted nothing. I wondered then if he was seriously ill; decaying people look back at the present from his kind of distance. Holding his hand was more my fear than my attempt to sympathise.

'Is it this part you're doing?'

'There's a lot in there that I recognise. O'Neill has a great love for Jamie; enormous compassion. I find it hard to balance that giving ... ' He looked for refuge in hopelessness.

'I didn't think that O'Neill liked Jamie very much.' I tried to budge him; I didn't know the plays that well.

'No ... no.' Billy shook his head. 'You have O'Neill, as Edmund, lying there on that damn couch. *Dying*. And he gives Jamie the line ... ' Billy searched. ' "Hell it" ... "you know I don't mean it." Something ... "Why shouldn't I be proud! Hell, it's purely selfish. You reflect credit on me. I've had more to do with bringing you up than anyone!" '

He looked away. It was unlike Billy not to need an audience. He said: 'Jamie doesn't even have to be right, you know? But there is the writer's love for Jamie. And O'Neill knows that he never turned round, right then when it happened, he never gave or admitted yes to his brother. Because they were a family of cowards.'

He stood rooted in self-disgust. I didn't know much about his family, he never talked about them. But I wouldn't have thought that he was being objective. I supposed that he was just testing me out again. I walked slightly ahead of him.

'So in the second play, he spends his whole time apologising, and by then Jamie needs apologising for.'

'I see. And is that the position you're putting yourself in?' I arranged some flowers which I had absent-mindedly picked from the side of the road.

'What are you on?' he demanded.

'Me? I'm not on anything.' It was one of those moments, with him, when I would have been happier with silence; but that was too much of a luxury.

'Has your relationship with Linda finished?'

'I think so. It's come up against a lot of dishonesty and a lot of changes which neither of us wants to get over together.'

'I'm sorry.'

'It's inevitable.'

'Why?'

'I don't know why.'

'That's not like you.'

'Diane, I've never known why anything; I've never stopped to think like that, not in my relationships.'

'When do you go into rehearsals?'

'In a couple of weeks.'

'You'll have people to play off. It'll be easier.'

'Yes,' he agreed vacantly.

We came across a clump of fern and I stopped to gather some. Billy walked on. It wasn't definite; I felt that he left part of himself trailing for me to follow, and he watched me closely as I straightened up and joined him.

'What is it?' I asked him, and I told him: 'You know, last year I wanted to have another child. Anyway, we didn't, or I didn't. The need went away, I just stopped wanting this child. I was surprised. It was against the fifteen-year plan. Almost everything went against the fifteen-year plan. In the end I dumped it and just put myself up for offer. I don't worry about it any more. You've never been any good at worrying; why start now?'

'I don't know.' Billy's eyes slipped to the ground. 'If I could find a reason, I'd tell you. I'd laugh and I'd go back to New York and forget about it.'

'Why don't you do that?'

'I don't have anything to give. I'm tired of being like that.'

'Why don't you come up here after Christmas for my birthday? I hate Christmas.'

Just to give him something beyond his present state. His face was pale and puffy.

'Sure. When is your birthday?'

'The fourth of January.'

'Okay. No serious play has that long a run. January is Martin's birthday too.'

'It is? That's a strange coincidence.' I smiled at him but he missed it.

'I don't know about coincidence. There's a kind of directness about everything which I don't know if I can accept. These years are flat, Diane. Flat dreams.'

'Flat plans too,' I said. His eyes strayed nervously over me, he grinned thinly.

'You didn't really want a baby, did you?'

'Yes, I did. I didn't find a father and I wouldn't have the child on my own.'

I put the flowers in a vase, and the vase in my bedroom, that particular created space. I didn't really believe his self-negation. He was a very straight man, he never tried to avoid anything except the responsibilities which people wanted him to carry, and he had a right to avoid those.

If there was one thing that made me angry it was the feeling Linda gave him that he had misused her for all these years, which I couldn't imagine to be true and which had cut him down. That made me angry. It was dishonest and destructive, a final spiteful peck at a wounded lover. So cruel.

Our evenings were spent apart, I walked the planks of my bedroom and Billy distracted himself with whatever feeling he could get from the guests, some optimism or the occasional strength. Only rarely, in the daytimes, did we talk, and I kept him to the subject of the plays. He was as ready as he could be, he would be grateful for a director. Instinctively, he had gone further than he might have done, walling himself into the character of Jamie Tyrone, taking his inheritance from the lonely, irretrievable mother.

Those around him he would touch only for reinforcement, and I started to wonder about Martin. He had no purpose in being here. He was held together by Billy's seriousness and his own admiration for Billy. He was being short-changed. I suggested to him that we escaped.

'I'd like to do *something*.' Martin was suspicious.

'*I'd* like to pick up a dresser I have waiting for me.'

'Yes, sure.' He was immediately deferential. And yet he was unwilling to join in, there was something tense and grudging in his acceptance.

'You'll be doing me a big favour, I don't know why I haven't been over there before instead of waiting for so long.'

'Did you want Billy to go with you?'

'He isn't really interested in that kind of thing.'

I called him at eight one morning, we drove over to the truck-hire garage and we didn't get on the road until eleven o'clock. I drove us up to Vermont in silence. I would have preferred him to drive, I would have enjoyed staring out of the window. But he didn't want to drive. I felt that I deserved an easier day. He didn't want lunch, just a sandwich while he sat in the driveway and dismantled the dresser into a dozen parts, and I sat in the house being sociable.

He was anxious to load the truck, he didn't want to sit around and didn't want a swim, didn't want anyone's interest in him; he asked if we could borrow some blankets. I made suggestions – how to protect the mirror, whether the drawers would be more secure if they were laid out rather than stacked, if the glass doors would be safer roped together, and he carefully rearranged the interior of the truck at each suggestion, with exaggerated formality.

It crossed my mind that he would break something deliberately, as a way out of his enclosure. I watched his every alienated movement. It became a ritual, and then a triumph, and involuntarily I put my arm around his shoulder when he had finished and the doors of the truck were closed. And my only other suggestion was that we head back, having delivered our gratitude and our apologies that we had to go because we had a lot to do.

Out of sight, along the road, I laughed. Martin smiled.

'That was a clean getaway,' he said, as though we had stolen the dresser.

'They didn't want it; we rescued it.'

'Oh, yes.'

He wasn't really sarcastic, he wanted me to know that he

hadn't been fooled, a truculent gloating which I didn't understand, along the lines of women getting things for free.

'Wouldn't you have liked to swim in their pool?'

'Not really.'

'We could turn back and arrive again, and unload the dresser and go swimming.'

He forced a laugh; that was better.

'You know ... ' he said, and he told me about a job he had once had for five days, in England, when he and a friend had answered a newspaper advertisement for sewage engineers, and they were supposed to construct two twenty-foot-deep circular pits, 'and we had these two JCBs, mechanical excavators, and we just dug ourselves twenty feet down from Monday to Friday until the arm of the digger couldn't reach over the top of the pit any longer. We didn't go back to work on the next Monday because there wasn't any way of getting the machines out of the pits.' He laughed, his eyes were bright with wonder. 'I don't know how they got them out.'

I laughed. I knew that he was inventing the story, but that didn't matter.

'I don't like rich people,' he said.

'Is that why you didn't want to use their pool?'

'Probably.'

'Tell me about yourself. I don't like rich people either.'

It took him about forty-five seconds to list his schools and his studies. 'It's all very normal,' he said.

'Much too normal to be true.'

'It *is* true. What do you mean?' He was unsure of me, I was prying.

'Well, when I was twenty-three I had decided that I didn't want to get married, and I was very ambitious; I wanted to change and open myself out to whatever experience I could believe in.'

Not true, I realised; I was concerned about who I was and how I could lose my concern. Strange how you pass on *hopeful* stereotypes to someone younger than yourself. And his response caught me by surprise.

'Had you met Billy then?'

'Yes. Why?'

'I just wondered.'

'That had nothing to do with it. It was what *I* wanted and what I went out to try, just to progress.'

'And you progressed in acting?'

'Through acting. It didn't matter to me if I was a successful actress although I wouldn't have wanted to be a failure.'

'And that's the same for Billy?'

'Billy may be different; I think he doesn't know any other way and for me there are any number of ways. Do you feel that?'

'Yes. But he has to make a living out of it ... '

That's how we talked: Martin was happier talking through Billy. Occasionally he would branch off to tell me about his past and his hopes. If he disagreed with Billy it came in a burst of severity, but he would always soften as though Billy was riding with us in the truck.

I suppose that I didn't have the heart to snap this format, but he was too intelligent to miss my amusement. And then I suddenly became very bored with talking about Billy; Martin, perhaps ashamed, retreated; and we drove in a stiff silence, limited by each other's presence. We were grateful when something clunked in the back of the truck.

I pulled over and Martin jumped out to check. It was a busy road and I worried that someone might crash into the back of us. 'I can't see anything,' he said at the window. 'It all looks the same. Nothing's broken. We'd have to unload it. This isn't a very good place to stop.' He looked at me to see what I thought. I wanted to unload it, to make sure, there didn't seem to be any point in slowly damaging the dresser. 'I think it's all right,' he said. 'We could go on until we find somewhere to have a better look. I'll bet you five dollars it's okay.' He sat in his seat and slammed the door hard, shaking the truck. There was no answering noise from the back. He accepted this as proof that nothing was wrong and I duly got us moving.

'Sorry,' he said after a while.

'We find it very difficult to be friends, I don't know why.'

'No. Do you mind if I smoke?'

'Not at all.'

He lit a cigarette, coughed quietly and swallowed. I didn't understand why we were so cold to each other, almost malevolent. He smoked very quickly while we were crawling along, and he looked nauseous.

'When I came back from Europe, I found that I couldn't stick American cigarettes.'

'It's just the first one. I feel poisoned and then I get used to

248

it.' He wiped the palms of his hands on his thighs. 'Like being married,' he hazarded.

I smiled, but I couldn't let it go. 'That's not what you believe, is it? Cynicism is a very thin disguise. It fits some people, but it doesn't fit you. Did your parents have an unhappy marriage?'

'No, they were very happy. You're alone,' he asked, 'aren't you?'

'Yes, and no; I don't think that's important.'

I remembered suddenly that when I first had Robby and John and was out for the evening I panicked at the thought that I might have left a cupboard door open and the boys might somehow lock themselves inside.

'I'd prefer to be on my own,' Martin said, so glumly that I laughed in sympathy. 'I'd have to change.'

'Would you like to drive?'

'Okay, yes.'

We pulled in at the side of a truck-stop diner. Martin untied the rope and we dragged everything out and put it back again. It was done suddenly, and done well, without our chattering to each other; we both stood in the back and passed the rope across after winding it around the hooks on our respective sides of the truck. Stopping to consider the arrangement I, I suppose, took his hand; and so when we turned, we turned inwards to each other, it was nothing when he put his arms round me other than that we were glad to have escaped words, and be relaxed.

I left him to shut up the back of the truck.

I don't like these diners, full or empty. This one was empty except for the server, and the yellow décor was overpowering. I was tired and I thought about John, stuck up in Montreal with Robby, I hoped that he would find someone to take care of him and that he wasn't drifting. Martin interrupted me, he asked me what I was thinking and I told him. I couldn't get him interested and I suppose I wasn't very concerned about John, I probably only worried when I wanted something to worry about. I went to the bathroom and when I came back Martin had paid and gone outside. He was sitting on the back flap of the truck. I chided us for our unnecessary devotion to the dresser. He said yes, and smiled, and didn't move. And then there was something between us, a jolt which I knew was ridiculous, sympathy and a desire for affection. I brushed the hair away from his ears, standing between his legs while he leaned forward and kissed my neck and breast.

'Can I see you naked?'

'Why?'

He mused, and then his head lifted. 'I don't know.' He held me away from him. He was trying to want me, rubbing his hands slowly up and down the backs of my legs, bending forward and kissing my stomach, undoing my shirt and jeans. I put my arms round his neck and held him, looking into the darkness of the truck, picking out the glass cabinets and the feel of his lips on my skin. He withdrew his hand and bumped his forehead, steadily, time after time, against my thigh. Until he stopped, and I stroked his back.

He cried; during the tears he said: 'It's something I want, isn't it?'

'You don't have to be embarrassed.'

'No. Don't tell Billy.'

'There's nothing to tell. Why Billy?'

I wanted him to talk it out but he wouldn't. He fastened my jeans. Pulling my stomach in; he must find the skin loose.

Should we clasp each other tightly, even embarrassed, before we sit in our two different seats, and I arrange my hair in the mirror, thinking how right I was not to wear a skirt; God knows why I should think that, confidentially, or why a boy shouldn't obviously be lost, or why I shouldn't be an executor of assurance. People have pulled me out of loneliness enough times, and I pretend to dislike them for it – much perhaps as Martin would feel.

Should I fight for Billy? Am I enough of a fighter?

'All right, let's go through it again. We arrived here at five, the two of you unloaded the dresser into the tool-room and I drove the truck back.'

'We put the dresser in there, and when you came home with the wood-preserver, we spread the dresser out and we treated the parts that had the wormholes.'

'And when you spread it out, did you see the marble?'

'I don't think so.'

'Martin?'

'I remember carrying it, but I don't remember seeing it. I

250

know that sounds strange. I just can't visualise it being in the tool-room.'

'We've looked through three times, and it isn't there. Do either of you *feel* that it's there?' They shook their heads. 'It *must* be there. It wasn't in the truck; I'm sure and I've checked with the rental office and he's certain. I trust him. So where the hell is it? It's heavy and it's big. Marble plaques don't just disappear. It's got to be here somewhere. Every second we're in that tool-room I just know that it's behind my back.'

'Yeah.' Andy was disenchanted.

'Martin?'

'Yes, it's got to be there. We didn't leave it at the house where we picked it up.'

'I've called them. That's definitely out.'

'So ... '

'I'm going out there for another look.'

'Diane, maybe we should let it ... '

Maybe we shouldn't. I went across the yard and turned the lights on in the tool-room. I expected to see the marble top leaning against the wall, so splendid that we'd missed it, so glaringly in the right place that we'd somehow ignored it. Damn it. I felt like crying with the frustration. *Why* had we been so late that I had to rush the truck back? *Why* hadn't I stayed with the boys? Had they broken it and they were too cowardly to say anything? Had they gotten stoned and dropped it? Yes, they had broken it. No, dammit, it was there! Where? Where? Everywhere. Underneath everything that we had moved backwards and forwards three times. Underneath the cabinets, underneath the chest, everything stinking of that wood preserver.

Andy's right. It's not here! But it is here, in here. I just have to happen upon it at the right time, turn my head and catch it.

'Did you find it?'

'No, Billy.' He looked around the room, standing with his arms akimbo.

'It'll show up.'

'But when? And how come we can't find it now? You see?'

'Sure.' Billy turned on his heel and went out. Screw you, darling. It's nobody else's problem, is it? He was replaced by Martin, who stood as still and as quiet as I did, glancing at me until I felt really angry at everyone's foolishness.

251

'There's another possibility,' he said.

'That it never existed?'

'That someone stole it out of the truck when we stopped at that diner.'

'Oh God, could they do that? I can't believe that.'

'It's quite valuable.'

'A marble plaque, on its own?'

'Maybe. I mean, it's not here.'

'No, it's not here.' I looked across at him, and I saw. 'We might have left it when we changed the rope.'

'Yes.'

'Okay. We'll drive up there tomorrow and take a look. We started this thing so we might as well finish it. I suppose that it has to be leaning against the wall of the diner.'

But it wasn't, and on our silent return Andy hadn't found it. I didn't want to be comforted, pulled out like some attractive fish by an inquisitive boy.

23

Martin stayed away from Diane. She was too inviting and then ... he couldn't resolve her, her kind of cold warmth. For all her caring, Martin thought that she was indifferent while Billy only pretended to be indifferent.

He began to go walking with Billy. They rarely said a word to each other. Martin hated walking with anyone. He wanted to feel that he surrendered to beauty; surrendering was impossible with another person on his shoulder, another set of observations.

If ever – while they were out – Martin became nervous, he complained to Billy about writing; usually dragging up some fancied frustration. Billy supplied the curt spur: 'Sure you can do it' or 'That's your problem.' Which killed the problem. Martin didn't mind very much about his writing; there wasn't very much of it and it was a mess. He guarded the words as brilliant and considered himself a useless interpreter. It was Billy who cast Martin as a writer as though this was a matter of fact.

On their return to the Farm, Martin went upstairs and daydreamed out of the window without ever writing a sentence; and Billy wandered into the meeting-room to listen to whoever happened to have something to say.

They weren't even particularly gleeful when they came across Diane's marble dresser-top sandwiched protectively between the snow tyres at the corner of the barn; they just carried it upstairs and fitted it into the dresser, and she took it pretty much as a matter of course. Although perhaps it was some kind of signal, because Billy spent a lot more time in the evenings sitting up there with her; Martin heard him laughing. They showed no public intimacy. When Martin asked Billy if he was looking forward to getting back to New York for the rehearsals, he just said: 'Yes, I am.'

They had all been very nervous at first, Martin realised. Now it was quieter. They didn't have to be together.

If he didn't ask what was happening, they would be fine. If they left it alone. Billy didn't want to say anything, to mess it up. There were times with Diane, over the years, when the mood had always been the same. Should he tell her that? But no one refurnishes a room and expects it to have the same effect. He could lose himself up here with her.

But she wouldn't have it.

She was restless.

She took them off in the car, over the State line into Connecticut, to something called a 'friendly'.

Braided horses, show-jumping, men in loud check jackets. And a very strange, unreal, soft sunlight.

And the stink of personal fortune which they should respect. Diane was amused by it all, smug and recognised. Martin got by, being English. Billy was supposed to talk with the men.

'That's a great-looking horse.'

'Harold told Frank Wheatley that he paid twenty thousand dollars for that horse.'

'I heard that. That has to be a great investment.'

Like a clutch of small dinghies at the mouth of a harbour, the men bobbed and righted themselves, trying to settle on the direction of the wind, stabilised only by their bank balances. Men are only on earth to be entertainers, Billy thought, and these men had paid to avoid being recognised as lousy entertainers. Diane would never have come here before. With this new air of naïvety at least she was free of the hawk-eyed resilience which most of the other women paraded. Well, perhaps they were less artificial, more bored.

Diane's party was invited to join the barbecue cook-out, an energetic conspiracy to harness the men once the horses needed a rest. Billy picked his way lamely round the order that passed for confusion. Station wagons disgorged coolers and baskets; Martin seemed to know what it was all about, Diane what it was down to. Billy wasn't in fancy dress, he felt like the only person in line at a huge soup-kitchen. He sat on the rug next to Diane.

'I have to make a little more effort.'

'Who with?' she asked.

'Martin. I'm responsible for him.'

Her smile demoralised Billy. 'He does well enough. We don't take account that he's a foreigner.'

'Everyone's a foreigner in this country, Diane. It sticks to us. He's had less of a family than we have. Now is this whole thing an act or ... '

'Not here, Billy,' she murmured, 'we won't stay long.'

They were joined by Martin; Diane started him talking. He told them about his sister and the horseshows in England. My kid sister, he called her, as though they did a lot of things together. Billy chose to doubt it.

And then Martin talked about the differences between England and America, quickly and stupidly and a lot of socialist bullshit as though America was some nightmare which was going to puncture England's blank, creative sleep.

Billy let it ride without saying anything. He no longer took America very personally. Having never had any faith, Martin had no right to disillusionment. I have that right, Billy thought; fuck you, I don't even want it. If America didn't exist, you'd have nothing to be for or against, you would die quietly. Maybe that's all they wanted in Europe.

Billy walked off round the horse ring, behind groups of lunchers – breeding and background, tweed discussion, the perfect blonde rinse. Well in from the cowboy boots and the handlers, well in from the shit.

So maybe he was shit. Tap on someone's shoulder and say, 'Pardon me, I've been through it all, here's how it smells.'

But dignified shit, at the end of the day. Yeah, his mother would be proud of him, wouldn't she. Billy. Went off and got half-famous. Not a household name, so maybe she wouldn't realise.

Made a living out of it, more than a living!

Don't mean to poison you. Don't even mean to look at you. Pardon me.

Billy realised that he was looking straight at the man in the photograph that was on Diane's desk. And that wasn't a co-incidence. It was why they were there. Why she was there, and why she had brought him along, to know.

So. He was glad.

He hadn't thought that there was anything between himself and Diane, he with his mongrel scabs sticking to her. She was out of his class, he was glad for her, he wouldn't have done her any good. She deserved better. He saw her patience, her kindness to himself and the advantage he took; he felt ridiculous.

Billy did the circuit, chewing on tears. She deserved; he was happy for her, like a fine clean mist into which he disappeared.

Without Billy, there was no contact between Martin and me. Neither of us would make the effort. I lay back on the rug while Martin helped to clear away the lunch things. We were both honest enough not to make any false attempts. Honest? Some people collect stamps, maybe we just collect people, silently, looking for something other than ourselves. I suppose the thing about Billy is that he makes me feel as though I'm still growing, on my own, as our relationship changes. He really doesn't care about the past. He is one of the few people for whom I don't find myself feeling sorry; and I don't like feeling sorry for people, losing my sympathy.

I had arranged to see Michael at three. See Michael at three, no more than that. We didn't want each other. Sometimes I had an irrational irritation at his side of the deficit, but that was only hurt pride. We were fair: I had been intrigued by myself as much as he had been intrigued by me. At the end of the Boston course he should simply have phased himself out, disappeared. His work is his religion; to pretend that I shared it would do no good to either of us.

'Martin?'

'Yes?'

'Do you know that carved elephant I have in the alcove in the meeting-room?'

'Yes, I noticed it. My grandfather used to have a collection of elephants.'

'Why don't you take it?'

'No, I couldn't,' he refused.

'We could go through this. I shall say: "Oh, I was just going to throw it out." Now don't be so English.'

'I am English.'

'Not utterly English.'

'No,' he said quickly.

'The elephant came from London. It was bought by an American tourist looking for something solid; I'd like you to return it. You can learn to accept, can't you?'

He smiled. 'Well, it's a bit heavy and I'm travelling around. I don't know if I'm going home.'

'So why do you call it home?'

'For no reason at all.' He stared at me. 'Are you nervous about something?'

I considered.

'Well, I dragged you and Billy here to help me meet a man who was, who is, my ex-lover.'

'Did you tell Billy?' he wondered.

'No.' But what is that to feel guilty about?

'Are you changing from him to Billy?'

'Billy has enough in front of him as it is.'

'The plays and everything ... '

We could both see Billy approaching, and if Billy *hadn't* been near I wouldn't have wanted to carry on this conversation, so bluntly. I wouldn't have talked like this to Pam, or to anybody. I wouldn't have been pinned down like this. 'Are you changing from Michael to Billy'! Is that how they see us? Slim calculators of love and need that slip easily from one pocket to another?

'Do you have the time, Mary?'

'Yes, let me see, it's a quarter of three. They should be starting the green hunter division right now.'

'Hi, babe.'

I looked at Billy, surprised at this old affectionate greeting, grateful for his easy warmth.

'Hi; have you made your tour?'

'I walked round the track.'

But with him too, I became suspicious of myself; the way he watched me, benevolently, as though he wanted me to share something, it was like a judgment. I steadied myself on his arm as I bent over for my shoes. No, not with Billy, Billy didn't make that kind of selfish decision; it was just that there was something on his mind, he should get away from these plays, shake himself out of himself; and I would stop imagining everything, these invasions, as if I were a set of crap dice banging around green baize walls.

'I thought that we should take one more look around together and then head for home.'

'Diane,' Billy grinned, 'he's about two hundred yards up on the left-hand side.'

'Is he?' I fixed on Billy, dealing with my fluster. 'His name is Michael.' I took Billy's arm.

Martin carried the rug over his shoulder and followed us. As we came up towards Michael, my hand tightened and I felt myself beginning to tremble. I made the introductions. Martin and Michael talked about the Cambridges. I felt Martin trying to shelter Billy, and that I was entirely superficial in such a simple, logical, male meeting. I suggested to Billy and Martin that they go on towards the car and I would catch them up.

Michael asked how I was, and I answered that I was fine. I thanked him and told him how I had been. I tried, but our procedure had already been set. I said nothing that would allow him to draw any conclusion. I wasn't dishonest; I told him that I was still private and that I had wanted to see how I felt when I saw him again.

'Naturally enough,' he said drily. He didn't ask me what my feelings were.

'But it's not easy.'

'You shouldn't expect it to be.'

'I feel as though I'm rebuilding.' That was a lie and he saw it. He let me off.

'Well, let me know how you feel around … when?'

'Not long. But not immediately.'

He laughed. 'Some time before Christmas.'

We separated. On my way back to the car, I was disappointed that he hadn't talked of his own feelings, hadn't tried to undermine the *fait accompli*. I reflected sadly that this kept me attached to him.

' ... get back to rehearsing, and we'll open it in four weeks. I might leave here the day after tomorrow.' Billy watched Diane walking over the grass.

Martin saw that he was hurt; but he was in some way resolved, almost cheerful. 'I'll go and you stay,' Martin said.

'That's not the question. Where will you go anyway?'

'I don't know. New Jersey, I expect,' Martin shrugged.

'You get out there!' Billy ordered softly. 'You decide what you want to do and you do it. Never mind the damn cost. If you play safe with yourself, you'll lose it.'

'What?'

'Don't ask me that, you shouldn't have to ask that. Find a good lie and hang on to it. Women know how to do that and they make it believable. Men are poison. No guts.'

As Diane came closer, Billy slid off the bonnet of the car and went to meet her.

'That's a lot of shit.'

'Sure it is,' Billy hung on irony, 'you should know.'

I sat up late with Billy in the kitchen. It went wrong and I don't know why. I wanted Billy to talk, I was sure that he needed to talk. But when Martin was there, Billy encouraged me to talk about myself. I wanted Billy to know that it was over between Michael and me – we had been together in a very small way for just two years. I stood up to make coffee, annoyed at the ease with which my own statements came and how impersonal they were, how irrelevant all this apparent honesty was.

Martin said that he was going to bed, he wished us goodnight. I awaited the coffee in silence.

'He doesn't know how to react,' Billy said, as though we were all some abstract problem.

'He's young. We don't have a lot to offer him.'

'You think I should stay out of it?'

'You're not responsible for him.'

'No.' Billy was restless.

'I seem to encourage people to stay out of me,' I snapped.

He lost himself in vagueness. 'Yeah, maybe that's the best way.'

I looked back over my shoulder. What is it with you? This isn't you, this hang-dog surrender.

'He certainly cares a lot about you.'

'I don't want that.'

'I hear you're going to be quite a success story when this movie comes out.' I brought our cups across to the table.

'It's a good movie,' he allowed.

'And your leg held up okay?'

'I had two months of complaining and then it forgot about me.'

He described the filming, the West Coast experience, the star routine.

'And you came back here?'

'I like the East Coast and I like the theatre. In movies it's in bits, you never get a chance to develop anything. The kind of relationship you have with everyone is slick professional. You hang around and you switch on and you switch off. You have to reach that level where you don't test each other. That's the take they always decide to print, they don't want to run any risks.'

'And now?'

'Now?' He shook his head, quietly uneasy. 'It'll come out when we're rehearsing.'

Don't go away from me like that; why can't we approach each other? We've never been this way.

He stood up.

'Where are you going?'

'To the men's room.'

I clasped him strongly, wanting something for him, wanting to see some of his pride and his humor.

When he returned, he found me snuffling; which I told him to ignore, I cried sometimes without it meaning anything. 'It's taking loneliness a little too seriously.'

'I never could take it. But I guess I can.'

I took his hand and steered him into the chair beside me. 'This course I did, that was lonely. It was going into yourself and not knowing what you might find there. I was on my own. I regressed right back, I went through everything. I didn't know at times if I would pull through. But you come right back up against yourself and then you *do* come through. Never mind the misconceptions and the paranoia, you survive all

259

that; and the part which is the plain, enduring *you*, that comes through!'

I demanded of him.

'Yeah. I know.' He lit another cigarette.

There is some terrible irony in this somewhere. I'm running up against a brick wall. He knows as much about this as I do, but it's all so introverted and trapped.

He said: 'I'm coming closer to something I don't know about. I'll tell you when it's over. I don't really know what it is.' He put his hands in the pockets of his jacket, wary and tired, his eyes blenched.

'Tell me.'

'No, I don't want to move it, you know? I don't know yet. I ... I don't know what it is. I'm not in love; that's the first time in my life for not loving, perhaps I even like the end of love.'

'It'll come through.'

Another ghostly smile, meant to reassure me. I saw that there was no point in pushing him further. He stood, leaning against the freezer.

'You know, we're leaving after tomorrow. I didn't have time to plan telling you.'

'Why?'

'Oh, Martin wants to get away, and I could do to settle back into the city before we start rehearsing. I'm dragging these plays around with me wherever I go, so I might as well get my feet in there.'

'Do you want me to go with you?'

'No.'

'You don't have to be proud about this.'

'That's not a stupid thing to say to me. But it wouldn't be right.'

By the time I had cleared the table and had done everything else I could find to do in the kitchen, I supposed that he was asleep.

The wood on my bedroom fire smelt like something horrible I had once tried for breakfast, in England, a kipper. I must be burning some of the old planking from the barn. I had a headache. I didn't want to be in that room. I could sit there all night, not thinking, allowing my mind to be on its own.

If I woke Billy, I would only apologise for waking him. We are very close.

So there is nothing to think about. Go out and get some air; jeans, sweater, shoes and a walk; let the fire go out.

Martin sifted through the sheets of paper. He had the images. He made a collection of them and started the process of extraction, smoking cigarette after cigarette. He crossed out the least striking of the images and he transferred the dozen survivors on to a single sheet of paper.

They were going to leave the Farm tomorrow. Martin picked out a clean sheet of paper and wrote:

> Donna
> Franco
> Billy
> California

He underlined these headings. He went to the bathroom, came back and glanced at them. Pushing the piece of paper to the top left-hand corner of the table, he started on the following sheets: 'Dear Jane and Philip,' and he wrote for the next half-hour.

By the time he had finished the letter, he had decided not to send it. It was too personal and yet too distanced. But he thought that he should send it. He added another page, telling them of his plans to work in New Jersey and then to go on to California. This was expressed with an assurance that he didn't feel, and he ended the letter this second time on a false, breezy excitement.

He then packed his clothes and tidied his room.

Though it was late at night, or very early in the morning, he sat on the bed and waited.

Nothing happened.

He decided that he would like to go downstairs. He thought of going naked, but he also thought better of it; someone might come down. But he wanted some sort of territorial affirmation. He wanted to be naked, moving around the darkened house, with his skin touched by objects. Restlessly clothed, he felt his way through the darkness along the corridor and down the stairs. He found Diane, sitting in the kitchen by the light of a table-lamp and a candle, writing in a large hardbacked exercise book.

He apologised for interrupting her. Diane blamed their insomnia on the full moon. She was composed, and the last thing Martin wanted to do was to talk. He sat for a moment, tense with his sexuality.

Diane offered him a drink, she wouldn't drink herself but if he wanted he could take the bottle back upstairs. He was blindly convinced that she was there to make love with him. But he did take the bottle, and he went back to his room.

He sat in front of his table, opened the folder and took out his papers. He sat looking at them and drinking. He drew lines between the images, building up a web. The web was secure, but he was still frustrated. He took a piece of paper and wrote:

She was a bit like the head porter at the hotel where our family used to holiday, in Devon. He fronted your arrival, you followed him while he smiled and dropped pleasing, raised-eyebrow comments to all the second-week guests who were hanging around in the hotel lounge as if they were fishing patiently at the edge of a pond. My uncle went in front of us, talking to the porter, a jerky one-sided conversation, usually about roads or décor, while Annie and I walked with my aunt, feeling idiotic. I wanted to be on the other side of the porter, coming towards him and receiving one of his easy non-inquiries. But instead I was knocking along in the rear, trying hard not to look at anybody and hoping that the tall warm-haired girl whom I had met last year and to whom I had written love letters from school hadn't arrived there before us and wasn't at this moment watching our entry – because I wanted to know if we were still going to get married and call our children by the same names. I wanted to know this before we really looked at each other. I had some trust, I didn't know if she did. She used to write about the Kenco coffee bar in her town. In our town there was the Black Cat. I did go in there once, but the place was occupied by old women pecking at cake. There wasn't a coffee bar at school. I wrote enthralling lies about the goings on at the Black Cat, pages of lies, and then pages of 'I-love-you's, cramped in small so as to up the numbers. She wrote back and I would count the numbers of her 'I-love-you's, the joy of my week being determined by arithmetical progression. We wrote only on Sundays. We met only for two weeks in the summer. The porter led us in. She walked in so well, that I was struck dumb by that violent explosion of belonging hopelessly to someone, there wasn't any I, only a gaze, my eyes and my mouth at odds. At the beginning of the second week, the porter led other people in, passing us, smiling at us, laying us a beautiful red carpet with his suggestion that we would win the tennis tournament. She turned to me and said nervously – do you think he knows about us – and I was sure that I didn't think so. How could anybody know about us? I don't think I ever looked at her body, but now I realise that she had wonderful legs, in the tennis skirt. But I was usually walking with her. I can't remember your eyes. We got to the final but we didn't win the tournament.

Why?
Legs, walking behind them. And lies. Writing. When they found us on the bed, not knowing what to do because we were so full of us, they sat around a table over coffee at tea-time. You didn't arrive next year. We were going to elope but neither of us wrote with instructions on how to do it.

The light switch at the end of the corridor, and the thin bar of light under the door. Diane came along the corridor, passed Martin's room, turned off the light and shut her bedroom door.

Martin felt bitter. He saw his list of headings, reached over for it and crossed out the name of Donna. Then he crossed out Billy. And he put a question mark before California. Because the sheet of paper was now untidy, he copied out the relevant points on to a clean sheet. Go to see Billy's play. Get married to someone rich. Write. That was enough.

The room was hot and full of cigarette smoke. He opened the window. There was a certain amount of silver glow, but the bare moon itself was on the other side of the house. Martin sat on the bed and waited for the smoke to disperse. He blew the smoke from the cigarette he was holding towards the open window. He put the cigarette out, he shut the window. Elephant? He wrote it on the sheet of paper, and laughed scornfully. He saw that there was nothing burning in the ashtray and emptied it into the waste bin. He washed the ashtray and dried it with a hand towel. He put the ashtray back on the table. He washed his hands and face and took off his clothes. He poured the last of the drink and sat back with his feet on the table. Legs. He smoked one more cigarette. Flakes of ash dropped on to his stomach. He rubbed them into his skin.

He finished his drink, cleaned his teeth, washed his hands again, for Diane. He caressed himself. He reared over the table, bucking and swaying on tiptoe. He pumped out on to a fresh sheet of paper. *Fuck* you, Diane, *fuck* you. Fuck writing. Fuck *you*. Fuck all.

Fat Shadows

24

Martin stayed at the penthouse for five days, mostly confining himself to the dining-room table. His anger had left him, he worked quietly, scribbling ideas and short scenes of dialogue. Billy ignored him. The apartment was quiet, Billy spending most of his time in his room. Donald was away.

Each evening they went out together to see a movie or some theatre. Martin suggested it, Martin cooked meals, Martin went to fetch Billy from his room. There was an unexpected homeliness about them. Billy's room now had a neat suburban formality, Billy lying on the bed smoking or reading when Martin knocked. Billy in a thin pullover with his shirt collar folded out at the neck of the pullover. There was a framed photograph of his mother at the head of the bed.

Martin had phoned Franco. It would fit very well; John the handle-smoother had met a girl and was moving out, Franco needed someone to take the room for a short while until he decided what to do with the apartment.

But Martin lingered with Billy. He didn't know why – except that it was calm between them.

Billy became inquisitive about what Martin was writing. Martin didn't want to show him and couldn't explain what it was about. Billy understood; he went back to his room. Martin sat at the dining-room table and didn't understand – neither his solitude nor the expanse of white paper before him.

He went down the corridor and into Billy's room. Billy seemed full and relaxed. Martin sat in the chair by Billy's bookcase and looked across at him; Billy glanced up from his book. It was Martin who felt observed.

'Are you trying to make it easy on yourself?' Billy said.
'Why?'

'Well, I don't have any answer.'

Martin watched him; Billy with his glasses on, the book across the pillow, calm intelligent eyes, like all those actors who played young university professors in continental films.

'We *did* have, didn't we?'

'We grew a little older, there's no harm in that. "We" is always one answer, as long as it lasts. If you're intelligent or capable you have to grow through that, you won't be able to help it.'

'That's not true.'

'It is, and it's painful. You'll have to ask a lot more questions of yourself.'

'Are you in love with Diane?'

Billy answered methodically. 'I'm not in love with anybody.'

'But you love, don't you?'

'Maybe, but I'm not in love.'

'Is that bad?'

'I thought so, but now I don't think so. I think now that it's a question of adapting, and Diane has enough problems adapting to her boyfriend.'

'Perhaps she doesn't want to adapt to him.'

'How do you know?'

'She loves you.'

'Sure. And I love her. She's a very determined woman, and she knows what she wants out of life. Don't imagine that you can play around with Diane. She is someone I respect right down the line.'

'Why don't you do something about it?'

'You're young, anything's possible if you get out there and see it through. You *will*.' Billy eyed Martin with a cold interest.

'So will you.' Martin hated him.

'Yeah. If you think that I talk a lot of shit then remember that if you have to go through it, at least do it on your own. Don't accuse the world, it's not a bad place to live in.'

'Okay,' Martin said facetiously. He stood and stretched self-consciously, reaching his arms out in front of him. Billy lit a cigarette. Martin went back to the dining-room table.

When Billy came through, hands in his trouser pockets, glasses half-way down his nose, he wasn't surprised to find Martin packed. Billy sat on the couch, Martin looked out of the window; possibly a beautiful city, New York. He couldn't not need Billy.

266

'I'll let you see when I've finished. The writing; whatever it is,' he said.

'Good,' Billy answered. 'I'd like to read it.'

Martin walked back across the room and sat down, facing him. Billy lit a cigarette. It was the determined detachment in Billy that nailed Martin's emotions down inside himself, Billy's cruel kindness and, as he thought, Billy's will. The tobacco stains on his teeth, the strong, imperious nose and those large, quiet, considering eyes.

'If you wanted to do it here then you'd be doing it,' Billy suggested. 'We're going different ways, that's right for both of us.'

Martin accepted.

It was absurd – they shook hands in front of the open elevator. Door closed.

'I'll see you, Billy.' Called through aluminium.

'Sure you will.'

Billy opened the door and stepped out on to the terrace with Rusty. He watched the dog meander around in the sunlight, and then he moved forward to look out over the black iron railings. It was four in the afternoon, a hot afternoon. The city, even from high up, had a Sunday atmosphere. A lot of people were off on vacation, he picked out the sounds from the streets below whereas he usually was indifferent to the daily cacophony. There were aircraft in the sky and rehearsals on Monday, there was nothing on Billy's mind, he was ready. The adrenalin would come. He would work. He went back inside and pulled a chair out on to the terrace. He sat and smoked.

When Martin left Billy, he took with him all the plans and the determination which Billy had made him create for himself. Somehow, now, it was better to be away from Billy and to find himself up against his own standards. He settled into Franco's spare room, borrowed a table from Franco's father and forced himself to sit silently with his papers for several hours each day. There was a residue of energy in him which he pulled out on to the paper; it didn't make much overall sense, but it gave him an identity and it filled his folder.

Franco was impressed by Martin's sense of purpose. They

had spent a couple of days drinking and talking and hanging around before Martin detached himself. Franco gave Martin the news: a girl called Donna had phoned from Trenton, he himself had found a piano player to work with.

'Donna?'

'She didn't say much; she said that she'd see you around some time. I didn't know what your plans were so I kept her, you know, at a distance?'

'That's okay.'

'Yeah, that's the way I feel. Sometimes you get a lot of directions thrown at you that you don't really want. Well, I don't.'

Martin observed him. Franco often looked as though he was daydreaming, his eyes slipped sideways, the ruminatory 'yeahs' were often grunted in agreement with himself.

'Is Chestnut around?'

'Yeah, she's around.' Franco wasn't sold on her. 'She wanted to move in here when John pulled out. I was seeing too much of her, I couldn't get on with anything. She's around.'

'What are you getting on with?'

'Hey, what is this?'

'Just interested.'

Franco chuckled. 'Yeah. Have you been hustling in the city?'

'In a way.'

'You get work?'

'No. I'm all right for money for about another month.'

'What do you figure on doing?'

'I'm going to stay in most of the time and do some writing.'

'That's fine by me.' Franco stirred himself. Martin saw that he was annoyed and nervous. Franco went across the room and opened his guitar case, he sat and tinkered with the guitar. 'Yeah, this guy on the piano, he's an older guy. Straight, but he plays okay; he's an old pro. We do old songs. You can learn a lot more off people like that.'

Franco was out most of the time, practising or moving some furniture or playing. Martin lost touch with him. They met up late at night over a drink in the apartment; Martin didn't look in on Franco's work, and Franco left his resident writer on one side.

Martin stuck it for a couple of weeks. It was more or less writing for Billy, trying to live up to Billy, maybe to challenge

Billy. But Martin wasn't ready for it. His day became very confining. He loitered in bed until noon. He got up and looked through several sheets of paper, to put himself in the mood. He left the apartment, to get some air; hot and fusty air, but air. He walked half a mile down the road, across the railway tracks, to a delicatessen, where he bought a torpedo – a stick of bread stuffed with peppery tomato sauce and meatballs – and a can of Coke. He ate and drank on a bench outside the shop. He felt ill for fifteen minutes. Writing was urgent. He felt more ill and nervous for another ten minutes. He walked back. On the third day, by accident, he arrived at the railway tracks when a freight train was going past; thereafter he timed himself so that he could watch the slow hundred cars clunt through. They lumbered so vagrantly that it would have been easy to hop aboard. But back to the four or five hours with blank paper and cigarettes, protective tiredness in the evenings, TV, beer and whiskies with Franco. If Franco felt buoyant, he would herald a pack of greasy cards with, 'Let's have a few hands of poker.' After a very few hands of poker, they always realised that neither of them liked poker. So they played seven-card whist with some music on the tape-deck, Franco tapping his foot, Martin wondering about words.

One night, Franco said: 'This guy keeps asking me to go back to his house when we finish.'

'Which guy?' Martin had good clubs.

'The piano player.'

'Huh. Does he play cards?'

'I don't know.' Franco laughed. 'I'm not sure that he's interested in that.'

'You could go and find out.'

'Yeah, but I don't think I will. I'll stick with cards and whisky.'

You couldn't look at Franco and say that there was any kind of defeat about him. He was suspicious of life and suspicious of himself, but he wasn't anxious or downcast. He wasn't bothered by a sense of worth. He dug out moods, they didn't settle on him.

Martin went to the bar one night to watch him play. He was surprised by the music. The piano player indulged in plenty of affected gesture, flirting with his audience. A large audience; the place was a cross between a bar and a club, most people sat and paid attention for some of the time, probably because the piano player was a showman. He wasn't bad, he was dexterous and the songs were arranged. Franco was arranged in with the songs, chumming away on his guitar.

Martin was amused, but it wasn't really his type of atmosphere; it was boyfriend and girlfriend, date territory. He didn't have the reserves to sit at a table and tip waitresses, so he went back to the bar. He found Chestnut on a bar stool. She was talking to the bartender. Martin understood that Franco wasn't going out with her any more, but no, she welcomed him to the stool next to her and she talked about Franco. Martin slowly became aware that she was under the impression that Franco spent his whole time practising the saxophone, and that they spent their days working on songs together. 'I hope something comes up,' she said, 'because he's wasting his time in here.' And she looked at Martin.

'I think it will,' he said.

'He really bristles about it.'

'About what?'

'Playing in here. Sure he does. Just look at that guy and the kind of music they're playing. He's better than that.'

'Yes he is.'

'And that guy won't allow Franco to do anything.'

'Then he won't go on playing with him.'

'You try telling him that.'

'No, I won't.'

'You know, both of you are really uptight. There's no way to get through to him.'

Then why bother? Martin left them to sort it out. Franco came home every night as soon as his session had finished, daytimes he sloped off somewhere with the guitar or the sax. For a while Martin liked the routine isolation; order appealed to him, the minutiae of laying out pencils and pens side by side, cleaning the kitchen, adding one scene to another, washing the ashtray, walking out into the living-room and across to the door of the apartment and back again after every fifth cigarette, adding a few lines, pondering, feeling self-satisfied. He rarely emerged.

One day, it struck Martin that his writing was utterly aimless. What would he do with it? He would give it to Billy. What did he owe to Billy? Thirty sheets of paper? Thirty sheets that were only another letter to Billy, and Billy never replied to his letters; and Billy was doing something else, and writing wasn't exciting. It was nothing, it was something he was doing to waste time and to get close to Billy. But Billy was expansive, he wasn't interested in small things, and each time Martin wrote he was getting smaller. Writing was a pernickety death. He couldn't deal with it. Both Franco's strumming and Billy's acting were more lively; Martin was boring himself for no reason.

He went out for his torpedo. On his agenda, he ate it ravenously. This one was a repulsive struggle. The delicatessen sold plenty of other take-aways, Martin wondered why he hadn't experimented. Fifteen days, fifteen torpedoes. Enough.

He went to take in the freight train. The wagons clunked past solemnly. Martin sat against the barrier post, a guard sat out on the caboose at the end of the line of wagons. Martin only noticed him when he drew level and then started to recede. Their eyes met; the guard seemed to realise his status.

'Going far?' Martin called.

'Dropping these empties down to Trenton,' the guard smiled and receded further, nodding calmly at Martin. Martin gave half a salute of farewell.

Trenton.

He went for a walk round the park. There was an impromptu soccer match going on, Italians versus others. It was fiercely contested in the afternoon heat, the players were quite skilful even if there wasn't much in the way of team tactics. Martin watched it. He got back to the apartment about six; Franco was drooling away on the saxophone. Martin went through the living-room, sat in front of his table for half an hour and doodled. Franco came in with four out of a sixpack. Martin took one. Franco said: 'Do you want to eat out at the diner tonight?'

'Okay. What happened to the job?'

'I quit.' The grin split open Franco's mouth.

'Because of Chestnut?' Martin smiled.

'Hell, no. I was bored. She was a good reason for staying put, I was pretty safe in there.'

Later Martin heard that Franco had got fired from the bar, he hadn't quit. He had gone off on his own with some drunken, slapdash blues, leaving his tinkling boss flustered and vengeful.

Franco had acted perplexed, but his indifference and finally his contempt shone through.

For the most part of a week, Franco lived off a lazy disdain and then – like a hangover – he worried about it, moodily, reproaching himself.

The phone rang. It was black Butch from down the road, hey, hey, and a lot of jive, how you doin' and sweet nuthin' mahself ah'm goin' on strike.

Martin relayed the news. 'He was *born* on strike.' Franco grunted from the horizontal. 'Ask him over. Tell him to bring some beer.' Martin asked him over.

You ain't understannin' me, we all goin' on strike.

So?

Sick people weren't going on strike. The hospital would still need cleaning staff. The hospital would need to pay out for scab labour. They would be paying out, for one shift, maybe two hundred bucks a week clear.

Clear?

As crystal.

Franco could move fast, Martin got the Kid's Social Security number off Lady, they shaved and put on a clean shirt apiece and drove down to the administration office where they smiled and were assigned to the natal unit. Double shift?

'Why not?' Martin tried to drawl.

'Yeah,' Franco said.

25

The bus came round to pick them up at seven in the morning. There were a few placards banged half-heartedly on the side of the bus as it went through the picket line but this was only for show. The hospital ended up with the worst workers in town so it was in the authorities' interest to end the strike before their patients died from lack of skilled attention. In return for the good money, the scabs paid out a percentage to the strike committee to ensure that the strikers didn't suffer too badly.

When Franco and Martin stepped out of the elevator on their first day, it struck both of them that they had drawn a good number out of the bag.

The natal unit was at the very top of the building and was spared the traffic of lower floors. It was quiet, of even temperature, and immaculate. It was like walking into one of those hushed control rooms that television spaceships seem to go in for; where the atmosphere is constant, the girls drift round in next to nothing, and no one ever smokes a cigarette or says anything angry to any other member of the crew.

Such was the antiseptic tone of the natal unit. The afterbirth had to be got off the floor inside a couple of minutes. And this was where Martin and Franco came in; they were the mop crew. There wasn't much to it. There were two delivery rooms, a tank room where the babies were stored, and a dozen rooms for the mishaps and the very rich.

Down the corridor a few yards was a different atmosphere. You pushed open a door; at peak hours there was a television set blaring and a half-dozen chain-smoking fathers stamping round in a litter of plastic coffee cups. Here was the human interest side of the unit and the ashtrays had to be emptied regularly.

When the unit got busy, the kids dropped in fast succession. Then Martin and Franco had to take the fathers to see their babies in the transparent perspex incubators. And in New Jersey, which was a good mix of colour and creed, it was important not to mistake any babies or lose the identification tags. This was one point the fathers tended not to miss in their anxiety. If they were white and the newborn was black, this was not an easily dismissed discrepancy in genetics, and no one was in the mood for jokes. It was not a good time to stand there with one hand behind your back, hemming and hawing and looking through a sheet of numbers suggesting 'Shall we try 37?'

Outside peak hours, it didn't take Martin and Franco long to get the place cleared and then they could laze around watching TV with a friendly nurse or a lone father.

It was a great job; there was so much innocent pleasure in it. Spontaneous joy and pride spread throughout the unit. It was a boost to lean on a mop and hear the cry of a newborn animal. Even the regular staff seemed beatifically drugged most of the time, and emergencies were few and far between. It was the only rewarding job Martin had ever done. And the tension flowed off Franco, who was often to be seen laughing quietly with an Italian father.

The days went quickly; the money mounted and the money faded into the background. Martin felt pampered by the sense of quiet fulfilment. They both worked Sunday without realising it. Life flowed by and there was always more of it around. When they went down to the canteen to eat, they never stayed, never talked to any of the other scabs unless they had to.

There was no point in going home at nights. The third night they slept in the staff-room, and after that a nurse usually managed to find them a couple of empty rooms in the hospital somewhere. They felt no desire to leave, or get out; none of that intense hatred for the place of work.

There was one disruption. Half-way through the second week, they were downstairs in the canteen for a sandwich, Martin was chewing absent-mindedly and reflecting on wet hair over babies' heads.

'Psst.'

They turned to look; they noticed the girl.

'Have you guys got any psilocybin?'

'Huh?' Franco wondered if she was on the same planet.

'Oh come on ... you guys are always stoned,' she smiled complacently.

'Always? How would you know that?' Franco picked at a piece of ham.

'So what's with you guys, are you gay or something?'

Franco's eyes plodded patiently down the table-top away from her. He looked at the wall, his eyes swung back, and he went on eating.

'We look after babies,' Martin told her, 'up there in the penthouse.'

'Oh, is that good?'

'Yes.'

There didn't seem to be much of anything left to say. She was young, Martin wondered how she managed to get a job in the hospital. She had the mannerisms of a speed-freak, being not quite attached to her body, having wrists as strong as a face flannel, pinprick eyes and she was very tired under the liveliness. Franco had seen a hundred of them. He got up and mumbled something and went back to the unit.

Martin had no wish to be unfriendly. The girl looked a bit embarrassed at butting in. There was something neutrally polite he could end with.

'And what do you do?' He stood up.

The floodgates opened; she was with her boyfriend and they were doing waste-disposal and he was with the junkies and she was scared and she needed the money and she'd left home and she didn't know any people in New Jersey and she was miserable. She was. It was monotonous misery; it was a shock. Martin hadn't seen a miserable person in days. He toyed with benevolence. She was silent and the onus was on him.

'Why don't you move on to babies for the afternoon,' he offered.

'I don't think I could do it.' She looked down into her lap and wound her fingers round each other.

'Anyone could do it. There's only me and Franco up there. And it's dopeless, if it's the dope that's getting to you ... '

'Oh no,' she shook her head resiliently. 'I can do a whole lot of dope.'

'Okay, leave it then.' He nodded at her and walked out.

She caught him at the elevator.

'Could I come up and see them right now, just take a look?'

'Sure. It's at the top.'

Martin showed her round the unit and showed her the babies in their tanks and the fathers; he left her and got on with his work. Franco was with the fathers and he was on mop-bucket. He noticed her occasionally. She got talking to a father, she asked Martin if she could help with the swabbing-up. At the end of the shift she came up to Martin and thanked him.

She went out of his mind. Franco and he worked through until midnight. There was only one delivery and they passed the evening playing cards and watching a movie on the television.

Martin awoke at seven-thirty, showered, ate and took the elevator. The girl was up there already, hurrying past with the mop as the doors opened. She looked a lot better, she said that she had slept thirteen hours and was feeling fine.

Martin went into conference with Franco. There wasn't the work up there for three, and if a supervisor came up it would create problems.

'Tell her to get fucked,' was Franco's line of thought.

'Let's give her another day.'

'Whose problem is she?'

'I'll take the waste job for today.'

'Suit yourself.' Franco wasn't worried.

'She can have a couple of days to cool out and then she can find something else.'

'Listen; just tell her to shift her ass out of here. There's a hundred fuckin' little girls like her running round the streets growing up ... this is a good job, let her do her own hustling ... '

Martin decided to take the break; he wanted to see what the rest of the hospital was like. When he told her, he realised that he'd been well hustled. She was a taker. She'd learn.

He certainly did; learn. The elevator doors were bare metal and cigarette burns, down in the basement. They pulled apart and there were a dozen people bent over brooms while a supervisor screamed at them. Martin was told that he was late and his pay would be docked and there were plenty of scabs after his job, so he'd better pick up that broom and clear out the loading bay, and put some sweat into it.

Immigrant labour, reality, capitalist exploitation, dehumanisation; you could call it what you like, and Martin called it a lot of things in the first four hours he was attached to the broom and the dustpan. Up in the natal clinic he never had much cause to notice the supervisors; and this must be because they were always on the backs of the basement boys, following the brooms from corridor to corridor, persuaded that they were the only people with eyes in their heads. All power of decision was removed; the worker with the broom became a listless object directed here and there, watched over and bullied; blinkered and defeated he drifted from room to room in the same daze. There was no sense of start or finish, the rooms were uniform. It was constant and draining and depressing.

There was only one chance of a break. Each person's head would lift when an elevator descended to the basement floor and had to be swept out in transit. It was a privilege to be chosen; once inside, the sweeper could knock against a button and go up a couple of floors to escape.

And then if an orderly descended and ground out a cigarette on the concrete, whoever was nearest would walk happily across to pick it up, just to break his monotony, and would do a little dance back to his broom, grinning inanely at whoever else took his chance to watch.

No such thing as a nurse ever appeared; it would have been too divine for the basement. When a drug truck arrived, smart men in white coats came suddenly from nowhere to wheel the cargo through, while the dopers leaned on their brooms, hungrily absorbing the mirage, and the supervisor barked at them and trailed them off to new wastelands elsewhere in the labyrinth.

At nine-thirty, Martin took a tab of speed which was silently placed in his hand by a passing realist.

At ten-thirty, a white guy with a damaged face swung a broom at the head of his supervisor and walked off the job. The other supervisors got no details and the casualty was sent upstairs.

At ten forty-five there was a break. People sat next to their brooms and smoked. At eleven, they got up and went on sweeping. They took their shirts off because there was no air-conditioning in the basement.

At noon there was the lunch hour. They were too dirty to be allowed up to the canteen. Martin threw his broom into a corner and went towards the elevator, intending to take a shower. He was stopped. He was too dirty to be allowed to use the showers. He should have brought his food with him. There was no argument. He wasn't the kind of person they could let walk through the hospital. The supervisor took his money and brought him a sandwich when he came back from lunch; Martin would have five minutes to eat it and drink a cup of coffee.

He joined the slumped labour force outside the loading bay in the humid, dirty sunshine, and sat with his back against the wall. There was little conversation. Half the people were junkies and the rest were drawn from every poverty-stricken nationality in the State. Only the junkies had a language in common, and that a dull and crumpled indifference.

'You get used to it,' said a prematurely ageing man from Eastern Europe. No, thought Martin. His sandwich arrived.

It would seem difficult for the supervisor to find any more sweeping after lunch, but they managed to spin it out for another hour simply because no one cared whether they swept dust or just swept. After this hour, there was a general consensus that you could lean on your broom and ignore the threats. The job was reckoned by hours, not by the cleanliness of the concrete. It was time to move on. The labour force stacked their brooms and wheeled out large garbage-bins. This was the appointed time to crash into your neighbour and play childishly.

They were assigned floors. They queued at the elevator doors like happy chimps.

'Not you, pretty boy.' Martin was held aside. The others smiled.

'I do it.' It was the East European who spoke.

'No y'don't, Polack, you take the third floor with the hippy. We don't want people to get the idea you're lookin' for food to take home every night.'

The supervisor took Martin back down to the locker room and gave him a full-length white coat to put on over his shirt and jeans, and there was another bin, lined with black polythene. Martin wheeled it out gladly. It was the only bin that didn't smell and he was seeing the advantages of a cleaner job.

'Round here.' The supervisor walked on past the main elevators to a service elevator by the loading bay. The two of them and the bin just fitted inside. The supervisor pressed the top button.

'I used to work up there in the natal unit,' Martin told him.

'That's where we're goin', the top floor.'

They rose to the top floor, and emerged in a part of it which Martin had never seen before. The supervisor told him to stay where he was while he went to check with the nurse.

Martin waited, the supervisor came back and motioned him into a small room next to the elevator, switching on the light and standing back.

Martin advanced with the bin. The room was bare except for a pair of rubber gloves and two large plastic buckets which were also lined with polythene sacks.

'Get 'em emptied and let's go ... ' The supervisor walked away.

Martin dragged one of the buckets towards him; he glanced into it as he lifted the lining clear of the edge. The bin was half-full of various sizes of foetus, each wrapped in its own clear plastic bag and sealed at the top. Martin looked in shock. There was a lot of death in the bucket.

'Hey ... ' he stuck his head round the door at the supervisor's back.

'Just get 'em in.'

As he pulled up the plastic sack, it was obvious that the weight was going to break it. He put on the gloves and pulled the foetuses out one by one and dropped them into his container. They just looked small; but one of them was deformed. And there were a couple of tiny twins, their heads close together, as though they were huddling, their tadpole legs intertwined. It was a sad job, and Martin had to turn his head away as he lifted the bucket to tip the last three out. The other bucket was full of female slops and insides, which was more nauseating because it was liquid. He tipped it in over the foetuses and shut the lid quickly so as not to witness the concoction.

'Is that it?' he asked, wheeling his bin across to the elevator.

'Next floor down,' said the supervisor.

There were more buckets on the floor underneath, which was the main floor for surgery. The foetuses had at least been whole, but now he was faced with collecting parts of bodies, anything from a liver to some sort of mangled arm. The supervisor tried the same joke on a doctor – 'Anything good to fry up in there, doc?' – and Martin dragged the slopping mass back to the elevator.

There was a slightly musty smell and there was too much time for reflection on the way down. Shocking images that had been quickly stored fell out in front of his eyes again. He felt a bit uneasy with nausea and was glad when the doors opened. It was a very hot afternoon as he bumped the bin down the ramp at the side of the loading bay. The supervisor pointed up the hill to the line of full bins. He was the last to get finished, everyone else was leaning against their charges, waiting to get into some sort of dump, Martin supposed.

'Up there, then wash out your truck.' The supervisor left.

The trailer wasn't heavy on the flat but it weighed a ton on the slope. Martin dragged it about five yards, then had to let it roll back to the loading bay. He walked up the slope to get help. It stank up there in the sunlight; old food, old medical dressings, old garbage in a temperature of over a hundred. Some of the saner basement boys wore masks over their noses.

They all shook their heads when he approached them.

'Wait for the Polack,' one of them said, 'he's first to dump when they get started up.'

Martin wandered back to his container. From five feet away

he could smell the sweet flesh, he retched, he didn't approach any closer. He looked around for some shade where he could wheel it out of the sun, but there wasn't any on this level and he didn't want to go down the slope any more. He sat on the gravel against the wall, waiting for the Polack.

Eventually the little man came down the hill smiling. He parked his garbage-bin in the loading bay and was delighted to have the opportunity to help Martin.

'Always they get the sick people to clean the bodies into the bucket,' was his cheerful summary of events, 'the people who are sick in the head.' He tapped his temple with his finger and grinned.

'Can we get it up the slope, with two of us?' Martin asked. The Polack affirmed; he knotted his handkerchief over his face. He took the handle of the truck and pulled, while Martin pushed from behind, his shirt pinned round his nose. It wasn't enough to get rid of the smell.

They set off up the slope with their tank of human remains. There was no way Martin was going to lean against the bin and wait in the queue. The other containers parted sympathetically to let them pass. Martin kept his eyes firmly on the ground that arrived between the wheels, the sweat trickling off the end of his nose and his back beginning to itch in the sun. He didn't want to think about his condition, he watched tarmac and gravel, his heart lurching at every bump, his hands balancing the lukewarm bin, his head swimming with attacks of nausea.

'Enough,' called the Polack as they hit level ground. Martin stood back and choked, whipping off his shirt in case he was sick. He wasn't. The Polack led the truck a little further and stopped behind two youths who were tipping their bin into the garbage dump.

Martin straightened up, his hands on his hips, and watched. The bin slid over and the garbage tumbled down a chute into a hole. One of the youths took off his gloves and went over to a control panel; he pushed a button. The machine started up; there was a scream of buckling metal and a scrunching of cardboard as the crushing block came across from right to left and condensed the garbage into an iron skip. The crusher pulled back and the engine switched itself off. The two attendants hosed down the chute; they pulled their bin out of the way.

The Polack beckoned to Martin. So immediately appalling had been his whole afternoon up to now, Martin hadn't had the time to consider what they were to do with their cargo. The crusher stretched his sense of belief.

The Polack handed him the hose; he was to keep hosing the smell and the blood down the chute. He stood on the other side of the hole while the Polack tipped.

He didn't look down the hole, but kept his eyes on a mid-point of the chute, past which everything cascaded and was gone. Then he levelled the hose into the bin and rinsed, then he washed down the sides of the chute. The Polack righted the bin and switched on the crusher.

Martin glanced down into the hole. This was a mistake; he didn't look again, he hosed quickly and blindly until the Polack stayed his arm.

His supervisor gave him a fifteen-minute break to have a coffee and get some colour back into his face.

He felt more relaxed when he was back with his broom in the basement. It gave him something to hang on to. He sank gratefully into the nullifying rhythm of the sweeping and the speechless presence of the other workers.

At the end of their shift, Martin sneaked upstairs, took a shower and changed his clothes, soaping himself methodically, the white tiles and the stainless-steel fittings glaring at him through the steam.

He took the elevator up to the natal unit. The early evening was the busiest time; Martin watched the bustle. Franco had a moment to slap him on the shoulder.

He wanted to get out of the hospital. He bought half a bottle of bourbon from a liquor store and ate his way through a plate of ham and eggs in a diner, pushing dimes into the small juke-box at the end of the table and choosing songs at random. He paid and left. He thought of going to the apartment but he hadn't his key on him, so he went back to the babies. It had quietened down, half the lights were off and Franco was sitting in the staff-room watching the movie on television. Martin reached for the bottle and took a pull, Franco was wary.

'Where's the girl?' Martin asked.

'Gone to get her stuff. Her name's Kathy.'

'How's it going?'

'In the next scene John Wayne gets shot.' Franco shrugged. Martin saw that it would be useless trying to tell him the story of the basement.

'Does he die?'

'Are you kidding?'

'Did you have a lot of births today?'

'Usual. The girl's a good worker.' John Wayne duly got shot and Franco changed channel.

'Does she get on all right?'

'Yeah ... ' Franco wasn't convinced. 'She's a pain. She's got no damn sympathy for anyone. She acts like a desk-clerk, telling everyone that they shouldn't smoke so much. Things have gotten tensed up. How's it with you?'

'Shit.'

'We'll get rid of her.'

'That basement is no place to send any human being.'

'That bad, huh?'

'Yes, worse.'

'There's someone coming.'

Martin pushed the bottle back down inside his boot and they watched television. The door opened and it was the girl, Kathy, carrying a guitar with her. Martin felt Franco stiffen.

'Hi, guys,' she said.

'Evening,' Martin nodded at her.

'I've brought my guitar along. Do any of you guys play?'

'No, 'fraid not,' Franco got in quickly.

'That's a pity. Do you?' She looked at Martin.

'No.'

'Well maybe I'll just play some songs. Will it be okay if I turn the television off?'

'Yeah, turn the sound down, we'll watch the pictures.'

'Oh come on, you guys, you can sing along. Do you know Janis Ian?'

'Did she play with Buddy Holly?' Franco lit a cigarette.

'Janis Ian!'

Franco subsided. Kathy warbled 'Jessie'. She wasn't bad; she was dreadful. Franco went out of the room, mumbling something about checking the unit.

'He's a lonely guy, your friend.' Kathy tuned the guitar.

'I don't think he is, he's just choosy; he likes to do what he feels like doing.'

'He's bitter.'

Martin let it drop and ignored her. She started again. 'He's scared in front of women.'

'Yes, maybe he is.' Martin yawned. 'It's not my business.'

'It would be cool up here if he could relax.' She tinkered with the guitar. 'Did you see my boyfriend?' she said.

'There were any number of junkies down there.'

'He's not a junkie; he needs a better job.'

Martin left her strumming the guitar and caught Franco in the fathers' waiting-room.

'Let's get her out. I'll see you tomorrow lunch break outside at the back.'

'Right.'

'Bring me down a sandwich.'

'Beef on rye?'

'Yes. Sleep well.'

'You'd better come up with a plan.'

'I will.' Martin descended and found a room. He lay in bed and thought of one obvious pulpy solution. He'd throw her in the crusher, guitar and all. He went to sleep before he could find an alternative.

He overslept and nearly solved everything by losing his job. But he swept like a maniac and grovelled sufficiently before the limited wit of his supervisor. The basement was its spotless, concrete self as he lazed through the half-hour before lunch, his eyes fixed on the ground, his broom assiduously gathering nothing but a few particles of dust.

When they were released, he went out and sat under the first tree. Franco showed up with the sandwich and a can of beer. He had no ideas and a lot of hatred. Martin laughed and led him up to the crusher. He threw in a cardboard box and they watched its reduction. Franco winced.

'It wouldn't work with a body; too much liquid, it wouldn't disappear so good.'

'It works.' Martin told him about the foetuses and the bits; Franco didn't believe him, he thought Martin's sense of humour a little vile and looked at him in disgust. 'We got a serious problem, and the only thing you can come up with is a sicko horror story.'

Martin realised that the basement crew probably had the nightmare all to themselves. No hospital committee passed minutes on the subject, or conducted feasibility studies. This emergency method of disposal must have been the result of a historic initiative.

Franco wanted to get back inside to the air-conditioning; besides, he took one look at the basement boys and decided that he was becoming class-conscious. They arranged to meet when Martin got off at half-four.

Two o'clock saw Martin and the Polack teamed up and collecting garbage from the second floor. A young longhair bounced out of the office and looked at Martin as though he had seen him somewhere around town. Martin recognised the face, but couldn't put a name to it. He nodded and the longhair came over to invite him to a party in room 323, the next floor up, when the shifts were over.

Leaning against the crusher and watching the discomfort of two dopers who were labouring up the hill with the meat wagon, Martin ticked over the possibilities for the party. The Polack took the hose and Martin tipped. The machine did its duty. He took the bin off down the hill.

Franco clicked on to the party like a gift from heaven; anything to get away from Kathy. He sized up the delivery schedule and foresaw liberation after seven o'clock, only one of them would have to stay around to keep an eye on the unit. Martin stood in for him on the rush hour while he shaved and changed. Kathy handled the mechanics of the job very well, it was true, but the whole atmosphere of the unit had changed. The fathers were shut out; they were kept informed in a well-regimented manner but the whole affair was now labelled as a woman's experience, and the waiting men were encouraged to feel only a sense of guilt before the pain and responsibility being shouldered by their wives. At best, Kathy treated them as being merely useless in this time of need.

Martin was relieved to get away. He and Franco took the elevator down to the third floor. When the doors slid open, they could already pick out the music.

'They're going to get busted,' Franco summarised the party's possibilities. They decided to look in for ten minutes to check out a job for Kathy.

Room 323 was in fact a suite, one bedroom and an anteroom where the relatives of the rich could no doubt console each other away from the hospitalised individual. Now, however, the room was full to bursting point with scab labour getting drunk and blowing dope and hustling pills.

Franco knew the longhair who had invited them, and after a brief talk about music, he explained the problem they were having with Kathy. The longhair considered that they could find one space on a floor crew, but two together would be impossible. Martin tried elsewhere and got a similar story.

The party was, incredibly, into its second hour. It was bald, out of order, and a blatant security risk.

'Real wow of a party,' Franco strode back into the natal unit, full of cheery propaganda, 'you should get down there and meet some people, we'll cover for an hour. Take your guitar along. We'll catch you later. There's nothing doing here.'

Franco's apparent change of humour swayed her more than anything. Martin took her down in the elevator and showed her into the room. There was even a drunken cheer as they caught sight of her guitar. Two guys moved in to hustle her. Martin faded out.

He and Franco sat upstairs, ate peppermints and waited.

'A half-hour,' Franco estimated, 'that's all they've got. There's a supervisor tour every two hours. They'll be too drunk to care.'

Sure enough, forty minutes later, Kathy arrived back with the story of the bust, and how everybody got fired, and how she escaped. Martin wondered if they were dealing with some supernatural force. Franco salvaged what he could.

'Well, if they all got fired, there'll be a lot of work around the building. You and your boyfriend can get a job together.'

Kathy smiled sweetly.

'I really like it up here.'

'Fuck it, lady, get outta here,' Franco lost his temper, 'we got the job and we're not gettin' hustled out of it. Now you can get fucked.'

'Oh you're such a big man,' she came back, 'you're full of shit. Finders keepers, right? You just try to get me out. Are you going to hit me now? I'll bet you like hitting women around.'

'Did a lot of people get away?' Martin asked. It didn't seem unlikely that Franco might hit her.

'Sure we did.' She revelled. 'Hell, the supervisor couldn't

285

watch all of us. Only the real winos got busted, and the guys in the bedroom. He locked them in there. Anyhow, there was a fight, the supervisor got his nose busted.'

'Yeah?' Martin saw that there would be the wrath of God going down in the hospital; there was bound to be a witch-hunt for anybody who was at the party. He left Franco smoking a cigarette and staring away out of the window.

He went down to the locker-room and collected the nearly empty half-bottle of bourbon. There was a witch-hunt in progress. There were four guys in the locker-room walking round in a stupor with their cards in their hands, and the security guards had been called in. He travelled back to the natal unit with the bottle in his boot.

He scattered some bourbon over Kathy's coat and left the bottle in a pocket. She was trying to rage at Franco in the staff-room. Martin walked round the natal unit, checking that it was in order. He got Franco and himself a clipboard with a sheaf of papers, and called him out of the staff-room.

Two security men stepped out of the elevator and they were angry.

'Could you keep it quieter please?' Martin asked them, 'we've got a lot of sleeping babies in here.' He hid his smile as they creaked across to him, hands irritating night-sticks, faces puffy with fury.

'Party? Where? There's no party up here,' Martin told them.

'You didn't even hear about it?'

'No, we've been upstairs all night. Ask the girl in the staff-room, she went downstairs a while ago; she might have heard something.'

Kathy was fired: they smelt the booze, they asked whose coat it was, they gave her fifteen minutes to clear her locker. They didn't hear her whines of protest, they went on checking the corridors of the hospital right through until morning. Franco and Martin got a few hours' sleep in the staff-room. Martin was finished with collecting garbage. They were right back in the nativity business.

26

Billy came out of the theatre and walked three blocks. He walked under the Westside Expressway and sat at the entrance to the pier. Further up-river, a Circle Line cruiseboat swung out a cargo of tourists and headed south over the Lincoln Tunnel. Two flat barges planed the mid-river. Apart from that, the Hudson was empty.

During the first week of rehearsals, Billy had played it quietly. There had been something detached about him, a feeling of routine. The two productions looked as though they might lose their edge. Billy deferred to the actress who was playing his mother; she was flattered, she took over the show and the show got stuck on her. In the second play, Billy fed the younger actress every feeling she had. He was brutal at first. There were days when from the front row of the seats you could feel his frustration roll over you towards the back of the theatre; having looked to the mother, he was angry at the girl's apparent incapacity. But she was patient. The director worked on her, and he let Billy work on her. Billy was finding his own way through to Jamie. Billy carried a lot, but Billy knew his resources. The first play was posing more problems and took up more of the director's time.

Billy *didn't* know what he was doing. He was adrift, he could make no contact with the mother. Nothing was worked out. He didn't know if he was missing everything. The director was laconic, the director said 'fine' occasionally. It all went past Billy. No one set any limits to the darkness. They weren't fixing him, they weren't interested in him. He wasn't coming up with it; he was insubstantial.

No one to talk to about it.

And anyway, goddam you, stop shoving your rotten soul in my lap, they were right.

Coming back from the pier, he passed by the theatre. The rest of the company had gone home, the crew would be resetting the stage for the current show. Billy hung around.

'Oh, Mr Maffett?'

'Yeah? Billy.'

'I work', it was the kid who worked out front of house, 'in

the box office, and we're sending out the complimentary tickets right now, if you would like to tell me what you want. If that's convenient for you.'

'Sure it is.' Billy followed him.

'We've just about chased everybody else up, I've been meaning to get round to you for some time.'

They went into a small office which was wallpapered with show posters; one of them was for the O'Neill festival, Billy had his name up there. The kid got out a folder from a desk drawer. 'What would you like?'

Billy asked for two opening-night tickets to be sent to Diane, he took one more for Donald, and he mailed two later Saturday-night tickets to Martin. He thought of buying the kid a drink, but he was involved in his office and what the hell would Billy say to him anyway, say to anyone. So it was back to the penthouse, staying clear of Donald, not picking up the phone to call Linda, leaving them alone, forgetting about Diane.

I have a pride in giving. Three years ago at the Farm I took from Billy – for all I know he felt the reverse, but that doesn't matter – and we went away guilty and loveless to pursue our plans and to cover the loose ends. We had both survived without any regret, we had even profited from our impatience.

When he said: 'It's the first time in my life for not loving', it was almost as though he had learned how to smile without having to laugh, as if he had grown out of a need. Much as I had grown out of the need for attention.

Strange for me that I can't begin to think what I want out of a relationship with him, nor what I would want for him. I would like to have him with me, to do things for him, to love him – certainly. But he changes by himself and on his own, I understand that and I don't want to monopolise it or to have my feelings for him become my exasperation with someone I have created. I am happier with my feelings at a distance. My weakness? But well balanced by Billy's huge reservoir of feeling, his strength.

He called several times, worried or excited about his rehearsal. His calls were sudden; I was always tempted to call him back an hour later, when I had found something to say. I did try to get back to him once, after he had come through to me with a long and uncertain tirade about self-deceit, but he had concealed his trail with an answering machine; I can't fill the vacancy of those machines.

Pam shouldn't have come with me to the opening night. Billy and I should have been alone after the show and perhaps we could have admitted how much we wanted to be with each other, we might have laughed at ourselves. I wanted to ridicule everything to do with myself. We might have talked the night free of all our moral seriousness and our small subtle offers which came like boxes out of boxes out of boxes.

It was a difficult experience, being anxious for him. I used to feel annoyed or appreciative or exasperated when watching other actors. That was a professional reaction. I would try to escape what was happening onstage, deliberately *not* believe, in order to find the different way in which *I* would have made the part truthful. Now I had none of that. I just hoped that Billy would get through it.

He was powerful. He has always had a strong stage presence, his main difficulty is in knowing how to shade it. He seemed irritable at being onstage, at being enclosed by the monotonous fatality of Jamie's character. His performance was disjointed. It was a stimulating experiment, but most of the audience wanted to see a well-varnished product such as they got from the girl in the cast.

We went backstage. His tiredness and preoccupation were probably exaggerated in order to disguise his uncertainty about his performance. He had given the character of Jamie more charm than it merited, he knew this and felt depressed at the evasion, he didn't want to talk about it. He wanted to join in the acclaim for the novice, Patti. It was her start, that was important. They shared full smiles and the self-contained embraces which try to fill an actor's need for replenishment.

Billy wanted to make it an occasion for everyone else. We went on to a late, large dinner party in a Village restaurant, Billy drew us in from the periphery. He and I rarely looked at each other, not even when the first editions arrived and the reviews were passed from hand to hand. Pam took everything very seriously, demanding to know what it all meant, making everyone laugh. I caught Billy's eye, wanting us to leave, we didn't need critics or good reviews; they hadn't changed Billy's concern. The most they might have done was distract him, and he seemed to be refusing the offer, despite Donald's pestering.

On our way out, when the party had broken up, Billy hugged Patti. She looked across at me, wondering what I was and what part I played in Billy's life, with that look which women never miss and which men think is women admiring each other. I was glad not to be a part of that scene, nor reliant on it, and to know that Billy was experienced enough to feel the same way. But he would need protecting. She gazed at him like a young cuckoo at a food-laden foster parent, and Billy, naturally enough, liked it and tried hopelessly and disarmingly to pretend that he didn't like it.

By the time that we walked into the apartment, it was two-thirty in the morning. Donald helped Billy carry the spare bed into Billy's room and he disappeared off to sleep. Billy dumped the newspapers on the dining-room table. Pam kissed him and said how much she had enjoyed it, we went to arrange the bedding.

I removed my make-up - except for the mascara - changed into a bathrobe and cleaned my teeth, brushed my hair. I laid my dress and slip over a chair, switched off the bedroom light and left Pam to sleep.

Billy was sprawled along the couch, smoking. I made a cup of coffee for us both and sat opposite him, feeling wide-awake, tucking my legs under myself to keep my feet warm. Billy noticed it. 'We should have a fire.'

'It's late; go to sleep, darling.'

'It's good that you came.'

'I wasn't sure if it would be uncomfortable for you, having me at the opening night.'

'Maybe confusing. I'm sorry. Are you going to sleep there tonight?'

'Yes.'

'It's better than nothing.' He opened one eye and smiled ironically.

'Go to sleep.'

'You look great,' he said solemnly.

'Dream about me then.' It was unfair but I enjoyed it, knowing that we couldn't lose.

'I didn't do too well tonight, it wasn't there for me.'

'I thought that you played it right, and it's going to come out more, isn't it?'

'I have this block about people believing in it. I don't *want* people believing in me.'

'You have that whether you like it or not.'

'I don't feel easy with it at the moment.'

'You don't have anything to feel sorry for yourself about. Patti believes in you,' I teased.

'Sure.'

'You can't screw them all, darling.' I laughed.

'I *can* screw them all,' he mumbled. 'I don't want to screw anyone out of what they believe in, but I don't want them believing in me.'

Most of him went to sleep. I carried the blankets through from the bedroom and put one over him, I turned out the light and lay along my own couch, wrapping myself up.

I couldn't sleep. I couldn't move my head on the small cushion, my hair got in the way, my left hand reached behind my head for nothing. One leg slipped over the side of the couch, delicious, and my foot pressed the tension against Billy's carpet. I touched myself under the blanket; but I was much too aware of trying to assert myself. Billy twitched violently in his sleep, trying to rid himself of something, very much on his own. Pam could have slept out here, we might have slept together in Billy's room. I wouldn't have let him sleep; I would have convinced him that it wasn't right to sleep, would have argued with him and kept him with me, loved him through it. I had the power to do that.

Meticulously I lifted the blanket and stood on the carpet. I placed the lamp on the floor and hung Billy's jacket over the side of the table so that he would be cut off from the light. When I turned the switch the darkness retired to the other end of the room. Billy didn't move. I suddenly wanted to drop something on to the glass-topped table, only something small like a cigarette lighter or a pen, not to wake him up but to have him stir.

Instead, I went over to the window and smoked one of Billy's cigarettes – my first in months – and I reflected that I ought to feel sentimental, or feel philosophical, or feel *something* about the whole bunched enormity of New York that was out there beyond the window, down six inches, across three feet, back eight feet. But it was just New York, that was all. And Billy's apartment, Billy and Donald's apartment, much the same as when I had called in before, years ago. Only now I was *with* Billy. Not an affair. An affair?

No. The apartment still didn't look as though he lived there, which I might find incomprehensible; irritating in the long term.

I wonder if tomorrow I will feel the need to leave something behind, a scarf or a cosmetic.

We've all done *that* before! It takes me too much effort, I don't even like throwing away paper in the street. I am really not very inquisitive about him. I'm not very inquisitive, period; nothing to do with age, I never have been inquisitive. But nevertheless, if I stand here looking out of the window at New York, if I don't close my eyes, I could list the things in this room. Dining area to the left, not a part of the main room, so: table with lamp, two tiers of bookholder underneath, chesterfield, table with lamp. Across in front of the door: couch, blankets, lamp on the floor. Etcetera and so on. All reflected in the window. I win.

I have sleeping pills. I don't *want* to go to sleep.

I ought to think about Billy's play, but it seems to exist only in as much as the reviews exist – inside the pile of newsprint on the table. He will read them time and time again, on his own, until they don't make any sense and he stops being impressed by them. He has it, I don't know what, quality, credibility, that's not my affair, *he* is my affair.

I said earlier that I was meticulous. I think that meticulous has no moral implication to it, it's not a question of confining other people to a framework of my acceptance or expectation. I was brought up inside a system that believed it wasn't a system, and this belief was the one reward that brought us up inside the system.

Great. Thank you, Diane. And what do you think of masturbation?

Well, the bed could be a little more comfortable, Billy could quit trying to drag half a seashore along the back of his throat, I'd rather get some sleep if you come right down to it. Or go to the freezer and pull out some orange juice.

Billy, Billy.

I want to touch him. We'll have it in January.

All the business of sitting down and figuring it out, doing a lot of nothing together. That would be enough.

Going over to my place on the couch, I upset a coffee cup. Unusual for me. Late. I cleaned the stain and washed my hands and switched off the light.

I would like a hand on my breast, for five minutes.

Slowly, morning. A dread of Donald waking and bringing in the day, which hardened into a personal dislike before I heard the sound of Donald's alarm clock and his movements round the bedroom.

I willed Donald away from us, and he duly stayed clear. He went to work, closing the door behind him.

I luxuriated carelessly in the thought of Donald caught up in the downtown rush. And in the knowledge that my face looked good after a sleepless night, the skin would have tightened, the eyes would not be bagged. Part of a love for Billy, a part of myself, a circle slowly moving outwards, recovering each other. I was happy to have spent the night here; I recognised pieces of the room, Billy himself looked small in the daylight, the room held out more confidence.

Pam appeared in the doorway. I put a finger to my lips; I quietly lifted the blankets and joined her. We showered and dressed. I took Billy's keys off the sideboard, leaving him a note, and we went out to breakfast.

Pam wanted to buy books; I came back alone. Billy was still asleep. Since there was nothing else for me to do, I started to tidy Billy's end of the apartment, placing my case in the corridor.

Billy came in, blinkered and puffy with sleep and innocence, an unlit cigarette hanging from two fingers. He embraced me and patted me absent-mindedly, going to lie on the bed.

I folded a blanket, very aware of him watching me, half-asleep but still a little sadly.

I wanted to be close to him. I wanted him to touch me. I wanted us to make love. I wanted us to be that close.

I sat on the bed and then lay along it, an arm round his neck, undressing with one hand. I wanted him right inside me. I felt enormous and in pieces. Still opening the buttons on my dress with one hand. Giving up.

Wanting him to put a cushion underneath me so that I was offered up. A huge reaching target. Want. And on top. Want. Want. Needing the sensation along inside me.

And I have you, I have you. I have you, Billy.

27

It was like being in an Aquarium amongst the hushed comment from the visitors before the rippleless tanks. Again the steady atmosphere of the chamber. The soft light filtering through the water over the large, blinking fish that hang motionlessly as if set in plastic and reduced to a work of art; while the tiny, bright minnows dart according to some preconceived pattern.

Here was Franco, suspended in the tranquillity of the natal unit, obese with stagnation and contentment. And Martin, having come back from the outside, from the basement, restlessly observing these creatures move to and fro behind the thick glass. He was searching for a brick. He found the atmosphere debilitating.

'If I stay here another month, I'll die here.'

'There's worse places to die,' was Franco's comment, 'you only have to go down three floors to get packaged up.'

They were sitting in the staff-room towards the end of the day, seventeen deliveries under their belts and waiting for a late dropper.

'What's wrong with the woman?' Martin looked at his watch.

'We couldn't take her in the afternoon rush; they gave her some drugs to hold it back.'

'Can't they give her some speed or something?'

Franco rested his eyes on the television.

'You're not getting bored?' Martin continued to nibble at him.

'Nope.' Franco brushed the question away. 'I'm going to get the sax up here and start practising. I've got the time and the place to do it; and I'm bein' paid. When I get out of here, I'll be the finest and richest sax-player in the country.' He grinned to himself.

The door opened and two nurses came in. Martin unwound from his slump and fetched some coffee. Franco made no move.

They were Sadie and Carol, they shared an apartment. They talked; or Carol did, sitting on the arm of a chair. Sadie smoked and paid some limited attention to the television.

Martin warmed to Carol. He made a play for her and got

nowhere. She was determined on Franco, hence their visit. Franco was at his most indifferent, dealing out very little of himself. To keep things going, Martin gave up on Carol and swung over to take her side in the assault on Franco. There wasn't anything they could do. Franco didn't want to be disturbed, and Martin ended up talking about nothing in an artificial way. Carol was attractive. The whole conversation was pointless.

It was Franco who killed it. Carol kept nagging at him until he flicked his eyes over her body and snapped at her: 'Do you want to get laid?'

She walked out of the room. Martin offered to take Sadie home in an hour, when his shift wound down. She said no, she would go with Carol, but she asked him to look in later for a coffee.

Franco was so touchy that Martin didn't ask him any questions.The mother came through with the kid soon afterwards; Martin cleared up and prepared to leave. Franco pulled on a cigarette. He asked Martin to apologise to Carol; it had been the only way to get rid of her. He was aiming to be self-sufficient at the moment and he wanted it known. He wasn't interested in her. His apologies. Not that it would break Carol's heart, she couldn't find it difficult to get hold of a man.

Martin bought some wine and went round to see the two girls, who lived in an upmarket apartment block in the centre of town. They had both been married and were now divorced, Carol living high off the alimony while Sadie made a lot of money out of her senior position at the hospital. He wanted to end up in bed with Carol, but she left the room soon after he arrived. He tried to readjust, but at midnight Sadie felt that he might leave.

He was back in the natal unit at eight the next morning with a sour taste in his mouth and even less enthusiasm for the job. He pushed the mop over the floor and showed three fathers their products, he argued with Franco about nothing at all. He wanted out. The hours dragged on. He called the physiotherapy department at lunch break. Carol was at lunch.

She was sitting with Sadie and two other nurses at a corner table, eating a salad and drinking coffee. Martin approached. Carol told him to pull up a chair.

He couldn't handle four girls in a group; and they talked

nursing, about which he knew nothing. Occasionally Carol would let herself out of the conversation and ask Martin about the natal unit or how he was enjoying it in America, but it was hard going, even tense. Martin wondered what he was doing there. She offered to let him talk about England. He couldn't find anything to say. He was stuck. Carol watched him, summing him up, and he was nonplussed. Their break ended. They wandered down the corridor. 'What's going on with Franco?' she asked him.

'I don't know. Nothing seems to interest him. He wants it that way. Do you know him well?'

'I heard that he was down.' She avoided any history. 'It's a small town when you've lived here for more than a year. You appreciate people you took for granted when you first arrived. Maybe we'll be seeing you.'

Martin took the elevator. He mentioned her to Franco.

'Yeah, rich bitches; they're all full of shit.'

Martin waded through the afternoon and wanted to get out on the town as soon as he could. Franco was annoyed at covering for him.

'Just tonight,' Martin asked.

'Okay, but if the supervisor comes on heavy then I'm not going to screw myself up with excuses.'

'Right.'

'You want to quit?' Franco eyed him.

'The money's too good.'

Franco snorted in disgust.

'I'll take a day off, and I'll cut back to doing just the one shift. Do you want to cut back?'

'Nope. I like it up here. Has Sadie got anything to do with this?'

'Sadie? No, not at all. Why Sadie?'

'She looks pretty sharp.'

He wasn't hard, not untouchable, not resigned, not careless, not cold, not playing any game. A lot of nots, with someone not knowing whether to emerge from them. Occasionally he and Martin were very close, but they rationed out their affection for each other.

'Are you still going off to California?'

'Maybe.' It was Martin's turn to play shy.

'Until then you're going to sit in Jake's all night and get drunk.'

296

'Yes.'

'You'd better take the keys to the apartment. I'll see you in the morning.' Franco flipped up and down the scales on the sax.

Martin passed by the apartment. Not a woman's touch anywhere. The bath enamel was crusted over, the bed sheets were grey, his papers had a settled covering of city grime which wouldn't blow off.

Martin made a start; he put on the television and cleaned out the stinking freezer.

Screw it. He looked at his writings. There was a lot to be crossed out. The television pandered through from the living-room. Martin collected the pages together and dumped them in his case. No point. Make some money and

Come back here. Come back *here?*

He walked from the room, turned off the television and locked the door behind him.

Rifling through the mailbox on the way out; there was a bill from the phone company which wouldn't cost him very much, and a letter from England with his uncle's handwriting on the envelope. Martin took a shallow breath. He read the letter, standing in the hallway, quickly, thinking that he would save the full impact until later. Philip thanked him for his letter and outlined the pleasant summer weather in England, Annie's inability to get over a cold and the rumoured entry of Aston Villa into the football transfer market; he wished Martin well.

Martin had never connected with his uncle. He never knew whether to feel it; whether he ought to feel it. He never threw away Philip's letters, he kept the single sheets and the envelopes. Martin and he had sometimes talked about the local football team.

And there was another letter, with the address typed. He opened it. There were two tickets for *A Moon for the Misbegotten* and a scrawled note from Billy – 'This is the play. I hope! Yours, Billy Maffett.'

Martin put the note and the tickets back in the envelope, folded all the envelopes in half, and pushed them down inside the breast pocket of his shirt.

Martin eased into the drunk slowly, not even keen on the idea or feeling any particular taste for the means of doing it. The beer was lousy, the Daniel's was too quick, the cocktails too much paraphernalia. If he drank Laird's he felt guilty about leaving Franco up in the unit alone. And the amount of orange juice they put in the tequila made it sickly.

It was out of this indecision that the drunk arrived. It crept up unnoticed and went past him, throttle wide open, dragging him along in its slipstream. He had nothing to say to anyone though conversation came and went with whoever happened to sit on the stool next to him. He was English, people wanted to talk about something meaningful, something comparative. As he got more drunk, it exasperated him. What do you think about England? Shit. What do you reckon to the States? Shit.

At times he tried to focus on Billy. He tried to convince Billy that he, Martin, was just taking time off from being creative.

Fuck Billy.

Chestnut came in on the arm of a new man, and Martin found it more difficult to talk with an acquaintance than with a stranger. They dissolved away from him into a far corner of the bar. Martin stuck to his glass, blindly.

Late in the night, he recognised a flash of blond hair. He turned unsteadily. The Kid was over by the door, feeding the cigarette machine for a pack of Kools. Martin was glad enough to see him. The Kid came over, peeling the Cellophane off the pack; Martin ordered him a beer.

'Whas going on?'

'I got back from a club in the city. We're doin' real good. Got a new keyboard player.' The Kid lit a cigarette and reached over the stool to get rid of the match. 'Hear you two are down at the hospital.'

'I'm drunk.'

'Yeah? I don't drink that much. I can't. I got a screwed-up liver. I dig smoking grass better; it's good for your head.'

'Right.'

'Yeah ... well ... I gotta get back and see my old lady, stop her bitching. If you show at one of the gigs, I can get you a couple of freeloaders' tickets.'

'Great.'

'Bring Franco along. Maybe it would do him some good to hear some music again.'

'Sure.'

And that was it. The Kid left. Martin was too drunk to detain him or to suggest going back to his place for a smoke.

He lit another cigarette out of nothing else to do, and couldn't handle it. He drank half the Kid's beer and caught himself in favour of letting his head go down on the bar; to sleep, to sleep.

He pulled himself off the stool and plodded his feet towards the exit, surprised and proud that his body was following. The barman called after him, something about his cigarettes; Martin waved a hand vaguely and stumbled into the night air.

It was a long way to walk, a long way. Martin sighed.

He leant against the wall but realised that if he sat down he wouldn't stand up again until morning. He wondered if he should make himself sick. Dialogue between brain and stomach which got repetitive, and he felt himself sleeping, the weight on his legs was terrific, he wondered that the tarmac took it. His shirt scraped against the wall.

There were other people coming out of Jake's, a long way away. Martin squinted out at them. He stuck his hands in his pockets and pretended that he was waiting for a bus with dignity. But there were no buses. He stumbled round the corner.

He wondered if he'd make it. There was nothing to sing.

His boots were too heavy. The hedge and the grass looked strange in the night-light, motionless. Same as it had done at Donna's. Hoped she was getting on all right. Small body, lovely. Skin was smooth. Pity. Nothing to talk about.

He yawned, and becoming more conscious of where he was, he felt more sober, or less incapably drunk. He walked on.

It came into his head that he should go to see Carol, talk things over with her, help her out a bit. He laughed out loud at this alcoholic shifting of responsibilities. The moment she opened her mouth, he would go to sleep.

Could he piss here? One of these wooden houses, behind the hedge. Which wasn't tall enough to hide him from the road. He ducked down and listened for the silence. Only the roar in his ears.

He got it out and bent over it, muttering to it and coaxing it. Cursing it as the pain in his back became apparent. Or was he going to be sick? Is that why he was here? What exit was everything going to take?

He looked up at the sky, where there was nothing further than the glow from the streetlamps, no moon, no stars, and the road with nothing on it. Strange how in English newspapers they always had bits about the violence and murder in America, nothing about the boredom of the whole place. He slipped backwards and looked down again to balance. He collided with the hedge. He laughed at himself, annoyed underneath. He would walk on, that was better.

He was going past her flat anyway. It was a tall building, he couldn't remember what floor, but there was a light on one of the floors, in one of the rooms. It would be hers. Things are made that way.

Martin took several breaths and wondered if he could handle it. Shit, he could wish her a good evening over the house-phone, joke a little, remind her that he existed, that he was a late-night creature like she was, the kind of person who was disinterestedly friendly.

The guard was at his desk, looking at Martin through the glass entrance, with his revolver laid out on the magazines.

Martin tapped. The guard looked at him and then at his watch. Martin went through some mimicry about wanting to get inside. The guard came round the desk with the gun in his hand, eyeing Martin while he turned the key in the door. He let Martin in.

'Who for?'

Martin gave Carol's name and his own. The guard kept an eye on him while he telephoned. 'It's gettin' on to be late, mister, and you've had a lot of liquor. You sure you don't want to call the lady up in the morning?'

'No, she might be expecting me.' Martin now knew that he lacked credibility. The light was dazzling him; he might just have the energy to leave his name. The guard hung on the phone.

'Miss Sadie? This is Bradley, ma'am. There's someone down here in the lobby. It's a quarter of three, ma'am. That's right. I will ... '

'Thank you, Bradley.' The guard handed the phone over to Martin, who didn't have a brain in his head. 'Hi ... '

There was no answer.

'Carol? Are you awake?'

'No, she's out. This is Sadie. I was just going to bed.'

300

'Oh.'

Bradley turned away and sat back down in his chair, utterly indifferent, noting down the time of the call on a printed chart. In case he got killed? Martin watched him blearily. Surely the killer wouldn't be so stupid as to leave the timesheet lying there for the police.

'Can I help you?' Sadie's voice.

'I was out on the town, I got drunk. It was a mistake. I'm sorry.' Pause. Silence. 'What've you been doing?'

She was still silent.

'What?'

'Okay,' she said, 'hand me over to Bradley.'

Martin gave Bradley the phone, having no idea what was to happen, thinking that now possibly was the time to bow out and make a last effort to get back to Franco's. The apartment, he realised, was in the other direction from Jake's Barn.

'Twenty minutes ... I'll do that, ma'am.' Bradley hung up. 'You got in; I hope you're goin' to behave yourself up there.'

'What floor is it?' Martin was elated.

'Four.'

'I'll take the stairs; I need the exercise.'

'You jus' take the elevator, it's right here.'

Bradley came round the desk and pressed all the right buttons for Martin. He arrived on the fourth floor without having said good-night to Bradley. He said it in the corridor, and thank you, Bradley.

He discovered the geography and pressed the buzzer to the apartment. Sadie looked at him.

'You *are* drunk.'

'I know.' Martin leant in the hallway.

'Very?'

'Yeah.'

'Bradley is going to phone through in fifteen minutes to check out that you don't have any ideas.'

He laughed hollowly. 'I haven't got any ideas.'

'I'll make you some coffee. Why don't you sit in the lounge? The lights in the kitchen will be too bright.'

'Thanks, Sadie.'

'In the lounge,' she called to remind him.

The cushions were on the carpet. Martin stretched out and took his boots off, then sat up to try to restore his consciousness.

'Where's Carol?' he mumbled. He cleared his throat. 'Where's Carol?'

'I stayed in tonight,' she came through with some black instant coffee, 'and Carol went out. Friday night for falling in love, Saturday for making love, Sunday for falling out of love.'

'That's terrible,' Martin mumbled. He felt himself going again. He put the coffee cup on the carpet.

'She sets her hair and goes to work on Monday.'

'And you?' He decided that Sadie was attractive.

'No.'

'No ... ' Martin agreed. 'Sadie, I want to go to bed.'

She looked at him from over the top of her bunched-up legs and considered.

'Drink the coffee.'

'I'm sorry.'

'That's all right.'

Now he had to walk, a long way, back to the apartment; but not yet, he couldn't. Drink more coffee. He would make it himself.

'Stay there,' she said, 'I'll do it.'

'Did you live here when you were married?' he asked, clearer, when she returned.

'I thought I swept the place out pretty good.'

'Rich husband?' he said bitterly.

'So so. I do all right on my own. I bought everything off him.'

'Yes,' Martin apologised.

'I wanted this apartment, and I wanted to be free of him.'

'Yes.'

There was a long silence.

'Is it still like that?' he asked her.

She took one of the cushions and sat opposite him. Using her hands, speaking monotonously, she built up the story brick by brick as if she wanted to make sure the wall was solid. It was all grey, though every now and then she would plaster it with some lurid poster to see how he reacted. It was a dull history, she had no anger or sympathy for herself; and she was very safe, looking at him from behind this wall. She had constructed her life out of calling-cards, the late-night massage service, the body, the throat and the warm, sticky oblivion for a hundred men on her taste-buds. She started by insuring the car and finished with the apartment. One night she was in a rush and didn't have time to change out of her nurse's uniform. The man liked it. It gave him some spice. *Then* she stopped, and went to lie on a beach for a month. She saw the need for some compromise and a friend. Carol helped out.

The coffee was finished. Martin was ashamed of just about everything, including himself. Most of all ashamed of himself, scab labour.

'What are you doing tomorrow night?' he asked her.

'I'm going out.'

He thanked her for the coffee. She picked up the house-phone and told the guard he was coming down. She saw him to the door. She averted her lips. He walked down the corridor to the elevator.

'Good night.' Martin walked towards the guard. He nodded and unlocked the door. He went back to his crime magazines.

Martin didn't have to alter his shifts. They heard on Thursday that the strike was to finish at the weekend, and their attachment to the hospital would be over.

Franco was depressed. He went to the office and asked if he could stay on. There was no vacancy; the administration would call him up if any of the regular staff failed to check in after the strike. He didn't have much faith in the outcome. But, unlike Martin who slackened his involvement, Franco dropped the saxophone into his downstairs locker and fussed and hassled and devoted himself to the natal unit as though he didn't trust the incoming staff.

'What is it?' Martin asked him.

'What do you mean?' Franco demanded.

'We're finishing here. You don't want to build a monument.'

'You're crazy. I'm not doing any more than I used to do.'

'Why don't we take the money and go to California?'

'Nope. The hospital might call up. If they don't, I'll try with the sax, take a look around for some other musicians.'

That *was* crazy. Franco on sax was like Nixon on honesty; fiddling over the scales was one thing, convincing people you could play was another. Martin looked up at him but Franco was already turned away and going out of the staff-room. Saturday was the night of Billy's play. Martin asked Franco if he wanted to go. Franco hesitated.

'Yeah?'

'What else are you going to do?'

'Okay. I never went to the theatre.'

'Let's start off in the afternoon.'

'What for? You got anything you want to do?'

'Not especially.'

'Maybe I should clean the apartment.'

'It's clean. I did it the other day.'

'Yeah?' Franco wasn't going to leave his base easily. He stood with one finger against his bottom lip. 'Well, sure we'll go, yeah.'

Friday night they collected their last wage packet, walked out of the basement exit and up past the crusher.

They went round the bars, avoiding Jake's Barn. Martin told Franco about the Kid's offer of free tickets.

'It might be a lead in for the music business.'

'That's not the kind of music I want to play and not the kind of people I want to play with.'

'But you're not playing with anybody.'

'Yeah, I know that. I'll wait. It isn't worth getting screwed around.'

They arrived in a bar where there was music, a band playing down one end. The band was lousy. When they heard this kind of band, Franco usually ignored the music; he preferred to talk, to throw in a little irony. Tonight he sat still, listening. He listened until the end of the set and then he said to Martin: 'Let's buy a bottle of Laird's and go back to the apartment. You feel like that?'

Martin concurred. When they were out in the street, Franco was enthusiastic about the band: they needed a little practice, a couple of new songs ...

'I thought they were crap.'

'Yeah, but that's an easy thing to say.'

'They'll never be a good band, Franco.'

'Yeah, they will.' He looked at the sidewalk. He wanted them to be a good band. He refused to let them go down. 'If people told you that you were a bad writer, what would you do?'

'I'd ignore them for a bit, and then if it went on I wouldn't write any more.'

'Right!'

'But if I was a bad writer, there wouldn't be any point in doing it.'

'I don't know if you're a good writer or a bad writer, but writing isn't something you have any choice about, is it?'

'Yes it is.'

'It is?' Franco stood stock-still, shaking his head. 'I didn't have that feeling about you before, when you were writing in the apartment. I didn't figure you'd take the hospital job.'

'I needed the money.'

'Yah shit ... '

'So did you,' Martin reminded him.

'Yeah, but I could have kept us going for a while. Jeez, I liked it up there. I had the time to do what I wanted.'

'It was a bit unreal.'

'What the hell do you want? What's unreal about people giving birth? It's pretty warm and creative. That's what I want. I can't deal in cold shit.' His eyes twitched sideways, as though he was trying not to see anything.

Franco wasn't keen to go into New York. They didn't have any plan for the afternoon; Martin didn't want to see Billy. He induced Franco to set off without any plan in mind; that they should walk around the city and do whatever took their fancy before going to the theatre. Franco armed himself with two packs of cigarettes. He called up a friend of his father's and arranged to leave the car in a high-security underground automobile bunker off the Park on 57th, where the office took his driving licence with the photograph on it and his keys.

They sauntered slowly down through the mid-town area, crossing from Fifth to Second Avenue and back again in time for Grand Central Station, not so much interested in the buildings as in the people and the whirligig of colour and impression. It was a lazy stroll. They took a sandwich and a beer at some place on 42nd Street and they decided to go down to Gramercy Park, if they got that far without succumbing to a music shop.

The buildings came down to meet them as they got into the 30s. They were a couple of blocks past 34th Street, beginning to think about heading towards the theatre. Martin glanced both ways at the lights and elected to head East. Franco wanted to stick on Lexington, but Martin thought it didn't look very interesting. They turned East.

This street was strangely artificial, it didn't look as though the Sanitation Department visited too often. It couldn't have been very dangerous for there was a cop car parked half-way down, and one cop chatted easily to a passer-by.

They threaded their way through the garbage in front of four old blacks sitting on beer crates, they were passed by younger, sharper blacks on their way into Harlem for the evening; they stopped to watch a delivery driver arguing with a line of waiting cars, he had a good command of the language, the irate drivers wound up their windows and blasted their horns. Franco laughed; they drifted on. Two orthodox Jews argued fervently under their hats, an old and a young; spicy smells distracted Franco into a delicatessen where he bought a huge torpedo, stuffed with meat and peppers; Martin refused to get involved.

A smart lady strutted towards them and disappeared up a flight of steps; there was a small, grimy bookshop and a bar buried underneath the building at the side. Franco tried to drag Martin into the shop, Martin said no, no, no; they laughed. A wretched white juvenile hooker paused against the wall to scrape at her hair, while a drunken failure negotiated the street, searching in his pocket for her fee. She didn't smile at him. A business man, rich enough to feel out of place, kept a steady direction and a preoccupied expression on his face. A guy in a mohair suit looked scornfully up at the sky while a punk held a hand out to him, jabbering his angle; the guy put on his shades as Martin and Franco passed. Franco wiped his mouth on the paper and threw the remaining half of the torpedo in the direction of a trashcan, which swallowed it neatly. Style, said Franco. Luck, said Martin.

They came up to and passed the two cops and their car. They were now involved with an informer, who sat in the back seat, leaning forward, gesticulating. Martin caught his eye; the informer wound up the car window. A nondescript man with a briefcase bumped against Franco and apologised, and went on ahead of them, those short American trousers flapping against the tops of his ankles. Two kids in white basketball boots skipped in and out and around the pedestrians, bouncing nothing between them; their ownership of the streets. Martin followed their progress, their mad dance as they weaved away past a big Italian lady with her arm under a sack of groceries, a youngster trailing along beside her, an old lady with a dog, a black activist, the back of the nondescript man – a paunchy guy in a white shirt, coming down the steps with a gun, pushing a woman away from him – it all froze, the people in front of Martin's eyes.

The black activist, perhaps his mind picked up on the wave of dangerous energy, he had a split second to look up before he died, he just folded on to the pavement, the gun was going off again, the nondescript man was lying down and coughing blood over his briefcase. Martin saw. It was random. He pushed Franco into the side of the wall. The gun pointed at them, held in two hands, Martin couldn't move.

The gun switched, the guy turned away and picked out one of the kids. Shame, thought Martin, the kid screamed violently and ran his death into the side of a car. The guy's woman was once again hanging on to his arm. He shook her off and killed the hooker who was on the other side of the street; it was a good shot – the drunk stared in disbelief, Martin couldn't move; people realised and started running; the groceries went down in the gutter; Martin knew that he wouldn't get killed. There was a moment when the crowd took over, the guy was filled with indecision. The gun flickered from target to target to Martin to target. The Italian woman was shot in the leg. The gunman's energy was running out. Maybe it was the noise from the rolling groceries. Martin was hit hard in the back and fell to the pavement. A cop knelt beside him, took aim, and shot the gunman in the chest.

Franco was huddled behind a garbage can, one hand clutching the rim, vomiting silently. The cop ran up the street to watch the gunman die over the railings. Martin lay on the sidewalk, peaceful for a moment, until the screaming disturbed him.

He got to his feet. The nondescript man was injured, there was nothing he could do. For some reason, he walked forward and lifted the dead kid on to the bonnet of the car. This seemed to arrange things better. He looked at the kid and put his hand into the gore coming out of the chest, it was warm, he put a smear of it behind his ear. He wiped his hand against the car. He looked up.

The cop car arrived beside him. He recalled that it had just travelled fifty yards with its lights and siren. He moved away from it. The blood on his hand was already drying and was like a thin rubber glove over his skin. He walked back. Franco's torment was wide-eyed and catatonic, he shrank away behind the garbage can. Martin pulled Franco out by the arm and looked at him. He slapped him twice, hard, across the face. Franco's eyes were dull.

'Franco! Franco!' he called. Franco wasn't there. Martin drew him close and whispered to him. 'Franco ... listen ... you're alive. There are people who are hurt.'

Franco wasn't there; he was far gone. Martin took his hand from Franco's back and tightened it round the handle of the garbage bin. He then put this hand round his other wrist, clutching his own flesh. It was still the same devoid material as the garbage can. Franco's whole body started to shake and Martin held on to him.

Martin knew that his balance was being overdrawn; when he had stood there confidently watching the psychopath picking his targets, watching the gun swing round at him, the barrel waver and turn away. Martin knew. He was low on assets but he wasn't broke, not yet. He knew also that Franco would have been shot when the gun came across, that the body against him would have been left uninhabited. Franco deserved better – slowly, painfully slowly, odd sobs ventured out of him and heaved up from his chest into the daylight, reasserting himself, cleaning him out.

They both followed the wounded and the dead to the hospital, their shirts covered in blood from the nondescript man who might make it if they pumped enough plasma into him during the ambulance ride. Franco hadn't wanted to visit the hospital, but Martin insisted and he unwillingly let himself be taken care of.

What else was there to do? You couldn't just stroll into a Eugene O'Neill festival after having been in a scene like that, you needed some special surroundings to woo you through the clear-cut impressions and the surges of re-enactment. And the hospital would be the nearest thing to going home, for both of them.

They sat in the staff-room over cups of coffee and a pill, recovering their strength. The pill took over.

Martin sat in a corner, wrapped in a blanket, smoking cigarettes while the electricity in his mind flashed and crackled and finally subsided under the influence of the drug. He fused slowly with his exhaustion.

News came through in jerks and snippets from the white-clad nurses who wheeled in and out of the room.

Excluding the killer, three dead and two wounded.

Six shock cases.

The nondescript man was critical.

The killer had shot at the first five people he saw, his wife was under sedation.

His wage packet had been stolen for the second week running, and he had lost his head.

Police would take statements from anyone who wished to file a complaint. For the insurance.

What? Against capitalism? File a complaint against capitalism? Against loneliness? Against a miserable job and a miserable wage? Against the deprivation of self-respect? Martin tittered. A lawsuit against God, he would sue God for everything the bastard had. Who would represent God? Wall Street. Would God win? Yes.

Franco didn't wish to file a complaint. Neither did Martin. The drug was balmy. He could watch any movie over and over again.

It was absurd how unimposing the experience was. They both felt tired, but mostly indifferent. After the initial glare of images, they dozed sluggishly.

Martin awoke first. His mind was functioning like a microfiche reader. It slid the index sheets in front of his eyes and magnified them. Billy, Franco, Donna, Diane, Writing, Blank. America, Blank.

It took something like the shooting for him to realise that it was finished. And Billy? He had even been prevented from seeing Billy's play. Martin loathed those who subscribed to fatalism. Billy didn't like that type of person either; Billy had bludgeoned Martin's pale grey fatalism. But they weren't fated to work together, Billy was right. Martin would have to do it on his own.

Martin picked up the payphone and dialled the penthouse. Billy's voice answered. Martin interrupted, burst in, cried. Billy's voice continued wearily. It was an answering machine.

Billy was uneasy with the machine – his introduction went on and on, about the theatre and the theatre number, about Donald and Donald's business number and Donald's hotel number in Philadelphia, and Billy said finally, 'Okay. After the tone. Okay.' Martin was calm now. The tone came. Of course, Billy was at the theatre, Billy was working. Martin had nothing to say, the tape went on. Martin said, 'I won't see you for a while, Billy. Until … I … ' he listened to the tape winding along. 'Good luck.' The tape went on. Martin put the phone down. A hollow, strong person, he watched Franco sleep.

By midnight, they were out the other side. Their shirts were brought to them from the hospital laundry and they each took a shower.

Franco didn't want to drive home yet in case the full effect of the drug or the shooting returned. He was still a bit dazed. They decided to have something to eat in the city.

They called a cab and Franco told the driver to find them a cheap restaurant. Martin played passenger, musing on his strange relationship with the dead kid. He had washed the blood off his neck in the shower. Franco interrupted him.

'How is it in England?'

'Boring,' Martin laughed at the presumable attraction of this.

'Underneath.'

'Tea and boring.'

'Hey … '

'It is. The country is geared for people between the ages of forty and fifty. There's no way round it. Until you reach that age, there's no point in staying there.'

'I might like it.'

Martin failed to notice what Franco said, he was thinking about himself.

The cab drew up, Franco was out first and paid. Martin shut the cab door and stood on the sidewalk. He looked up at the humiliating buildings and lost himself for a moment. Franco walked past him towards the restaurant, Martin caught him at the door.

'Franco, have I taken anything from you?'

Franco looked blankly at him. 'No. We're quits, aren't we? Yeah.'

Even at one o'clock in the morning, the restaurant was crowded. It was one of those international spartan-cult places, all stripped wood and art posters, servers in long cotton dresses or blue jeans, a lot of dopey smiling and soft voices. There was only one place to sit and that was in the corner, opposite a fat man who was poking daintily at a small salad.

They ordered.

The great fat man opposite was chewing over his greenery. Martin expected to see a string of cud-juice hanging from his mouth. Two small piggy eyes flicked over at Martin and must have noticed his distaste. Three chins wobbled and the mouth-load sank down somewhere into the vast bulk. The pudgy hand reached out and squeezed a glass of water which it brought up to the lips. Once more the chins wobbled and the man swallowed. Martin had to remove his fascination.

'Not a pretty sight, heh?' the man asked him, self-conscious but not perturbed. Martin smiled wanly. Not a pretty sight. It was a strange thing to say.

Their food came. Martin asked for more bread and made a series of sandwiches, which he shovelled down with the help of some wine. He noticed the fat man stirring his coffee for about three minutes. He then drank it, one-off, and ordered another cup. There was a pause when Martin had cleared his plate and Franco was still eating. Martin pushed his chair back; he met the eyes of the fat man. This time there was no getting out of it. The fat man spoke.

'You're English?'

'Yes. And you?'

'American. Or should I say, New Yorker?'

Martin didn't care what he said. 'Is there a difference?'

'There certainly is. New York is something on its own.'

Franco nudged Martin under the table.

The fat guy might have been a tramp, his suit showed no great signs of any devotion to appearance; it was threadbare, shiny and carried several foodstains. And either he had no mirror or else he had a razor which couldn't handle overhangs. Franco carried on eating, his face fixed firmly on the other tables.

'What do you do?' Martin asked.

'I believe that everybody is beautiful.'

Martin had to fumble around with the water in order to

suppress the explosion of laughter which mushroomed up from his belly. The fat man wasn't at all concerned. He said: 'Are you friends?'

'Sure,' Franco said.

'Well, you're very lucky.' The fat man finished his coffee and seemed to be about to leave.

'Why don't you have a glass of wine?' Martin asked him.

'That's very kind of you, I thank you. I feel that your friend would like it better if you were alone.'

'We've had a hard day; we got mixed up in a shooting. Franco?'

'Sure, let's drink.'

Martin poured the fat man a wine. 'We're both a bit exhausted.'

'Your very good health.' The fat man raised his glass. 'The city's a dangerous place. Not many people talk to strangers. It isn't a wise thing to do.'

'Yeah,' Franco said, 'but if you don't do it, you end up talking to yourself and maybe shooting at other people.'

'Why do *you* talk to other people?' Martin asked.

The fat man shrugged. 'I was always ugly. I was very unhappy when I was a child, I didn't have a woman until I was twenty-eight and then I paid for one. I thought then that I'd got nothing to lose and my experience tells me that I was right. I started doing it out of desperation, there are a lot of losers in this town, there's no point in getting hung up about it. Together you can have some success. Togetherness brings ripeness and its own reward.' The fat man paused to let the words sink in.

It would be difficult to continue. Franco raised an eyebrow. Martin shamelessly offered another banality in part-exchange: 'Action brings good fortune.'

'Truly,' said the fat man, sipping his wine.

'So what do you *do*?' Martin blurted at him.

'I'm a psychotherapist.' The fat man looked across at him, heavy-lidded with credentials.

'Hell no … ' Franco grinned. The fat man smiled and indicated Franco's pose. Martin smiled back. 'My name is Paul,' the fat man beamed.

'Martin.'

'Franco.'

'We were in the medical profession, the afterbirth side, mop therapy.'

'Not for long, surely, the mopping?' The fat man was perplexed. 'You both seem to have more intelligence.'

'Not for any longer than we needed to. It was a question of money rather than intellectual involvement.'

'It wasn't a bad place,' Franco said.

The fat man addressed himself to Martin. 'Sanitation doesn't have its own reward?'

'Maybe, but I should imagine that those receiving it spend it pretty quickly on psychotherapists.' Martin thought suddenly of the Polack and what he had said about the intimacy between the sickos and the crushed foetuses. He wondered if Franco had kept the memory of that crushing plant.

The fat man took up the conversation. 'You should transfer to my business. I remember what you said. Action brings good fortune. That's good, people like to hear it, they like to hear it spelt out. And you're also a good listener. You could make it.'

'Action brings good fortune?' Franco considered it. 'Yeah, it's off an old rock and roll album.'

Martin laughed. The fat man merely shrugged.

'It's a good slogan, people like to hear that kind of thing. It gives them confidence. Who cares where it comes from? You don't tell them that. You got to see it this way: that painter guy, Andy Warhol, he paints bean cans, people pay a lot of money for them and what are they? Bean cans. You can't even get any beans out of them and half the world is starving.'

Martin laughed; Franco smiled, a bit distracted.

'Soup,' Martin said, 'he paints soup cans.'

'Soup, beans, Marilyn Monroe, who gives a shit ... you think some kid in Africa, or the Bronx, can afford to get choosy? Hell, you sell them democracy; you sell them beans if they're poor and pictures of beans if they're rich. That way you cross-section the world's market.'

Martin thought that he was marvellous, but he could feel Franco's benevolence evaporating.

'You want some more wine, let's drink some more wine.' The fat man turned to contact the waitress. Franco shook his head. It was reasonable, the restaurant had nearly emptied, there were only three other tables occupied. Martin held up

313

both hands in a ten-minute suggestion. Franco nodded. The fat man eased himself round on the chair to face them again.

'Is that how the psychotherapy business works?' Martin asked, and was delighted with the answer.

'It is. I try to keep people happy, beautiful, sane and in contact with each other. Pain out. That's a chant, like a mantra. Pain out.'

'Do you have any training?' Martin asked.

'All the training you need. There's no way I don't know about problems. I've been fat and ugly since I was a kid, right on through adolescence and high school I was ugly.'

'Don't you need a licence for what you do?' Franco muttered.

'Do you think that the administration should control psychotherapy? You're young. Don't you think that's dangerous? I was under the impression that young people were against that kind of thing; the administration controlling the people.'

'No ... but do you know what you're doing?'

'I don't do anything.' The fat man held Martin's eye. 'I don't do a damn thing, I don't read any books, I don't tell people what to do.'

'Well how do you get any patients?'

'When I started I put an advertisement in the newspaper.'

Martin was incredulous. The fat man pinned him down.

'Lemme tell you. This is America. If you got the guts to be a salesman, you can sell anything. There's a whole dumb mass of buyers. One thing this country has got is money; so much of it that people have the feeling that it can't buy anything of value. So you charge a high enough price and people relate to it as being worth something, not so much the end product but the actual experience of spending money. They walk into Sears and the experience lasts them five minutes; they come to an encounter session and it lasts an hour. And because I don't give them an object to take home with them, they don't get bored with it, and so they come back.'

'And they don't blow your cover?'

The fat guy poured more wine. 'What cover? I don't kid them. I pay taxes, and you should see the taxes in this city. You may be a genius, I'm no genius. I was ugly and fat and fucked-up. I went to see this guy who had an advertisement in the *Village Voice*. You pay five bucks for an hour. What's five bucks? Who hasn't got five bucks? It's a democratic figure. The room was full of people; twenty; maybe twenty-five. They all had problems, they wanted to talk about their problems; they didn't need him. They acknowledged that it was his apartment, he gave them coffee, maybe some pot and a few words as he walked round the room. He'd met a lot of people; he wasn't dumb; his words were objective. He didn't have to get involved in the encounter, he could keep a clear head. Everybody knew that everybody else had problems or they wouldn't be there. So they talked to each other about their problems; they helped each other. You can't do that in the city; you have a telephone and a book of numbers, the music is too loud in the clubs, you feel like an asshole in front of somebody who hasn't got problems. So I went there twice and it was doing me a lot of good. I went to bed with a girl the second time. So I ask the guy, what credentials has he got? None. What harm is he doing? None. What is the effect? Good. How much money is he making? A hundred, a hundred and fifty a night. With that kind of money you can retire in two years, you can afford to go to a therapist with a string of letters, you can fuck the best-looking broads in the city, you're beautiful.'

Martin was hauled back into the present. The chairs were on the tables around them. The restaurant's music system was off and the sound of a piano drifted in from somewhere down the street.

The fat man wanted to pay for their dinner, but Martin refused. Franco was tired and finished and they still had to drive out to Jersey. They stood on the sidewalk, waiting for cabs.

'New York ... ' the fat man breathed his loneliness upwards the sky. 'It never sleeps.'

A cab arrived from downtown and swung across to them.

'Can we give you a ride?' Martin asked.

'Thank you, we're going different ways,' the fat man said. Franco disappeared into the back of the cab.

'See you, Paul. You take care.' Martin shook the pudgy hand and followed Franco. The face looked into the cab.

'You enjoy yourself while you're here.' He closed their cab door and the driver didn't loiter.

'That guy is fucked,' Franco said.

'How much is a plane ticket to California?'

'Not too much.' Franco kept his eyes on the road.

'I'm going to stand on the side of the road and see what happens.'

'Do it Monday. Nothing happens today except for families.'

They arrived at the toll-booth and Franco leaned out of the window to drop two quarters into the basket. There were six lanes. To the left was a family, with children sleeping; and three lanes to the right a shaded man in a light-blue Mustang looked them over and revved his engine before accelerating away in excessive style. Martin lit two cigarettes and passed one over to Franco. 'I might as well go while I've got the money. Can I leave the suitcase at the apartment?'

'Sure.'

'And I'll give you a month's rent.'

'Screw it, there are always people looking for places. I'll stash the suitcase in my parents' basement.'

'Are you tired?'

'Yeah, but I don't feel like sleeping. I'm going to do nothing next week, just stay home and wait for my ass to drop off.'

They nearly missed their exit road, Martin pointed it out as a lost cause but Franco swerved the car across the expressway and down the ramp.

'Pretty good, huh?' He was upset. He checked out the VW guiltily, slowed it down, grunted a nervous chuckle and speeded it up again.

'Shall we stop off at the park?'

'You want to?'

'Yes. Then we can wait for the shops to open and buy some food.'

'I know where we can get some food.' Franco looked in the mirror and whirled the car round a hundred and eighty degrees without braking. The tyres petitioned the road, Franco changed down and they skedaddled off like a clockwork toy. They went to Herbie's Diner. Neither of them was hungry. Herbie packaged up the food.

'I hate parks', Franco said, 'where you can see the city on both sides.'

The food was in the backseat of the VW, Martin and Franco were fifty yards into the grass, coughing on warm cigarettes. 'Parks make me paranoid.' Franco cast a suspicious eye around them. 'I couldn't make it to California.' He rubbed his chin.

'I don't know why I'm going. There isn't any reason. It's just something to do.'

'Yeah.' Franco stood sideways. 'You want to head across to the bandstand?'

They went back to the apartment. Martin packed up his clothes, he would leave most of them in the suitcase and travel with a small bag. He threw away every piece of writing he had into the bin, and felt better. Franco handed him a drink.

'You think there's a connection between the guy in the shooting and the guy in the restaurant?' Franco put the Laird's back on the floor and swigged at his glass before going across to change the tape. He had been wired up for a couple of hours, sometimes sitting stunned and vacant and shying away nervously when Martin came into the room, sometimes bursting in on him. Martin was quite drunk by now, Franco was drunk and his questions came more infrequently and more laboured.

'There isn't any connection. Things just happen. We work for a month in a maternity ward and then we see five people shot.'

That wasn't a good example of random flux. Martin's voice rose, he stood up and walked towards the wall.

'No, fuck it, why should there be any connection! The guy in the restaurant was a successful hustler and the guy with the gun wasn't! You just get out there and you see it through!' Martin pleaded.

That was Billy.

Martin came to the wall, his fist clenched. He closed his eyes. And they only leaked, like condensation at the foot of a window, the mist awaiting finger-patterns. He was still staring at the wall, and then up to where the wall met the ceiling. Franco was crouched by the tape deck, peering blindly at the title of the last track.

They were on the side of the Turnpike, confused with farewell, messing around with luck. Franco drove off. Martin watched him go, almost without registering, and watched him circle and return. Franco got out of the car, Martin approached him. 'Send me a postcard from Kansas City,' Franco said. 'That sounds an interesting place. Yeah. Shit.'

317

28

Behind Billy, the city buses collected late tourists from the waterfront and ran them up into the mid-town area. The Hudson wallowed murkily, the same old barges philandered downriver with their bouquets of trash for the ocean. Billy would stand up and walk towards the theatre at six-fifteen.

He came down to the pier every day around five o'clock. The fall afternoons were chilly. Billy wore a sweater and a jacket and he smoked a dozen cigarettes during his waterfront solitude. He considered that he smoked these cigarettes to supply himself with enough nicotine to see him through the performance. The smoking was a ritual and so now was his presence here on the edge of the Hudson each afternoon before he played in the O'Neill.

The powerful, sluggish meaninglessness of the river anchored him. Over his shoulder were the brief linear bursts of traffic, burning itself out on the gridded rectangles of a darkening city. Downtown, the towering control panels of Wall Street arrayed their circuitry; occasionally the West side Heliport would tunnel a winking chopper out over the river against the silhouette of New Jersey.

Up past the shadows of Riverside Park, people were driving home across the Washington Bridge, getting out of New York, back to their homes in the suburbs. North and west there was Diane. Billy saw the one-way current of the traffic, that arc of red and white pinpoints fireflying against the dusk. Night-life would awake in an hour's time, the city was adapting.

Water slapped against the wharf like two middle-aged bellies during copulation. In front of him, the warehouse was dark and rotted by the waterside climate. Summer gave it a false reprieve; fall restored its swollen decay. It was still used, it had had a couple of afternoon visitors in the time that Billy had been coming to the pier. Three weeks ago there had still been winos arguing and lurching on the jetty; they had now taken up a winter haunt somewhere else on Manhattan. Somewhere more lucrative, warmer. The jetty wasn't dangerous, its piles were driven deep down through the water into the Hudson silt, but the pier was chained off with a red metal warning-plate hung in mid-swoop.

The warehouse carried the smell of its mildewed growths. Decomposing, moving sideways. Stubborn against the water. Billy dropped another cigarette stub over the edge of the bench. There were a dozen cigarette stubs and a scattering of ash in an uneven circle. Always by the next afternoon they had gone, no sign of them, somebody swept the pierfront each morning.

He had sent his mother and father two tickets for the première of the movie. His mother had written back, saying that his father was not fit to travel, that they both wished Billy luck and that they would see the movie when it came to their neighbourhood.

He might have called Linda. It crossed his mind and he set himself to think about it. There would be nothing to talk about except for where they had gone wrong, and the prospect of her being either indifferent or convincing flooded him with gloom. In the run-up to the première there was a lot of publicity work in the daytime. He let that swathe him, he didn't want to know about Linda. There would be no conversation they could rise to without feeling the vertigo of loss. He knew that he couldn't talk about anything else with her and the back-tracking had been going on too long. He hadn't the courage for analysing failure, or sufficient strength to pore over the molecules of his particular deficiency.

Billy was doing *Long Day's Journey* and so he didn't go to the film. The theatre could have used his understudy but Billy wanted to stay and he could make the journey across town in time for the social duties and the offers of work.

He asked Patti to meet him at the reception. Donald was there already as his business manager. The reception had all that buzz of smoothly-prepared success, finished product. No doubts about it; Billy had done well, the movie would do well. Song and dance.

Patti had watched the movie, she adored it, Donald adored it. Donald kept raising an eyebrow and confiding to anyone that Billy had done it all on one leg. On one leg? That was a long time ago. That was a time of making love on a rock in the middle of a creek, searching for Diane when they were both down. He looked inside himself and he couldn't find her now.

Several people in the business had the impression that Billy had a strong relationship with Patti, they were like two people who were going to get married but who just hadn't stopped to make the arrangement. Billy laughed a lot, agreed with any positive comment, toed the line. He seemed to have lost his bitter restlessness. He was a good bet.

Billy had always been the wired-up, insecure force at these film gatherings; he was renowned for it. She appeared to have taken the edge off him. She obviously relied on him and he reached for her instinctively, pleased to have her near. He was assessed as reliable. Donald didn't have to approach anyone, the inquiries came to him.

She clung to Billy and waited to go home with him. As the night died down, he asked her what she wanted to do and she told him that she wanted to be with him; she saw that it was a mistake. He could easily have covered this over, because they were both tired and that excuse alone would have served. But she couldn't understand how it was that he seemed to feel snubbed, as though *he* had made a serious offer and had been rejected, how it was *his* eyes which slipped sadly away.

'It wasn't meant to be a threat.' She made light of it.

'I know that,' he thanked her, clasping her hand. 'Are you about ready, Donald?'

Part of the trappings; a limousine. They dropped Patti off, Billy got out of the car and hugged her firmly. 'I'll see you up there tomorrow night.'

'You sleep well.'

'You too.'

Billy had the limo wait until she was inside the building.

'Are you getting involved with her?' Donald was dwarfed by the accommodation.

'Leave her out of it. She's a sweet girl.'

They hadn't had much audience for the plays to start with. Billy was conscious of this, but it didn't greatly matter to him. The reviews didn't help. They were neither good nor bad, they simply didn't touch on what Billy suspected about the character he was playing. The critics had a total complicity with Jamie which Billy could only wonder at and accept. His own playing was described as detached and ponderous, Patti got the credit for trying, for her warmth and the empathy she invited across the pit. Billy wouldn't hear of any complaint.

Then the movie emerged, and during a couple of weeks they had large audiences for Billy, which was a drain on him. He

320

had to force himself to get up there. He didn't know where he was with Jamie, he was groping around and he didn't want a public. When Martin failed to materialise, Billy didn't notice; Martin's message drew it to his attention. Billy laughed, he was bitterly glad that someone understood *something*.

Long Day's Journey was a twisted experience for him. When he wasn't onstage he watched the play from the wings, watched the old actress clawing out every bit of luxury. Billy loathed her. He bottled up his insecurity. Their onstage contact was limited, offstage he stayed well clear of her and her swanning exhaustion in the bar after the show. She pointedly ignored *A Moon for the Misbegotten*.

Patti offered him her support, Billy demurred. She started to lose him during their performance together. He would come back to her, gentle and kind, from a ghostly distance.

She felt that something was falling apart; the play was falling apart or he was falling apart, or that which was underneath and between them was disintegrating. At her request, the director came in to see the show and ran some of it through with them the next afternoon. 'It's developing, Patti.'

'Where am I going wrong?'

'Nowhere. You have your character perfectly, you don't have to change that.'

'I just don't have the feeling that he's there sometimes.'

'Oh Billy is very much there, he has it. He's finding out now what to take from you. Stay right with it. In the second act, you could try moving across when he ... '

And the director talked with Billy.

'How is it?'

'It's around. I hope I can make something of this.'

'It's really starting to have something.'

What? Billy reached around himself like a blindfolded man at a houseparty; and the blindfold was coming off and the house was dark and empty, just the voices hanging in the corners of the rooms. Which room was his? There was no way of seeing; the objects he touched were round and pliable and increasingly obsolete.

The star-gazers dropped off, *A Moon* started pulling in a different audience. More of a cult audience. It was like playing in front of predators who were hungry for the actors' pain.

The Festival was scheduled to run for two months. As if

fitting in with the programme, the audience for the other O'Neill plays started to taper down. But *A Moon* was playing to full houses. The producer wanted to book the theatre through until Christmas. Billy hated it; he wanted to get it right; he said yes. Patti agreed. She stuck with him as long as she could, and then she stuck to herself.

'You should be thinking about the next job, Billy.'
   'Screw off, Donald.'

He dithered around the stage, an early dawn shadow, washing up against Patti. The audience strained towards him, willing him through, appalled at his laceration. Some nights the play finished to a shocked silence, into which the first handclaps pecked like flimsy stiletto heels along a concrete alleyway. At other times the applause inundated Billy – as though the audience were evacuating themselves after an embarrassment of gluttony – and he was expected to bob up and show the consumers that it was all only a trick, this desperation. Billy and Patti led the cast out to face the acclaim. She was numb and exhausted. But scared; because each time she took his hand she felt his shuddering.

She went home. She counted the days until it would be over, she bought new clothes, painted her apartment, played loud music and got out of New York whenever their schedule allowed her.

Billy became meticulous. His day had a stark routine. His room was tidy and his favourite objects were dusted. He ate alone at the same restaurant at three o'clock in the afternoon and at midnight; he listened either to Bach or to Irish folk music until three in the morning; sometimes reading haphazardly, sometimes just lying along his bed, smoking, the bedside light often staying on until he woke at noon. Coffee and cigarettes, nothing else.

'Hi, Billy.'
   'Hi, babe.'

And the river.

The director presented Billy with a small stereo system for his dressing-room. He felt that he must say something to Billy, cautiously. About losing sight of the play, about Billy being into his own thing; pulling Jamie back. Billy: 'I know what I'm doing. I understand this character. You don't understand it at all.'

Brooding across the Hudson. Can't break Jamie Tyrone down; out there, the actor, bravura on a dead soul.

PART
5

Desertion of the Confederate

29

I was uneasy about seeing Michael, I put it off for as long as possible. The Farm got tidied and arranged and over-arranged, I sent a couple of chairs off to be re-upholstered and a crew came in to lay a fresh surface on the kitchen floor. Usually I would have retreated into my winter by now, the calm day-to-day reading and lazing and going through business papers in the office or the bedroom.

It would have been easier if Michael had pestered me, or at least made contact, but he didn't call. I was cooped up with the mixed blessing of letting the matter slide and yet knowing that I would have to go out and present my decision.

When the kitchen floor was finished and the men moved out, I tried to get down to the paperwork. The question of Michael proved to be a block. I called him and asked him if we could have dinner together in Cambridge on Saturday. It was a short conversation; I deliberately called him at the Center. He said: 'Yes. Certainly. I'll look forward to seeing you. Why don't you drop by some time in the afternoon and we can take in an exhibition or something?'

So we looked at paintings. He more calmly than I, I touched his arm too often to draw his attention to paintings I looked for us to share.

I was overdressed, almost classical in costume, a little out of date, but the outfit suited me, it gave me a comfortable feeling of distance. I thought that everything might be all right, a false feeling which I played with, that we might not even talk about a future because we both understood.

We left the gallery and went back to his house, and the feeling became oppressive. We sat and talked, a bit about myself and my reaction to the course, in perspective, and a bit about his work and the atmosphere at the Center, Tom and other therapists, Tom's impending divorce, the short-term effects of leaving a relationship. Time passed, and I asked: 'Do you mind if we don't go out to dinner?'

'No, I don't mind at all. I don't have very much here at the house. You'd like to *eat*?'

'Something. But nothing special. Maybe later.'

Michael stood up and went to the lower half of the split-level room, he looked through the kitchen cupboards. 'We can get something together.' He returned with a bottle of white wine, glasses and ice. He felt along the central heating. 'Do you find it cold in here?'

'I'm fine. I'm used to the Farm.'

'Ah yes, sure. Well, this temperature is fine by me. Some visitors find this house draughty.'

'If we're going to stick ourselves into this bottle, I'll cut something up so that it can cook slowly.'

He brought the bottle into the kitchen and started to help me fix a spaghetti sauce. I didn't leave him much to do, so he sat at the table over his wineglass. I moved between the skillet and the chopping board, quietly at home.

'You're very beautiful,' he said.

I had my back to him and didn't answer for a moment. Glancing round at him, I saw that he was cowed, slowly revolving the wineglass by its stem. I blushed frantically at the wall. I didn't dislike his remark, although I thought that he might give me something to worry about.

'All men say something like that when they watch a woman cooking a meal for them.'

'Do they? I suppose it's obvious. You seem relaxed and self-contained in your own rhythm. I like to watch it. There's no act about it.'

'It's a timeless, reliable picture.'

'And saying that you're beautiful is just as obviously an anxious way of trying to get in there and state it and dominate it.'

'Perhaps.' I smiled across at his self-detraction. 'That's a bit hard.'

'Or share it?'

'Yes.'

'You know?'

'Yes.'

It was getting more difficult.

'What *really* worries you?' He cheered up, sensing that we should reserve any seriousness for later. 'The one thing you think about in yourself – in your character or your behaviour – that worries you?'

I laughed. 'A hundred things.'

'So?'

'One thing?'

'Yes.'

I paused. 'I suppose that I think I am boring.'

'Boring! *Do* you?'

'Yes. There are even moments when I bore myself. Not often,' I smiled playfully and he laughed.

'Not flirting?' he asked.

'Does it worry me? Oh no, flirting is fair. You're pretty good at it, *you* should know.'

'*I* am?'

'Yes,' I told him, 'as in now.'

It was better, we would get along okay.

'Will you stay tonight?' he said.

My heart hovered. That was the wrong thing for him to say. No, it was the right thing.

'Yes, I will stay. Because we have things to talk about and to sort out. But I don't want you to expect anything of me. If that's a promise then I will stay.'

'Sure. It's good to have that nervousness out of the way.'

'Yes it is. Especially with you because I feel a lot for you.'

'Morbidly?'

I started to cry, damn it. 'I hope not.' I pressed my forehead against his nose. A dozen tears trickled down, but I wouldn't sob. He comforted me. 'Not a mess, are you?'

'No.'

He manoeuvred me backwards, he stood up, holding me. I whispered: 'I didn't want you to be hurt.'

'That's okay ... that's okay.'

It was over. I went to the bathroom to fix my face.

There was no bitterness between us, and we didn't feel deceived by any expectations. I didn't have to tell him about Billy. We switched to talking about Michael, condemning our future contact by agreeing on what we thought about each other. I asked him the same question, about the one thing that worried him. He said he worried that he was superficial.

I stayed the night. We drank a lot, ate and laughed and surfaced. It wasn't so difficult, we had only ever lived together in someone else's home – and that for me was only a dream, and Michael now worked for the government.

I wanted Billy.

Some weeks ago, Robby and John had asked me up to Montreal for a long stay, and I had refused, not wanting to tread on anybody's toes. I had suspected the formality of inviting mother for Christmas. But I was restless, the more so beside the excited intimacy of Pam and Andy's preparations for their winter in Florida. I called Billy to wish him luck for the final weeks of the show, I wished him everything and I flew off to Montreal.

30

It had been a long, hard, purposeless haul across America. Chico and Martin broke into a house just off Venice Beach and slept on the floor of the front room. The house was semi-derelict, the beach an expanse of yellow-grey sand, the sea post-industrial.

Chico had been sitting on the side of the six-lane highway that sweeps down from the hills into LA. They hitched a final ride together down the hill and took a bus to Venice Beach because Chico could start by stealing from that area until he learned his trade better. Then he would move into Beverly Hills.

The people who lived in the neighbourhood had settled like sludge in the stream of American progress. It was a sediment area of no-hopers with plenty of time on their hands. Several called themselves artists or lovers – some made films of each other, others put all their creative energy into the way they dressed up and draped themselves over a bar stool.

Martin got a job on the other side of the bar counter, as a way of side-stepping the question of whether or not to stay. The bar clientele were mostly whiners looking for an ear; there was more self-pity than heavy drinking. They talked monotonously. There was no sense of humour in the area.

Very rarely did anyone leave. And the only visitors from outside were the police who cruised up and down the road between the sand and the buildings, ceaselessly checking identity cards to relieve their boredom.

It was supposed to be a violent place. The bar customers would gibber briefly with delight at each new incident, reinforcing their own sense of the huge risks they were taking in life. But the violence was rarely public. It all happened in back rooms. People got bored. Old friends knifed each other rather than use the energy to move away; the neighbourhood hooker took a beating from one of her regular customers; someone found an old pill and went beserk. The offenders would disappear, the customers had their quick burst of titillation, and general apathy plumped its fat arse down in front of the beer.

Chico found his own way around the beachfront; he did a bit of dealing, there were a good number of houses to be broken into. Martin kept him going with food from the bar until he started to fence the stuff he had stolen. They slept at opposite ends of the downstairs front room, coming in through the window at different hours.

Chico liked a free beer but he didn't spend much time in Martin's bar - it was too close to his sources of income. Sometimes Martin overheard the complaints that there was a thief about; no one ever considered calling the cops so obviously Chico wasn't over-demanding. He kept the money under a floorboard. He would count it out in front of Martin, he was open rather than ostentatious. Chico was impressed by Martin's complete lack of interest, Martin was impressed by the way the pile of notes thickened.

He came back late one night and Chico was sitting in the far corner, lit up by the candle in front of him, brooding. Martin sat on the other side of the candle and rolled a strong joint. He took a couple of draws and passed it over. Chico broke the quiet. 'Someone's looking for a guy who can do an English accent. Some crap on the radio at the university. It pays. He'll come into the bar tomorrow around midday.'

'Thanks.'

'Time I go to work.' Chico put his tools in his pockets and climbed out of the window.

Martin met the student in the bar and agreed to do the job. He would spend two days reading bits of Sherlock Holmes into a tape machine at five bucks an hour; he would have to pay for accommodation on campus.

They must have liked his voice because they decided to do further recordings and gave him an hour-long disc jockey spot twice a week. He spent his time in the tiny recording-room being more English than the English. He wasn't sociable. He negotiated the wage for the whole series of readings and churned them out; he dumped the music spot when listeners started phoning in to complain about the haphazard cynicism that was creeping into his comments. He slept uneasily, his weight crashed down. He hated Sherlock Holmes; that smug, boyscout logician with his Englishness.

The day after he finished the tapes, he picked up his money and caught a bus back to LA. He had no business in the town and it didn't attract him any more now than it had done with Billy, four years before.

He thought of going to San Francisco, maybe to Seattle, maybe to Canada; but he caught a plane back East and called Franco from La Guardia. The number was disconnected. Finally he called Donna.

She seemed to know about him, she asked about the West, as though he had been away on business, something that didn't concern her.

'How was your writing?'

'Pretty good,' he lied. 'And you?'

She told him that she had written some poems, she had several projects which she wanted to get on with. She had cut down her involvement with the women's group because she didn't want so much responsibility for organising it.

Martin wanted her to go on talking. He tightened his grip on the telephone. Donna was stuck in the silence, not understanding it. He missed her, he had missed her.

'I know that we didn't have much to say to each other. That's part of what I'm working on,' she laughed.

'Can I come and see you?' he asked.

She paused. 'I don't feel that would be a good idea.'

'No?'

'I have the same apartment and I guess the same thing would happen over again. Just now I need more security. I guess we both feel the same way about understanding ourselves, maybe being on our own to think things through ... '

She was probably sitting, framed, on her couch with her legs folded under her, comfortable with herself, smoking, the cat was advancing cautiously over the notes she had made and the passages she had copied from books. He knew that he couldn't reach her again.

'What are you wearing?' he asked.

'Me? Why?'

'I don't know.'

'A pair of jeans and a sweatshirt. All American.'

'Okay.'

'Do you have somewhere to go?' she worried.

'Yes.'

He heard in her voice the relief she couldn't hide, that she had no need to offer him anything of herself. She assumed that she would see him again, next time around, when she was settled; she hoped so, he hoped so, so they said.

He wouldn't go to Billy. He dialled Franco's parents and found Franco there, a thoroughly contented Franco, back at home, his apartment burnt out in a fire, a Franco who had just heard something on the television about Kansas City, a Franco with yeahs and belches and a need to get out for a beer at Jake's Barn, a limo, a train and a cab away.

'So that's it?' Franco grinned.

'Yes.' Martin hunched over the bar.

'Well, the fire cleaned me out – clothes, furniture, guitars, everything. Your suitcase was at my parents' house.'

'How do you feel about it?'

'I couldn't give a damn. I don't know why. I'll get a job and save some money, go back to something simple for a change. Live on my own and see what happens.' Franco was almost exuberant, Martin saw.

'Are you finished with music?'

'I'm sick of the egos. That fire was all right. It got rid of everything. I can breathe again, there's nothing to chase around for.' Franco knocked back his whisky. 'Are you going home?'

'I don't know. I've paid for a ticket but I haven't decided to use it.'

Franco was ruminating gently. 'I live in my parents' basement. It's small. Good for two or three nights but not like the apartment.' His eyes apologised generously. 'Nothing much I can do for you.'

'No, no, I wasn't expecting anything.'

'Yeah, you look that way.' Franco's eyebrows met in concern; a bit like Annie, Martin recognised. He glanced away and pulled out another cigarette.

'I don't know what it is … '

'Sure.' Franco saddened at the restrictions. 'Anyways, sitting in this lousy bar gets you down. I'm supposed to be fixing a tuna fish salad. This girl Mollie is coming round, an old teacher friend of mine.'

Franco drove them up the road. He had borrowed a tapedeck from somewhere but there wasn't much else in the basement besides the unmade bed and another mattress and a piece of carpet. Martin met his parents, pleaded exhaustion and waited downstairs. He sorted through his suitcase, discarding most of the clothes for Franco's use, should he want them. Franco appeared at the door with a sleeping-bag thrown over his shoulder. 'Best I could find.'

'You take what you want from these clothes, I'd like you to have them.' Franco was wary about accepting them and the terse sincerity with which they were given. 'Take what you want, these shirts are good.' Martin held one up by the collar, offering it across.

'I'll look through them.' Franco bent and laid a hand on his shoulder. 'It's okay, you know, it'll pass. You want a beer?'

'No. Yes.' Martin didn't know what to want.

'I've got a sixpack upstairs. I'm cooking. You want to stay down here?'

Martin looked uneasily at the carpet; he didn't know if he wanted to stay down here. Over his head, boots clunked across the porch. The doorbell chimed, a stoned chuckle penetrated the walls. He watched Franco estimate, Franco's finger scratch the bristles on his chin, the words fall over Franco's lips in pieces of sound. 'That's not Mollie. I'll get rid of whoever it is.' Franco looked into Martin's mute eyes. 'Yeah; no people. We'll take a peaceful evening. Okay.'

He was gone upstairs. Martin heard him reach the front door.

'Hey, how you doing?' From the visitor.

'Great. Hey, how're you making out?' From Franco.

Martin rehearsed the format of greeting in case the people should come downstairs to see him. The door shut and the conversation went off into the back of the house. Martin tightened; his mind raced through possible introductions, he planned ways of not getting involved, excuses for leaving the room, something he could do where he wouldn't have to be noticed by anybody. The palms of his hands were wet, although he was sure that he was in control and that he had

334

the anxiety in its place. The walls of the room leant over him. It would be best if he started now to make his excuses and leave, they would think him strange if he left just after they had been introduced and he didn't want to be strange. He got to his feet, despite a feeling that he was too weak and it was impossible. He prepared to open the door. He heard boots going across the hallway, the conversation again.

'Be seeing you.'

'Yeah, I'll check you out later.' Franco's voice. The door shutting and the boots walking off the porch.

Martin sat down quickly, trying to rearrange himself exactly as he had been before so that Franco wouldn't know he had been to the door and wouldn't worry about what he was doing, if he was acting strangely.

Franco came down. The reassuring efficiency with which he opened the door – he had no worries, he was normal, he didn't want anything.

'That was the Kid. He brought round this old guitar.' Franco's eyes beamed with pleasure.

'That's good.' Martin evinced a desire to fit in, waiting for Franco to tell him exactly if it was good or not so that he knew how to react without upsetting him, so they could agree.

'Sure is. Old buddies ... ' His eyes crooned sentimentally for a moment, and he sniggered. Martin was unsure what this meant. Franco lit a cigarette and checked the guitar. He started tuning it. Martin looked at his clothes. He pushed them away into the corner, where they would not be so unworthy; the suitcase he hated as well, who would want that? It was too big to hide. He held his hands round his knees and tried not to notice the suitcase, he was intent on watching Franco's fingers in their experiment with the neck of the guitar. This was important.

'Lousy guitar.' Franco let it drop negligently against the wall. 'It'll have to do for a start.'

'Yes,' Martin agreed, 'it doesn't look much good.'

'As whoever said, it's the thought that counts.' Franco stood up and went out of the door. What did he mean by that? Martin couldn't think clearly. He was on some race with himself; he felt his pulse, it seemed unnaturally fast and strong, the pumping.

'One beer.' Franco poked his head round the door and

handed Martin the can. 'Food later.'

Martin sipped at the beer and food seemed an insuperable problem; perhaps in the future he would need food and would have an appetite, food would go down and find a space, but it was foreign and he couldn't deal with anything foreign inside him. Cigarette smoke was more at home.

The doorbell chimed again and he was in such a rush of himself that his mind gabbled away in its own irrelevant blankness while he said how do you do and sat down, rubbing the skin on his forehead like parchment as she sat down on the floor at a decent distance and Franco did the introductions. For some reason she rather ignored Franco. She devoted herself to looking at Martin in silence, some soothing way that enabled him to have the confidence to conduct the rigmarole of talk in a fashion which would give her no opportunity to get close to him but would not leave her insulted. He never had to think of anything to say, he hardly recognised her except as an extension of himself into which Franco came and went as a deferential guest, benevolently uncertain as to what was happening.

She talked. He listened to the sound of her voice, where she hesitated, lowered her eyes, picked at a bit of dirt on the carpet and rolled it round between her forefinger and thumb; he listened to her pauses, he looked at the soft spread of her on the floor, the lines of her lips, the roughness of the skin on her cheekbones.

When she looked at her watch and said that she must go, she saw that he didn't understand. She explained. 'My son is on his own. That's all right until eleven; after that I feel that I should be at home.' She shook hands. Franco saw her to the front door.

'Good woman,' Franco returned and sat down, 'always been a friend of mine.'

Martin needed nothing else now but a sleep.

'She invited you round for dinner tomorrow night. I think she saw you didn't eat much. Why don't you go?'

'I will. What about you?'

'Yeah?' Franco chuckled and picked up the guitar; Martin folded into sleep as Franco trained the strings.

He awoke suddenly to Franco's heavy snore, and lay for a time, trying to meditate, with his arms stretched down his sides and the palms of his hands open to the ceiling. Once more, his mind was working overtime; he had achieved no calm in sleep, he had suffered nightmares. The glaring visions zig-zagged across his nervous system; he let them go without resistance, feeling that the effort of control was beyond him and that they would wear themselves out. A fierce roar in his ears seemed to divorce him from any other sound in the room, though when Franco turned over and broke the rhythm of his breathing, the shock of this plunged in on him and his legs moved nervously, according to some elusive power source. When Franco showed signs of awakening, Martin pretended to be asleep; and he did finally stumble across a series of dozes – like stepping stones – after Franco had left the room.

By noon, he was exhausted with himself. He forced himself to get up and get dressed, marvelling at how little time this took and how much time there was left. No noise in the house, so he took himself upstairs into the kitchen where he saw a note propped against the cooker. 'Working till one, then two thru six. Food in freezer.'

He managed a glass of milk; the sight of food didn't stir his appetite. He thought that he should take a shower to get rid of the sweat, and dress himself in clean clothes. He did this; each moment seemed to rush by – it struck him as strange that he could sweat and yet that the water from the shower couldn't find a way into his skin; he hung on to this thought doggedly, to slow himself down, doubting his ability to cling on to anything else.

He was aware of the need for outside stimulus, something to come up against; the balance was all wrong, he was shaken by an energy that came only from himself.

He took a snap decision to go for a walk and adhered to this with determination. Standing at the front door, he worried that he could not lock the house enough. There were a great number of bolts which could be drawn only from the inside, and one main lock for which he had no key. He would leave the door secured only by the latch-lock. What else could he do? He couldn't stay in the house and wait. Already from the front door, he didn't want to go back into the house; he didn't want to sit down. The street was so much more something to aim for, with its humdrum activity.

He closed the door and walked hurriedly away, keeping his eyes on the ground and his hands in his pockets. He wanted to guard the number of the house in his head, he repeated it to himself over and over again until it slowed to keep time with his footsteps. He walked efficiently, pushing his own space along in front of him, glancing up at a grey sky.

He walked uphill, not having made any choice. It worried him. But he congratulated himself when he realised that it would be sensible to be coming downhill on the way back, when he was tired. He walked quickly, up past the suburban houses, past the mansions and on by the reservoir to the plateau at the top. The view across New Jersey to the city was still there, the weather was cold now and only a few people looked out from the warmth of their cars. He didn't want to be taken for a lonely voyeur, so he swung round the perimeter of the plateau, casting his eyes over the distance spread beneath him.

He needed to know the time; he tapped on the window of the next car he came to, interrupting lovers.

'Have you got the time, please?' he asked.

'Quarter of three.' The man replied shortly, annoyed. Time seemed to matter to them.

He turned on his heel and strode away, uncertain of where to go next. He was at the furthest point of his circuit; it remained to go back and then maybe to start again. Downhill would mean that he arrived at the house around four. Possibly three hours with himself until he could set off to see the woman, what was her name, Mollie. He could only vaguely remember her. He supposed that she might want to make love, they usually did. Perhaps he would sleep better afterwards.

Downhill was difficult; he kept wanting to run and fall, but he knew that he must keep himself back. He imagined the sharp crack of his forehead against concrete, his nose being suddenly jolted up into his brain; he had to sit for a moment, resting back against a wall, to smoke half a cigarette and deal with the vision. He must buy some more cigarettes, which meant that he must walk past the house towards the town. Once more, the time of his arrival was indistinct; he was glad to say. He said it out loud.

Feeling weary, his legs thin and useless. He should have food, it was necessary to put food in at the top. The cigarette made him retch emptily, he spat out the bile. If he walked on down here, he would stop at Jake's Barn for a drink, carry on into town for something to eat and to buy more cigarettes. There were only ten left in the pack. Falling short. He continued downhill.

Only half-way through the pack. He smiled, sarcastic and defensive, so he laughed, jerking out the laughter for several yards. He embarrassed himself. He worried openly for a moment about himself, what he needed and what was wrong with him. Billy would know.

He stopped.

He took several deep breaths and unclenched the hands in his pockets. He dug his nails into the cushions at the back of these hands. He belched, to try to relieve the nausea floating over his stomach. He tried to relax.

Seeming to succeed, he walked on. He shut out the desire to whistle. The walking braced him. He had to stop to relieve the pressure on his bladder - he shook the few drops out, zipped himself up. He realised that this might have been a criminal offence, pissing in the street when he wasn't a dog.

He went down Main Street and chewed on half a meat-roll before dropping the rest into a litter bin. He thought that he wouldn't need the cigarettes but he bought a pack anyway for some time in the future. He had a large roll of damp money in his pocket. He entered a milk bar and ordered a banana shake - slurping it through a straw until it filled him. He felt better, watching the kids. Cigarette smoking wasn't allowed, he didn't miss it. A warm tiredness steeped him; he stayed in the milk bar until way after six, a funny sad scarecrow smile on one side of his mouth and his hands lying open on his lap like a labourer. He would have liked to lay his head on a woman's belly.

They were sitting down to a huge meal when he arrived back at Franco's; the parents, the sister, her husband, and Franco dashing round the table with wine. The family were generous-hearted in their welcome; Franco's mother fussed with common sense about his exhaustion, his father motioned him forward to the food.

He was calm, smiling quietly. His mood had switched into a sublime detachment; he felt a fool, wide-eyed and the little smile, he felt childish and without the need to be responsible for himself. He said nothing, he loved to watch them eat. Franco explained, between mouthfuls of pasta.

'He's got a date with Mollie.'

'Hah!' old man Laverno grunted in appreciation; his wife pushed a napkin across to him.

'Will she cook him a good big supper?' she warned.

Franco laughed. 'Sure she will. Maybe not as good as this.'

'What do you mean, maybe?' the father growled. 'You eaten better than this in the last month?'

'Lemme see … ' Franco teased.

'Tuna fish salad … ' his sister smiled. 'Do you still make that?'

'Yep,' Franco grinned, 'now and then.'

'Six times a week maybe,' Mr Laverno suggested.

'He makes not a bad tuna fish salad,' Franco's mother supported him, 'you think so?'

'Yes, I like it.' Martin burst out laughing. Franco grinned. 'I'd better get cleaned up I think.' Martin wanted to leave them, perfect as they were in the family.

'You give him a towel.'

'Sure.' Franco rested his fork on the plate and pushed back his chair. He went first up the stairs.

'You've got a good family.'

'Yeah, very good. Sometimes gets to be a bit much, but they're all right. I can't see any towel. You better use mine.'

'Go and eat your food before it gets cold.'

'Yeah. Knock on the window tonight if you come back late. My father doesn't sleep too good.'

'I'll remember.'

Franco was in a hurry to get back to his food. Martin left his clothes on the floor and sat under the shower, hot water pouring down around him.

He changed only his shirt and came up from the basement to find the family watching television with Franco helping his mother to clear the kitchen.

'That's better, he looks better,' she said to Franco. 'You eat a good supper with Mollie,' she commanded Martin.

'You want the address. One fifty-seven Park Street, ground floor apartment.'

'One fifty-seven, okay.'

'And you go down to the right. Five, six blocks?' Franco sought his mother's confirmation.

'No, you take him in the car. He doesn't want to walk a

half hour in the cold after his shower. You leave the dishes.'

'That's all right,' Martin protested. 'I can find it.'

'Better he drives the car than he does the dishes.' She was already more efficient without Franco.

'Yeah.' Franco was in favour. 'Let's go.'

'Can I borrow a coat?'

'Do I have a coat?' he wondered.

'In the closet upstairs – an old coat,' his mother said.

'Yeah?' Franco's right eyebrow lifted. 'No kidding. I'll get the coat, you get the keys from the basement.' He went upstairs to investigate this old coat. Martin watched Mrs Laverno push the table-cloth into a washing machine and stack the dishes on the side of the sink unit.

'Thank you very much,' he said to her.

'It's a long time since my son brings his friends home, and now he sleeps in the basement. Crazy.' She was amused; she shrugged, understanding Franco. 'When you get tired of sleeping in the basement, you take the bed upstairs.'

'Thank you. I don't know if I'll be staying.'

'Then where will you go? You should make a home, find a nice girl.' She was moved. Martin saw that she was talking about Franco, how she wasn't too well suited to America perhaps.

'Maybe I will,' he said.

'You will, you won't,' she was joking again.

'D'you get the keys?' Franco stood with the coat at arm's length. 'You want to wear this?' He couldn't believe it, this old coat.

'It looks warm.'

'Take it.'

'I'll borrow it for tonight. I didn't get the keys.'

'I'll get them.' Franco burped his way to the basement door. 'Too damn full of food.'

Franco dropped him off at the end of Park Street, such as it was. There might have been a park once, with traditional trees, grass, a lake or whatever; Park Street now was just one side of a large car-park which served people who commuted into New York by train. It was almost deserted by this time of the evening, its emptiness highlighted by a scattering of street lamps. He walked through the pools of light and the shadows in between. It was like a series of scenes, brief illuminations cast on the evasive central character. In one scene there was an empty beercan, which he didn't kick; in another a small dog standing in the wings; one more, and a car polished by the glow of the lamp. He started to feel different in each scene.

He escaped. He cut away from the lights and hugged the line of houses on his right, quickening his pace as the numbers increased. One fifty-seven. He stopped, composed himself, rang the bell.

She welcomed him, everything was taken for granted, she didn't expect any chess-like conversation. She wore a long deep-brown skirt and a sweater.

They went into the kitchen because she had only just come in from a parent-teacher meeting and the lounge was not warmed up yet. She sliced vegetables and talked about vegetarianism, while he sat, mostly silent, grateful for her lead. She moved easily – not a noisy cook – he fed off her warm sureness as she padded between the table and the cooker, her eyes watching what she did in the same way as they looked at him every now and then. She didn't summarise or challenge. He was part of a unity.

While the food was cooking, she told him about her son, she pointed to a photograph on the shelf over the table. He looked for a decent time and when he turned back, she was regarding him hesitantly. She backed off. She spoke about aloneness, not upset at it; she was objective without being cold or seeking sympathy. She talked about being at one with the way of the world. She took lovers, not many, three in the last two years; he could stay the night and sleep with her if he wanted to, her son was sleeping at a friend's house. She talked about vitamins.

The meal was good; he ate while she picked at hers. She fetched him a beer, drank a little of it herself. He felt contented and drowsy.

'I managed to get some dope,' she said.

'Yes?' Martin had no wish to be stimulated by any interference.

'Will you roll it? I'm not used to doing joints, it seems to be a man's thing. I haven't got any acid or anything like that,' she apologised. She seemed suddenly unsure of herself; her eyes a bit lost behind her glasses, she fingered her hair nervously. 'I really get high on dope,' she said wilfully. 'Why don't we leave all the dishes, leave everything where it is and go into the lounge. It's more comfortable. Do the joint in there, on the table.'

'Yes, okay,' he said, collecting the papers and the small piece of tin foil. He felt as though he was put to one side, as though a function was about to take over. He glanced at her, she was restless and uncertain. He became worried as her mood spread to him; he felt clumsy.

He sat in the lounge on a high-backed chair in front of an oak table and applied himself to making the joint.

'Mollie?' he called, wondering where she was.

'I'm just changing out of these work clothes. I won't be long.' There was a calm matter-of-factness in her voice. He relaxed. It was only the changing of rooms that had thrown him for a moment. He rolled the papers and licked the glue, smoothing the lip down with the moist pad of his first finger. He inserted the roach. It was an exact joint, a perfect cylinder. He twisted the end and left it on the table in front of him.

'Is it made yet?' she called.

'Yes.'

'Can you light it for me?' She came out of the bedroom door and stood in front of him, her crotch against his crossed legs, which tensed involuntarily. He looked at her, not knowing her.

She wore a long blonde wig and a flimsy Indian shirt with a black bra underneath, the shirt pulled tight by a black leather belt. She rubbed her leg against his and stood back. Her skirt was made up of a dozen chiffon scarves, hanging separately from the belt. There was the pink skin of her thighs and knees; the pair of high-heeled black shoes; she had done away with her glasses.

She posed, concentrating on inhaling the joint which he had passed to her. He shuddered.

'I get so high; I like fun,' she intoned, never looking at him. She swayed with the joint, rolling her hips. She reached for one of the table lamps and turned it off.

She was determined; she wasn't stoned because she didn't smoke cigarettes and was having a hard time inhaling the thinnest stream of smoke, however much she concentrated on it. Without her glasses and with the room so dim, she must hardly be able to see him.

'What did I do to deserve you, babe?' she said appreciatively. 'Why don't you lie on the couch over there ... ' she pointed with one foot. He did as he was told, he lay down uncomfortably on the double-tiered mattress. 'I get so high,' she chanted to herself.

He had never been happy as an audience, not at rock concerts or plays or weddings or football matches. He always drank at these times, but she had no more drink in the apartment; she was a healthy macrobiotic. She handed him the end of the joint to put in the ashtray. He was anxious to get the show finished.

'Music?' she suggested. She swayed over to the bookcase and pushed down a button on the transistor radio. Frank Sinatra sang. Martin started to panic, feet shifting uneasily.

'That's better,' she said, 'so much better ... '

She pirouetted gently round the room, unbuttoning her shirt. He watched as it came off, and the bra, hugged to her and then held out for him to take. She rubbed her breasts together, looking at him naughtily.

'You want to see more?' she asked.

'Yes,' he said politely, because there was no option.

She pulled the scarves off one by one, passing them between her legs and letting them float to the floor. Frank sang and was replaced by a rumba. She rolled and gyrated, stroking her body with her hands, removing the scarves. Martin began to fear for the moment of reckoning. The last scarf she rubbed rhythmically back and forth across her groin, as yet covered by a pair of red pants which were stained with her wet.

'Do you like it?' she murmured.

'What about the pants?' He tried to sound excited; he felt false and lost. He didn't want this.

'You're not doing anything, come on, babe, come over to me ... ' she beckoned for him.

'Mollie ... ' he tried to get through to her. She danced close and put his hand against her crotch, massaging it to and fro. He pulled the pants down.

'That's better,' she said, running her own hand through her hair and pushing the wig back on to the floor. 'How do you want to do it?' She crouched on the mattress, on her elbows and knees. 'Like this,' she murmured into the cushion. 'Put it inside me ... '

344

'Yes,' he said numbly, looking at the widespread arse and the hanging pouch, pulling his jeans down to his knees, feeling his prick come out like a crippled animal from a cave. Somehow he managed to slip it just inside her, it hovered limp, he came quickly without getting a full erection, the sperm dribbled out of her vagina, he never lost his awareness.

He reached under and rubbed her breasts in a desultory fashion, trying to offer her something; he was stone cold with the feel of the wind across a razed city, his mind howled blankly and his hands sweated.

'I think I must go home,' he said, as though reading a newspaper placard in the street. He looked at her body. She felt with her hand the sticky residue between her legs.

'I thought you'd stay the night, lover.'

'No, Mollie, I *must* go; I have to catch a plane early in the morning.' He arranged his jeans and walked nervously into the hall. She followed him, she collected a dressing-gown from the bedroom and wrapped it round her.

'Stay ...' she crooned.

'No.' He fought shy of her. 'I'm ... I've got nothing to give. I'm not well enough.'

'All right,' she said, going with him to the door.

'Goodbye. Many thanks for everything.' He kissed her abruptly on the lips and shook her hand. She shut the door.

Franco was picking the guitar apart when Martin tapped on the window. 'It's pretty early,' Franco remarked.

'I didn't feel sociable.' Martin's eyes twitched away.

He told Franco about it as they sat over a half of Laird's.

'There's always something strange about teachers,' Franco said, 'they like their own power.'

Martin kissed him at the airport.

31

Billy started taking uppers to see him through the last two weeks of the show, to give him some fight-back against the weariness and defeat of Jamie. Just a couple of pills around midnight for three or four hours of high times before going to bed; hanging out at a club, dancing. And then sleepers, just a couple.

Donald noticed. At first he was angry at being woken up at four in the morning by Billy's loud arrival home. He kept an eye on Billy. But, he thought, at least Billy was coming out a little more, he was no longer wedged into the bitter silence of the last months.

No more classics, Donald promised himself, it's the last time Billy does that.

He set aside a Friday night to talk with Billy about the future. He went to see *A Moon* again; he thought Billy was way off-key, a real mess; but Billy had the audience in the palm of his hand, out beyond Donald's range. In the dressing-room afterwards he came across Billy sitting in a corner, shaken and exhausted.

'Will you damn well wait for me in the bar!' Billy shouted. Donald waited.

A half-hour later Billy appeared and had a drink. People came up to him, Billy thanked them for their appreciation, he was stuck for anything to say and he stayed close to members of the crew. Patti went over to sit with Billy. Donald felt out of it.

Billy revived, he was laughing, he wanted action. Patti detached herself from his plans and went home. Donald moved in, Billy greeted him playfully. Donald tried to calm him.

'No one *else* is doing anything. Why don't we go home and talk?'

'We'll go to a club, we can talk there.'

'Billy, it's one in the morning.'

'What the fuck, I feel good.'

'All right, we'll talk in the morning.'

'Okay, all right. Hey, let's go!' Billy put his arm around someone Donald didn't know. 'Let's go dancing, let's go.'

Donald went home.

Billy slept through until two in the afternoon; he came out of his bedroom bleached and sagging.

'Do you have anyone with you?' Donald asked.

'No.' Billy made some coffee and went back to his room.

Donald knocked.

'Yeah?'

'Billy, why don't we take a vacation over Christmas?'

346

'Where do you want to go?'

'You should get away after the play is finished, go somewhere and relax. You should start pulling out of it. I don't *have* to go with you. As a matter of fact I have some things to catch up on over the holiday ... '

'Yeah.'

'What is that supposed to mean?'

'It means I'll go away if I want to.'

'Well ... ' Donald's eyes cast around him. 'Or maybe we should spend some time – '

'Doing up the apartment,' Billy droned. 'Yeah, maybe we ... should spend ... some time ... doing up the apartment.'

'I don't think you should go straight away into anything new. I think you should take a rest.'

'Oh thank you. Thank you, Donald. You don't think I should go into anything new.'

Donald retreated to the lounge. Billy followed him. 'I don't know why the fuck we bother to talk.'

'No.'

Billy went back to his room.

Donald stretched out along the couch and lay looking at the ceiling. Billy's tiredness? Linda's absence? His own increased involvement with the electronics side of the business? Try and get Linda back in there, get them back together. Goshsakes, dealing with it all. He added up the several offers of work which were banked for Billy. And really that was his job done. If Billy wanted to blow it then Billy would blow it.

'I want to have a party here for the cast at the end of the run.' Billy came forward in his overcoat, on his way out to the theatre.

'What kind of party?'

'Just some party. A happy party. I'm telling you so that if you don't want to come then you can stay out of the way.'

'Shall I invite anyone special?'

'Anyone you like.'

'Diane?'

'She's away. She has Christmas with her kids. Her life is down to a pretty fine art. I don't want these serious people, they're no more truthful than anyone else anyway.'

'I don't know how you can say that about Diane. That's a little too careless.'

'Screw it.'

Billy went over and looked out of the window.

'I only have another week in this thing, this play. It's a success and I've made it a success. I'm sorry for all the *shit!*'

The same old shock. The same Billy. Donald lifted his glasses and rubbed his eyes. 'That's the way it always is.'

He didn't mean anything by the remark.

That was a down, Billy thought. It became hard to lift your head. There was nothing much to look at.

Better not to have anything to do with anybody, no harm in that, it's just a change in fashion. No we. Let them all down sooner or later anyway. Nobody's fool, Diane.

The whole damn destructive game of getting there.

Acting, goddam it I hate acting. With all of them. That kind of dim peace up there always with your heart out on the floor all lit up – Jesus Christ I know every fucking knot in every fucking board on the right-hand side of that stage. Lying on her lap with her hands there, damp, that kid. Every fucking night open; invite it. Women get you to admit things. So damn pointless being that naked. So damn empty. We can't get it right.

Jamie arrives drunk, Patti gives him a drink, start Act Three, 'Hi, babe', 'Hi, Billy', go up the steps, go into the bedroom, leave the audience in their own shit, fuck them they've only paid they'd rather know people are having a good time.

Fuck writers. How many times did he write it through, twice, three times? He should write it through a hundred times, keep on writing it through, the same fucking mess every fucking day. With no soft chair and no happy kids downstairs. And he'd crack, he'd have one fucking hope somewhere, one thing, person, relationship that worked out somewhere.

'Hey!'

'Yeah?'

'You want to look where you're going.'

'I didn't see. I'm sorry. Hey, fuck you, I said I was sorry!'

Two, getting into a cab. Yeah, well, go home and breed. Leave your mark on society. Get her legs over her head, she looks good that way, she appeals, make a good impression, keep trying to get up there somewhere quiet and warm, never as far as herself, cold outside buddy, don't let her kid you that it isn't. All these people coming out of nowhere, in control, great personality, real entertainers, you can't put your finger on the movement, how children do it so well. We're nothing, we can't even laugh about it because it means so much.

A great maker of love. What does it mean, Diane? I don't know where it all went.

Actor! You can fool yourself like you can fool the others if you try hard enough.

There's only sometimes that you can't get away with it and it comes right down off your shoulder and settles with you, some part you take up and it comes home, stays. You've never done right and you've never done wrong, but you have to move out, hug it. In some fucking cold city it's there. More than the memory of any love or any mother or any hope. Shit. In front of everyone. On a warm stage.

We don't mind that, Patti, it's afterwards I hate; just that kind of it not being finished, it tagging around inside you. I should know this by now, deal with it.

One more week, Eugene.

My party: '... a lot to drink, and it's way into dawn, Patti. It doesn't mean anything. Everyone's gone home, Donald's asleep, your boyfriend will be worrying about you. Listen: you know how you do a play together and you get to know each other very intimately. You're a beautiful girl and a really good actress. Each ... experience ... has those limits. Outside that you have to live and you have your *life* outside that. I've been in love with a dozen actresses. All ages. You cry a little and you grow up. I have a lot of people and ... '

'The wonderful thing about you, Billy, is that you've stayed a virgin.' She got up off the couch; kissed. 'There's a lot of love in you.'

She called again. 'I miss you.'

'I miss you too. It'll go away, it's just the habit.'

Christmas Day: a Diane like the effervescence in that first splash of champagne to hit the bottom of the glass, Diane in Montreal. 'Darling, you know what these family occasions are like; we're sitting around hating each other ... ' They were partying, whoops and laughter interrupt her call.

'Hi Billy, happy Christmas ... we'll see you ... '
'Take it easy, Billy ... '
Robby and John. Diane's.

Silence. Cold around this time of year. I know this apartment, the accumulation of so much; hug it tightly. Nervous days, very sad about everything.

New Year: our party. Linda came. She left early because she wanted not to be alone later on, meeting someone else somewhere. We had fifty people, we didn't miss her when she went out of the room. I don't know why I was ever with her – that's kind of confusing. Scaring in a way. No base at all between us. We didn't even have to try to ignore each other. There wasn't anything out of the ordinary. She didn't dance. That's because she doesn't dance, not well. She won't try to do anything she doesn't think she can do well.

Escorting Patti to her boyfriend. Linda left early. It figures. We had really loud music, didn't we? And the people who wanted to talk sat in the other room; we have sitting in the sitting-room, dancing in the bedroom, drinking in the dining-room and pilling in the bathroom. Like the old times and the beautiful people and the great loud music.

> 'No one else can do it for me
> No one else gets through to me
> Nobody holds me
> Like you do – '

We're up there, we're keeping it going. We're going to get them all out of that nothing. Patti danced. She dances well. She enjoys herself. They all sit in the fucking sitting-room. We dance really well. We party. Linda went to see a New Year somewhere else. We have a great party, darling. We don't have any realism, the kind of realism was in the sitting-room; lounge, Donald, you asshole. Probably still is there, the realism, I don't know if those people have gone home. I guess they're my friends as well as Donald's friends ... think badly of them ... don't care about it ...

Talking with each other in the lounge. I can lie here and not listen to it. *My* damn party. Look in and say good-night, and thank you and thank *you* for coming to our party. So high. Take a little pill now and get some sleep without them ...

Stage in front; large stage. Black and that beautiful blazing red sky. Diane, help me!

32

Donald found Billy's body on New Year's Day. I was on my way back to the Farm, I could think of no better way to spend New Year's Day than carrying a sparkling Diane back towards the place where she and Billy would be assured of each other; one of the few travellers over a motionless landscape. On the plane I stood in front of the mirror, making faces at myself; and on my walk through the airport I matched Diane joyfully against the appraisals.

Three hours after I arrived home, Donald called with his short message. I believed it immediately. I could almost pick up the little sentence of words from the desk top, as though it was bracketed and stiff, between my two middle fingers. Perhaps I worried that this thin sentence might snap and the words tumble, out of order, to remain embedded in the desk, and there would be no further opportunity to arrange them.

I left the telephone and went upstairs, I refreshed the make-up on my face. I placed my Christmas cards from Bobby and John on the marble top of the dresser, and I put some cards that I had bought in Montreal to send to someone some time in the future when I needed to send a card, I put them in the cabinet. And I thought that I would have a bath, later; I had already switched on the small water tank in order to have a hot bath. But I had just refreshed my face, and I didn't really feel so uncomfortable after the journey. I called Robby and John to wish them a happy New Year and to let them know that I had arrived safely. I didn't tell them about Billy's death because it would have spoiled their party. If people try too hard to be sympathetic, they usually become guilty and irritable.

Did Billy think about me before he died? Yes, almost certainly, he would have thought about me before he died.

I could start talking to the fireplace, now or later.

How did Billy die? I called Donald. A coma and respiratory failure; after a party, and drink, and pills. Most certainly an accident. Yes. Naturally. No early death is reasonable.

I wondered why the line had been free. Somehow I should have had more difficulty in reaching Donald at the apartment, I shouldn't have got straight through to him. On Christmas Day it had taken several attempts to reach Billy. The line had always been occupied. So I had been obliged to call during the Christmas fancy-dress games, in the pandemonium when we couldn't hear each other too well. Whose fault was that? He had the number in Montreal.

Billy had once been hit by a car in an accident, but he was not accident prone, it wasn't in his character.

At least my ambivalence about having or not having some-one, at least that is solved. The tight little circle is back, and it is *mine*, it *is* mine. It is *his* decision again to scatter those plans.

I am not obliged to have a bath purely because I have heated the water, although I see it as something to do. Something utterly unimportant one way or the other.

I called Donald. 'You'll let me know about the arrange-ments?' Billy had always wanted to be cremated, what did I think, of course he didn't leave any instructions. If that was what he wanted; I would like to be buried, I think, not burnt.

There was no one I could notify. What was Donald doing? Billy's body was at the City Morgue. I had never seen the City Morgue; jealous of the place where Billy spent his time when he should be here talking with me.

Poor Billy. Not to see the patterns of the fire.

'He was a man who ... ' This and that and everything. Left you with the last word.

There's nothing to do in January, nothing I want to see.

January. Shropshire. Piercingly cold before dawn when the blackness is thin and sheer. A vast space, a field; a twenty-yard pit in the middle of the field with earth piled at one side, solid blackness against the silver snow which crunches and puffs underfoot. A gate is open in the corner of the field, and through it stumbles a herd of cows like so many people leaving a cinema. Conveniently distant from farmer and dogs, the cows at the front stop. They consider the field and the night. They turn their heads and they look back and they are persuaded to continue by the inconvenient jamming at the back of the herd. Cows are nothing if not socially aware.

A generator starts up. The cows watch expressionlessly as two arc lights shine amber from the top of a pole in the middle of the field. They see the lights and they see the newly constructed pen, and, what with the whistling and the dogs, they trudge on towards the pen, heavy with milk, licking their lips, painfully, a sandpaper tongue over blisters.

Behind and above the amber lights, the darkness hangs now like a black, felt screen; in and out of this screen two men appear and disappear in a clinical pantomime, quietly, considerately, two small pants of steam in front of the approaching nimbus of cow-breath.

When the sixty cows are in the pen and the farmer has gone back across his field, the two army marksmen – on loan to the Ministry of Agriculture and flown back from Belfast – shoot the herd. As they finish, a dark grey prises open the night. The men pack their guns, putting the gun cases in the back seat of their car; one of them opens the boot, pulls out a tin of disinfectant and slops it over the wheels. The other man goes over to the generator and switches it off. The lights die and a pale grey morning is allowed to droop across the field. One of the men looks at his watch.

I like this time and this colour. We always arrive just after dawn, in the back of a blue Wimpey transit, from Drayton. Everyone in the van talks except for Patsy and me, but then these other Irish are all regularly winter-contracted to Wimpey whereas Patsy and I come from notices in two different Social Security offices. Patsy is slow to wake up and I am even slower; sitting in the van, watching the pale grey rush motionlessly past the windows, until we arrive at another diseased farm.

And then Patsy and I stand in a peaceful daze while two drivers trundle their JCBs over from the hedgerow and lift the first of the cows out of the pen, corpses gripped by the teeth of the bucket, spots of red blood machine-stitching into the snow.

We have to pour petrol on to the straw at the bottom of the pit. We have, when the arm of the JCB comes across with the dangling cow, to slash open the stomach so that the corpse will not bloat while it burns.

Jokes: dropping a dead cow next to someone when he isn't looking.

And once, towards the end of the day, when the flames from the pit are dying down against a quiet, cold semi-gloom, a coach draws up in the lane. And a procession of besuited men, mostly in sheepskin coats, walk across the field towards us on a sort of guided tour. They receive a short lecture and then they ask us questions. They are from the Ministry of Defence, from the National Association of Funeral Directors and from the American Defense Department, and they want to know what to do after a nuclear war.

Oh Billy, you scare me, America scares me and I scare myself.